From the Author of the Best-selling
Liz Talbot Mystery Series . . .

. . . comes a novel about family and secrets, and the lengths we'll
go to in order to protect both.

Praise for the Liz Talbot Mystery Series

"Plenty of secrets, long-simmering feuds, and greedy ventures make for a captivating read . . . Boyer's chick lit PI debut charmingly showcases South Carolina island culture."

— LIBRARY JOURNAL

"Boyer delivers a beach read filled with quirky, endearing characters and a masterfully layered mystery, all set in the lush lowcountry. Don't miss this one!"

— MARY ALICE MONROE, NEW YORK TIMES BESTSELLING AUTHOR

"Has everything you could want in a traditional mystery: a credible and savvy protagonist, a meaty mystery, and setting that will make you want to spend time in South Carolina. I enjoyed every minute of it."

— CHARLAINE HARRIS, NEW YORK TIMES BESTSELLING AUTHOR

"Imaginative, empathetic, genuine, and fun, *Lowcountry Boil* is a lowcountry delight."

— CAROLYN HART, AUTHOR OF THE BAILEY RUTH RAEBURN SERIES

"The local foods sound scrumptious and the locale descriptions are enough to entice us to be tourists . . . the PI detail is as convincing as Grafton."

— FRESH FICTION

"Boyer deftly shapes characters with just enough idiosyncrasies without succumbing to cliches while infusing her lighthearted plot with an insightful look at families."

— OLINE COGDILL, SOUTH FLORIDA SUN SENTINEL

"This light-hearted and authentically Southern mystery is full of heart, insight, and a deep understanding of human nature. Susan M. Boyer is a fresh new voice in crime fiction!"

— HANK PHILLIPPI RYAN, AUTHOR OF *HER PERFECT LIFE*

"It's a simmering gumbo of a story full of spice, salt, heat, and shrimp. She had me guessing, detouring for a few laughs then doubling back for another clue right until the last chapter."

— THE HUFFINGTON POST

"Twisted humor has long been a tradition in Southern literature (maybe it's the heat and humidity), and Boyer delivers it with both barrels. In lesser hands, all the hijinks could be distracting, but not in *Lowcountry Boil*. Boyer's voice is so perky that no matter what looney mayhem her characters commit, we happily dive in with them. An original and delightful read."

— BETTY WEBB, *MYSTERY SCENE MAGAZINE*

"Susan Boyer delivers big time with a witty mystery that is fun, radiant, and impossible to put down. I love this book!"

— DARYNDA JONES, NEW YORK TIMES BESTSELLING AUTHOR

"*Lowcountry Bombshell* is that rare combination of suspense, humor, seduction, and mayhem, an absolute must-read not only for mystery enthusiasts but for anyone who loves a fast-paced, well-written story!"

— CASSANDRA KING, AUTHOR OF THE SAME SWEET GIRLS

Big Trouble on Sullivan's Island

Also by Susan M. Boyer

Big Trouble on Sullivan's Island

A CAROLINA TALE

SUSAN M. BOYER

STELLA MARIS BOOKS
LLC

Big Trouble on Sullivan's Island

A Carolina Tale

First Edition | April 2023

Stella Maris Books, LLC

https://stellamarisbooksllc.com

Cover Photo © 2022 by Susan M. Boyer

Cover design by Elizabeth Mackey

Author photograph by Mic Smith

This is a work of fiction. All of the characters, organizations, and events portrayed in this novel are either products of the author's imagination or are used fictitiously.

ISBN 978-1-959023-13-5 (E-book)

ISBN 978-1-959023-14-2 (Trade Paperback)

ISBN 978-1-959023-15-9 (Hardcover)

ISBN 978-1-959023-16-6 (Large Print Paperback)

ISBN 978-1-959023-17-3 (Audio Download)

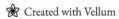 Created with Vellum

For Jim, always

Chapter One

Sunday, June 6, 2021, just before noon
Mount Pleasant, South Carolina
Hadley Scott Drayton Legare (luh-GREE) Cooper

Driving through the Old Village of Mount Pleasant always takes me right back to my childhood. "We Are Family," by Sister Sledge, played on the sound system, then and now, though back then it was via one of my mother's cassette tape mixes. Two blocks from the harbor, I turned off Royall Avenue and pulled into the driveway at the Kinloch house. As I climbed out of Jolene—my 1966 teal blue Ford Fairlane convertible—I drew a deep breath, savoring the sweet blend of star jasmine and magnolia blossoms seasoned with the salty breeze off Charleston Harbor.

The thing I loved best about this neighborhood was the sprawling live oaks that offered shelter from the Carolina sunshine. By June, it was plenty warm. Later in the summer, the Lowcountry sun would fry you up like bacon in a cast iron skillet. But beneath the canopy of gnarled limbs, you could find refuge. Interspersed with the venerable grande dames grew a mix of crepe myrtles, pines, palmettos, and all manner of trees, shrubs, vines, and flowers. All that vegetation seemed to soak up the unrelenting rays, keeping them at bay. There's respite here in the shade.

I was home.

I'd grown up in the house next door.

Massive round blue blooms drooped from overripe hydrangeas that have flanked the Kinloch's front porch steps since before I was born. Maribel, Gavin's late wife, planted them when they first moved into the hundred-year-old cottage built by Gavin's grandfather. Standing in Gavin's front yard, enveloped by the flamboyantly lush landscape, I'm ten years old again, and the biggest problem I have is finishing my homework before I can ride my bike down to Pitt Street Bridge to meet my friends.

I slogged through the simmering June air and climbed the steps to Gavin's front porch. The couple who'd bought our house —the one my mother was raised in, the same one she raised me in —had remodeled it into a sprawling affair I barely recognized. But the Kinloch house appeared as it had throughout my childhood. The bungalow sported robin's-egg blue paint, a color originally chosen by Maribel. Twenty-five years after a drunk driver killed her in a hit and run, Gavin still kept the robin's-egg blue paint and everything else about the house exactly the way Maribel liked it. There were more stately homes in the Old Village of Mount Pleasant, but none more welcoming. A gust set the wind chimes to jangling.

I would turn forty tomorrow. Not for the first time, I wondered if I was officially "a woman of a certain age." I stopped celebrating my birthday in 1998, when my mother died on my seventeenth. The next year, Gavin made me lunch and a cake the day before my birthday, on June 6. That's been our custom ever since. At some point, Gavin's best friend and my mentor, Joe Vincent, started joining us.

Gavin and Joe are my family, and I know exactly how lucky I am to have them. I don't mention that to them often. They make these godawful faces, like maybe they're trying to pass simultaneous kidney stones, at the first sign of emotion. They don't fool me, these prickly old codgers. Gavin had no doubt been cooking for days for my prebirthday, and I'd bet my mother's pearls Joe had bought me a present, likely some personal-protection gadget. Joe worried about me too much. They both did.

It was sweet of them to want to make a fuss over me. And hey, not every girl gets to spend her prebirthday with two crazy widowers and a foul-mouthed parrot. As was his custom, Gavin's military macaw greeted me as I walked through the door. "Bonjour, bitch."

He'd called me worse, so much worse. His favorite word of all is one I've never in my life said out loud—I don't even *think* this word. It rhymes with runt.

"Can you say taxidermist?" I asked the bright green, blue, and red-plumed rascal.

"Rudi, that's it. Say night night." Gavin dove for the black cage cover and quickly draped Rudi's six-foot-tall wrought iron cage.

"Night night," said Rudi.

"Sorry about that, Twinkle." Gavin lifted his large palms and shrugged. He flashed me an expression that said, *What are you gonna do?*

I'd known Gavin Kinloch my entire life. He and Maribel had lived here when my mother's parents bought the house next door. Contemporaries, the two couples became fast friends. Gavin was a Marine before he became a Mount Pleasant police officer in the early seventies. Rudi had belonged to one of Gavin's buddies. Rudi had lived all over the world with a bachelor Marine. When Gavin's friend passed away, he bequeathed Rudi to Gavin. Rudi had the foulest mouth imaginable.

"Ah, no worries." I pulled Gavin in for a hug. "Thank you for making lunch."

He hugged me hard, then patted me on the back. "Nothing to it. Come sit down. It's almost ready."

"Hold up there now." Joe stepped around Gavin and opened

his arms wide. "I'd best get a hug too before we take our lives into our hands eating whatever mess that one threw together." He crushed me to him.

Gavin moved through the dining room towards the kitchen. "Nobody said you have to eat it." Friends since their paths crossed on a case in the late seventies, the two of them bickered like an old married couple.

"Do I smell fried green tomatoes?" I asked.

"Is it June 6th?" Gavin called, in a tone that notified me I'd asked a ridiculous question. He knew how much I loved his fried green tomatoes with pimento cheese.

"Is there anything I can do to help?" I asked.

"Sit, sit," said Joe. "I'll pour the tea."

I settled into my customary spot at the pine farmhouse table, facing a fireplace flanked by long double windows. All three of us preferred to sit facing the door, but we observed a pecking order.

Joe set a glass of iced tea in front of me. "Hadley, it's so good to see you. Happy Birthday, Darlin'."

"Idiot," Gavin yelled from the kitchen.

I pulled back, gave Joe a mock-exasperated look. "The whole point of celebrating today is that it's *not* my birthday . . . yet."

Joe threw up his hands. "I know, I know. Sorry about that. It's just . . . aw, screw it." He slid into the chair across the table. "Talk to me, while Gav puts his apron on and rattles his pots and pans. What's new with you? Any interesting clients lately? I haven't heard from you in weeks."

"Let's see," I said. "I told you about the workers' comp case."

"Cleaning woman with migraine headaches from the chemicals moonlighting as a stripper over at the Cheetah Club?" asked Joe.

"Yeah, you would've enjoyed that one. I did not. And I'll likely end up having to go to court to testify because the Cheetah Club was hyperalert to cameras, so I got zero incriminating photos. Fun times."

"Umm, umm." Joe shook his head, a gleam in his eye.

"I just wrapped up a couple domestics. Things are pretty quiet at the moment," I said.

"You need me to make some calls?" Joe asked.

Joe was an FBI agent before leaving to open his own PI firm. I'd interned with Vincent Investigations for three years, then worked for him another three prior to opening Cooper & Associates Investigations. Joe was retired now, but he still had friends in several Charleston law offices.

"Thanks," I said, "but I'm fine. Middleton, Bull & Vanderhorst has been keeping me busy. I'm actually grateful for the break." I had a loose arrangement with the high-dollar Charleston law office. I worked cases important to them, and they occasionally sent me the kinds of cases I preferred, the ones involving clients with neither blue blood nor trust funds. Also, Middleton, Bull & Vanderhorst paid me well. Oh—if you're not familiar, Vanderhorst is pronounced VAN-dross in the Lowcountry. Crazy, I know. Lots of historic family names—and thus, street names—aren't pronounced the way they're spelled at all.

Joe shrugged. "Just say the word."

"Thanks, Joe. I appreciate you."

With the flair of an experienced waiter, Gavin carried three plates from the kitchen and set one in front of me. It was piled high with all my favorites: Swedish meatballs, mashed potatoes and gravy, macaroni and cheese, squash and onion tart, and fried green tomatoes layered with Gavin's homemade pimento cheese.

I inhaled deeply and closed my eyes. "Gavin, you have outdone yourself."

"There's biscuits in the bread basket." Gavin set an extra bowl of gravy by my plate and took his place. He sat closest to the kitchen, facing the row of windows along the front porch. Through the pass-through to the living room, he had a view of the front door.

I reached for a biscuit, opened it on my plate and poured gravy all over it. Gavin watched with a grin on his face as I took my first bite. I picked up a spoon and the bowl of gravy and ate it like soup, savoring the decadent umami flavor. My eyes may have rolled back in my head from pleasure. After a moment of silent appreciation, I sighed. "So insanely delicious."

When I opened my eyes, both men were shaking their heads at me.

"That's not real gravy, is it?" Joe made a face like he had a plateful of mud pies, but he nevertheless picked up his fork and dug in.

"It's utterly divine," I said.

"Why certainly it's real," said Gavin. "What's the matter with you?"

"You know what I mean," said Joe. "It's got no meat drippings whatsoever in it, like proper gravy."

"Yeah," said Gavin, "I'm real sorry it won't make your heart explode."

"You need to work on a more nutritionally balanced menu," said Joe. "Get this girl to eat a steak. We've prob'ly all got anemia."

"This is a celebratory meal. I'm serving the celebrat-ee's favorites. Doesn't matter if it's balanced or not. If you'd rather not risk it, I'll save yours and have it for lunch tomorrow." Gavin reached for Joe's plate.

Joe scowled at him from under bushy eyebrows and slid his plate out of range. "Getting a little sensitive, aren't you?"

"What I thought." Gavin flashed him a knowing look.

Since I was sixteen, I've eaten a whole food plant-based diet. Most days, I don't eat any animal products at all, nothing processed—no oil, no sugar—and I limit my salt intake. Gavin learned to cook this way to support me and my mother, and he'd fully embraced the lifestyle. Everything on our plates was made from plants, even the macaroni and "cheese," which really didn't have any cheese at all, but could fool most people. He was an excellent home chef, and he made a lot of things with plant-based substitutes that were so delicious we stopped making the distinction. We'd stopped calling it fake pimento cheese because it didn't taste fake. The fried green tomatoes were made in Gavin's oven on the air-fry setting, and they had no oil in them at all. Joe cleaned his plate every time Gavin cooked, and he always asked for seconds. But his story was that we were both nutty and in dire need of a cheeseburger. Joe only ate this way when we were together.

"What have you two been up to?" I put together the perfect bite of fried green tomato and pimento cheese.

"We're too old to be up to anything, dammit," said Joe. "We live vicariously through you."

"Oh, I think the two of you have a few tricks left up your sleeves," I said.

"Speak for yourself." Gavin looked at Joe. "I'm what they call an active adult. I engage in various hobbies to keep my mind and body sharp. I'm a regular Renaissance man. Dylan taking you to dinner tonight?"

"Yeah," I said. "I'm meeting him at Hank's at seven." Okay, I did occasionally eat seafood. And if I were having the odd meal at a nice restaurant, I didn't ask a lot of inconvenient questions about what they put in the sauces and the sides. But this was a rare indulgence.

"Meeting him?" Gavin looked like he'd taken a bite of something sour. "A gentleman picks up a lady and escorts her to dinner. Opens doors for her, like that."

Joe wore a disgusted look.

I shrugged. "Yeah, well, he asked me to meet him there."

"You know he sells insurance." Joe tossed a look at Gavin that said, *I bet he posts porn videos from his parents' basement.*

"Yeah, I recall that," said Gavin. "You ran background on him, right?"

"You know I did," Joe said. "No clear indications he's a psychopath. But that's the thing about psychopaths. They're clever."

I swallowed a bite of meatball. "You can*not* be serious. Please tell me the two of you did not go digging into Dylan's background."

Gavin squinted at me, gave his head a small shake. "Na, na. We just told you. Joe did the background check. He's got access to much better systems than I do."

"That's not the point," I said. "Do you do that for everyone I go out with?"

Joe waved a hand at me. "Course not."

"We never checked into Cash Reynolds." Gavin raised his eyebrows innocently.

I rolled my eyes, closed them, and shook my head. Cash Reynolds was a Charleston police detective. He and I dated for four years. We'd broken up a year ago in July, and Gavin and Joe were still in mourning. The biggest problem they had with Dylan was that he wasn't Cash.

"How long you been seeing this Dylan anyway?" asked Joe, the expression on his face making it clear he considered Dylan a dime-store knockoff.

"Since January." I popped a bite of macaroni and cheese into my mouth.

Gavin turned to Joe. "If he's having her meet him at restaurants, and she's going along with that, it's not serious."

"That's ridiculous," I said. "What's wrong with me meeting him at a restaurant? This is the twenty-first century for heaven's sake. Besides, it could mean he has something special planned." I was still trying to convince myself of this.

Both their brows lowered.

"Something special?" asked Gavin.

"Like what, for instance?" asked Joe.

"I don't know." I searched the ceiling for an idea. "Maybe he had to stop and pick up a gift."

Gavin laid down his fork. "You don't think he's fixin' to propose do you?"

"Of course not." Was I having heart palpitations? I gulped my iced tea.

Please God, don't let Dylan propose. He probably wasn't going to. I mean, if this were a big night, surely, he *would* pick me up and take me to Hank's Seafood—hands down my favorite mainstream restaurant—instead of arranging to meet me there. But that was the thing. Dylan was a reliably mischievous sort, taken with frequent bouts of whimsy. Sometimes he surprised me in ways that warmed my heart and made me smile from the inside out. Other times, he annoyed the pure-T-fire out of me.

"I wish you would carry the Glock I bought you in your purse," said Joe. "Do you at least carry a stun gun with you at all times?"

This was an ongoing argument. They wanted me to carry a gun. I hated guns. They scared me. I had zero confidence that I could use lethal force if push came to shove. "You think I should shoot him if he proposes?"

"Answer the question," said Gavin. "Streets of any city aren't safe anymore for a lady to be walking alone at night."

I closed my eyes. "Yes. I carry a stun gun in my purse. Y'all do remember that I'm well trained in self-defense?"

"I gotcha something else too." Joe laid his napkin by his plate, stepped into the living room, and returned with a gift-wrapped box sporting a huge yellow bow.

"Let the girl eat," said Gavin. "We'll open gifts before we cut the cake. I got you a little something too. Eat. Your dinner's getting cold." In our part of the world, dinner was often referred to as the midday meal. We had supper in the evening most days, yet the evening meal on fancy occasions was also called dinner. I would have dinner twice that Sunday.

Later, after we'd cleared the table and done the dishes, after I'd opened my gifts—a pepper spray gun with a fifty-foot range from Joe and a gift certificate for Krav Maga lessons from Gavin, Gavin brought in a tall birthday cake decorated with daisies, streamers, and four candles. He set it in front of me. "Now, it's not your birthday, of course, but by the power vested in me by the South Carolina Old Coot's Association, I officially confer upon you one prebirthday wish."

They were both watching me, waiting.

What to wish for? I had my health. I loved my job. I had good friends.

"Hurry up now, before we burn down the house," said Gavin. "That's lemon blueberry pound cake with cream cheese frosting, by the way."

"Of course it is." I smiled at him, tearing up a bit. Since I was six years old, that was my favorite cake.

I closed my eyes and wished for the same thing I always wished for. Sometimes it was a wish, sometimes a prayer. I wanted to help someone who felt hopeless, someone whose back was slammed flat against the wall.

Chapter Two

Sunday, June 6, 8:50 p.m.
Charleston, South Carolina
Mrs. Josephine Huger (you-JEE)

I was there. I can tell you precisely what happened. Arthur and I were having dinner at Hank's, like we've had every Sunday evening for Lord knows how many years. We'd had our first martinis and finished our crab cakes. Honestly, I say Hank's has the best crab cakes in Charleston. Arthur likes their oysters, and they are quite nice. But that evening we had the crab cakes.

Now, normally, we sit in one of the banquettes along the wall. But that particular evening, several people had made reservations and apparently requested those way in advance. I'm certain they would have seated us wherever we wanted anyway—we are regulars, after all—but Arthur doesn't like to make a fuss, so we sat at a table directly across from one of those booths—right in the center of the room. We had a front row seat, is what I'm telling you.

Well, right after we sat down, I said to Arthur, "I believe that's

Swinton Legare's daughter." Naturally, he had no idea. Men don't pay attention to certain things. But Judith Legare is a friend of mine, and nothing against the daughter—I can't recall her name, something with an 'H,' not Helen, nothing traditional— but Swinton treated Judith abysmally. Of course that was all so long ago, and I suppose we've all done things we regret. Judith and Swinton have been married for more than forty years, and they're very happy from what I understand.

I have to say, the daughter is quite lovely. She looks like Swinton—has that rich, glossy brown hair he had when he was younger. His is solid grey now, but it's a nice shade of grey. Thank goodness the daughter's had the good sense not to color her hair aside from a few tasteful highlights around her face. Now she does wear her hair quite long. It's past her shoulders. She has Swinton's eyes too. I always said Swinton had kind eyes. They're sort of a soft dark chocolate color. And she's very fit, the way Swinton always has been. Some would call her skinny, but I think quite trim is more appropriate myself. To tell you the truth, she looks exactly like a female version of John Thomas, Judith and Swinton's son.

I'm telling you, they could be twins. Born two days apart, in the same hospital, to different mothers, but the same father. *Two days.* Judith and Swinton were married in mid-October, and both those babies arrived the first part of June, so you do the math. It would've been a scandal, but no one knew about the daughter, not even Swinton himself. Not until years later, after both children were nearly grown. I understand they actually have a good relationship now, John Thomas and his sister, that is. Judith says Swinton adores the girl, but she won't have a single thing to do with him. Blames him for her mother's death. Of course, I never met the mother. I understand she was a clerk at Burbage's Grocery, and that's where Swinton met her.

So, the daughter and her date—I should add here, I noticed immediately he was dressed rather oddly. Black slacks, black long-sleeved shirt, black blazer, and quite dark sunglasses. He looked like a vampire. Anyway, they were seated in the banquette right across the aisle from us. We were close enough we could've heard their conversation if we were the sort of people who engaged in eavesdropping.

As it was, we didn't know anything was amiss until the waiter had served our entrées. I had the roast grouper, that's my favorite. If you haven't tried it, I highly recommend it. Arthur had the shrimp and grits, which is also quite good. Well, we barely had a bite in our mouths when that young man dressed in black pulled out a harmonica. A *harmonica*. Right there in the restaurant.

He stood up and played a few bars. I didn't recognize the song at first. Then he stopped playing and sang to the girl. I thought it must be some sort of proposal, so at first, I thought, well, he's making a fool of himself, but if it's in the name of love . . . but then, I worked out what he was singing.

Arthur said, "Now it makes sense. He's dressed up like Johnny Cash." And I guess the young man was. He sang "It Ain't Me Babe" to her. In front of half of Charleston and a whole gaggle of tourists. The restaurant was completely full. I felt really bad for the girl. Of course she must've been humiliated, but she sure kept her composure. I'll say this for her, her posture was impeccable.

When the young man finished his song, he said to her, "I know you'll hate me for this, but I think that's for the best. This'll be a clean break." Then he strolled right out the door. Left her with the check. Can you *imagine*?

I think everyone in the restaurant was in shock. No one knew what to do. I seriously doubt anything like that has ever happened in Hank's before. And it was all over so quickly.

Well, she ordered another drink. A Holy City Smoke—it has mezcal and a few liqueurs. Sounds intriguing. I may try that next week. Anyway, she sipped her drink and held her head high. Looked anyone looking her way straight in the eye. I have to say, I admired her grit.

I guess someone with the restaurant must've called the police because the next thing that happened, a gentleman with a badge on his belt sat down with her. It was very discreet. I almost didn't see it under his jacket. Now, he was quite handsome, actually.

Arthur felt sorry for the girl. He has a soft heart. He asked the waiter to take her anything else she asked for and bring him the entire bill for the table. It's a sad state of affairs, really, that people will behave so outlandishly in public nowadays. Clearly, that young man was from off.

Chapter Three

Monday, June 7, 5:00 a.m.
Mount Pleasant, South Carolina

As it does most days, my body clock roused me at five a.m. My brother, John Thomas—I call him J. T.—texted me at 5:02.

> You all right? Heard what happened at Hank's. Want me to have his legs broken?

> I'm fine. Should've broken up with him a month ago. Was never going to be anything serious. Actually relieved. Getting on the bike. Have a good run.

> So you haven't seen the video then?

> Me: There's a video??? 😮

> Afraid so. Appears you've gone viral. Nearly half a million views already on YouTube. It's on Facebook, Instagram, Twitter and possibly TikTok.

I'm going to kill him. Please post bail.

My pleasure.

I ride my bike from my apartment off Rifle Range Road in Mount Pleasant to Thomson Park at the east end of Sullivan's Island most mornings to watch the sunrise over Breach Inlet. The morning of my fortieth birthday, I left at 5:10 as usual. It was still dark, and the traffic along Ben Sawyer Boulevard was sparse, the air soft, and not yet saturated with exhaust fumes. This was my favorite time of the day.

That particular morning, the first mile of my ride was fueled by rage. How dare Dylan create such a public spectacle and humiliate me so? Of course someone videoed it. Someone *always* had a smartphone handy to commit every waking moment of any given day to film and broadcast it to the known universe. Privacy was a thing of the past. Of course, when one sets out to stage a musical breakup in one of Charleston's most popular restaurants, one is not courting privacy. What madness had possessed him? It clearly wasn't drugs. The whole thing had been far too well orchestrated for that. The only thing I could come up with was sudden onset impulse control disorder. Dylan always had been a little on the theatric side.

And then Cash showed up and made the fiasco even worse. Someone called the police because of Dylan's public spectacle, and the call had been handed to Cash as a courtesy. Everyone in the department knew our history. I'd almost married him. Or almost wanted to marry him anyway. He never actually proposed. But he and I see things too differently to ever make things work. Don't get me wrong. Cash is one of the good guys. He takes the whole "serve and protect thing" very seriously. But there's no ambiguity in his worldview, no room for extenuating circumstances at all. And a lot of people are saddled with really grim circumstances. I've seen some things, let me tell you.

But even though Cash and I wouldn't be settling into a house with a white picket fence and rocking chairs on the front porch, when he thought about me, I wanted him to imagine me with someone who looked a little like Brad Pitt, only taller, with a great job, an expensive car, and a nice home. I wanted him to imagine I was being swept off my feet, wined and dined, and treated like a queen. I did *not* want him to have the image in his head of Dylan the insurance salesman—completely respectable, but not the most romantic-sounding job, is it?—playing a breakup tune on the harmonica to me in public.

My jaw ached. I forced the muscles to relax, practiced my deep breathing exercises, and let the morning wash over me. A warm wind blew off the ocean and made its way across the marsh. It pushed against me as I approached the Ben Sawyer Bridge. I pedaled hard into the wind. By the time the wheel of my bike touched Sullivan's Island, I had reclaimed my joie de vivre. Who cared if Dylan was a world-class idiot and a YouTube sensation? *I* hadn't created the scene. I was an innocent bystander, just like every other restaurant patron last night—like the lovely couple at the next table who'd insisted on paying my check. I wondered if Swinton the Swine would see the video. Probably not. I doubted he spent much time on the Internet. But the thought made me giggle. He'd no doubt be appalled. Public displays of any sort were an anathema in his world.

First light would arrive at 5:42. I made it to Thomson Park with a few minutes to spare. I parked my bike, grabbed a rolled beach towel out of the trunk bag, and made my way down the path to the sand. I had Breach Inlet—the inlet between Sullivan's Island and Isle of Palms—to myself that morning, at least on the Sullivan's Island side. It was so peaceful at that hour. Just me and the shore birds. What the waves in the inlet lacked in drama, they made up for in enthusiasm. The waves were reduced to ripples but seemed to roll in at double time. I spread my towel on the narrow strip of sand, sat down, and leaned back on my outstretched hands to watch the miracle of morning unfold.

Before the arrival of the British, Sewee Indians hunted on Sullivan's Island and Isle of Palms. Two hundred and forty-five years ago, in this exact spot, the Battle of Sullivan's Island was fought between Americans led by Colonel William "Danger" Thomson and British troops. The Americans prevailed, and the place made quite an impression on the Brits. Breach Inlet was a mile wide back then. Historical markers in the park document how one of the British soldiers described Long Island—as Isle of Palms was then called—as what sounds like one of Dante's circles of hell—one big rattlesnake pit, with suffocating heat, relentless mosquitoes, alligators, crocodiles, and gargantuan spiders. Sullivan's Island is now home to some of the most expensive real estate in the country, and Isle of Palms is no one's idea of a bargain. Still, nature holds her own. The spiders, snakes, mosquitoes, and alligators are still around.

Twilight appeared, lifting the veil of night. Homes across the inlet slipped gradually into sharper relief. The first hint of orange glowed over top of the line of houses, then spread and grew until the edge of the fireball was in sight. After it first appeared, the sun seemed to climb the sky impossibly fast. Later in the year, the sun would rise over the water. But in June, the sun rose over Isle of Palms.

Forty didn't feel one bit different from thirty-nine. In fact, I felt the same inside as I had at twenty-five. Would it always be this way? I had no idea forty would arrive so soon. In some ways, I was still trying to learn the steps only to find the dance halfway over. But I was happy. I had my dream job and friends I could count on. As far as I knew, I was healthy. My list of counted blessings was long.

I shook out my towel and made my way back to my bike. Many mornings, I had to rush home, get showered, and start my workday. But today was my birthday, and even if I wouldn't celebrate, I was going to stroll down the beach a ways and soak in the salty air. I did this as often as I could, but today I did it for my mother, who couldn't. I felt her presence here.

You couldn't walk down the beach from Breach Inlet. The thin strip of sand ended, and a band of rocks struggled to protect the homes near Station 32—the northeasternmost end of the island—from the Atlantic. Beach access points were still called stations, a throwback to the days when the island had a trolley. Middle Street ran from one end of the island to the other. The streets corresponding with the original beach access points intersected with Middle Street.

I rode my bike down to Station 29. There wasn't a bike rack, but I'd left my bike to the side of the path many times over the years, and no one had ever bothered it. Sullivan's Island was rarely troubled by any crime to speak of.

From the end of the short wooden walkway, the ocean called to me. When my shoes hit the sand, I scurried to the right, nearly getting my sneakers wet as I passed the first house. The northeast end of Sullivan's Island fought a continuous battle with the Atlantic, which chewed away at the sand. The homes here held tenuous positions. Ahead of me, the beach widened enough for a walk. I inhaled deeply, savoring the briny breeze.

The rhythm of the surf soothed my soul as it always did, the gentle rumble of each wave growing until it dashed itself on the sand and then sluiced back to the sea. I meandered down the beach, not walking for exercise, but just to revel in the peace and beauty of the morning.

Mostly, I liked to watch the surf, but every once in a while, I looked to my right and admired the houses. The closer you were to Station 32, the better you could see the oceanfront homes. Farther down the beach, owing to the jetties in Charleston Harbor, rather than eroding, the island is actually accreting sand. The beach has widened up to fifteen hundred feet in some places over the past fifty years, with underbrush and trees flourishing between the oceanfront homes and the beach. On this end of the island, most of the homes were newer, the original homes having been wiped out by Hugo in 1989.

Between Station 29 and Station 28 1/2, for the thousandth time, I admired the newest oceanfront home. This was my fantasy house, the one I planned to buy if I ever won the lottery. I'd watched the house go up over the past two years. It was a soft grey poured concrete affair with tons of huge windows and sliding doors. Typically, modern-looking houses like this didn't appeal to me. But something about this one was special. Perhaps the landscaping softened it. The trees had gone in back in March: young live oaks, palmettos, palm trees, and all manner of tropical-looking plants. It looked like the Garden of Eden. An infinity pool was situated in the middle of all that foliage. This was my idea of paradise. I wondered when the lucky homeowners would move in. The house looked like it was ready and waiting for someone to call it home. I can't tell you why, but I hoped it wasn't going to be a rental. I wanted better for the house than a constant stream of temporary residents. It needed someone to care for it, I thought, make it truly a home. I shook my head at my own silliness.

Occasionally, I passed another walker or a runner, but for the most part, I had the beach to myself. I'd just passed Station 21 when a figure walking towards me from the other direction came into focus. She was an older lady, older than me, anyway, but how old was hard to guess. She moved with an easy grace. Her short hair was either pale blonde or perhaps white. An adorable bichon frise scampered ahead of her, tormenting the shorebirds.

The dog charged a seagull, who laughed at him as he flew off low over the water.

The white ball of fluff gave chase.

"Faulkner!" The woman called. "Come here."

Faulkner didn't even look in her direction. He was gonna get that seagull.

A wave crashed over top of Faulkner. He rolled in the surf, then disappeared.

"*Faulkner,*" the woman cried out. She dashed towards the water.

Faulkner's head surfaced, but the current sucked him farther offshore and down the coast. The flat break between two sets of waves was likely a rip current. I scoured the beach for anything I could use. There. Someone had left a longboard near a cluster of sea oats.

I dashed for it. "Hold on!"

"Faulkner, I'm coming!" the woman yelled.

I glanced over my shoulder to see her high-stepping over the waves.

"Ma'am," I called to her. "Ma'am, wait."

"I've got to save my puppy." She was up to her knees, pushing through the water at an angle.

"That's a rip current," I shouted. "You can't go in after him."

She stopped and looked at the water. "Faulkner! Oh no, no, *no.*" She turned to me, her palms flattened on each side of her face. "He'll drown."

"I'll get him." If only I possessed the confidence I was trying to project.

The board was long, maybe eight feet. I grabbed it—I wasn't a surfer, didn't know what to expect—and was relieved to find it made of lightweight foam. I ran for the water. The top of Faulkner's head was barely visible.

I leapt over a wave, then laid the board in the water, hopped on, and paddled hard towards Faulkner. He had been sucked out awfully far, awfully fast. Please, please, please, let him be okay.

"Be careful," the woman called after me.

Faulkner went under, then bobbed to the surface.

I plowed through the water as fast as I could.

Just as I reached the pup, I saw the dorsal fin.

I grabbed Faulkner by the top of his head and plopped him onto the board in front of me. He sputtered violently, coughed, and sneezed.

"You okay, Faulkner?" Miraculously, he seemed to be. "Let's get out of here." I scanned for the shark. There. At my ten o'clock.

Operating on adrenaline more than skill, I turned the board around and paddled away from the current, parallel with the beach for a few strokes, then turned towards shore.

Faulkner whimpered, cuddled up to my chest, and commenced licking my face with gratitude. He licked me all the way back to his momma. She waded out to meet us.

"There's my precious puppy. Oh, Faulkner . . . I thought I'd lost you for good." She cuddled the dog to her chest, kissed him on the top of the head, and closed her eyes, nearly fainting with relief. "I'll never be able to thank you enough for saving him," she said to me.

"I'm so happy I was here to help," I said. "And grateful someone left their board out, which really surprises me."

"That is odd. But quite fortunate. Where on earth are my manners? I'm Eugenia Ladson, and this, of course, is Faulkner." Her bright blue eyes sparkled warmly, but she didn't loosen her grip on Faulkner to offer me a hand. I doubted she'd let him down for days. Her hair was a very pale blonde in front but blended to a soft strawberry color in back. It was the kind of hair a highly paid professional spent hours coloring, then styled at least once a week. Eugenia had good posture, high cheekbones, and the look of regular maintenance about her.

"Nice to meet you. I'm Hadley Cooper."

"Hadley . . . that's a lovely name. You've no doubt saved Faulkner's life. I'm just so, so very grateful to you."

"My pleasure, really."

The expression on her face shifted. She blinked at me, tilted her head, and looked at me sideways. She licked her lips, started to say something, stopped, then changed her mind again. "Forgive me, my dear, but you seem to have had an adverse reaction to the seawater this morning—perhaps some sort of bacteria? It's been in the paper up the coast. I believe you're breaking out in hives. Your face is positively covered."

I winced but wasn't surprised. "I uh . . . I'm actually allergic to dogs."

"To bichons?" She drew back her chin. "I don't think so. They're hypoallergenic."

"They don't shed like some dogs, that's true. Perhaps they have less dander? I don't know. But I'm highly allergic to their saliva. Faulkner was profuse with his thanks. That's a well-mannered puppy you have." I aimed for a smile, but my face itched. "I guess I should get back." It was going to be a long ride home.

"Do you live close by?" Eugenia's face knit with concern.

"Just over the bridge in Mount Pleasant."

"Where are you parked?"

"My bike is at Station 29. It was lovely to—"

"I'm afraid that won't do at all. We need to get you some Benadryl, quickly. And some calamine lotion. I live just up the beach. Do you need help with that surfboard?"

"You're very kind," I said, "but that's not necessary, really."

"Well, just leave it on the beach where you found it, then. Come along." She started up the beach.

"No, what I mean is . . ." She wasn't paying the slightest bit of attention to what I was saying. Eugenia Ladson was on a mission.

I did as she said.

I'd walked right by her home earlier. The two-story raised white beach house sat in the middle of a small compound a few houses down from the new modern house I so admired. Eugenia led the way across the sandy path, through the gate, past the pool house, around the pool, and up the back steps. Along the way she alternated between cooing at Faulkner, thanking me, and reiterating her bewilderment at my allergic reaction—*bichons are hypoallergenic*. I imagined I looked a sight.

Eugenia opened the back door. "Please come in. Make yourself at home, and I'll get the first aid kit and some towels." She moved from a back hall into the kitchen, and I followed.

"I appreciate this, really, but I should just go home and—"

"Don't be silly. Sit." She gestured towards a row of counter stools and disappeared. We'd only just met, but I already knew this much about Eugenia Ladson: she was accustomed to offering direction to anyone she deemed in need of it.

The kitchen was the stuff of magazine layouts: tall ceilings and big windows with views of the pool area and the ocean beyond, white cabinets, hardwood floors, a huge island, industrial appliances, white glass tile backsplash, and grey-surfaced counters, likely quartz. Sweetgrass baskets and seagrass rugs softened the room. Pops of orange—the mixer, a large ceramic fruit bowl, and a utensil caddy—accented the neutral palette. I climbed into one of the deep leather cushioned stools and waited as instructed.

Eugenia reappeared and handed me a fluffy, oversized towel. I wrapped myself in it, and she commenced doctoring me. For his part, Faulkner climbed into the leather sofa-style dog bed with fleece cushions that occupied a nook in the kitchen. No doubt tired from his ordeal, he conked right out.

When Eugenia had a Benadryl in me and calamine lotion dotted all over my face, she looked at her handiwork and nodded in satisfaction. "Now, let's get you some breakfast."

"Mrs. Ladson—"

"It's Eugenia, please."

I nodded and smiled. "Eugenia, really, I should be going. You've gone to enough trouble on my account."

"Nonsense." She raised her chin and squinted at me, taking my measure. "Are you vegan?"

That seemed random. Why would she ask me that? "I'm a high-maintenance eater, Mrs.—Eugenia. Really, feeding me is more trouble than it's worth. I'll just—"

"So that's a yes, then? You are a vegan? You're thin as a blade of marsh grass, and yet seemingly quite fit."

I sighed. "It's complicated. I eat a whole food plant-based diet, no oil, no sugar, little salt. That's a mouthful, so usually I just say plant based when people ask. Well, I eat that way 350 days of the year anyway. But seriously—"

"Really? So do I. Although I have much more frequent lapses in self-control than you. It's not the same as being vegan at all, and I know that. But most people have no idea what 'whole food plant-based' even means. Vegan is a more familiar term, I guess, and it gets the main point across—no animal products."

"Exactly."

"Not that there's anything wrong with veganism. I have no issue with the ethical treatment of animals, mind you. I'm all for that. But I started eating this way for my health. It had nothing to do with the animals at all. But after I'd been off animal products a while, the very idea of eating a chicken, or milk or eggs from another species, well, it seemed bizarre. Juanita left granola and berry bowls." She moved to the refrigerator and swung open the door. "Her granola is homemade, and I have to say, it's excellent." She pulled out a large bowl of mixed berries and a carafe of what I assumed was plant milk and set them on the island. "How do you take your coffee?"

"Eugenia . . . really—"

"Resistance is futile, my dear." She offered me a benevolent smile. "Now, how do you take your coffee?"

I shook my head with a chuckle. "Do you have any date syrup?"

"Naturally."

"I'd like some of that and a plant-based creamer if you have it, please."

She nodded once, then went about the business of grinding beans and boiling water. "You're originally from here?" she asked.

"Mount Pleasant, yes."

"I've seen you here before." She raised her eyebrows at me in a gesture that encouraged me to talk.

"I'm not surprised," I said. "I ride my bike to Sullivan's Island most days. Whenever I have the chance, I walk on the beach."

"I love it here too," she said. "I grew up in Charleston, lived there most of my life. On Tradd Street. My father left me the house that's been in our family for generations."

Bitterness flitted across her face. What was that all about?

"But I've always loved it here," she said. "I bought this house two years ago, and I've rarely spent a night anywhere else since. There's something awfully special about this island."

"There is indeed. My mother loved it. She brought me here for the first time when I was only three days old. We came here at least once a week until . . . until she passed away. The island's always been a magical place for me. I have a lot of happy memories here."

Eugenia poured water into a French press. "I'm sorry to hear about your mother."

"Thanks. It was a long time ago. Twenty-three years today, actually."

"She died when you were quite young. Tell me about her." Her voice was gentle, her eyes soft.

"Mother was this life force who took up all the air in every room—she was larger than life. Always planning something. We never had much money, but she always found ways to make our lives adventurous. We sang, we danced in the kitchen, in the den —all over the house. And we spent every moment we could here, on Sullivan's Island. This was our happy place. We'd take a picnic and beach chairs Mamma had pulled out of someone's trash and asked the next-door neighbor, Gavin Kinloch, to fix. Gavin is a widower. Lived next door all Mamma's life. He still lives in the same house."

"She sounds like an exuberant spirit," Eugenia said softly. "It's heart wrenching for a girl to lose her mother. My own mother died when I was fifteen. Breast cancer."

"My mother had ovarian cancer," I said.

A look of silent understanding passed between us. We were members of the same sad club, she and I. For all the ways we were different, we shared a common heartache.

"You start eating plant based when she was diagnosed?" Eugenia asked.

"Yes," I said. "We were trying everything we knew to try to keep the cancer at bay."

She nodded in an *I've been there* kinda way. "Are you an only child?"

"I have a half brother. We . . . ah . . . we didn't grow up together."

Eugenia continued, "I was an only child myself. My father did his best, but, well . . . fathers are hard pressed to raise teenage daughters alone, aren't they?"

That thought yanked me right out of that moment of reverie, like someone had tossed an icy bucket of water in my face. "I couldn't say. My father wasn't—isn't—in the picture." It was time for a new topic. "You have a lovely home. Two of them, I suppose. I mean, I'm sure your home on Tradd Street is lovely too." I mentally whacked my forehead with my palm. Could I possibly be any more conversationally awkward?

The bitter expression returned to Eugenia's face. "Yes, it's quite lovely. My husband lives there now." She spooned granola and berries into two large bowls and poured milk over them.

I'd plowed straight into a painful subject, of course. "I'm so sorry to have mentioned it."

"Oh, please, how were you to know? Honestly, our living arrangements are my doing, not his." She poured coffee into two large mugs and passed me one. Then she slid me the date syrup and the cream pitcher. "Shall we eat on the deck?" She picked up her bowl and her mug and headed towards the back door.

"Sounds good." I stirred cream and syrup into my coffee, then gathered my bowl and mug and followed her outside, where the melody of the surf provided the perfect soundtrack for breakfast.

We settled into chairs at a large teak table, with her on the end and me facing the ocean. She adjusted her chair at an angle to enjoy the view. After a moment, she said, "I stare at the ocean all the time, listen to it. It's hypnotic. It's why I bought this house, the soothing rhythm of it. I'm a cancer survivor myself."

What did one say? "That's . . . wonderful."

"It is. Everette was, shall we say, less than supportive during testing, surgery, chemotherapy—all my hair falling out—and radiation. He had no patience whatsoever with my healthy diet. Nothing will stand between Everette and a steak. When I tested clear after one year, I bought this house. This is where I want to be for every day I have left. Life's too short not to do what you love."

To the extent you had the means, sure. "It is." I nodded, felt my eyes widen. We both contemplated the ocean for a few moments. The need to make conversation weighed heavy on me. "So, you live here by yourself?"

"Mmm . . . well, yes and no. I have the house to myself. An old friend who's hit a rough patch lives in the pool house. He's good company. What do you do, Hadley? I assume you have a career of some sort."

"I do. I'm a private investigator. I own my own firm: Cooper & Associates Investigations. There really aren't any associates. Just me, Hadley Cooper. But I like the way it sounds, and I plan on having associates one day."

"Ambition." She smiled, nodded. "I like that. And how intriguing your work must be."

"It is never dull." I took a bite of my granola and berries. "This is delicious."

"It's amazing how Juanita makes even the simplest things taste so good. I don't know what I'd do without her. Well, I'd eat out a lot, I guess. I used to like to cook, but I guess I've done so much of it that it feels like a chore, so I've given it up."

"I like to cook," I said. "But it's hard to find the time."

"I would imagine you're on stakeout at dinnertime." Eugenia smiled.

"Sometimes." I nodded. "My schedule is pretty erratic. I try to cook a couple times a week and make enough for a few meals. I freeze things in individual servings, then I always have something in the freezer I can pop in the oven."

"Smart." She seemed lost in thought for a moment, then she

sipped her coffee and eyed me over the cup. "You're Swinton Legare's daughter, aren't you?"

Of course. Eugenia must be around the same age as Swinton. Charleston is a small town in a lot of ways, especially if you live South of Broad. Naturally, they knew each other. I closed my eyes and nodded. "Guilty as charged."

"Now why would you say it like that?" She leaned into her head tilt with an expression of consternation.

I searched the horizon for ships and an answer. "I imagine Judith is your friend."

"She's like a sister to me. Has been my entire life."

I nodded, "So you must think me some sort of home-wrecker. A scandal. I'm the bastard child that forever marred Judith's perfect life."

"My dear, Judith Legare is one of the happiest people I know. Her home isn't wrecked. Her life hasn't been marred." Eugenia waved away any objection I might consider mounting. "Yes, there was quite the scandal. But everyone survived. And my heavens, it was hardly *your* fault. Or are you going to tell me you're some sort of alien species uniquely responsible for your own conception?"

"My father is a womanizer—a notorious philanderer. Clearly, I come from a questionable gene pool, on that side of the family, anyway."

"Why, that's utter nonsense. Swinton—"

What had possessed me? I had spoken the truth, but no doubt offended this poor woman in her own home after she so kindly invited me to breakfast. "I apologize. My mother raised me better. I know they are your friends. I should never have spoken ill of him to you. Please forgive me."

She waved away my apology. "There's nothing to forgive. I just think it's all quite sad." She reached out and patted my hand.

We ate in companionable silence for a few moments. I studied her from the corner of my eye. Her eyes widened and danced with mischief. She had the look of someone with an idea she was rather fond of.

I finished my breakfast and sat back in my chair, elbows propped on the chair arms, hands wrapped around my mug. The view from Eugenia's deck was simply too sublime to waste by stressing over anything. I watched the waves. My breathing synchronized with the rhythm.

"Hadley, are you terribly busy just now? Work wise, I mean?"

Her question caught me off guard. "No, I'm actually having a bit of a break between cases." I squinted at her, inviting her to explain her inquiry.

"The thing is," she said, "I could use a private investigator. I've been thinking about hiring one, but I really didn't know who to call. I had planned to ask my attorney for a referral. But I do like dealing with people I know a little about. I know who your people are. And despite what you may think, they're fine upstanding members of the community. Besides, you saved my Faulkner. That's the best reference anyone could possibly have as far as I'm concerned."

I tensed. I really liked Eugenia. But I didn't want to be anywhere near Swinton's world. That's ridiculous. It's not *his* world. He doesn't own his friends. For heaven's sake, Sullivan's Island can be a whole different world from Charleston. It's possible they haven't even seen each other in years. If I could help a new friend out . . . "What do you want investigated?" I asked.

"My husband."

Domestics were my bread and butter. "I see. With a goal of . . ."

"I know he's cheating on me. I want you to get incontrovertible evidence that I can use in a divorce action. I have an ironclad prenuptial agreement. My father saw to that. Which is ironic, considering he cheated on my mother. The money, you see, is mostly mine. I'd like to keep it. But not him . . . Everette. My husband."

"I've handled quite a few domestic cases. I'd be happy to help. I'll need to get a services contract filled out for you. Perhaps I could drop it by later?"

"That would be lovely. Come at five. The girls and I have happy hour every weekday at five under the beach cabana. You'll join us, of course. You'll fit right in."

I seriously doubted that. But happy hour under a beach cabana on Sullivan's Island . . . this was not an invitation I could pass up. "Isn't alcohol on the beach illegal here?"

"Why, yes. It is indeed. And if you carry it out in containers that advertise what you're drinking, one of our fine young patrol officers will write you a ticket for $1,100. Don't worry about a thing. Just meet us on the beach at five."

Chapter Four

When I finally got back to my apartment, I had a message from a guy named Beckett Driscoll who professed to be a Manhattan resident in urgent need of my services. My first thought was that Beckett Driscoll sounded like a made-up name. I did a cursory check and learned that there was an actual Beckett Driscoll, originally from Mystic, Connecticut, who lived in Manhattan and worked for JPMorgan Chase. I couldn't imagine why a New York banker would need my services, but I was curious enough to want to find out.

I called and arranged to meet him at Brown Fox Coffee at ten. Cooper & Associates Investigations didn't maintain an actual office at present. That was a luxury that would need to come after the 'associates.' Meeting clients at Brown Fox had its advantages. I loved the Mexican Fox Mocha. Gavin seems to think I suffer from a caffeine addiction. Addiction is such an ugly word.

By the time I'd had a quick shower, the last of the hives had vanished, thanks to Eugenia's expert ministrations, no doubt. I pulled on a pair of white, ankle-length chinos and a crisp black and white gingham shirt and sat at my dressing table. Scrutinizing my face, I applied eye cream, moisturizer, and sunscreen. You couldn't be too careful with forty-year-old skin. I probably needed to look into something a bit more concentrated. It was a challenge. I was picky about what I put on my skin, choosing only all-natural products. As I ran a brush through my hair and put on a smidgen of mascara and lip gloss, it occurred to me I probably wasn't what a New York banker expected in a private investigator. I fit none of the stereotypes. This might be a short meeting.

Brown Fox Coffee Company occupied one end of a grey-painted brick building on Simmons Street, near its intersection with Coleman Boulevard. I arrived at ten till ten and ordered my coffee at the walk-up window. Then I stepped around to the packed-dirt courtyard, which provided the only seating. There was a row of wooden picnic tables with grey-striped umbrellas, and a row of smaller bistro tables. My potential client hadn't arrived yet. The courtyard was deserted.

I collected my coffee from the pickup window, then grabbed the picnic table in the back. A few sips into my iced Mexican Fox Mocha, a tall guy in a dark grey business suit stepped around the side of the building. He was Beckett Driscoll, all right. I recognized him from the photos I'd seen online. He lifted his chin in greeting and headed towards me.

I stood and watched him approach. Handsome with dark wavy hair, he had the buffed and polished look of money about him. "Ms. Cooper?"

I nodded and held out a hand. "You must be Mr. Driscoll."

"Beck, please. Interesting office." He perused the courtyard.

"The rent is reasonable. And it's a public place. Comes in handy, in case a prospective client turns out to be a sociopath." I returned to my seat at the picnic table.

His eyebrows darted up his forehead in surprise. "Well, I assure you, I am not."

"Good to know. Did you order coffee?"

The clerk called his name. He smiled at me. "Be right back."

He had a nice smile. And a heavy-looking wedding band, not that I noticed.

He retrieved his drink and folded himself into the picnic table across from me. When he'd settled, he took a sip from his cup. "Excellent coffee."

"It always is. What did you order?"

"Coffee. Black." He dipped his head with a half chuckle, as if he understood how predictable that was. "I have a rather unusual request."

That put me on high alert. Heaven only knew where this was headed. He hadn't been referred by anyone I knew. "Oh, no. I don't do unusual. Just . . . regular. Common, everyday investigations."

"Now hear me out," he said.

I sighed, took a long drink of my mocha, then set down my cup. "All right. What is your unusual request, exactly?"

"I need a house sitter."

My eyebrows drew together. "N—"

"On Sullivan's Island."

"For how long?" I asked.

"Indefinitely."

He had my attention. "Explain."

"It's quite simple, really. I live in Manhattan. I'm an investment banker. A couple years ago, I bought a lot between Station 28 1/2 and Station 29. Did you know, it's actually as easy to get to Sullivan's Island on Friday afternoon as it is to get to the Hamptons?"

"I've heard that, yes." Beckett Driscoll wasn't the only Wall Street banker to discover Sullivan's Island.

He nodded. "Well, I contracted with a builder. The project took longer than expected for a number of reasons, but the house is finally ready. Unfortunately—well, actually, that's not right. *Quite* fortunately, I've met the love of my life. We were married just two months ago."

"Congratulations." Wait. Was he talking about my fantasy house?

"Thank you. But the thing is, you see, Philippa isn't a beach lover. She prefers the mountains, cooler climates. We've just bought a weekend home in Telluride. Philippa loves it there, so naturally, that's where we'll spend our weekends. And I've promised her we'd spend time in the UK. She has family there. In fact, we may buy a home there as well."

"Why not sell the house on Sullivan's?" I asked.

"Eventually, I probably will. But I've put quite a lot of money into it. It's state-of-the-art hurricane proof, all the latest technology. I think I'll get a better price if I hold on to it for a while, let it appreciate. But I can't let it sit empty. The builder offers a warranty, but some items are only covered for a year, others two years. Structural things, of course, are warrantied longer. But I need someone to actually live there and use everything the way it's designed—to make sure everything works properly."

"So when you say indefinitely . . ."

"I mean at least a couple of years, possibly longer," he said. "It all depends on property values and how the rest of my portfolio is performing."

Butterflies fluttered in my chest. This was inconceivable. The only brand-new house between Station 28 1/2 and Station 29 was *my* house. The one I'd admired the entire time it was being built. Could this possibly work? "I'd . . . I'd have to give up the lease on my apartment. I'd need sufficient notice to get a new place before you sold it."

"Perfectly reasonable. How about we stipulate I give you six months' notice at a minimum before I sell?"

I might have been the slightest bit gobsmacked. "I need some time to think this over."

"Ah . . . well, that's a problem. I need to finalize arrangements. I've got a meeting in New York in the morning I can't miss, and I'm not sure when, or if, in fact, I'll be back in town. Perhaps I should move on to the next name on my list. Thank you for your time." He turned his head, moved to stand.

Had I lost my mind? "Wait." I raised both hands in a stop motion.

He froze, lifted his eyebrows in a question.

If I agreed to this, I could still check him out further, and his house too . . . make sure this was all aboveboard. I offered him what I hoped was a radiant smile. "I'm in. It sounds good . . . really good."

"Are you sure?"

"Yes, positive."

"I can't allow pets," he said. "Though there is a saltwater aquarium. There's a service who'll take care of that weekly."

"No pets. Sadly, I'm allergic to cats and dogs both. I love fish. I've always wanted an aquarium."

"Me too." He heaved a deep sigh. "I think you'll like this one."

"Anything else I should know?"

"You may need a storage unit. A decorator has completely furnished the place, artwork and all. I wouldn't want to move the new things out. If you'd like to hang a few personal pieces, that's fine, of course. You'll be there a while. I want you to make yourself completely at home."

Words failed me. This whole package was just too good to be true. "Is there a storage room?" I asked.

"Several of them, actually. I haven't moved any of my things in at all, so the closets are empty as well. Tons of storage."

"I really don't have that much, in the way of furniture," I said. "There are only a couple of pieces that have sentimental value. Most of it is probably not worth what it would cost to store it."

"I'm prepared to cover the storage fees. It wouldn't be right for you to incur expenses on my behalf. And I'll cover the utilities, of course."

"Of course." I nodded, though this shocked me. Why on earth would he pay for my utilities? "Why?" I felt my face twist and my head tilt.

He shrugged. "You're testing appliances, sound systems, televisions, security, the plumbing . . . all the systems in the house. You can hardly do that without basic services. Besides, all the utilities have been set up to be paid automatically. There's no point in changing all that. Too much paperwork."

I continued to nod.

"Problem?" he asked.

"No, not at all." I was going to check this man out all the way back to the delivery room.

"Excellent. Here are the keys and the gate and garage door opener." He laid two heavy keys and a gadget on the table, then reached into his jacket and laid a piece of paper beside them. "Everything has a keypad, and the combination is the same for everything: the security system, the garage doors, both gates—one just off the street in the driveway, and a walk-thru that leads from the patio to the beach—and the doors. The doors are all keyed alike. They'll all open with either the code or the key. If you have a button on your sun visor, you can program the gate and garage doors to open with that.

"Here's a list of everyone you might conceivably need to contact in case you do run across issues—and I'm sure you will. It's new construction. Things are not going to be perfect. Don't hesitate to call the builder, but he's asked that you try the subcontractors first. If there's a plumbing issue, call the plumber, and so forth."

"Right." My head was spinning.

"Everything should be covered under my warranty, but if there is a charge for anything, they know to bill me directly."

I kept nodding.

"The pool company comes on Wednesdays."

"The pool company?" Of course. That gorgeous infinity pool.

"Yes, there's a saltwater pool and a spa. The pool is heated, of course. Not that you'll need to heat the water for a while, but when it does get cool this winter, don't hesitate to use the pool. The heating system needs to be tested just like every other system."

"Naturally." This could only be a bizarre dream, from which I would soon wake.

"My contact information is on the sheet as well, though I'd

like you to try my administrative assistant first. Her name is Romilly, Romilly Yearwood."

"Call Romilly, check."

"Any questions?" he asked.

"How did you get my name, again?" How had he found the one private investigator in Charleston County with a lifelong, burning desire to live on Sullivan's Island?

"I Googled private investigator, Charleston County, South Carolina. My thought process was that a PI has to go through a vetting process to be licensed. And a PI is additional security in the event of a break-in. They're trained to handle situations the average college student is not. I assume you're armed?"

"Oh yes, I'm well armed."

He didn't ask for specifics, so I didn't volunteer the exact nature of my arsenal, or how I was terrified of guns. Surely, he knew how low the crime rate was on Sullivan's Island. He hardly needed an armed guard. Or was there something he had left out?

"Excellent."

"That Internet search gave you at least twenty names. How did you settle on mine?"

He shrugged. "Most of them are married, some with children, grandkids, even. I didn't want a family, per se. Even an empty nester with grandchildren, they'd want to have the family over."

"You don't want kids in your house?" A new house with what must be expensive artwork and high-end technology, naturally that wasn't a kid-friendly place. But . . . if he didn't *like* kids, maybe that pointed to a fussy disposition. In the unlikely event I wasn't dreaming, I didn't want to go to the trouble of moving only to learn he was impossible to deal with.

"It's not that, exactly. I like kids just fine. I hope to have a couple, in fact. But if someone were to be hurt . . . a swimming accident, or even falling in the bathroom . . . the liability is less with one person than a whole gang. I'm extremely risk averse."

"So I shouldn't have friends over?" No doubt the expression

on my face notified him this was a deal breaker. I wouldn't spend the next however long this arrangement might last in isolation.

"Not at all. I didn't mean to imply that you shouldn't have company. Please, have anyone you like over. Have houseguests. There are five bedrooms, though one of them is set up as an office and another an exercise room. Still, plenty of room for company. Truly, have anyone you like. You asked, and so I explained my thought process as I was evaluating potential candidates. I didn't intend any commentary on how you should live. As I said, make yourself completely and utterly at home."

"So if I wanted to throw my niece a birthday pool party, that would be all right?"

"Well, it would, except for the matter of you don't have a niece. You're an only child—you do have a half brother—but neither of you have ever been married."

"You checked me out," I said.

"Of course I checked you out," he said. "You'll be living in my home indefinitely. I ran a full background report. I'm not foolish."

Neither am I. "Okay then."

"Okay then. But if you'd like to throw a birthday party for any random child, by all means, feel free."

"I'll need that six-month notice clause in writing. For my protection, I'd like our entire agreement in writing, please."

"Naturally." He pulled out a folded set of documents and handed me one. "Let me know if there's anything you'd like to add."

He waited while I read through it, then signed. I signed, but I was also planning my argument to invalidate the agreement if he'd misled me in any way. And I was absolutely certain this too-good-to-be-true offer came with undisclosed irritations. Perhaps the foundation was faulty, and the house was ready to collapse and be swept away by the Atlantic. That stretch of beach was awfully narrow at high tide.

Or maybe there'd been a horrible crime on the construction

site that had somehow been kept out of the news. Maybe it was infested with snakes . . . or black mold. Mold. I'd bet that was it. I was his guinea pig. If I didn't get sick, the house was safe for him and his family.

Except there were eminently cheaper ways to test for mold.

There was a catch. I was certain of it.

Chapter Five

Some people's lives are open books, the milestones and special occasions publicly chronicled in small-town newspaper announcements, society pages, social media, and public records such that it's difficult to conceive how they could hide bad behavior. Beckett Driscoll's was such a life.

I spent the rest of the day checking into him and his house on Sullivan's Island. I walked onto a renovation job site on Pirates Cruz in Old Mount Pleasant to speak to the builder who'd built my fantasy house. He confirmed that Beck had spent big money designing and building his dream beach house, only to marry a woman who relished mountains, snow, and cocoa by the fire.

Technically, the house was owned by Extraordinary Measures, Inc., the name likely a commentary on a tax loophole he'd somehow slipped through by creating the corporation. According to the South Carolina Secretary of State's website, the entity's registered agent was a CPA in Charleston, but that tracked. The state required corporations to have a registered agent with a physical address inside the state of South Carolina. The company was in good standing. Every jot in Beckett's story checked out. He was who he claimed to be. His situation was as represented.

Was it perhaps a little too perfectly laid out and easily established? That thought crossed my mind, but I immediately tossed it out the window and drove over it. Why critique the gift horse's flossing habits? Besides, it simply wasn't credible that anyone would go to the elaborate steps and expense necessary to create this kind of background with the sole purpose of convincing me to live in his magnificent new beach house.

I was ecstatic. I also felt like I'd landed in a strange but wonderful dream. This couldn't really be happening. It was absurd. But there was no harm I could apprehend in riding this ride as far as it would go. With my Southern Rock playlist shuffled on my iPhone, Jolene and I drove towards Sullivan's Island, with Molly Hatchett singing "Flirtin' With Disaster" over the sound system. Maybe I should've recognized that as a portent, but I can't honestly say that I did.

I was eager to toast my outrageous fortune with my new neighbor, Eugenia Ladson. Despite our age difference—and our wildly divergent financial situations—I'd felt a connection to her. We'd both lost quite a lot to cancer, her more than me. I admired her take-no-prisoners attitude—her sass. And now that I knew I was going to be moving to Sullivan's Island, I was eager to meet more of my new—if temporary—neighbors.

I turned off Marshall Boulevard into the driveway of the home of my wildest dreams. Twin concrete columns that matched the house marked the entrance to the property. Between the columns hung a steel gate that was both formidable and stylish, with crisscrossing bars in a pattern that left no hole larger than a bread box. The street number, 2859 Marshall Boulevard, was forged into the top left grid. With a glance over my shoulder to see if perhaps anyone was making a note of suspicious activity, I pushed the button on the remote marked "gate," and the panels slid open. I pulled Jolene through like I owned the place, and the gate slid silently closed behind me.

The raised two-story house was even more imposing up close. I parked and stared at the modern, pale grey concrete and glass home surrounded by verdant trees, shrubs, and plants. The landscaping alone must've cost more than most homes I'd ever set foot in. Four stained-wood garage doors stood in front of me, two on either side of a wide set of steps that rose to a deep covered porch running the length of the first floor.

I hadn't been inside yet, and I positively itched to see it. But happy hour wouldn't wait, and I knew as soon as I walked through the door, I'd want to take my time exploring every nook and cranny. I climbed out of the car and strolled down the path to the left side of the house. The pavers, which appeared much more porous than concrete, were separated by grass. Through a veritable jungle of fronded plants and flowering vines, I found my way to the lower level of the patio.

At the center rear of the garden, I passed through a gate that led down a boardwalk to the beach. When I reached the sand, I pulled off my sandals and headed right, towards Eugenia's house. I chuckled as I caught my first glimpse of her "cabana." No doubt astronauts could spot it from space. It was a large, turquoise affair with four poles, roomy enough for the eight comfy-looking striped beach chairs and two rolling coolers beneath it. Eugenia held court from the center of the tent, surrounded by five other women. A bare-chested guy in shorts with shoulder-length dark blond hair handed Eugenia a large pink tumbler, the kind that shouted fruity liquor drink. How did they get away with this? As I got closer, I could see the bartender had grey in his hair. The tie-dyed headband looked like a remnant from the sixties. Most of what I know about the sixties I learned from Forrest Gump, but I digress.

"Hadley, I'm so happy you made it." Eugenia motioned me closer with the brightly colored church fan she held in her left hand and raised the glass in her right to take a sip from the straw. "Come meet everyone. Fish, get her a drink."

A happier looking group I could scarcely conjure. Everyone had the big pink cocktail glasses and the cardboard church fans. They sipped, stirred the air, and welcomed me with wide smiles.

From up close, I could see the women were from several different generations.

Eugenia executed a sweeping gesture to her right. "That's Sarabeth Boone on the far end. She and her husband, Tucker, moved here a few months ago. As you can see, she's fallen in with a bad crowd."

A honey-blonde woman with wavy shoulder-length hair, Sarabeth grinned, flashed Eugenia an affectionate little eye roll, and gave her a dismissive wave of the fan.

Eugenia continued. "Next to Sarabeth is Libba Graham. Libba and Elliott have been here five years or thereabouts. They have three teenagers. Add them to your prayer list, would you?" Libba was a lighter shade of blonde who wore her hair in a smooth chin-length bob.

Eugenia dropped her fan to her lap and rested her hand on the arm of the woman next to her. "This is my dear friend, Tallulah Wentworth. We've known each other a thousand years. She's lived on this island her entire life, and she knows everyone and everything. But don't believe a thing she says about me. She's bad to make things up."

Trying mightily to commit their names to memory, I noted how Tallulah's hair was platinum blonde. It was nice the blondes in the group, Sarabeth, Libba, and Tallulah, were all on Eugenia's right, and lined up darkest to lightest shade.

Tallulah grimaced. "Oh, *please*. If I stopped telling lies, who would cover up your notoriously bad behavior?"

"You see what I'm tellin' you?" Eugenia raised her right palm and gestured with the cocktail glass in her left. "Anyway, you sit here by me." She nodded towards the chair to her left. "That's Camille Houston on your other side. She moved here from Texas. I've forgotten how long ago. Seems like she's been here forever. Never play poker with her. She'll rob you blind."

Camille, a redhead, tilted her head, nodded, and made a face that seemed to acknowledge that Eugenia spoke the truth.

Eugenia continued. "On the other side of Camille is Quinn

Poinsett. She moved here with her parents as a child. She and her husband, Redmond, also have teenagers, but just two of them—twins, actually—and they're perfect angels. Probably growing psychedelic mushrooms in their closets and selling them on YouTube or Tiktok or some fool thing. *I'm kidding.* But pray for Quinn and her husband too because with teenagers, you just never know. *Sit, sit.*"

I laughed, dropped my sandals and my backpack by my chair, and sat. Quinn was a brunette, her hair a shade or two lighter than mine. But where I generally wore my hair straight, hers was wavy. How would I keep them all straight? Sarabeth, Libba, Tallulah, Eugenia, Camille, and Quinn. Sarabeth—

"Now listen, 'eah?" said Eugenia. "Don't fret a solitary second about remembering who's who. There's not going to be a pop quiz or anything. You'll get to know everyone in time."

Had she read my mind?

Eugenia winked at me, and I had to laugh.

The hippie bartender handed me my own pink cocktail glass, which I now saw was actually a large pink insulated tumbler with a matching straw and lid. He wore a wide grin and a pair of faded blue twill shorts that had likely been expensive a decade ago.

"It's a prickly pear margarita. That okay?" he asked. "Eugenia loves her tequila, but I have some Frozé in the cooler if you'd rather have that."

"This is great. Thank you," I said. "Cheers, everyone. It's lovely to meet y'all."

They all said cheers, nice to meet you, and all like that.

Fish handed me one of the handheld fans. "You'll need this. It's warm out this evening."

I hadn't seen one of those things in years. I waggled it back and forth in front of my face. It's crazy, but before I had a second taste of that drink, a peaceful, easy feeling settled over me.

"My goodness, where are my manners?" said Eugenia. "I forgot to introduce you to Fish. Fish is one of my oldest and dearest friends. Of course, Fish isn't the name his momma gave him. His birth certificate reads 'Hamilton Alexander Hughes Fisher Ravenel Aiken,' but that's quite the mouthful, and he prefers Fish. He's kind enough to set things up for us for happy hour and play bartender. The stories Fish could tell would fill a set of Encyclopedia Britannicas, if they even made such a thing anymore."

This must be the friend who had fallen on hard times and lived in Eugenia's pool house. "Nice to meet you, Fish." I smiled and lifted my glass to him.

"The pleasure is entirely mine." Fish settled into the chair on the end by Quinn, nearest the coolers. "Let me know if that drink doesn't suit you, 'eah?"

I sipped my margarita. "This is delicious—thank you." Oooh, this concoction might go down a little too easy.

Fish smiled and nodded. His eyes were a touch glassy. How many margaritas had he had already? It crossed my mind that having one of these every day at five might cancel out all of Eugenia's healthy eating. But that was between her and her doctor. Who was I to say what she should or shouldn't do? People were often contradictions. Besides, as much as Eugenia had been through, if she wanted a margarita, she should have one.

"Eugenia, where's Birdie today?" asked the platinum blonde to Eugenia's right—Tallulah. That was her name. Oh, good grief, there was another?

Eugenia raised an elegant eyebrow. "She and Vernon had some business to attend to." Eugenia turned to me. "Birdie Markley has been my dear friend since our mothers planned their baby showers together. She's married to an absolute trial of a man. I adore him, of course, but he's a constant torment."

"What's Vernon done now?" asked Camille, the poker-playing redhead of Eugenia's generation to my left. To keep the women straight, I mentally grouped them by age. Camille, Tallulah, and Birdie (who was absent) were Eugenia's age or thereabouts. Libba and Quinn were somewhere around my age, I figured, and Sarabeth was somewhere between the two groups.

Tallulah said, "I can't confirm to a certainty he's keeping goats in the house, so let's say no more about it."

"Goats? *Goats?*" Camille tilted her head in incredulity, then closed her eyes. "Poor Birdie. Bless her heart. What on earth?"

"Ladies, for goodness' sake," said Eugenia, "that's quite enough about Vernon. Better to save some of our crazy for another time. We want Hadley to come back. Hadley dear, did you bring my contract? Forgive me for jumping straight to business. Terribly rude of me, I know. But I am eager to get things rolling."

Did she really want to discuss her personal business in front of the group?

Reading my mind again, she said, "We have no secrets. The girls know all about my lying, no-account, cheating husband. Fish and Tallulah have known him as long as they've known me. They can vouch for his general jack-assery."

"Well, all right then." I reached into my backpack and pulled out my standard contract, personalized with Eugenia's name and address. "This just outlines the basics: my retainer, fees, and deliverables." I handed the paperwork to Eugenia.

"What she wants delivered is Everette's staff of life on a polished silver platter," said Tallulah.

"Preferably presented to her at the top of the steps at Old City Market at high noon on a Saturday," added Camille.

I nodded. "Understandable."

"But I will settle for ironclad evidence of his current affair that I can use in court," said Eugenia.

"His current affair?" I asked. "Has he had more than one?"

"Well if he hasn't, it's not for lack of trying," said Eugenia. "He's been on Tinder for two years, at least."

"Eugenia set herself up a profile to catch him," said Sarabeth.

"My, my. That was clever," I said. "Did you print the screens?"

"Well, of course I did," said Eugenia. "But I suspect his

attorney would try to cast doubt on any evidence directly produced by me."

"Prob-a-*blee,*" I said. "Not to mention that you'd have to explain what you were doing on Tinder."

"Well, it was for the sole purpose of seeing what he was up to, I assure you," said Eugenia.

"Tinder is more for hookups, isn't it?" asked Libba. "I heard that anyway."

"I don't know the first thing about all those dating apps," said Quinn. "Thank goodness. It all sounds positively miserable to me."

"I know someone who used a couple of them for a while," said Camille. "She kissed a battalion of frogs, then had a date with a psycho stalker she had to take out a restraining order against. The whole ordeal scared her so badly she deleted all her profiles. Said she'd rather be alone."

"I don't know," said Sarabeth. "I think those apps must help some folks or they'd all go out of business. I mean, I hope to never have the occasion to *need* one, but I think they help lonely people make connections. There's nothing wrong with that."

"Not at all," said Camille. "As long as you're not set up with a serial killer. It's a dangerous proposition, going out with strangers. Better to meet men the old-fashioned way, through friends and family. Maybe at church."

"Because there aren't any crazy people at church," Tallulah said dryly.

"Well, not many serial killers are regular church attendees, I bet you that much," said Camille.

"Oh, don't get me started on church," said Eugenia.

The women all hooted in laughter.

"Everette thinks Eugenia's joined a cult," said Tallulah.

"Have you?" I asked. She didn't strike me as the cult type at all.

"Of course not." Eugenia scowled. "I am a member of Cornerstone Community Church in Mount Pleasant. It's a lovely church. The people are warm and friendly. Not stuffy at all. And it's certainly not a cult. Fish invited me. He's been going there for years."

Fish nodded. "My former ex-future mother-in-law invited me. She no longer attends services, of course. The entire family moved to Kissimmee, Florida to be near her father. He's developed a skin condition and can't wear clothes anymore. I digress. There are fine people at Cornerstone Community Church. Fine people. They don't concern themselves overmuch with the size of your bank account, or what car you drive. Just nice folks."

"Everette's problem with Cornerstone is twofold," said Eugenia. "First, it's not an Episcopal church. Everette's family, and mine, for that matter, have been Episcopalians forever and ten years, and specifically, members of St. Michael's since 1761 when the doors first opened. Everette is a fan of tradition. His second issue with Cornerstone—and by far the closest to his heart, I can assure you—is that he knows it is my custom to give generously. Everette doesn't like me giving my money to a church—any church—because he wants it all for himself. Cult, my Aunt Fanny."

I nodded in sympathy, then made an attempt to dispose of the business at hand, so as to give my margarita the attention it deserved and share my news. "Does the contract meet with your approval?"

"What?" Eugenia squinted at me. "Oh . . . right." She glanced at the paperwork. "I'm certain it's in order. Do you have a pen?"

I reached into my backpack and handed her a ballpoint.

"Fish, would you be a dear and bring me my checkbook?" Eugenia said.

"Of course," he said. "Back in a jiffy."

"Hadley," said Sarabeth, "what an exciting life you must lead."

Libba said, "That *is* quite an intriguing career choice. How did you end up a private investigator, anyway?"

"Well . . . it's complicated." I gathered my thoughts. "I grew up next door to a Mount Pleasant police officer. He was a father figure to me, I guess. Or grandfather, maybe. My grandfather died when I was four, and my father was never a part of my life. So I looked up to Gavin—I still do. He's a hero to me. For a long time, I wanted to be a police officer."

"You couldn't pay me enough to take on that dangerous, thankless job," said Quinn. "What brought you to your senses?"

I said, "A couple of things, I guess. Gavin's wife, Maribel, was killed in a hit and run car accident when I was in middle school. The guy who blew through a stoplight and plowed into her was never even arrested because he's a highly intelligent sociopath who had contacts in an elite car-theft ring, and he was able to dispose of all the evidence quickly and efficiently. Of course, that couldn't be proven without jeopardizing the FBI's case against the car thieves. Which left a complete lack of evidence. But they know who it was, just as sure as I'm sitting here.

"And then, a completely innocent friend of mine ended up going to prison because he was handy and an overzealous district attorney had an agenda. It impressed upon me how our justice system doesn't always deliver justice. I mean, yeah, he might've made a questionable decision, but that's not against the law."

"It's a very fortunate thing for me that it isn't," said Eugenia. "I'm sorry about your friend."

I winced. "Thank you. I guess it's obvious his story had an impact on me. Sometimes innocent people go to prison. And then I think maybe I have too much empathy for the guilty people driven to crime by desperate circumstances to ever be a good cop. I came to realize, I guess, that the police aren't in the right and wrong business. They're in the legal and illegal business. I was more concerned with justice than the letter of the law. I wanted to be in the 'setting things right' business."

"So you're a vigilante PI?" asked Libba.

I laughed, might've snorted. "No, not at all. But I choose my cases based on if I think I can right a wrong. I majored in computer science and minored in sociology, thinking that would give me a good solid, related background. Now, I don't want to give the wrong impression. I have an awful lot of respect for police officers. I just don't think I'd make a good one."

"Interesting." Libba stretched the word out, enunciating each syllable. "Well, nailing Everette's 'credentials' to the wall definitely counts as righting a wrong in my book."

"Precisely," said Tallulah, and everyone murmured their agreement.

"A man who cheats on his wife certainly shouldn't be allowed to profit from the divorce," said Tallulah.

"I'm counting on Hadley to make sure he doesn't," said Eugenia.

"Not to change the subject . . ." Camille regarded Eugenia from over the top of the frame of her sunglasses. "But did things calm down at Dunleavy's after I left? I truly hated to rush off, but it takes six months to get an appointment with Peter. I can't afford to miss a touch-up."

Eugenia turned both hands palm up and gestured dramatically. "Can you believe how positively ungrateful some people can be?"

"What happened at Dunleavy's?" asked Libba.

"What'd we miss?" asked Sarabeth.

"Have you been terrorizing the bartender again?" asked Quinn.

"I haven't terrorized anyone," said Eugenia. "And I don't appreciate that mischaracterization of my actions."

"Well," said Tallulah, "I couldn't say if Kateryna was terrorized or not. But she certainly was fit to be tied."

"I'm only trying to help the girl," protested Eugenia.

"I don't think she sees it that way." Camille attempted to smother a grin.

Eugenia turned to me. "Kateryna Petrenko is one of the bartenders at Dunleavy's Pub."

"Doesn't she normally work nights?" asked Libba.

"Yes," said Eugenia. "I understand she picked up a shift to

help someone out. In any case, she was there when they opened at two today, when Tallulah, Camille, and I went for our monthly Reuben. We all love Reubens, but they're not at all healthy, of course, so we limit ourselves to one a month."

"Hadley doesn't care a fig about the culinary adventures of three old women," said Tallulah. "Tell her about Kateryna."

"Who are you calling old?" asked Camille.

Tallulah slid her sunglasses down her nose and raised her eyebrows. "Oh please."

"Speak for yourself," said Camille. "Personally, I feel as good as I did when I was thirty. You're as old as you feel."

"All of you are marvels, testaments to the importance of regular maintenance," said Libba. "Now would you please tell us what happened?"

"Yes, of course," said Eugenia. "Provided I'm allowed to speak uninterrupted."

Tallulah's patience apparently ran out. "Eugenia got Hayes Middleton to offer Kateryna a job at the law firm."

Hayes Middleton I knew. He was the senior partner at Middleton, Bull & Vanderhorst, the law firm that sent me the lion's share of my work.

"And I say that was very nice of her," said Camille. "I'm not sure exactly what qualifications Kateryna has aside from, well, she makes a very good martini. But it was kind of Eugenia to take an interest and *extremely* generous of Hayes to find a position for her."

"I'm guessing Kateryna wasn't overcome with gratitude," said Sarabeth.

"She most assuredly was not," said Eugenia. "I suspect she cursed me, in Ukrainian, or perhaps Russian. Who knows? I was only trying to help the girl. I declare, the more I do to try and help her, the more hostile she becomes."

"She doesn't speak English?" I tried to keep up with the story.

"She does," said Tallulah. "Her accent is pretty thick, exotic, if you ask me. But I understand her just fine. It's only when she's angry and starts talking fast that she reverts to Ukrainian . . . or Russian. I honestly wouldn't be able to tell the difference."

"So the Irish pub has a Ukrainian bartender?" I asked.

"Yes," said Eugenia. "And she's quite a lovely young woman. Lots of potential. She could be so many things—have a future. She shouldn't be limited to service-industry jobs with notoriously bad hours and . . ."

"Optics. I think optics is the word you're searching for." Tallulah wore a grin.

"Oh, for heaven's sake, Tallulah," said Eugenia. "You know as well as I do that in Anson's position, optics do matter."

"And who is Anson?" I felt myself squinting.

Tallulah said, "Anson Gibbes Jones is the reverend at Eugenia's church. He's quite the eligible bachelor, and he's been dating our Kateryna."

Fish returned from the house with Eugenia's checkbook. He chuckled as he handed it to Eugenia. "The lovely Kateryna is a recent Ukrainian immigrant. Fascinating story. She won the immigration lottery."

"That's an actual thing?" I asked.

"Indeed," said Eugenia. "Our government selects fifty thousand winners every year. It's a global program. The countries vary. It depends on which countries have sent the fewest immigrants."

"And they can stay forever?" I asked.

"They apply for green cards," said Fish. "They have to go through the regular process. There's an interview, a background check, a medical exam. I think you have to show you can support yourself. About half of the lottery winners actually end up getting green cards."

"Forgive my ignorance," said Camille, "but do green cards expire? How long do lottery winners get to live here?"

Eugenia dashed out a check for my retainer and handed it to me. "Green cards don't expire. People who have them can live here permanently as long as they obey the law, file their taxes, et cetera. Now, if they want to become a citizen, they can apply after they've lived here five years. In Kateryna's case, she's got a year to go before she can apply for citizenship. If I understand her correctly, she's counting the days until she can take her test. Frankly, she knows more about this country than a lot of college students who've lived here their whole lives—and she appreciates it more."

"But the issue is her job." There was a mischievous note in Quinn's voice. "Eugenia thinks it's unseemly for a minister to date a bartender."

"It is *quite* unseemly," said Eugenia. "A minister, and by extension, his family, or those who might aspire to *be* his family, should set a good example. Impressionable young ladies in the church look up to Kateryna. She's very glamorous, naturally, and they all think she's just the coolest thing since sliced bread. The next thing you know, they'll all say they've given up college plans because they want to tend bar like Kateryna."

"Really, do you think so, Eugenia?" Sarabeth's forehead creased skeptically.

"You mark my words," said Eugenia.

"And then there's the matter of her wardrobe," said Camille.

"What's wrong with her wardrobe?" I asked.

Eugenia grimaced.

Tallulah said, "Well, she dresses quite provocatively."

"Come on now," said Fish. "She dresses like young attractive women dress . . . she accentuates her positives."

"Yes, well, women who date ministers need to dress modestly," said Eugenia. "Set a good example. She's a beautiful young woman. She doesn't need to flaunt her wares."

"Her wares?" Fish's voice rose an octave. "Eugenia, really."

"So, I take it you didn't ask Kateryna if she was interested in working in a law office before you arranged a job for her there?" asked Libba.

Eugenia blushed. "Well, no, as a matter of fact. It never occurred to me for a single second that she wouldn't be thrilled to death."

"Hmm . . . ," mused Quinn.

"Did you just walk up to the bar and tell her you'd found her another job?" asked Sarabeth.

"Something like that," said Eugenia. "I thought it was a happy surprise."

"And then what happened?" asked Libba.

"That's when we think Kateryna might've cursed Eugenia in Russian," said Tallulah. "Some of the words were in English."

"I had to leave right after that," said Camille.

"So you said," said Tallulah. "Are you sure you went to the hairdresser this afternoon? Your hair doesn't look any different to me."

"That's the point, isn't it?" said Camille. "It was a touch-up."

"No good deed goes unpunished," said Eugenia.

"Perhaps when she's had time to think about it, she'll change her mind," said Tallulah.

"You really think so?" asked Eugenia.

"No," said Tallulah, "but there's never harm in hoping."

"As if being publicly cursed wasn't bad enough, why on earth did Everette have to be at Dunleavy's today to witness that scene? He needs to stay on the other side of the Cooper River Bridge. What was he doing over here anyway?" asked Eugenia.

"It's the first Monday of the month," said Camille. "Doesn't he always have lunch with a group of other retired judges on the first Monday?"

"He does." said Eugenia. "And that's the group he was with. But they don't typically come to Sullivan's Island. They generally prefer peninsula restaurants with wood paneling, white table-cloths, and water sommeliers."

"I wouldn't give it another thought," said Tallulah. "No one cares what Everette thinks about anything. You'll be shed of him soon enough. And he'll be greeting people at Walmart to earn his Medicare deductible."

"Everette will land on his feet," said Eugenia. "But he'll be someone else's problem."

"I'll start to work tomorrow," I said. "Normally, I would've hopped right on it. But it's been a banner day. I actually have some interesting news."

"Well, spill it," said Eugenia. "Don't just tease us."

"We're officially neighbors," I said. "I'm going to be living in the new house just up the beach."

Eugenia lowered her sunglasses and peered at me. Her expression demanded I elaborate immediately and leave nothing out.

"I'm going to be house sitting for a new client indefinitely," I said.

"I guess it has been an eventful day," said Eugenia. "That's fabulous news, Hadley. Welcome to the island. I've been positively dying to see inside that house."

"Me too," I said. "I haven't even crossed the threshold yet."

"Well do let us know when you're receiving guests," said Tallulah.

"I'm thinking now is good." The words just slipped out of my mouth. Normally, I'd be a nervous wreck and over-plan and fret for at least a month before having friends over. Actually, I'd never really had a close circle of girlfriends, the way many women do. For some reason, I'd just never clicked with other women. Until today. Maybe I was getting ahead of myself, but as unlikely as it seemed, I felt right at home with Eugenia and her friends.

I didn't have to ask twice. Everyone hopped right up. Fish refreshed all our drinks, then stayed behind to dismantle the cabana. Chatting, laughing, and toasting my new home, our boisterous group swarmed up the beach.

Chapter Six

Since the first anniversary of my mother's death, I'd kept a ritual. I briefly considered skipping it that year, mostly because it had been a crazy eventful day and I was exhausted. But letting it go felt like the first step in forgetting her, and I was damned if any of us would be doing that. It was just something I needed to do. After my new friends cleared out, I stopped by my apartment to grab my solid maple Louisville Slugger, then drove over to my father's waterfront, brick Colonial Revival mansion on Murray Boulevard, two blocks down from White Point Garden. He was sipping bourbon on the portico overlooking the gardens.

"Evening, Hadley," he said easily as I opened the wrought iron gate and strode towards the garage.

I didn't respond. I'd come here to remember. To make sure *he* remembered my mother. She'd died alone, except for me and Gavin, worried about the medical bills, worried about me. He had more money than Croesus. He could have—should have—made sure she'd had the latest in treatments. He should have seen to it she was taken to MD Anderson, or Sloan Kettering, gotten her into a drug trial. He should have done *something*. He owed her that.

But he did nothing. He let her die, and he did not one thing to stop it. Not only that, he did nothing to ease her mind. So many things he could have done.

That same year, the year she died, he'd started his classic car collection. How much had he spent on cars that just sat in his massive, climate-controlled garage 99 percent of the time? It was obscene. Now, in the interests of full disclosure, a part of me knew there was more to the story with the cars.

Jolene was my mother's car—the only car she ever owned. She loved that car like crazy, and she left her to me. If I hadn't needed a less flashy car for my job, Jolene would've maybe been my only car too. She was a connection to my mother. Also, she was a thing of beauty, fully restored, mint condition. The only thing that wasn't original was the stereo—which looked like the original but was actually a modern sound system that paired with my iPhone.

I kept Jolene the same way Mom did—under a protective cover—and I babied that car. I asked Mom once why she named her Jolene. She just said Jolene could have her choice of men. I know that's a line from an old Dolly Parton song. Mom always had a thing for classic cars, though the Ford Fairlane, as far as I knew, wasn't especially valuable like some American muscle cars were.

She never told me anything about the part of her life before I was born. I don't know what the story with Jolene was. But clearly, Swinton Legare also had a fondness for classic cars. On the first anniversary of my mother's death, I bashed the fool out of a 1953 Corvette—that was the first year they made Corvettes. He watched me do it, didn't say a word. Now he just waits on the portico. Some years he tries to talk to me. Others, he just drinks and waits.

That year, I chose a red, 1956 Ford Thunderbird convertible.

I swung my bat true, landing the first blow on the windshield. I remembered my mother's face, lined with worry, not for herself, but about me. Before she died, my mother made me promise, no matter what, I'd go to college. She was a clerk in a grocery store, and later a waitress. Mother wanted me to have choices she never did. She knew my father had offered to pay for me to go wherever I wanted. Since he didn't spend one thin dime trying to save my mother's life, I was up front with her and told her I would never take his money for any reason. We'd argued about it. Her solution was to insist I sell the house.

"There's been too much sadness here," she said. "Don't chain yourself to this house out of sentimentality. The taxes are so high the house will own you. Not to mention the upkeep. It's a hundred years old. Something always needs fixing. Sell it and put the money in the bank. Go to college. Travel."

I did as she asked as soon as I graduated from high school. Property values had gotten so crazy in the Old Village, I would've been able to pay for college with money left over. But as it turned out, the financial aid office found a small scholarship and a few grants I qualified for. They put together a package that covered everything and gave me spending money as well. The money from selling the house set me up with a nice nest egg. I wasn't wealthy by any means. But I wasn't destitute, either. I didn't need one damn thing from Swinton Barnwell Drayton Legare.

I smashed a taillight, then realized he had me thinking in cuss words. I whacked the other taillight harder.

My mother raised me by four rules:

1. Always be a lady—and if you ever have to tell someone you're a lady, you're most certainly not one. Ladies do not curse.
2. Always be kind.
3. Be smart—don't ever be anybody's fool.
4. Know how to cook a proper meal.

I tried my best to honor what she taught me.

I didn't need one *single* thing from Swinton Barnwell Drayton Legare.

Except this. I raised the bat over my head and brought it down on the hood.

When I was satisfied with the amount of damage I'd done, I headed out of the garage and back across the yard.

"You're exactly like her." His voice was a low, weathered drawl.

"Thank you." I kept walking.

"She didn't want my money any more than you do. I don't understand why you won't believe that, when you're the same, damn stubborn-headed way yourself."

I spun towards him. "That's different. If there'd been a way for her to live, she'd have taken money from the devil."

"Maybe," he said. "But she wouldn't take it from me."

"You're a damn liar." I ground my teeth.

"Sometimes. If it's necessary. But I'm not lying to *you* about *this*."

"That's awfully convenient, isn't it," I said. "She's not here to set the record straight."

"No. It's not convenient at all. Vivienne may have been stubborn, but she would never . . . *never* . . . have wanted things this way. She would have wanted you to be with your family."

"I have a family. You're not part of it. Why do you think she hid me from you for sixteen years? It certainly wasn't because she thought you'd make an excellent father."

"All I know about that is what she told me. What she told us both, Hadley. She was afraid. Afraid you'd want to be a part of a world she did not want any part of. It wasn't because she thought I was evil. She told you that. She ended things with me before you were born. I did not abandon her, and I didn't know you existed until she got sick. She told you all this."

"She was dying. Her head was fuzzy from all the drugs. If she'd trusted you to be a good dad, she would never have kept us apart."

"I can't win this. I know that. But still, I have the damndest need to beat my head against this wall, occasionally."

"Don't waste your breath."

"This is such a damn shame. Hadley, you always think there'll be more time. But often there's not. Your mother thought she had more time. Time to fix things with you and me. Time to explain to you why she *did not* want to go to MD Anderson, or any of the other specialists. Her mother died of the same thing. She was convinced it was a lost cause. She didn't want to spend her final days in a hospital across the country. She wanted to be with you."

"She didn't mention it," I spat. "We talked about a lot of things before she died. You offering to help with treatment . . . that wasn't one of them. And she knew how important that was to me. She would've told me."

"Time was short. She didn't want to fight with you, Hadley. She told me she was going to put it all in a letter."

"Yeah, so you said. But she didn't, did she? My mother did the things that were important to her. Every. Day. When she knew she was dying, she said the important things. You offering money . . . that never came up."

"She thought she had more *time*," he said slowly. "Time is the one thing no one can make more of."

"I'm aware." I turned and walked through the gate.

Chapter Seven

It was a Monday night, so I had to see about North. I stopped by Publix on the way home and bought two foot-long turkey subs with extra meat and all the trimmings except onions. North doesn't care for onions. I didn't argue with him about the meat. He needed the extra calories, and frankly, North had bigger problems than a healthy diet. I took the subs home and put them in the small refrigerator cube on my covered patio along with several bottles of water, chips, and a package of Nutter Butters, North's favorite. Then I sat in one of the Adirondack chairs and waited.

North Pickens was the first friend I made in kindergarten, and the first boy I ever kissed. I was eight years old when he suggested we should find out what kissing was all about, and I was curious enough to give it a try. He lived with his grandmother in a townhome a few blocks away on Center Street. There was a rumor floating around when we were at Moultrie Middle that North's IQ was higher than 160. I don't doubt that's true. North is the smartest person I've ever met, and he's one of the kindest souls God ever made. He was a classic nerd, awkward with most girls, but not with me. In high school, he had a crush on me. I told him I'd always love him as a friend, and he accepted that. He was my best friend—he still is.

North went to Georgia Tech on a full scholarship, was studying information technology. There's no doubt in my mind he was destined to be another Steve Jobs, only nicer, at least from what I've heard about Steve Jobs. North was a genius with computers, still is, I guess. But then the computer that assigned his roommate junior year changed his life.

Mark Godfrey was another brainiac who was majoring in robotics. He was smart like North, but he had no conscience whatsoever. He talked North into driving him to a party one night. If North had a flaw, it was that he was too nice, maybe a bit naive. Mark—and other people, too—took advantage of North. Somehow, Mark claimed he'd been invited to a frat party, which isn't the most unlikely lie he told, but it was on the list.

North never planned to stay at that party, just drop Mark off. But Mark took his keys so he'd have to stay. Mark was looking after Mark and wanted to be sure he'd have a ride home when he wanted one. Then when the liquor was running low, Mark offered to take a couple of the guys to someone's apartment to get more, likely to score points with the pretty people.

Mark was driving North's car when it plowed into a light pole killing David Fesperman, the front-seat passenger. Mark and the two surviving frat boys fled the scene. They later testified that North, who had hopped in the back seat because he couldn't get his keys away from Mark, had left the party with David to get more liquor. They claimed they tried to stop him from driving because he'd been drinking. North was the only one in the bunch who *hadn't* been drinking. That's what he told me, and I believe him. Aside from the fact that he's never lied to me, here's why: North never drinks alcohol. Never. His father was a mean, ugly drunk who beat his mother to death and is rotting in prison where he belongs. North's grandfather was an alcoholic. His grandmother, who basically raised him, called alcohol the devil's elixir. He's properly terrified of alcohol. He'd never touch it.

David's father was grieving, wealthy, and connected. The district attorney had run on a platform of cracking down on drunk drivers. North was never given a field sobriety test, and yet somehow, even though a top-notch attorney from Middleton, Bull & Vanderhorst went to Atlanta to defend him, North was convicted of felony DUI homicide.

My sweet, funny, brilliant friend went to jail for ten years and came out irrevocably broken. But not for the efforts of Middleton, Bull & Vanderhorst, he would no doubt still be in prison. North is the reason I lost my faith in the system that utterly failed him and David Fesperman and Mark Godfrey as well. North is the reason I know for a stone-cold fact that karma is hogwash. In a world where karma ruled, we'd all get what we deserved. How often have you seen that work out? Frankly, I'm certain I've gotten far better than I deserve thus far. But North . . .

North came back to Mount Pleasant after he was released, but his grandmother had died while he was in prison, so he had nowhere to go. Anyway, I tried to get him to stay with me, but the thing is, since his release, North can't abide being indoors. He has debilitating panic attacks anytime he tries to go inside.

North Pickens, the smartest person I've ever met, is homeless. He rides a bike around Mount Pleasant and makes a pseudo-living doing odd yard chores for whoever will hire him. Occasionally, he'll let me hire him to do something, but he's proud, and sensitive to anything he perceives as a handout. I have no idea where he sleeps. He made me promise I wouldn't try to find out. That's our deal. I don't try to force him to come inside, and he comes by once or twice a week and gets food I leave for him. He particularly likes the subs from Publix.

North has good days and bad days. When he's keeping his demons at bay, we sit and talk, and he's almost like the North I remember from before he went to prison. On those evenings, he comes by between 11:00 and 11:30. Other times he waits until after midnight, when I'm inside and my windows are dark.

At 11:30, I went indoors and turned out all the lights. But on that particular evening, I didn't go upstairs. I waited by the window in the kitchen. I needed to talk to North, and it couldn't wait. At 12:05, I watched him park his bike, take off the sling-style backpack he wore that held a rake, a hoe, and the few other worldly possessions he owned, and creep up to the porch. He took a seat in one of the Adirondack chairs. Carefully, so as not to startle him, I eased the kitchen door open.

"North?" I called softly.

He turned and looked at me, his eyes shining in the moonlight. I could feel the anxiety rolling off of him. "Hadley." His voice was low and even.

I stepped outside and settled back into my chair. "I'm so sorry, but I needed to talk to you."

He let out a long sigh. "It's fine. Good to see you."

"It's real good to see you too. You doing all right?"

"I'm good. What did you want to talk about?"

I told him about Beck Driscoll and his house.

"You checked him out?" he asked.

"Of course. He's on the level—100 percent."

"I doubt that."

"Well, the worst thing that can happen is it doesn't work out and I have to move again."

"That's not the worst thing." North knew a thing or two about worst-case scenarios.

I inhaled deeply and let it out slowly. "No, I guess it isn't. But it's the most likely outcome." I gave him the address and the gate code. "I know it's farther for you, and I'm sorry about that."

He shrugged. "I'll enjoy spending some time on Sullivan's Island too. You been by to see your dad this evening?"

"I paid him my customary visit, yes."

He winced, shook his head. "When are you going to make peace with him?"

"I'm thinking probably never."

The sadness in his face deepened. "He's your dad. At least he's trying."

I felt my hackles raise. "Oh really? Tell me about that, why don't you? What's he trying to do, exactly?"

"He's trying to connect with you. He's tried a hundred ways. But all you can see is the ways he failed you. And I'm not saying he didn't fail you and your mom. But we all fail each other. Not everyone walks away."

"You can't compare your parents to mine."

"No, you can't. That's my point exactly." We'd had this conversation many times. North had been there for me when my mom got sick, through everything. We were both quiet for a minute, then he said, "Hey, Had, would you happen to have an extra bar of soap?"

Lots of folks in the Lowcountry had outdoor showers, especially those who lived near the water or had a pool. North borrowed their facilities on a rotation, spreading out the water usage. But he always brought his own soap, and he did something for the homeowner every time—usually raked up something that needed raking, or weeded a bed, like that. Folks who woke up to yard chores that had been completed overnight knew North had been by, and most were okay with that. Some of them had lived here long enough to have known him before.

"Sure. I'll be right back." I went inside and came back with a bar of Irish Spring, his favorite. "Is there anything else you need?"

"Nah, I'm good. I think I'll just sit here a while, if that's okay."

"You know it's okay. Anytime. And, look . . . don't be intimidated by the house I'm staying in, okay? There's an outdoor shower there you can use every day if you like. And the yard is big. It has lots of trees and bushes. It's private. There's plenty of room for you to, hang out . . . if you like."

He stared off into space for a minute, then said, "We'll see. Thanks."

But I doubted he'd take me up on that. North lived like something was after him and he didn't dare stay in one spot very long.

North had to keep moving.

Chapter Eight

Tuesday morning, I walked as far as the beach would take me and back. The music of the surf whispered to me of the mysteries of the universe, all the things it had seen, all its depths. As it always did, it put the problems of my world into proper perspective.

I'd spent the night in my apartment—I didn't even have sheets for the bed over here yet. Actually, all the beds had the silkiest, softest sheets I'd ever touched. But they weren't my sheets, and I had no idea if squatters had broken in and spent a night or twelve here while the house was empty. It happens, or it certainly could anyway. I would not be sleeping on these sheets until they were washed, nor using the impossibly fluffy towels either. I had a lot to do to settle in. But I couldn't resist working from here today.

This house . . . I couldn't even take it all in, couldn't process it. It was massive, overwhelming, and gorgeous, and everything I'd dreamed of and more. You know how some people dream of what they'll do if they win the big pot—the Mega Millions or Powerball? I do that, anyway. I have plans in place, though I seldom buy the tickets. I'd set up a charitable foundation to help people caught up in the legal system with no hope, like North. And I'd have another charitable foundation that focused on the needs of children in foster care . . . and one that's sole mission was nutrition—getting the word out about how many of our modern health problems could be solved by a plant-based diet.

And I'd have a house exactly like this.

The views were incredible from every room. Most of the windows were floor-to-ceiling sliding glass panels. In several cases, the panels slid back into the wall, opening the room to the massive patio. There were exterior hurricane shutters that deployed at the flip of a switch, wrapping all the glass in metal. Inside, it took me a while to figure out how the shades worked. They were hidden by sleek valances that blended with the woodwork. At a flip of a switch or by remote control, either light-filtering or blackout shades were raised or lowered. I needed an instruction manual for this house, and possibly a map. I would have to digest it bit by bit.

The office was on the second floor, on the corner looking out over the ocean. The room jutted out a few feet from the one adjacent to it, giving the office two sets of corner windows. As I stepped into the room, which had its own little foyer, the wall ahead of me and the perpendicular wall to its left were glass. The wall to my right featured three framed dry erase boards and a wide section of floor to ceiling windows. The remaining wall, now behind me as I stared out at the ocean, housed a closet and a wall of bookcases.

I crossed the room and opened the heavy, solid wood, five-panel door. The walk-in closet housed the modem and router, the security system, complete with dual hard drives, a couple other gadgets that were completely foreign to me, a safe, and a fire-safe file cabinet. On top of the file cabinet was a set of three jumbo three-ring binders. I picked up the first one and perused the table of contents. I wanted a manual for the house, and I had one. It might take me six months to get through it, but I had a manual.

I stepped back into the office and closed the closet door behind me. I'd never seen a desk like the one floated at an angle off the glass corner. The top was a slab of solid wood with sinuous edges, like someone had carved it from a slice out of a massive tree and finished it to a silky gloss. It was perched on top of eight little wooden rods, four on each side, that floated it above two drawer pedestals, also made of solid wood. I sat in the cream-colored leather-looking desk chair. *Frogs raining from the clear blue sky* . . . I had no idea chairs could be that comfortable. I opened the top right desk drawer. It was filled with standard office supplies. And thankfully, the instruction manual for the chair, which apparently had massage and heat settings.

I could've spent all day just ogling that office, which seemed designed especially with me in mind, spinning around in the chair, alternately staring across the Atlantic and up the beach towards Breach Inlet. But I had work to do. I pulled my laptop out of my backpack and set it up on the desk.

Beck had named the house Stella Marina—it was in the paperwork. The Wi-Fi was up and working just fine, with two networks: Stella Marina, and Stella Marina Guest. He'd given me passwords for both and encouraged me to change them immediately. I did that, then checked and upgraded the network security. Then I got down to business.

The Ladson case started out like a hundred other domestic treachery cases I'd worked. As was my custom, I began with an electronic profile of my subject. I have subscription software, created especially for licensed private investigators that makes this easy, pulling information from a variety of databases. I found everything I could about Everette Ladson online. There were quite a few mentions in news articles due to his long career as a judge, and before that, an attorney. What he didn't have that was often helpful in a domestic case was a social media presence. Apparently, he'd limited his online activities to Tinder.

Next, I used online maps to scour the area around his home for the best places to watch him without being spotted. Tradd Street was a difficult area to run surveillance. It was narrow and well traveled. I needed all the information I could get. His home was a few houses down from the intersection with Meeting Street, with the First Scots Presbyterian Church across the street facing Meeting.

After I'd done all my homework, I headed to Charleston and commenced surveillance. Since Jolene tends to stand out in a crowd, I alternated vehicles, mostly using the 2013 white Honda Accord I'd bought precisely because it was one of the most common cars on the road. For the next three days, I took turns following him all over Charleston, washing sheets and towels, and carrying boxes from my apartment to the house.

Judge Everette Ladson was clearly enjoying his retirement. He played golf at the Country Club, tennis at the Citadel, and poker with his buddies at a historic home on Church Street. He lunched at the Yacht Club, had drinks at two different private residences South of Broad, and dinner at Halls Chophouse and Bistronomy by Nico on Spring Street, a newish place I'd heard a lot about and hoped to try.

On Thursday, the third day of surveillance, after a power walk along the Battery and through the neighborhood near his Tradd Street home, which took the entire morning because he stopped to chat with every neighbor and random stranger, he drove his very large, metallic-blue, late-model BMW sedan to Rodney Scott's Whole Hog BBQ on the corner of King and Grove Streets. The idea of all those pit-cooked farm animals made me a little squeamish, but hey, I went where the job took me. It's funny, I didn't think about it much, but what Eugenia had said was true for me too. I started eating this way to support my mother, and later, I stuck with it for my own health. But after I'd done it for a while—detoxed, if you will—the idea of eating a cow or a pig or a chicken seemed absurd.

Everette parked in the Food Lion parking lot and crossed Grove Street. That's when my father met him on the sidewalk, yanking me out of my food reflection. Everette slapped him on the back, and the two of them headed around the corner, towards the King Street entrance. Great. Now I was going to have to slip into a disguise. Everette didn't know me from Adam's house cat, but there's no way Swinton wouldn't notice me immediately. What's worse, once he saw me, he'd maybe make a casual remark to Everette, drawing unwanted attention my way, which would complicate my surveillance, even if Swinton failed to mention I was a PI, a career choice he no doubt disapproved of. I considered my options as I parked the Honda one row over from Everette.

Sometimes I want a disguise to be low-key, to not draw attention to myself, the point being to blend in. Another option that can be just as effective is to dress so outlandishly that people immediately look away, dismiss you as a nut, or both. Given that the only person I needed to be invisible to was my father, I went with option two.

I hopped out of the car, scooted around to the back, and opened the trunk. I kept a plastic tote filled with disguise components, one with spare clothes, and another with my more commonly used surveillance equipment in the back. First, I grabbed a GPS tracker from the surveillance tote.

I walked towards Everette's car, eyes on the horizon, shoulders back, chin high, arms swinging, imagining myself in slow motion, like they do it in movies. Oops—I fake dropped an earring and bent down to attach the tracker to his wheel well. Then I straightened and pantomimed *forgot something* with a dramatic gesture and glance to the sky and walked back to my car. I do a great many things in my life with the audience in mind, because I never know when I have one and when I don't. But I never forget that I might, at least when I'm working.

I rummaged in my wardrobe box and pulled out a purple, pink, and green striped shoulder-length wig, a pair of big-rimmed yellow plastic sunglasses, a lime tie-dyed cropped t-shirt, and a pull-on ankle-length white skirt, the flouncy kind, with tiers and crinkled fabric. Fortunately, I'd worn a tank top and a pair of shorts that day. I slid the skirt and t-shirt on over my clothes, quickly pulled my hair up and snugged it under the wig, swapped my sneakers for a pair of sandals, and popped on the sunglasses. Then I crossed the street, rounded the corner, pushed the wooden door with the sign that said "One Way In" open, and stepped into Rodney's.

The long, narrow dining room was between me and the wooden, white-topped counter, where a line formed for ordering. Neither Everette nor Swinton were in line. I scanned the dining room. This was odd. Everette was immediately to my left. I could've reached out and touched him. He'd taken a table in the front corner by the window. He was by himself and had opened a Wall Street Journal.

Swinton was seated across the room, also by himself, at the front window table on the right. Both men had ordered, as they had numbers on their tables. So they had just run into each other outside, okay, fine . . . but surely they weren't both here to eat alone. Old friends like them would've decided to sit together if they were both by themselves.

I crossed the room and got in line, turning my attention to the menu, scanning for something I could eat. When my turn came, I stepped to the counter, and the smiling woman at the register greeted me. If she had any opinions about my appearance, she didn't let on.

"Hey, how are you?" I smiled. My mother had waited tables in a restaurant from the time she was seventeen until the year before she died. She worked hard and put up with a lot. I made a point to be kind to folks in the service industry.

"I'm good, how are you today?"

"I'm great. I'd like a Pig Out Salad, no bacon, no cheese, please, and an unsweetened iced tea."

"What kind of meat with that?"

"No meat." I smiled at her.

She blinked, confused. "What dressing?"

"Do you have balsamic vinegar? Not the dressing, just the vinegar." Oil is pure fat, even olive oil, the "healthy" oil. All the fiber and water has been removed, leaving only the calorie-dense fat. It's like the processed sugar of fats. You think when you adopt this way of eating you can never give up the oils. But a month in, anything with oil makes your mouth feel like an oil slick, and you feel queasy after eating it.

"No, ma'am," said the woman behind the counter. "We have ranch, thousand island, blue cheese, honey mustard, and Italian."

"Just some lemon slices, please."

She scrunched her face into an expression that inquired why I'd chosen a BBQ restaurant for a salad with no dressing and no meat. I just kept smiling. She shook her head, took my money, and gave me a number.

The dining room was halfway full, and the line at the counter had grown in the last few minutes. The noise level was building. I snagged a table near Everette, settled in, and fake scrolled my phone. After a few minutes, a server brought Everette a brisket sandwich with fries and an order of hush puppies.

From the corner of my eye, I caught movement in the direction of Swinton's table. I glanced his way in time to see a blonde who had to be close to my age approach the table. He stood and spoke to her, then gestured towards the table and waited for her to be seated before sliding back into his seat.

Just exactly who was this? I continued to fake scroll my phone as I snapped a few pictures. Her back was to me, so I couldn't get a shot of her face, which was unfortunate. She was dressed for the role of an assistant district attorney on one of the legal TV dramas, but I knew all the ADAs in Charleston County, and she wasn't one. They appeared engrossed in a conversation that indicated they were familiar with each other on some level. This didn't seem to be a Tinder date. I wished I had a microphone planted on the napkin holder.

I glanced at Everette, who was thoroughly enjoying his brisket and reading a folded-over page of the paper. No sign of *his* floozy. Was the blonde Swinton's? Was he cheating on Judith again? When I looked back Swinton's way, a server was delivering sandwiches and fries. He must've known what to order for her. Could this be some flavor of business lunch?

Swinton wasn't retired. He'd turned over a lot of the day-to-day operation of his real estate development company to J. T., but he still did whatever suited him. I knew this because J. T. told me, in the casual way he shared things related to our common parent. J. T. never pressed me to embrace Swinton. He knew better. But I knew it hurt him that I hated the father he adored. J. T. and I may have shared a father, but we had vastly different relationships with him.

The blonde leaned in and placed a hand on Swinton's arm in a not-very-businesslike manner. Had I finally caught him in the act? Off and on as time permitted, for years, I'd tailed Swinton, as a sort of penance to Judith. The thing was, I liked Judith. She'd always been kind to me, or tried to, anyway.

When I first found out Swinton was my father, my mother was so sick, and I wasn't feeling all that charitable towards the woman who'd occupied her place in his life. I may have been a teeny bit obnoxious to Judith. Later, I came to understand she was a victim just like my mother. I figured if I could catch him doing what he no doubt was, she could take him to the cleaners, and perhaps I would have squared a debt with her. I probably needed to talk to a shrink about all of this, but who had the time for all that navel-gazing?

A server set my salad in front of me with a quizzical look. Whether that was to do with my outfit or my food, I couldn't say. I squeezed the lemon wedges on the mixed veggies, sprinkled on some walnuts I had in my purse, and dug in. Twenty minutes later, Everette folded his newspaper and rose to leave. I hated leaving without getting a license plate number for the blonde lunching with Swinton and a closeup of her face, but I wasn't being paid to document *his* infidelity. I would have to pick this up another day. I waited a couple beats, then stood. Instead of following Everette out the door on the Grove Street side of the building, I walked out the "in" door, on the King Street side, pausing in the doorway long enough to fake something important on my phone and snap a quick photo of Swinton's lunch date from the front. Then I hurried around the building and caught up with Everette.

His next stop that afternoon was back at his Tradd Street

home—Eugenia's home. Everette's sleazy behavior had rendered him not much more than a squatter in Eugenia's house. Was I judging him harshly? I hadn't actually *seen* him with another woman yet. Lots of wives suspect their husbands of infidelity. Sometimes they were right. Okay, usually, by the time they hired me, they knew their husbands were cheating, but they needed proof. Once in a blue moon, the spouse I was investigating was innocent. Typically, I withheld judgement until I actually caught the guy—usually, not always, it was the guy—in the act. Why had I assumed out the gate that Eugenia was right and Everette was a louse with no proof? That was unlike me. But I found Eugenia to be highly intelligent and not prone to emotional decisions. And Everette was a big-grinning, back-slapping friend of my father's.

Everette pulled into the basement garage of the house, a three-story brick Georgian affair. I'd lucked out that morning and snagged a parking place on Tradd, but that afternoon my luck didn't hold. I drove on past, then made a left on Meeting and circled back around to the First Scots Presbyterian Church parking lot off King Street. A small lot, perhaps for staff, it was virtually empty. I borrowed a spot and made a quick call to the church. I'd saved the number during my research, just in case.

"Hey, my name is Darcy Singleton?" I said when a woman answered, my voice raising at the end in a question where there was none, a habit carved in my DNA by generations of Southern women who were bred to be pleasing above all else.

"How can I help you?" She said it real friendly, like she truly did want to help.

"I'm afraid my car is giving me trouble. It has died, right here on King Street. I didn't want to block the road, so I pulled into your parking lot."

"Oh no. I'm so sorry to hear that."

"Would it be okay if my car stayed here just a little while? My husband's going to come see about it when he gets off work. I don't know a thing about cars myself."

"Why sure, that'll be fine. Just so I know which one it is, what does your car look like?"

"It's an older white Honda Accord."

"All right, Miss Darcy. I hope your husband gets it fixed for you. Thank you for calling and letting us know."

"Thank you so much." I hated lying to people, but it was honestly a big part of my job. Pretexting. That was the official name for it. But I comforted myself in the knowledge that I only ever did it in service to the greater good.

I popped the trunk and hopped out. As quickly as I could, I peeled off my bohemian ensemble and tossed it in the back. I pulled my hair into a high ponytail and put on a faded navy Charleston RiverDogs baseball cap. Then I swapped out my sunglasses for RayBan knockoffs, changed back into my tennis shoes, grabbed a folded tourist map, closed the trunk, and high-tailed it down King Street.

As I rounded the corner onto Tradd, I spotted Everette on the sidewalk across the street, heading in the opposite direction. He carried a reusable grocery bag. I faked an untied shoelace and bent to fake fix it, then I followed him at a safe distance over to Burbage's Self-Service Grocery on Broad Street. This case was rattling the skeletons in my closet every which way I turned. Burbage's and I had history. To be accurate, my mother and Burbage's had history. I'd never set foot in the place. But she worked here as a clerk for two years. It was her first job. And it's where she met Swinton.

Just before you get to Colonial Lake, Savage Street runs at an angle between Broad Street and Rutledge, cutting a triangle into the neighborhood. Burbage's sat in the point of the triangle, facing diagonally across Broad. The store was a Charleston institution. It occupied the lower floor of a white wooden two-story building that dated back to 1874, with a dark green awning and light green shutters.

Originally a combination store and saloon, it was built by the Lutjen family, who immigrated to Charleston from Hanover,

Germany. As Burbage's Self-Service Grocery, it had served the neighborhood since 1948. Burbage's was the kind of neighborhood grocery store that delivered groceries to residents, and at one time—a simpler time—even put them away in cabinets, or so I'd heard. It was the only grocery store South of Broad. Everette carried his reusable bag inside, and I followed him.

Naturally, the place had a nostalgic feel. With a black and white checkered tile floor and several artful displays of specialty items, it exuded charm. It wasn't a large store at all, so I needed to busy myself not looking at Everette. I approached the row of coolers along the left-hand wall and browsed drinks, listening to Everette chat up the lady behind the counter in the back. Thirty minutes later, after shooting the breeze with two other customers, Everette left with wine, chocolate, truffled ravioli and sauce, salad, assorted cheeses, and fresh flowers. This had romantic evening in written all over it. I needed to figure out my best vantage point to get photos. I hung back, paid for a bottle of water, then followed him.

Since I knew where Everette was headed, on the way back I lagged way behind, gave him plenty of room, and plotted my strategy for capturing him on film in midcanoodle.

I called Eugenia. "Where is the master bedroom in your Tradd Street house?" I asked when she answered.

"Why, it's upstairs. The master suite runs along the front of the house. Why do you ask?"

"I'll explain when I see you. Gotta go."

"Had—"

I ended the call. She'd put two and two together fast enough anyway. I didn't want to share my suspicions prematurely. The front of the house looked out across Tradd Street and the First Scots Presbyterian Church. What I needed was access to the second floor of the church, which occupied the corner of Meeting and Tradd. It would have an excellent view of Eugenia's house, and I could stay out of sight. Tradd Street was narrow and well-traveled. The church really was my best option.

It was nearly two thirty. If Everette were entertaining this evening, he likely wasn't expecting company for a while yet, but there was no guarantee. I needed to get into position as quickly as possible. But what if Everette went out in the meantime? What if he was going to her place and taking dinner and all the trimmings? He could disappear while I was figuring a way into the church. Even if he didn't, sure as shrimp, I'd be on the second floor of the church when he backed out of the driveway. I did have a tracker on his car, but I didn't want to miss anything while he was out of sight. I needed to attack the afternoon and evening surveillance in two phases: ground level until he either left or his company arrived, and then later from the second floor of the church.

Parking on Tradd Street was problematic for several reasons, but the biggest issue was it left me very exposed to being spotted, not to mention it was a sunny day in June in Charleston. I wouldn't be able to stay in a closed-up car without the engine running for very long. I needed to find a better option. I stepped up my pace and jogged past Everette, then back to my car. The church parking lot off King Street backed up to the church, which faced Meeting.

I stopped near the car and pretended to consult my handy tourist map, for the benefit of anyone who might stumble upon me. The parking lot was empty, and fairly well screened by trees and surrounding buildings. I walked in the direction of the church, then bore left across a herringbone brick walkway, towards the back property lines of the homes across Tradd Street from Everette's house.

I scanned the area. The neighboring yard closest to the church was separated from the parking lot by a brick wall more than six feet tall. Interesting . . . the wall was lined with historic grave markers, some too worn to read. I'd lived just across the Cooper River my whole life, and I'd never seen this. Where were the people buried? Under the wall? There was a story here, but not one I could investigate today.

There was an alley at the end of the wall that ran between the church and the house next to it, accessible from Tradd Street. The alley was completely blocked by scaffolding and construction equipment—work was apparently being done on the church. A chain link fence—who knew they even allowed those South of Broad?—separated the alley from the neighboring yard. Fortunately for me, the fence was lined with trees and shrubs, which completely screened it. Unfortunately, the people living in the house could look out a window and they'd no doubt see me in their bushes.

I went back to the car and changed outfits in the back seat. Everette might remember seeing me in the grocery store if he spotted me again today. This time, I put on a long green sleeveless sundress that buttoned up the front and sandals. I pulled my hair into a low ponytail and donned my big straw hat. Then I walked at a leisurely pace back over to Tradd Street via King, ending up back on Tradd just as Everette passed out of sight on the way back to his house. Most of the homes on Tradd were so close to the sidewalk the line of sight didn't extend very far. Crepe myrtles were planted in cutouts all along both sides of the sidewalk, adding to the visibility issue. I stayed on the right-hand sidewalk and sped up until I could see him.

The ground-level floor of his home was the basement, which housed the garage and what appeared to be storage. The entrance was situated on the right-hand side of the first floor above the basement. I watched as he climbed the steps to his front door, slowing my gait, meandering along, admiring the crepe myrtles and the flowers spilling out of window boxes. Then I dillydallied long enough to get a good view of the house next to the church and its yard from this side of the alley. I would be well concealed along that narrow strip of side yard that ran beside the chain link fence.

I crossed the street, ostensibly for a closer look at the window boxes adorning the house next to Everette's. I've never had the time or inclination to garden, but I surely did enjoy looking at the flowers. Yellow, purple, and white blooms cascaded all over each other and out the front of the containers, with some type of ivy adding a touch of green. Maybe one day I'd give gardening a try, but I didn't see that in my near future. I studied the garage door and the front door a little closer. These were the only two ways into the house. I'd used mapping software to look at the lot. You could access the long, narrow courtyard from a set of French doors off a sunporch, but there was no way out of the courtyard unless you climbed over the tall brick wall or went back through the house.

Everette was likely inside getting spiffed up for his evening. I headed on down Tradd and circled back to my car. I rolled down the windows and got a breeze blowing through to cool things off. Then I pulled out my laptop and checked property services for who owned the house across from Everette—the one that adjoined the church parking lot. Once I had a name, I searched my consolidated databases for a cellphone number for the lady of the house. I looked up the number for Edible Arrangements, then opened my spoofing app, typed in the number I was calling and the number I wanted to appear to be calling from.

She answered on the third ring. "Hello?"

"Good afternoon. Mrs. Williams?"

"Yes."

"This is Monica Ferndale from Edible Arrangements. We have a delivery for you this afternoon. Are you at home to receive it, ma'am?"

"What? Why no, I'm out of town at the moment."

"Is there someone else at home who can accept delivery?" I asked.

"Not just now. My husband won't be in until very late this evening."

"Perhaps there's a housekeeper at home?"

"Not today. There's no one home at all. Can you bring it tomorrow?"

"Yes, ma'am, we surely can. What's the best time?"

"Any time after nine tomorrow will be fine. Francesca will be there until five."

"All right, we'll see her then."

"Thank you so much. I appreciate your being flexible. I can't imagine who sent it."

"Oh, I wouldn't want to spoil the surprise. There'll be a card, ma'am."

"Thank you again."

I hung up and called Edible Arrangements and ordered a small Rainbow and Butterflies bouquet, made from pineapple, melon, and chocolate covered strawberries with swizzles. It looked delicious. I considered it a thank you to Mrs. Williams for unknowingly providing me with the perfect spot to watch the Ladson house across the street. I asked for the card to read, *I hope this brightens your day the way you have brightened mine,* with no signature. The card I paid with was a prepaid card I kept on hand for such things, so there was no way to trace the purchase.

It was three fifteen. There'd been no alert from my tracking app that Everette had left the house. I rolled up the windows and opened the back of the car. My iPhone took great pictures, but some jobs called for a longer lens. I unpacked my good camera and slipped the neck strap over my head. Then I grabbed a compact canvas folding chair, my backpack, and an outdoor speaker and closed the trunk.

Keeping my eyes peeled for church employees and neighbors, I set my things on the other side of the four-foot chain link fence, then climbed over. So far no sign of a dog, which was a blessing. I gathered my equipment and moved quickly towards the line of tall, sculpted bushes along the perimeter. Turning sideways, I threaded myself and my paraphernalia between the bushes and navigated to the far-right corner of the tree line. Looking through the foliage, I could see Everette's house clearly. No sign of activity.

Making sure I was screened from both Tradd Street and from the church parking lot, I set up my chair. The green canvas fabric on the chair, my green dress, and my natural woven hat helped me to blend in with the greenery. I set up my speaker and plugged it into my phone. Now it was all about the waiting, which was ninety percent of all stakeouts.

I passed the time scrutinizing the bedroom windows along the front of the house. Sadly, they had plantation shutters which were already closed. I couldn't imagine anyone would be opening them for the evening's entertainment. There was no sense in sneaking into the church. No matter how good my angle, I couldn't see through wood.

At precisely six o'clock, a brunette in a black skirt suit tailored to fit her real good approached the little wrought iron fence that surrounded the entrance to Eugenia's house. I needed the potential floozy to turn around so I could get her face, and I came prepared. Did you know that you can download audio files of animal sounds from the Internet? There's a whole library of them. Cell phone ring tones are so common no one pays any attention to one that's not their own. But animal noises get their full and immediate focus. I pressed play on "Monkey Excited Screech" and got my camera ready.

The monkey screeched.

The brunette whirled my way and stared hard at the bushes. The look on her face screamed, *What the devil was that?*

I started snapping.

She was a looker, with long, sleek dark brown hair and makeup that looked like it could've been professionally done, but not with the goal of appearing natural. I'm not saying it was overdone, just obvious. She was gorgeous. And I'd guess at least ten or fifteen years younger than Everette, maybe more.

The monkey didn't screech again, and after a few seconds, she blinked and shook her head, perhaps thinking she must've imagined the wild animal in the bushes. She turned around, opened the gate, and climbed the steps. Everette must've been waiting for her. He immediately opened the front door. As she stepped past him, he leaned out and scanned the street. He looked guilty as a kid with his hand in his little sister's Halloween candy. I took his picture too.

Everette closed the door, and I made note of the time. If she was his date, as opposed to someone with legitimate business, she'd be in there a while. I got out a bag of popcorn and a bottle of Bai Nariño Peach tea.

It was a long evening. At ten fifteen, someone driving a late model Lincoln SUV parked in front of the house and entered through the wrought iron gate. I assumed it was Mr. Williams, coming in late as expected. Fortunately for me, it was too dark for him to see me in the lushly planted border bed, either from the street or inside the house.

At five past one, Everette's front door opened. I took a few quick snaps of the as-yet-unnamed brunette coming out the door. Everette was standing in the doorway, but he failed to oblige me by kissing her goodnight. I couldn't make out what he was wearing. She was in my line of sight. I laid my camera on my chair and grabbed my phone. Through the bushes, over the fence, and across the parking lot I dashed. I darted down King Street and pulled up short at the corner of King and Tradd. Then I strolled casually down Tradd towards Everette's house.

The brunette crossed the street and walked towards a red Tesla. I discreetly snapped photos of her, the car, and the license plate, as she got in and drove away. I would have her name as soon as I could run the plate. I didn't have enough proof yet for Eugenia's purposes, but it looked mighty suspicious. And since they were apparently bold enough to commit marital misbehavior in Eugenia's house, getting proof would be ridiculously easy.

Chapter Nine

Friday, June 11, 7:00 a.m.
Sullivan's Island, South Carolina

The master suite in the beach house occupied the entire righthand side of the second floor—opposite the office, on the other side of the area open to the family room below. I spent my first night there with the sliding doors that opened to a balcony wide open. The song of the surf gentled me into the deepest sleep of my life. Eugenia yanked me straight out of it when she showed up at the door unannounced at 7 a.m. the next morning, hammering out Chopsticks on my doorbell, which was jarring, as the doorbell played, "I Love Beach Music," by the Embers.

"Who exactly is Everette having carnal knowledge of in my family home?" she asked the second I opened the door.

"I figured you'd work that out," I said. "Let's get some coffee." I turned around and headed towards the kitchen.

Eugenia followed me through the foyer and past the living room and dining room, which was really all part of the same space. The floor plan of my dream house was very open, the ceilings crazy high. She stopped in wonder to stare at the aquarium. "Oh, my."

"It's mesmerizing, isn't it?" It filled the entire wall between the kitchen and dining room. Brightly colored fish of many different species swam back and forth, in and out of the coral towers, and around a sunken boat. "I just want to sit in front of it and watch them swim."

"It's quite relaxing. I may need to come sit and stare at this for therapeutic reasons."

"Anytime," I said.

"How do you get in there to clean it?"

"Well, actually, I don't. A service takes care of the fish and the aquarium itself. But to answer your question, there's a closet around that corner that runs between the aquarium and the kitchen. Everything's handled from there."

"Amazing."

I continued into the kitchen and Eugenia followed.

She climbed onto one of the cream-colored leather counter stools with the metal pole base. They looked very modern to my eye, but they were growing on me. The entire house was decorated in a very minimalist, contemporary style that was unlike anything I'd ever had, but somehow calming. Virtually everything in the kitchen was white or cream, except the stainless steel appliances, a couple of plants, and a bowl of Granny Smith apples someone had left for me. I set about the business of boiling water and grinding coffee beans.

"This really is a lovely house." Eugenia seemed to gather I needed a moment to come fully awake before launching into work. "These hardwoods are exquisite. And I love that they run throughout the house."

"I love them too," I said. "They're light, but not too light. Rustic, not shiny. And I particularly like the wide planks."

"So much light—so open to the outdoors. I like the way the indoor living, dining, and breakfast rooms are all mirrored with the same spaces outdoors. And you open up that wall and it all flows together. And that aquarium . . . that's a masterpiece. You could throw the consummate party here. It's a shame the fellow who built it won't ever get to enjoy it. It looks like he put a lot of love into it. But what good fortune for you."

"I still keep thinking I'm going to wake up from a dream." We were both quiet while we waited for the coffee to brew. I'd stayed up far too late profiling Everette's mistress. This was one of those mornings I needed caffeine to function. I poured us each a mug of coffee and set the oat milk creamer and the date syrup where Eugenia could reach them.

She fixed her coffee, took a sip, and met my eyes over the top of her cup. "Now . . . what have you learned? Tell me everything."

"He's seeing Jordyn Jackman. She's a local realtor, about fifteen years younger than him. She's divorced, and yes, they appear to be spending time together in your Tradd Street home."

"I will *kill* him." Her voice had sharp, lethal edges.

"No," I said. "You won't. You will hurt him much harder and longer than that. Just give me a few more days. I need to set up cameras in the house. You okay with that?"

"Of course." Wheels spun at a frenetic pace in her brain. I could see it.

"I'll install several . . . one in the bedroom."

"Do whatever you need to do." She pulled her key chain from a pocket in her shorts, slid a key off, and laid it on the counter. "Get me a pen and paper, and I'll write down the alarm code."

I grabbed a notepad from the built-in desk off the kitchen. "Eugenia, as tempting as it may be, now is not the time to confront him with this knowledge. Wait until we have the evidence."

She narrowed her eyes, shot daggers at me, and gave her head a little shake, like she was sorely vexed. Then she rolled her eyes dramatically and sighed. "I know," she said, with a guilty look that told me I'd read her intentions correctly. She'd been planning her retaliation until I called her on it. "I'm not an idiot."

"Of course you're not," I soothed. "I just need you to be patient a while longer."

"I can be patient." She tore off the page and handed me the code, wearing an angelic expression.

"That's good. Because as long as they don't suspect anything, they'll give us the evidence you need for court. I need an hour or so with him out of the house so I can set up the cameras."

Eugenia's eyes glistened, her tough façade crumbling. She wiped away a tear. "I had hoped . . ." She looked down at her hands and sniffed. "I knew he was cheating, but I suppose after everything, I'm still heartbroken to have it confirmed. Everette was my first love. My high school sweetheart. We've been through a lot together. A part of me held out hope."

My heart broke for her. I reached out and put a hand on her arm. "Of course you did. That's only natural. I know how difficult this must be for you."

Eugenia sniffled once more, then rallied. "Can we post the video footage online? I'd like nothing better than to plaster his wrinkled rear all over the Internet. It would serve him right."

"Nooooo. No. No. No. No. We can't. First of all, they'd know right then we had cameras in the house, and we'd lose our advantage. Secondly, judges rarely enjoy one party turning the other into an Internet sensation."

"Oh, he'd be a sensation all right."

"Eugenia, please—"

"Oh, all right, fine."

"I have your word? You won't confront him?"

"You have my solemn oath as a card-carrying member of Costco's warehouse."

Somehow, I was not reassured as to her intentions.

Chapter Ten

Friday, June 11, 11:45 a.m.
Tradd Street, Charleston, South Carolina

Given that Everette had entertained Jordyn Jackman the evening before, and it was the first time I'd seen him with her in the three days I'd been following him, I reasoned he was unlikely to see her that morning. I'd worked many a domestic case. Sometimes, especially when one party was quite a bit older than the other, you ran into adults with raging enthusiasms who behaved like hormonal teenagers. Thus far, I'd seen no evidence Everette fancied himself in love. I decided to focus on getting my cameras in place for their next rendezvous.

When Everette left just before lunch, I didn't follow. From behind the dark tinted windows in the back seat of the Honda, I watched him pull out of the driveway. Then I watched the car icon on the tracking app on my phone as he drove to the dry cleaners, the bank, and the Walgreens on King Street before parking in a garage on Cumberland near East Bay. If his habits of the past few days were any guide, he was headed to lunch.

I grabbed my backpack and let myself into the house with the key Eugenia had given me, then punched in the code to disable the alarm. What a lovely home. I admired the wide-plank heart pine floors and the details in the trim work as I surveyed the foyer, living room, dining room, kitchen, and sunporch. The key to hidden cameras is strategic placement, that and disguising them, of course. The best place to put them, in my experience, is in smoke detectors. You get a bird's-eye view, and they're impossible to detect without getting on a ladder and taking the unit apart. The downside was you had to get on a ladder and take the smoke detector apart to install one. When one was surreptitiously in a residence while its occupant was out to lunch of an undetermined length, one kept the ladder climbing to a minimum.

Attempting to cover the entire house was overkill. There was an 83 percent chance the money shots would come from the master bedroom. But, a certain percentage of the population will get frisky in the kitchen on occasion, and then there's always the possibility of one thing leading to another while relaxing on the sofa after dinner. For my purposes, three cameras were sufficient.

Kitchens were tricky. Most people knew what was on their kitchen counters. A new item would be noticed. The kitchen in Eugenia's historic home featured antique plates hung on racks along one wall and over what had once been a mantle. I chose the plate with the best angle and twisted an anchor wire around the frame. Then I pulled up the feed on my app and verified coverage.

My eyes in the living room were hidden in a book added to a stack on a table by the window. I grabbed a step ladder from the broom closet and put in the extra time upstairs in the master bedroom to put the camera in the smoke detector, which ensured I wouldn't miss a shot. It took me less than thirty minutes to get all three online. I checked the app for the GPS tracker and verified Everette's car hadn't moved, then I reset the alarm and let myself out.

All I had to do now was sit back and wait for Everette to entertain his mistress. The cameras were motion activated. The footage I needed would be automatically shot. Within a week, I would have everything Eugenia needed to send Everette packing and embrace the future on her own terms. I was so happy to be able to help my new friend.

And really, the job had been easy compared to most domestics. Everette had made it easy by being careless enough to entertain his mistress in his wife's home. The Ladson case would be wrapped up in record time, with minimal expense for my client. Feeling pleased with myself, I went back to Sullivan's Island to finish settling into the beach house.

Chapter Eleven

Friday, June 11, 1:45 p.m.
Tradd Street, Charleston, South Carolina
Mrs. Josephine Huger (you-JEE)

I'll say this much . . . I have never seen such an unpleasant display in all my life. I was walking Petunia, our tricolor English bulldog over on Tradd Street early this afternoon. Petunia and I had just turned the corner off of Meeting Street when we first heard the commotion.

Everette was bellowing at poor Pepper Townsend to get off his property. You may know Pepper. She's a real estate broker, one of the best in the city, if you ask me. Pepper is not from here, but she made enough money selling historic homes to live in one. She bought a single house over on Gibbes Street ten years or more ago, and it's been very tastefully redone.

Apparently, Eugenia had asked Pepper to sell the house on Tradd Street, because there she was, putting up a For Sale sign on the fence. Technically, when Petunia and I arrived, Pepper wasn't even in the yard. She was standing on the sidewalk. But Everette could not be concerned with this technicality. He was howling at her like one of the hounds of hell. Pepper was unperturbed by his antics. She's a professional.

Now, everyone knows of course, that home has been in Eugenia's family for generations. I understand she's been living over on Sullivan's Island recently. I do recall hearing that she had a bout with cancer, bless her heart. Goodness, I haven't spoken to Eugenia in years. If memory serves, the last time was at a fundraiser for the Coastal Conservation League.

Eugenia became quite the philanthropist, didn't she? Who would've ever guessed it? She was quite the party girl back when we were in school. Wherever a good time was being had, Eugenia and Everette and Swinton and Judith were always right in the middle of it. I suppose we all grow up. And too, things changed after the accident. You remember, when Amelia Simons and Charles Butler were killed in that boating accident on the Stono River? I guess we all changed after that. It's downright sobering when it dawns on you that you're not immortal after all.

Where was I? Anyway, Everette has been living in the Tradd Street house by himself for quite some time. I don't have any idea what their marital situation is, or at least I hadn't any idea until I saw Everette's hissy fit. Apparently, there's trouble in the Ladson marriage.

The open house is scheduled for tomorrow, Saturday, from ten until four, if you know of anyone looking South of Broad.

Chapter Twelve

Friday afternoon, June 11–Saturday, June 12

Friday afternoon, I took my time getting acquainted with my new home. After I'd finished unpacking, I went through it room by room, marveling at the blend of style and function. I was relieved none of the electronics operated on voice command. Those things freaked me out a little, the way they were always listening.

I got takeout from Poe's Tavern—a veggie Amontillado burger with no cheese or sour cream—and ate on the deck. Since I'd gotten in late and Eugenia had interrupted my beauty sleep that morning, I turned in early, again sleeping with the sliding doors open so I could hear the surf.

I couldn't tell you what prompted me to drive by Everette's house the next day. It was Saturday, and since the Ladson case was on autopilot, I had the day off. I'd texted J. T. and arranged to meet at Gnome Cafe over near MUSC for lunch. We typically got together during our birthday week, and I hadn't seen him yet. Anyway, I had a few minutes to spare, so Jolene and I tootled down Tradd.

The first thing that caught my eye was the small crowd just

inside the gate. Was Everette entertaining? Seemed an odd hour for it. I rolled closer. *Sweet baby Moses in a basket.* The house was for sale—and there was an open house in progress.

I voice dialed Eugenia as I looped around the block searching for a parking place.

"Eugenia, what have you done?" I asked.

"I have sent Everette a message."

"What were you thinking? Explain it to me, please. Start at the beginning."

"I was thinking that my husband is sleeping with his mistress in my mother's house. The house where my grandmother gave birth to my father. I was thinking selling the house and putting his sorry ass on the street would be immensely satisfying, and I have to say, based on what Pepper told me about him foaming at the mouth in the street, so far, I've not been disappointed."

"You hired me to do a job, and you're making that job very difficult, Eugenia. I want to see you annihilate him in court. But the cameras I just installed yesterday are useless now. He'll never take Jordyn to your house again. He knows you know. You've given up your advantage."

"Do you imagine he'll stop seeing his harlot?" she asked.

"Well, no, I seriously doubt *that*."

"Then you should still be able to get the evidence, shouldn't you?"

I took a deep cleansing breath and pulled to the curb on Meeting Street. "It will be infinitely harder now, but yes." Only twenty-four hours ago, this case had such a positive outlook.

"Well, then. This will cost me more money, as it will take more of your time. I'm perfectly fine with that, Hadley. This was something I needed to do. I probably should have told you, and I apologize for not doing so. But I'm not one bit sorry I did it."

I thought back to Monday night and my annual visit to Swinton's garage. I understood needing to make a point. "I get it, Eugenia. I do. Have you heard from him?"

"He called. I didn't answer. He declined to leave a message."

"He would've had to've left for the open house. Let me go find him. I'll talk to you later."

I opened the tracking app on my phone.

What the devil? Everette was on I-26 near Summerville, moving northwest towards Columbia. Where was he headed? So much for my day off. Helen of Troy.

I called J. T. and canceled on my way out of town. It was very fortunate that I kept an overnight bag packed and in both cars for such occasions. It was not so fortunate that I was driving Jolene, as she tended to stand out in traffic. On the other hand, I wouldn't have to worry about Everette spotting a tail when he was forty minutes and a county away.

Since I had no idea where he was headed, I set the tracking app to route me to Everette's location. My destination would continuously update. With my phone mounted on a vent clip so I could see the screen while I drove and "Hold On Loosely" by 38 Special playing on the sound system, I followed Everette.

We drove up I-26 nearly to Spartanburg before getting off on I-385. I was near Gray Court when the tracking app showed Everette's car come to a stop immediately behind the Westin Poinsett hotel in Greenville. Was Jordyn Jackman with him? Was this some sort of romantic getaway? Or was Everette so humiliated by Eugenia's stunt with the open house he'd fled Charleston and the gossip that was sure to spread amongst the South of Broad gentility? I needed to determine whether or not he'd checked into the Westin.

When I arrived in Greenville, I found his car parked in one of the valet spots on the ground level in the Poinsett garage. He could've valet parked just to go to a restaurant in the area. But it was nearly four, late for lunch and early for dinner. Odds were, he'd checked into the hotel. I parked one level up, then walked down the steps. Fortunately for me, the back entrance to the hotel wasn't key card controlled this time of day. Perhaps more hotel guests self-parked in the garage and used this entrance than dropped their cars with the valet at the fountain out front.

The lobby was elegantly appointed, with coffered ceilings that soared to the second floor. Originally opened as the Poinsett Hotel in 1925, the building had fallen into disrepair after changing hands several times. Developers purchased it in the late nineties and restored it, turning it into arguably the nicest hotel in Greenville. I took a seat in a club chair, part of a grouping of four chairs around a coffee table in the back corner of the lobby lounge. There were many such conversation areas, some with sofas, scattered across the room. It was early for happy hour. I had the place to myself except for a pair of ladies who might've wandered in for a drink after lunch that had turned into several. Their conversation was punctuated with occasional laughter, the volume rising, then falling.

From a house phone in the lobby, I called and ordered room service for Everette. Nothing big—a pricey bottle of wine would make him wonder. But a pot of coffee and a couple cookies . . . well, that could easily be compliments of the hotel. Later, if he even noticed it on the bill, there was a remote chance he'd challenge it. In the unlikely event he did, both he and the hotel would assume it was an honest mistake somewhere in the process. There'd be no way to trace it to me. Meanwhile, I'd confirmed he'd checked into the hotel.

When the waiter rolled the cart up to the eleventh floor, I rode in the elevator with him. We chatted about the stage production of Tootsie, which had been at the Peace Center recently. I also mentioned to him how delighted I'd been to receive my complimentary coffee and cookies the afternoon I'd checked in because I'd needed the caffeine boost to perk me up in time for dinner with my parents. It's such a thoughtful thing for management to do. He hadn't known they were doing that, but he was happy to know it now. With a pinch of luck, due to the power of suggestion, he'd mention that to Everette.

When the waiter knocked on the door of room 1103, I smiled and waved bye-bye. After he was through the door, I headed for the stairs. I grabbed the well-worn leather duffel bag my mother had given me when I was sixteen from the back of Jolene and checked into the hotel. Before I returned to the lobby lounge, I stopped by my room on the third floor and changed into a long summer shirtdress with cap sleeves and a white sweater. White canvas tennis shoes and ankle socks completed my ensemble, while a blonde bob wig and blue and green cat eye framed glasses rounded out my disguise.

Just before six, Everette came off the elevator and headed towards the front door of the hotel. I followed him a few steps south on Main Street, then across it to Soby's New South Cuisine, where he met a group of friends. This wasn't looking like a romantic escape. I debated whether or not I should check out his hotel room, just to verify he was traveling alone. Best to err on the side of dotting my i's. I doubled back to the hotel.

If one knows where to shop, one can purchase gadgets that will open hotel room doors as magically as if one had a key card from housekeeping. Fortunately, Joe had taught me all the best places to buy such tools of the trade. I let myself into Everette's room. It didn't take me five minutes to ascertain he was by himself and he was only planning to stay the one night. No need to leave a camera here. I'd just have to let myself back into the room later to retrieve it. Every time I did that, I risked being discovered. There'd be nothing to see here. He was in town to see his buddies, or business associates, or whoever they were.

By the time I got back to Soby's and smiled wide at the hostess as I slid on by saying, "I'm meeting friends," Everette and his friends were getting their first round of bourbon. They'd been seated upstairs. I discreetly snapped a few pictures of the party of four as I passed by the table. The popular restaurant was packed, every table full. The noise level in the brick-walled building was such that I'd never be able to hear what they were talking about even if I'd had the table right next to them. I made my way back to the hostess stand.

I offered her another sunny smile, my eyes wide with innocence. "You'll never believe this, but I just called my friends because I couldn't find them. Our reservation is for *tomorrow* night. But I'm only in town this evening. Would you happen to have a table anywhere? Or a place at the bar, maybe?" Hey, a girl had to eat. And Soby's was one of the highest-rated restaurants in Greenville on TripAdvisor.

"Oh—I'm so sorry. Let me see where I can put you. I have a table on the patio, if that's okay . . ."

"That'd be great. Thank you so much." I could hear myself think outside. Everette would most likely walk right past me on the way out. Even if he went through the bar, I'd see him when he crossed the street and went into the Poinsett.

I settled into my table and relaxed. It was a beautiful almost summer evening. The air was soft and warm with a slight breeze. A street musician across Main serenaded the diners on the patio and the passersby with a cover of Amos Lee's "Southern Girl." White lights strung through the trees gave the street a festive vibe. I ordered a glass of Pinot Grigio and sipped it slowly.

The waiter was eager to help me find something that would thrill me, his words. I settled on a veggie plate, which was nothing less than a work of art made from field peas, cauliflower, brussels sprouts, carrots, squash, and baby greens. A light balsamic glaze finished the vegetables nicely. Eating in restaurants was sometimes challenging for me. My entree was a pleasant surprise. I lingered over my food, knowing Everette would likely be a while with his friends.

It was nearly ten when the red-faced band of merry men wobbled out the door. How many rounds of bourbon had they had? With toothy grins and much backslapping, they said their good nights. Everette's dinner companions dispersed in three different directions. Alone, Everette weaved diagonally across the street, barely looking for traffic. I followed him, thankful he wasn't driving. I would've liked to've gotten a license plate for one of his buddies, but I had to make a choice, so I stayed with Everette. Anyway, I couldn't see how knowing who his dinner companions were would help Eugenia's case. Everette nearly tripped over one of the black permanent traffic barricades near the door, then apologized to it. He was three sheets to the wind, no doubt about it.

While he waited for the elevator, I dashed up the stairs. On the eleventh floor, I passed him in the hallway, then nonchalantly glanced over my shoulder as he let himself into his room. In the lobby, I ordered myself a cup of peppermint tea. At eleven, Everette hadn't come back downstairs, and his car hadn't moved from its spot in the valet parking section. I went to bed.

Chapter Thirteen

My cell phone rang just as I was getting out of the shower the next morning. I didn't recognize the number, but it was from the 843 area code, which was eastern, mostly coastal, South Carolina.

"Hadley?" a male voice inquired when I answered.

"Yes, who's calling, please?"

"This is Fish."

"Oh, hi, I—"

"I'm afraid I have dreadful news."

Every fiber in my body tensed for the blow. "What's happened?"

"It's Eugenia. Hadley . . . someone's killed our Eugenia." His voice broke.

"*What*? No—" Oh, please no.

"I found her early this morning in the kitchen. It was . . . I'll never get over it. I've called Tallulah. She's here. She thought we should tell you."

"Was it a burglar?"

"Not unless they took something very specific. Something I can't even tell is missing. The police asked Tallulah and me to take a look at her jewelry. As far as we can tell, that's all here. There's cash in her desk. There's a safe in the closet in her office, but we don't have the combination."

I fought for air. "Oh my God, Fish, I just can't believe it. Who? Who did this?" Everette. Was he still here? Had he gone back to Sullivan's Island while I slept? How? He could barely walk.

"I can't imagine," said Fish. "Everyone loved Eugenia."

Not everyone.

Fish continued, "Except . . ."

"Except what, Fish?"

"It's inconceivable. I hesitate to say this, but I suppose I have no choice. Eugenia told me a while back that should anything untoward happen to her—should she have a mysterious 'accident,' or what have you, that I should assume Everette was responsible."

"Fish, I've got to check on something. I'll call you back. Is this your cell number?"

"It is."

"Are the police there?"

"Yes, the entire Sullivan's Island force is here, as well as contingents from the county and the state."

"Listen to me carefully. Call Middleton, Bull & Vanderhorst. That's—"

"Yes, of course. Her attorneys will need to know what's happened."

"Fish, you and Tallulah need representation, and anyone else who is questioned. These things can get turned sideways so, so easily. The police could get a wrong idea. Sometimes when they get wrong ideas, they get invested in them. You hear me?"

"Well I—yes, all right. I'll speak to Charlie Vanderhorst. Hadley?"

"Yes?"

"Should we mention that Eugenia had hired you?"

"Yes. Don't withhold any information. I hope you don't think I was suggesting that. I'm not. Not at all. I just don't want to see this godawful mess get even worse. It's just better to have someone there who speaks cop."

"I understand. Thank you, Hadley."

I ended the call and opened the tracker app on my phone. I'd checked it when I first woke up, but I looked again. Everette's car hadn't moved. At least the tracker hadn't. I threw on my clothes and sprinted down the stairs, through the lobby, and into the parking garage.

The car was still there. I put my hands on the hood. The engine was cool.

Where was Everette?

I called the hotel and asked to be connected to his room.

No answer.

I headed back towards the lobby. This time, I scanned every chair in the lounge. No Everette.

I crossed the room and approached the hostess stand at the entrance to Spoonbread, the hotel restaurant. It wasn't large. Table by table, I scoured the dining room. No Everette, but the person at the banquette in the corner was reading a newspaper.

"One for breakfast?" The hostess asked.

I smiled, hesitated.

The newspaper folded in as someone turned the page.

Everette. It was Everette.

"Ma'am?" the hostess inquired again.

Did he know? Surely someone had called him if they'd called me. But there he sat, lingering over breakfast.

"Yes, please," I said to the hostess.

She sat me diagonally across the room from Everette, but I had a clear view.

The hostess brought me coffee and a menu. I needed the coffee, but knew I couldn't eat a thing. Eugenia . . . I just couldn't believe my friend was gone. She was such a force of nature. To have stared cancer down only to be murdered in her own home . . . It was just unthinkable.

Everette laid the paper down and picked up his phone.

I couldn't hear what he said, but he raised a hand to his head, a shocked expression on his face. Was he putting it on? For whose benefit? He ended the call and signaled the waitress with a check mark in the air. Had he just heard? He was subdued, but rather composed for someone whose wife had been murdered. He signed the check and left the restaurant in a hurry.

I asked the waitress for a to-go cup for my coffee.

It had to have been Everette. He had all the motive in the world. Eugenia had known he might kill her. She'd warned Fish.

It couldn't have been Everette. I was his alibi.

He must've hired someone to kill her and made sure he was out of town when it happened.

With God as my witness, I was going to see to it his sorry hide rotted in jail.

Chapter Fourteen

I stayed a half mile or so behind Everette on the way back to Charleston. The tracking app showed me not only where he was, but how fast he was going, so it was easy for me to stay out of sight. My mind raced round and around. It had to've been Everette.

It couldn't't've been Everette.

Or could it?

Was it possible that after I saw him go to his room, he could've driven home, killed Eugenia, and been back in time for me to see him in the restaurant at shortly after eight?

It was three hours and twenty-six minutes door to door, best case scenario. I'd last seen Everette shortly after ten, when he was drunk as a skunk. Could he have faked that? Why? It's not like he knew I was watching. But say he did fake it.

If he'd somehow slipped past me and left the hotel, the earliest he could've possibly left was 10:15. He'd have arrived on Sullivan's Island at 1:41. If it took him thirty minutes to get in the house and trick Eugenia into coming downstairs, he could've left to come back to Greenville at 2:11. That would've put him back in Greenville at 5:37.

With more than two hours to spare.

But, I'd had a tracker on his car. It hadn't moved. I'd checked the engine. It was cool. If he'd driven home, he would've had to've taken another car. He'd driven straight to the hotel from Charleston. He hadn't left to Uber to a rental car company.

If he'd done that—gone home and back—he would've had to've had help. Anyone who knew him would've heard about Eugenia's death, would've known immediately what Everette had done. So, anyone who helped him was a willing accomplice. And if he were going to have an accomplice, wouldn't he have taken the easier route, and just had the accomplice commit the murder?

I was right back where I started. He'd been convincingly drunk. His car hadn't moved. It couldn't've been Everette. It still nagged at me.

We were on I-26 near Summerville when my phone sang out the piano riff I hadn't heard in a while, the intro to "Bad to the Bone."

Cash's picture displaced the tracking app map on the screen.

Something grabbed my stomach and squeezed. I tasted metal.

Deep, slow breaths. Why was I so anxious? We were still friends. He'd been very kind to me Sunday night at Hank's after the humiliating debacle with Dylan.

I cleared my throat and pressed the button to answer the call. "Hey." I tried so hard to sound nonchalant. Was I *too* nonchalant?

"Hadley. Am I catching you at a bad time?" His tone was uncharacteristically businesslike. It was disorienting, and I was already a mess.

"No. Not at all." Did I sound like he'd interrupted something? What? *Why* was I scrutinizing every syllable either of us uttered?

"Good, good. Listen, I meant to tell you this Sunday, but I didn't get around to it. We were preoccupied, to say the least. I've changed jobs."

"What? You love your job. Why—"

"I've taken a job with SLED. In Investigative Services, for the Lowcountry region."

"SLED? Really? I'm surprised. I mean . . . when did this happen?" I'd never heard him mention being interested in working for the South Carolina Law Enforcement Division, our state-level agency. Also the group who oversaw private investigators, not that *that* was of any consequence whatsoever.

"I started about two months ago. Anyway, I'm the primary investigator on the Eugenia Ladson case. I understand she was a client of yours."

Oh, *dammit*. Dammit. Dammit. Dam—

"Hadley? You there?"

"Yeah—sorry. I'm driving. Service is spotty. Yes. Eugenia. Well, I mean, yes, she was a client." Why did I sound like a blithering idiot?

"Could we get together this afternoon? I have a few questions. And I'd love to hear your thoughts."

"Ah, sure. What time?"

"When's good for you?"

It was almost one p.m. "How about six?" I needed enough time to see if Everette met anyone, perhaps to pay them for a job completed in his absence. Though he might do that after dark . . . six actually wasn't great. I should've thought this through. Moron.

"I can make that. Your apartment?"

Ah, crackers. "No. I've moved, actually."

"Moved? When? Where?"

"I'm housesitting for a client." I gave him the address. He'd think this whole arrangement was odd, no doubt. It was odd, wasn't it?

"Wow. That's . . . amazing. Okay. I'll see you at six."

My phone screen switched back to the tracking app map. Everette was still on I-26. I focused on my breathing until my stomach settled and my heart rate returned to normal. Cash had been a Charleston police detective the entire time we'd dated. I'd been a private investigator. We'd sometimes brainstormed cases with each other, but we'd never, ever worked on the same case.

And to say I wasn't eager to do that now was a ginormous under-statement.

But wait . . . my client was dead. My involvement with this case was over. Except I had to make sure Everette paid for what I knew in my bones he'd done to my friend. No . . . I needed to walk away and trust Cash to do his job. He was very good at it. We may have had our differences, but I was absolutely convinced he was a top-notch detective. He would handle Everette. That was that then.

My decision notwithstanding, something compelled me to follow Everette all the way back to Eugenia's Tradd Street house. He didn't make a solitary stop en route. But after he parked the car in the garage, he strode out to the fence surrounding the front stoop and yanked the For Sale sign right off. Then he stomped back in through the open garage door and closed it.

I waited until three o'clock. When Cash climbed the steps and rang the doorbell, I headed back to Sullivan's Island. Everette would be home for a while. And I needed to tell Cash everything, walk away, and trust him to do his job, didn't I?

Cash and I settled into the living room in front of the fireplace, me on one of the twin camel-colored leather sofas, him in a side chair looking like he'd maybe been spending more time in the gym. He'd always been fit, but . . . he looked really good, is what I'm saying. Six foot three, rich toffee-colored hair, soft brown eyes, and just a shadow of a beard and mustache. Cash Reynolds was my strongest weakness, and he had been since the day we'd met.

He stared at the fireplace wall. Then he stood and walked over to touch it. "I wonder what kind of wood that is?"

"I have no idea." The wall was a work of art. Like several pieces in the house, it seemed to be carved from a tree. A modern gas fireplace was set into the wall, and above it was what appeared to be an oil painting, a seascape, but with the press of a button on a remote control, revealed itself to be a television.

Cash raised his eyebrows. I knew what he was thinking. He was thinking this was awfully fancy. He was right. "The house is nice," he said. "It suits you." He returned to his chair but continued to survey the room.

I shrugged. "As well as someone else's house can, I suppose. It is truly beautiful. I just keep pinching myself."

"Is that how you met Eugenia Ladson? When you moved here? She bring you a pound cake or something?"

"No, actually. I met her first." I gave him the CliffsNotes version of how I'd met Eugenia and how she came to hire me.

"And the husband, Everette, was he having an affair?"

"Yes, with Jordyn Jackman, a realtor." I briefed him on the case, more or less, leaving out the parts involving hidden cameras, tracking devices, possible breaking and entering, et cetera. "I didn't have the proof Eugenia needed for court just yet. But if there's one thing I can spot, it's a cheating spouse."

"So you saw him go into his hotel room in Greenville at what time last night?"

"Around ten."

"And he was clearly inebriated?"

"He appeared to be, yes."

"And then you saw him this morning at breakfast, at what time?"

"About eight thirty."

Cash nodded. "Okay. Anything else I should know?"

"I'm convinced Everette Ladson killed Eugenia."

His brow lowered. "How's that? I mean, yeah, usually spouses are the first ones we suspect. But, Hadley, you're his alibi."

"I think he hired someone. He wanted to be free of Eugenia, but he wanted the money. Her money. Virtually everything they have, she inherited."

"I'll definitely check into his finances. If he did that, there'll be a money trail. Why are you so convinced it was him?"

There were things about Everette Ladson I could observe that were hard to put into words. He was smug. He was slick, in an unwholesome way that screamed *Hell yeah, I did it, and I'll get away with it too. Watch me.* He was a friend of my father's. "They were separated. The marriage was over. He was having an affair. He wanted out, but the money was Eugenia's. She had an iron-clad prenup. If he divorced her, he got nothing."

"And with her dead? Have you seen her will?"

"No, of course not. There was no need of that, not for my purposes."

"So he might not be any better off with her dead than if she'd divorced him."

"Maybe not." I needed to get a look at that will. No, I did *not*. Cash needed to take a hard look at it. "But what's important is, what were his expectations?"

"That's a good point. I'll check into it."

"And Eugenia told Mr. Aiken—he's an old friend of hers who was living in her pool house—that should anything happen to her, it was Everette. Not a month ago, she told him that."

"Well, that certainly speaks to her state of mind," said Cash.

"She knew Everette better than anyone. She was clearly afraid of him, or at least afraid of what he might do." And yet she'd held out hope that she was wrong. Poor Eugenia. My heart ached for her.

"You've known Eugenia Ladson for less than a week?"

It seemed like I'd known her much longer. She was my friend. The way he said it seemed to belittle that relationship. "It would've been a week tomorrow."

"Not very long, then."

My feathers ruffled. "No."

"But clearly you had a connection with her."

"Exactly. We've faced some of the same challenges."

"Like what, for example?"

"We both lost our mothers to cancer. Eugenia was a cancer survivor herself. And Everette was a complete cad to her when she was sick."

Something changed in Cash's face. He seemed to catch himself, slid a neutral expression back in place. He nodded. "Okay. I think I have what I need."

He was shutting me down. "You think I'm being emotional." He *always* thought I was too emotional, that it clouded my judgement.

"No." He shook his head, looked innocent. "I didn't say that at all. I just think we've covered everything. Haven't we?"

"I suppose we have." He would be better served, as would the people of South Carolina, if he were in touch with a solitary emotion on occasion and didn't behave like some android. When, exactly, had compassion become a liability?

He stood. "Well, if you think of anything else, you know how to reach me."

I led him to the door.

He stopped on the porch and turned around. "It was really good to see you, Hadley. Sunday. And today. Even though the circumstances have been less than ideal. It was good to see you." He looked like he had more to say but couldn't quite get it out. That was his default setting.

I felt my lips curl, but knew my eyes weren't smiling. I nodded, looked over his shoulder. "Good to see you too, Cash."

I meant that. It was good to see him. *So* good to see him. Except in the respect that it stirred up an old hurt that had taken a long time to finally settle to the bottom of my heart, where I needed to let it lie.

Chapter Sixteen

There was a tune stuck in my head. No . . . someone was playing the same tune, over and over. "I Love Beach Music." The doorbell. I sat straight up in bed. It was seven a.m. Eugenia?

A bolt of hot lightning sliced through me. It couldn't be Eugenia ever again. Something swelled in my throat, making it difficult to breathe. The song rang out again.

I grabbed my phone and opened the security system app. Tallulah and Camille waved at the front door camera. I scrambled out of bed, threw on a robe, and dashed down the stairs. When I opened the door, they plowed right in.

"Hadley, we need to talk," said Tallulah.

"It's urgent," said Camille.

"I'll put on the coffee." I led them into the kitchen, and they settled at the bar while I filled the electric kettle.

"What's happened?" I asked.

"Have you spoken with the police?" asked Tallulah.

"I did. I met with Agent Reynolds yesterday afternoon." Deep breaths. *Iiinn, ouutt.*

"You didn't have him in your home, did you? By yourself?" Camille's voice climbed the scale, the word "yourself" ringing a note of disbelief.

"I did. I uh . . . I actually know him."

"You can't be too careful," said Camille. "I know he's an officer of the law, but still. Sadly, that's no guarantee he's always a gentleman."

"What did he tell you?" Tallulah's voice dripped impatience.

"He mostly did the asking, and I did the telling," I said.

"So you told him Eugenia hired you to get the goods on Everette?" asked Tallulah.

"I told him everything I knew, yes." Well, except the parts I left out, but those details weren't really pertinent. Like the cameras I'd installed in Eugenia's house. What was the point of telling him that now? I needed to retrieve those, as soon as possible.

"About Jordyn Jackman?" asked Camille.

"Eugenia told you?" I asked.

"Of course she did. She told us all at happy hour on Friday," said Tallulah.

I sighed. "I wish she'd've kept that to herself. Yes, I told him all about Everette's affair, including the part about how I don't have any proof of that just yet."

"Everette killed Eugenia," said Tallulah. "I'm absolutely certain of it. Fish said Eugenia was stabbed several times with one of the kitchen knives. That's a crime of passion if ever I've heard of one. Everette has a temper. Eugenia's stunt with the open house set him off."

"He certainly had motive," I said. "And I feel it in my bones that he's ultimately responsible for Eugenia's death. But I don't think he killed her himself."

Tallulah squinted at me. "Why not, precisely?"

"Because he was in Greenville at the time." I gave them the broad strokes of my trip to the Upstate.

"Then he hired someone," said Camille.

"I'd bet good money on that," I said. "I hope Agent Reynolds goes through the Ladson's finances with a fine-tooth comb."

"You should recommend that to him," said Tallulah.

I scoffed. "Tallulah? He's not interested in any recommendations I might have to offer. Generally, sworn officers of the law are unenthusiastic about my entire profession. They don't hold private investigators in especially high regard." Maybe Cash was different on that score, but there was no doubt in my mind as to how he would feel about me weighing in on his case, one of his first in his new job.

"I don't understand that," said Camille. "Why on earth not?"

Tallulah rolled her eyes. "We are wasting time. What's your next move?" She was looking at me.

"*My* next move?"

"Yes, of course, *your* next move," said Tallulah. "How do we go about proving Everette killed Eugenia?"

"Oh no." I held my hands up in a stop motion. "We don't. We can't. This is an open police investigation. Three different agencies are involved. The Sullivan's Island Police Department, Charleston County Sheriff's Office, and SLED—the State Law Enforcement Division. Trust me. They're already crawling all over each other. The last thing they'd welcome is my involvement."

"They don't have to like it," said Tallulah.

"They certainly do not," added Camille.

"Ladies, I appreciate your concerns. I share them. But my case ended when my client died. Now, would I *like* to see to it Everette goes to jail for the rest of his life? Yes. Yes, I would find that immensely satisfying. But we're going to have to trust Agent Reynolds to do his job."

"Is he the lead investigator?" asked Tallulah.

"That's my understanding," I said. "He's the lead agent, and SLED is the lead agency. I doubt the Sullivan's Island Police Department has the resources to investigate a murder. Thankfully, there's not much call for that sort of skill set here."

"I just don't have any degree of confidence they'll get this right," said Tallulah. "The problem is that Everette is a retired judge. He knows everyone involved in the legal system in this part of the state. He's everyone's buddy. Their golf buddy, or their poker buddy, or the buddy they meet at the Cheetah Club when their wives are out of town. They like him. They're not going to want to believe he did this. They'll find someone else they like better, you mark my words."

"Ahh, Tallulah." I sighed. "I do understand what you're saying. But as much as I'd like to help, I just don't think I can. Look . . . I lay awake all night long wrestling with this. I'm convinced Everette is guilty, and there's nothing I'd like better than to be the one to get the proof needed to put him away. But it's pretty obvious he did this, don't you think? Surely, they'll arrest him before the day's out. There are limits to what even good ole boy retired judges can get away with."

Tallulah raised an eyebrow and looked at Camille, who shook her head. They were not buying what I was selling.

Marimba music announced a call. We all looked at our phones. Tallulah answered hers. "Birdie?"

She listened for a moment. Her left hand fluttered to her chest. She met Camille's eyes, then mine. Tallulah's eyes telegraphed that Birdie was telling her something appalling.

"Thank you for letting me know. We'll talk soon." Tallulah ended the call, took a deep breath. "They've arrested Kateryna."

"The bartender? *Why*?" I asked.

"That's outrageous," said Camille.

"It is outrageous," said Tallulah. "But apparently, it didn't take your Agent Reynolds long at all to find someone he could railroad into taking Everette's rightful place in prison. Kateryna has no family here to rely on. Very little in the way of resources. She doesn't know our legal system well. She's perfect for his purposes. He'll likely get a promotion for closing his case so quickly."

"He's not *my* agent," I said. "He's not my anything. Why would you say such a thing?" Now was not the time to tell Tallulah and Camille I'd almost married the object of their justifiable scorn. I couldn't imagine what poor Kateryna must be going through right now. She must be scared out of her mind.

"Clearly, you have confidence in him to deliver justice," said Tallulah.

"Wait—"

"Isn't that what you said?" asked Tallulah. "It was obvious, you thought? Everette's guilt, that is."

"Okay, so I guess it's not obvious to everyone." How could Cash have gotten this so wrong so fast? He clearly didn't ask the right questions, talk to the right people. Murder was a highly personal thing.

"Indeed." Tallulah stared at me hard. "Do you believe me now?"

I massaged my scalp with all ten fingers. "What exactly are you proposing we do?"

"What I was getting to, before Birdie called, is that Camille and I would like to hire you," said Tallulah. "Actually, all of us are going in—Camille and me, Sarabeth, Quinn, Libba, Birdie, and Fish. Well, Fish is with us in spirit, anyway. His means are quite limited. Whatever contract you had with Eugenia, I'll sign one just like it on behalf of the group. Eugenia had faith in you. We do too."

I'd never had a group client before. This sounded messy. And it was Cash's case, so, messy didn't begin to cover it. I had fully intended to walk away, but that was before he apparently suffered a stroke, or perhaps an alien abduction. Why, oh why, had he not even mentioned Kateryna to me? Why was he so secretive? "Precisely what would you like to hire me to do? Because I can't guarantee an outcome. You get that, right?"

"Of course," said Tallulah. "We're not fools."

"No, I never meant to imply that you were. It's just that all of our emotions are high right now. We all want justice for Eugenia. And we all think we know who's responsible. But it might not turn out that way. If I take this case, it has to be with a clear understanding that I'm searching for the truth, no matter what that is."

"Understood," said Tallulah.

"Can you live with it if it turns out Everette didn't kill Eugenia, and I end up proving that very thing? Because as it stands right now, I'm his alibi."

"That's not going to happen," said Tallulah.

"But if it does?" I asked.

"Well, then it does," said Tallulah. "But it won't."

"Just help poor Kateryna," said Camille.

"Yes, of course," said Tallulah. "Let's put it that way, now that she's been arrested. We'll hire you to help Kateryna. There's no way on earth she killed Eugenia. You just find out who did and provide the police with the evidence they need to make a proper arrest."

I nodded. "I will do my best. Honestly, I would do this pro bono—"

"Nonsense," said Camille. "You're not a nonprofit organization. This is your livelihood. You need paying clients to keep food on the table. We understand that. And frankly, I can't think of a better use of my money."

"I'll get a contract."

Chapter Seventeen

I met Dana Smalls, the public defender assigned to Kateryna's case at Home Team Barbecue on Williman Street—her choice—for lunch. I'd been inside more barbecue joints in the last few days than I had in my entire life before that. We sat outside at a picnic table under the shade of a live oak.

Dana had Halle Berry's luminous light-toffee skin tone and a mass of striped caramel-and-blonde colored hair pulled high into a knotted ponytail. She had a solid look to her. I'm not saying she was fat, not at all. But she was substantial, with the bone structure and height of a super model, or a warrior princess.

She piled brisket from her platter of nachos onto a chip and embellished it with salsa, cheese, and jalapeños. "So tell me again how you know Kateryna. Because she says she's never heard of you. Tell you the truth, she thinks you mighta been hired by Everette Ladson to see to it she spends the rest of her life in jail." She raised an elegant eyebrow at me.

"I've never met Kateryna. I've been hired by a group of ladies, friends of Eugenia's, who *do* know Kateryna, though not well. They are convinced of Everette's guilt, actually."

"Interesting."

"I thought you'd be happy to have my help," I said. "I don't imagine you often have the luxury of having an outside investigator on board."

"No, I do not, and that's a fact. Because it's so unusual, you'll excuse me if I'm a touch skeptical."

"Sure, I get it. Listen, I've been hired to do a job. We don't have to work together for me to get it done. I just thought I could help you. And I wanted you to know I was working to help clear your client." I took a bite of my salad. Thankfully, they had black beans on the menu. I'd had them add some to a Home Team salad, which turned out to be pretty tasty.

"I appreciate that. I do," said Dana.

"You sound as if there's a 'but' coming."

"Not a but. You and I just need to get to know each other a little better."

I nodded, put together another bite of salad. "Why are you staring at my food?"

"There's no meat on it."

"I only eat plants."

Her face twisted into an expression that suggested maybe that made me untrustworthy. "Hmm." She picked up a fried tot and swirled it in queso. The tots were one of two side dishes she'd ordered with her nachos, the other being an order of smoked chicken wings with something called death relish. I reserved comment.

"Do you know why they arrested Kateryna?" I asked. "I mean, I know she'd recently had a public quarrel with Eugenia, but my understanding is that it wasn't anything to rise to the level of a motive for murder."

Dana took a chicken wing apart. "Yeah, I know why they arrested her."

I waited.

She took a sip of her Cheerwine and seemed to be taking my measure.

"Would you care to share?" I asked. "We're on the same team here."

"I've worked in the public defender's office in Charleston County for eighteen years. Our paths have never crossed, yours and mine."

"Most of my clients come through an attorney's office, so by definition, they are someone else's clients, not yours."

"People who can afford high-dollar attorneys." There was a touch of a sneer in her voice.

"Listen, lady . . . I do not have to justify myself to you or anyone else. But just so you know who you're dealing with . . . first of all . . . people with money are no less deserving of justice than anyone else. That said, nothing would make me happier than if the county paid me to help people with no money. Like they do you. But they don't. So I make it my business to seek out pro bono cases. My arrangement with the so-called high-dollar attorneys allows me to choose to work for people with bad luck and trouble and no cash on a regular basis. But I do have to buy groceries and pay the rent, just like everyone else. So I help those I can, the ones who can pay and the ones who can't, every chance I get. And I've accepted payment in everything from eggs to lingerie to limo service."

"Well. As my sainted momma used to say, pin a rose on your butt." She heaved a heavy sigh, rolled her eyes, and then her voice softened. "My problem is, I don't know you."

"Yeah? Well, I don't know you either." This was ridiculous. For Kateryna's sake, and to avenge Eugenia, I needed to work with this woman. I sucked it up, reached for a soothing tone. "Surely we have friends in common."

"You married?"

"No, I'm not. Are you?"

"No. Got a boyfriend? Girlfriend?"

"Not anymore. A boyfriend. I don't have a boyfriend anymore."

"Yeah, I heard that. Which attorney's office you work for?"

"I have a loose arrangement with Middleton, Bull & Vanderhorst." Vanderhorst is one of those names that, in Charleston at least, isn't pronounced anything like it's spelled. It came out of my mouth the way I'd always heard it, "VAN-dross."

"You know Charlie Vanderhorst?"

"I've known her for years."

"She vouch for you?"

"Look, I really don't need—"

"So she won't then?"

"I didn't say that."

"Will she, or won't she?"

"Yes, she will. If I need her to. Which I don't."

"Yeah, you do."

"Look. I'm just going to finish my salad and go about my business. If I come across anything you need to know, I'll let you know. I'd appreciate if you'd do the same, but if you're not comfortable with that, somehow, I will manage to go on breathing."

"Touchy, aren't you?"

"I most certainly am not touchy. You have a suspicious nature . . . and you're completely unreasonable."

"Unreasonable? I have a client facing murder charges. A client, I might add, who is uniquely vulnerable. She has no family in this country and few resources. English isn't her first language. She's charged with killing someone whose family has lived in Charleston for centuries. There are streets named after the families on both branches of that family tree. The victim's husband is a *retired judge*. These people sit on boards and spend their weekends going to coming out parties that ain't got nothing to do with closets. My client is up against not only our legal system, but money and power. For her sake, I don't trust anyone right now until they prove they can be trusted."

"And I'd rather spend my time clearing Kateryna than convincing you I'm on her side."

Dana put together another bite of nachos and delivered it to her mouth. She chewed thoughtfully and took a sip of Cheerwine. "Her fingerprints were on the murder weapon. That's why they arrested her. That, combined with the argument she had with the victim at Dunleavy's Pub Monday afternoon. Oh, and a witness saw her car there at two thirty in the morning, which is during the window the coroner says Eugenia was killed. Between midnight and four a.m."

Ah, crackers. That's not good. Could Everette have hired Kateryna to kill Eugenia? "Who was the witness?"

"Mr. Aiken. The gentleman living in the pool house."

I needed to talk to Fish. "Agent Reynolds wasn't exactly forthcoming, but I heard Eugenia was stabbed with a kitchen knife." Had I known I'd still be working this case, I would've asked him a few more questions. But at the time we'd talked, I thought I was leaving it all with him.

"That's right. Eight times."

Something bitter roiled in my stomach. I couldn't bear to think of what Eugenia had been through, how terrified she must've been. "Was it a knife that belonged in her kitchen?"

"It was."

"How does Kateryna explain her prints on the knife?"

"She can't," said Dana. "She believes the police are framing her."

"What do you think?"

"I think someone is framing her. I seriously doubt it's the police."

"My money is on Everette," I said.

"I wouldn't bet against you."

"My clients have asked me to inquire about bail."

Dana's eyebrows climbed her forehead. "Her arraignment was this morning. Bail has been set at $500,000. Might as well be a billion."

"I've been instructed to arrange payment."

Dana's eyebrows lowered. She pulled back her chin. "A-you should've led with that, and B-I'm still not sure about you. How do I know someone doesn't want her free because she'll be more accessible? If she dies, she's presumed guilty, and the case goes quietly away. That would be very convenient for some people."

"I imagine you're right. Look. Eugenia was my friend. She hired me to get proof Everette was cheating on her. She was going to divorce him. He knew she was on to him because she put their house, where he was living, on the market without telling him and scheduled an open house. I am convinced Everette is responsible for Eugenia's death, but it is my great misfortune to be his alibi."

"What the—"

"I was following him at the time she was killed, and he was in Greenville."

"Mother—" Dana smothered the curse.

"But here's what you need to know. There is no scenario in which I would help Everette. I think he's the slimiest scum at the bottom of hell's pond. And I'm convinced he's behind Eugenia's death. And I plan to prove exactly that. So, get over yourself. And let's go get Kateryna out of jail."

Chapter Eighteen

Dana gave me Kateryna's address and told me our newly sprung client would meet me there around three—after she'd had a chance to get home, shower, and change. Dana was due in court on another case. As I pulled into the North Charleston neighborhood, I was thinking Dana likely hadn't had the chance to meet with Kateryna at home just yet. The entrance to Southern Shores was marked with a pair of decorative aluminum fence sections with the name on a sign in large swirling letters. In small print underneath. it read, "an active adult community." This was unexpected. Wasn't "active adult" a euphemism for over fifty-five?

The neighborhood was nice, with a mix of single- and double-wide mobile homes on large, well-kept lots, along shady tree-lined streets. Mature landscaping, featuring mulched beds with azaleas, hydrangeas, and gardenias had the look of professional maintenance. Several of the homes sported full-size metal poles out front flying Old Glory. I passed several groups of walkers on my way in. Everyone smiled real big and waved.

I pulled into Kateryna's driveway and parked behind her grey Honda Accord. From the shape of the car, I guessed it was five to seven years old, but it was clean and appeared to be taken care of. I climbed out of the car and snapped a picture of the license plate, then took a series of photos from every angle.

Next door, the woman watering her flowerpots stole a glance my way as I ambled down the front walk and climbed the steps. Kateryna must've been watching for me. She opened the door before I could ring the bell. For a moment, we took each other's measure. She was exotically beautiful, with straight, dark brown hair that hung to her waist, big blue eyes that flashed with intelligence, and plump lips. She was trim but curvy in the places guys liked best.

After a moment, she said, "You are the private investigator?" Kateryna's accent was thick.

"I am. Hadley Cooper." I smiled, handed her a business card, and showed her my PI license and driver's license.

She scrutinized me, my ID, and my business card, then waved me inside. "This is not the way I keep the house. Dana tells me the police destroyed it while they were searching. What they were searching for is not very clear. They must not have found it."

The place looked like it had been ransacked. Cushions were off the sofa, and the stuffing had been torn out. Chairs lay on their sides. Books, framed photos, and magazines littered the floor. Kateryna bent to pick up a figurine of an angel. "My mother gave me that before I left Ukraine. Animals."

She set the figurine on the coffee table and grabbed a chair and righted it. I set another upright and looked around. "I'm really sorry about this. Let me help you straighten up."

"You didn't do it. Thank you, but I think you have more important things to discuss. Dana says you will help me."

"I'm going to try my best."

She slid the chair she'd righted into position at a right angle to the sofa and sat, gesturing for me to join her. "Eugenia was your friend? This is what Dana tells me."

"Yes, she was." I moved my chair to the other end of the sofa, opposite hers, and took a seat.

"And they are saying I killed her. Which I did not do. But they are saying this anyway. If you were her friend, explain to me, please, why you would want to help me?"

"Because I believe you're innocent, and I want to see the guilty party prosecuted," I was still mulling the possibility that *maybe* Kateryna was Everette's accomplice. But I honestly saw that as unlikely. For the time being, I was operating on the assumption she was innocent. "Is this your home?"

Her eyes hardened. The wary expression she wore deepened. "Yes, I live here."

"For how long?"

"Nearly three years."

I squinted at her. "How old are you?" I knew the answer to this. She was thirty-seven. I'd done a basic profile before I left the house.

"Look, I moved in with my friend, Oscar. This was his place. He passed away three months ago and left it to me. But, it's tricky, because obviously, I am not over fifty-five. But this is my home. I have nowhere else to go."

"How old was Oscar?"

"Ninety-four. He was very healthy and active, but his heart failed him anyway."

I nodded and reflected upon that information.

"I know what you're thinking, but it wasn't like that. Oscar was my friend, my mentor, and my roommate. We were not romantically involved. We kept each other company."

"Of course." Surely a roommate closer to his own demographic . . . I shook the thought from my head. It didn't matter. "Where were you between midnight and four a.m. Sunday morning?"

"I worked Saturday night. I'm a bartender at Dunleavy's Pub on Sullivan's Island. I got off about 2:15 Sunday morning and came straight home."

"You didn't swing by Eugenia's for any reason on the way?" I asked.

"No. I told the policemen this. I did not go to her house. I've never been to her house. We weren't that close. And who goes visiting at 2:15 in the morning?"

"A witness apparently saw your car there at 2:30 a.m., which lines up pretty well with the time you left Dunleavy's."

"No. They did *not* see my car at her house." Her eyes flashed. "Because my car was not there. It is not possible that someone saw my car there because I was driving my car, and I was on my way home at that time."

I held her gaze. She was either telling me the truth, or she was a convincing liar. "Do you have any idea how your fingerprints came to be on the knife used to kill her?"

"It's very simple. I am being framed. I am . . . what is the word? Unimportant . . . ex . . ."

"Expendable."

"Yes. I am expendable. Someone important needs to hide what they have done. I was an easy target. Who cares about Ukrainian immigrant?"

"Well, I do, for starters. Have you ever met Everette Ladson?"

She muttered something that may have been a Ukrainian swear word. "That pig. Yes. I have met him, unfortunately. He sometimes comes to Dunleavy's. He asked me out once. I had to try to be nice about it because he is customer. But there is no way I would date a married man, even if he were young and handsome. Certainly not an old goat married to a woman who goes to my church." Her lip curled in disgust. "Besides, I am in relationship."

"You've never crossed paths with Everette anywhere else? Besides Dunleavy's?"

"Not that I can remember."

"All right. Back to the murder weapon—"

"I've been thinking about this. I don't know how they did this, but it's possible someone switched our knives."

"What do you mean?"

"Eugenia goes to my church, I told you. She has made it her

mission to fix me, even though I am not broken. She bought me a set of knives."

"Why did she do that?"

"Because I should learn to make a proper chicken bog for the church cook-off. It is a regional dish I should know how to make, and you have to chop all the little vegetables. I told her I didn't have a sharp knife to cut all the vegetables. She got me a set." Kateryna stood, strode into the kitchen, and came back with a knife block. "They probably cost more than my car. She told me they were exactly like hers. I don't know if that's true or not, but she told me that more than once. She said I could cook the chicken bog and everything else a good Southern cook should know how to make now that I had the proper equipment."

I took the block from her and set it on the coffee table. "All of yours seem to be here. But someone certainly could've swapped one of yours for one of hers. If they're identical, that is."

"I only know what she told me."

I pulled a glove from my purse and slid it on, then took the chef's knife out of the block, laid it beside the block, and snapped a picture of it. "Have you noticed any signs of someone breaking and entering?" I slid the knife into an evidence bag.

"You mean before the police did it? Before I was arrested, if someone broke in here, they were careful to not leave a trace."

"How well do you know your neighbors?"

She shrugged. "Not that well. They all liked Oscar, but they loved Oscar's wife. She died a year before I moved in. They don't approve of me. They think the worst."

"I'll see if anyone noticed a prowler. Who all knew Eugenia gave you the knives?"

"Anson—my fiancé, Anson Gibbes Jones. He's the minister at Cornerstone Community Church in Mount Pleasant. We used to joke about Eugenia trying to make me into a proper wife for him. But he really loved Eugenia. She could be very nice. When she wasn't finding me a job or telling me how to dress."

"Anyone else?" I asked.

"Probably some of her friends knew. Her gang." Her lip quirked up in a little sneer.

"Did Dana tell you who was paying me to help you?"

Her eyebrows lowered. "No. Someone is paying you to do this?"

"I make my living as a private investigator. Someone has to pay the bills. Aside from the cost of my time, there are expenses for any investigation."

She waited, wearing a suspicious expression.

"Tallulah Wentworth, Camille Houston, Birdie Markley, Sarabeth Boone, Libba Graham, Quinn Poinsett—oh, and Mr. Hamilton Aiken. Eugenia's 'gang' paid your bail, and they're paying me to help you."

The suspicion and scorn melted into shock. "Dana did not tell me that. We didn't have much time. She had to be in court. She said you would explain everything. Why would they do this for me?"

"For the same reason I want to help you. They think you're innocent."

"But they barely know me."

"They know Everette pretty well."

She nodded, a knowing look on her face. "I am so very grateful. To you, and to them. I would still be in jail—probably forever —if it weren't for all of you. Truly. I—thank you." She swallowed hard. Two tears slipped down her face.

"Do you have any kind of security system?"

"No. This neighborhood is very safe."

"It may be, but I'm concerned for your safety, as is Dana. Whoever killed Eugenia, and I have a theory about that, but whoever did it, they've already tried to frame you. They may see an opportunity in your freedom. Were anything to happen to you before trial, well, the case would likely be shelved. The police have what they think is convincing evidence. Given the opportunity, the killer may want to avoid having this all play out at a trial."

"So I'm better to him dead than alive."

"He may see it that way," I said. "I can install a basic system for you if you like."

"Thank you, but Anson will help me. I'll call him before I go to work."

"You're going to work this evening?"

"I don't have a choice. Oscar left me this house, but the taxes, insurance, utilities, homeowners association fees—all that adds up. Anyway, I don't know how long they'll let me stay here. I'm a violation of the restrictions. I expect the property manager to come every day. I keep a very low profile and hope they'll forget about me, at least until I have my citizenship."

"You said Anson was your fiancé?"

"Yes." She smiled and held out her left hand to show me a round cut solitaire.

"Oh how pretty! Have you set a date?"

"Not yet." Her lip trembled, and her eyes filled with tears. "Now that I am really a scandal, his church members will not be happy for him to marry me."

"You're not a scandal. We're going to get this figured out. You just focus on staying safe. Could you stay with Anson until all this is over?"

Her eyes grew, and she shook her head. "He's a minister. His congregation would think that's inappropriate."

"Surely if your safety is at issue . . ."

"No. I cannot ask him to do this. And he will try to get me to stay with him, probably. But I can't. I can't make trouble for him. Do you see?"

"I do." What I could see clearly was that she loved Anson Gibbes Jones. And she was scared.

As I was leaving, I perused the neighborhood. Four of Kateryna's neighbors had a view of her house and could've noticed a prowler if they'd been looking at the right time. I knocked on doors. The three couples I spoke with were retirees from different parts of the country. They were all nice enough—they seemed to be focused on enjoying their retirement and not so much concerned about their neighbor Oscar's roommate. None of them had noticed a prowler, but they all went to bed early and slept soundly most nights.

The fourth neighbor—Kateryna's next-door neighbor to the right, a Roger Riddle, according to property records—wasn't home. But I spied security cameras on all four sides of his house. I scrawled a note asking him to call me and left it with a business card inside the storm door.

Chapter Nineteen

Monday, June 14, 4:30 p.m.
Legare home, Charleston, South Carolina
Mrs. Josephine Huger (you-JEE)

Well, if you ask me, it's high time John Thomas Legare settled down. I would never say that to Judith, of course, but some things are entirely obvious to the casual observer. He's just turned forty, after all.

Judith is throwing him a huge birthday party Saturday evening. Now, his birthday was on the ninth, but I think there was a conflict last Saturday. Anyway, I'm helping Judith pull together gift buckets for all the guests. Yes, you heard me right. We're using galvanized oyster buckets rather than gift bags, or boxes. It's different, but a clever idea, in my opinion.

Judith let John Thomas choose what he wanted to include, and we're putting in some of his favorite treats—cake pops, of all things, a bottle of Elijah Craig Barrel Proof bourbon, a special blend from Charleston Coffee Roasters, benne wafers, a box of cheese and chive biscuits from Callie's, and oyster knives with the date carved on the handles. It's an eclectic combination, I'll say that. But it is his birthday, and he is Judith's only child, so what harm does it do?

Judith and I worked on packing those buckets for hours Monday afternoon—two hundred and fifty of them. We had a few extra pairs of hands helping, but it was a job, I'm telling you. One of the women who works for Judith spent most of the day polishing the silver, but then she helped us finish up. We finally finished just after four, and we were chatting on the verandah, sipping our mint juleps. Judith doesn't drink much. Did you know she's diabetic? Anyway, we were having cocktails when John Thomas came home.

Now, I wasn't paying close attention because Judith and I were talking, but I think the young lady actually arrived just before John Thomas. I think they came separately, is my point. But they did walk up the steps together, and they seemed quite friendly.

Judith introduced her, and her name is Alexandra Ireland. I'm reasonably certain she's from off, though Judith didn't specifically say that. I don't believe I know any Irelands. She's a lovely woman —tall, with long blonde hair, and good bone structure. She was well spoken, and she was dressed in a skirt suit, like she'd just come from the office. John Thomas could do a lot worse.

Now of course, I don't know that they're an item. No one said as much. But if they're not, John Thomas is missing an opportunity there. Perhaps she'll be on his arm Saturday evening. If he has a special lady, surely she'll be with him at his birthday party. It should be an interesting evening.

Chapter Twenty

I barely made it home and down the beach by five. The happy hour crowd at the beach cabana that Monday was utterly heart-broken. Fish made Eugenia's favorite prickly pear margaritas. Her chair sat empty save for her drink in its holder and a single blue hydrangea blossom in her chair.

"I just can't believe she's gone," said Camille. "It's like I'm in a dream, and I just know I'll wake up soon."

"I feel the very same way. After all she went through. She beat the cancer, and now this. It's just so unbelievably unfair." Sara-beth's voice broke.

Murmurs of agreement, sniffles, and sobs rumbled through our group. The next minute we were all crying and hugging and falling apart together. Finally, Fish said, "Ladies, we've got to do better than this. If Eugenia could see us—and I for one don't doubt that she can—well, she's probably fit to be tied right about now. If she were here, she'd tell us not to waste a single instant of this precious life being sad. Of all of us, Eugenia appreciated the value of every moment. We should honor her by living the way she lived. Seizing every day and sucking all the marrow from it. To Eugenia." He raised his glass.

"To Eugenia," we echoed in unison, then drank.

"Why, Hamilton, that was quite poetic," said Tallulah.

"Well done, Mr. Aiken," added Camille.

"You should speak at her service," said Libba. "When is the service? Does anyone know?"

"Eugenia has everything planned," said Tallulah. "I know that much. She took care of all that a year or so ago. She was quite specific. The pastor over at Cornerstone has his marching orders."

Fish poured us all refills. "I bet there's something on the church website. I'll check and let everyone know."

"Well," I said, "I haven't known Eugenia, or any of you, very long. But I just want to say how grateful I am to have gotten to know her, even for such a short time. She was a blessing to me, and she brought all of you into my life. To Eugenia."

We took turns toasting Eugenia, then cursing the vile creature who took her from us. Finally, Tallulah said, "Hadley, bring us up to speed. I'm positively dying to hear what you've learned."

"There's not much to tell at this point. It's early yet." I briefed them on everything that had happened since that morning, and the evidence against Kateryna. "Fish, are you certain that was Kateryna's car you saw?"

"Why, no. Not at all," said Fish. "I don't recall ever seeing her car. Naturally, I never claimed to have seen it here Sunday morning. What I *saw*, was a grey Honda Accord, and that's what I told the police officer."

"The Accord is one of the most common cars on the road." I pulled up the photos of Kateryna's car I'd taken earlier. "Is this the car you saw?"

Fish took my phone. "Hmm . . . well, it could be. It's hard to say for sure, of course. I didn't take down the license plate. Didn't see the need at the time. But the car I saw had a sticker on the back windshield, one of those things with a stick-people family and a dog. It caught my attention."

"Kateryna doesn't have one of those," I said. "At least today she doesn't. And it wouldn't make any sense, anyway. She doesn't have a family. But that doesn't prove anything. The sticker could've been on the car when she bought it. Are you familiar with Eugenia's security system?"

"I am," said Fish. "She often asked me to do one thing or another that involved turning it on or off. Why do you ask?"

"I'm wondering if the outdoor cameras caught the car or anyone coming or going. How long does it keep recordings, do you know?"

"The cameras are motion activated," said Fish. "The system saves a clip anytime one of them is triggered. I think they're kept for thirty days unless someone saves them," said Fish. "The police already looked at whatever is there. It's all stored in the cloud. They downloaded what they needed, but whatever was captured is still there."

"Do you think I could see it later?"

"Of course. The house . . . well, there's still crime scene tape everywhere, you understand. We're not supposed to be in there. I'm not sure why, exactly. The police've already gone over everything with a fine-tooth comb. Took lots of little baggies with them. I'm sure this is important to your investigation. We'll just have to be cautious."

"Thank you—that'll be a big help," I said.

"Not at all," said Fish. "Whatever you need."

"Fish, is Faulkner with you?" asked Quinn.

"I'm keeping him with me at the pool house for now," said Fish. "Neither of us needs to be alone. I doubt Everette will fight me for custody. I expect this may be a permanent arrangement. Which is fine with me. Faulkner is good company."

"Faulkner will be much better off with you than Everette," said Libba.

"Everette's not really the kind to have pets," said Fish.

"That's an understatement," said Tallulah. "Hadley, how is Kateryna holding up?"

"Remarkably well, all things considered," I said. "She did tell me one thing I'm hoping you ladies can verify. Do y'all recall Eugenia buying Kateryna a set of knives?"

"Oh my stars, those knives." Sarabeth covered her mouth. Her shoulders shook with laughter, which proved contagious. Giggles turned to guffaws, then they were all laughing.

"Classic Eugenia," said Fish. "Yes, she bought Kateryna a set of knives. It was part of Eugenia's campaign to turn her into an acceptable pastor's wife."

"Were they just like Eugenia's?" I asked.

"Identical," said Camille. "I was with her when she bought them at Williams Sonoma on King Street. She was very specific. It had to be the precise set. Zwilling J.A. Henckels Professional sixteen-piece in a bamboo block."

"Do any of you know if Kateryna ever visited Eugenia? Did she ever come to the house?"

"Not that I'm aware of," said Fish.

"I wouldn't think so." Tallulah took on a thoughtful look.

"No," said Camille. "I'm almost certain she didn't."

"They weren't that sort of friends," said Libba. "It was an involuntary mentoring situation."

"Listen, I just need to cover all the bases here," I said. "I know we all think we know who's responsible for Eugenia's death, and I'm not saying we're wrong. But I have to explore all the possibilities. Is there anyone else who might've had a motive to kill Eugenia?"

"Of course not," said Camille.

The rest of the group echoed her with a chorus of "nos."

"I wish Birdie could've been here this evening," said Tallulah. "You need to speak with her as soon as possible."

"Why is that?" I asked.

"There are things Eugenia didn't tell you," said Tallulah.

"Like what?" I asked.

Tallulah winced. "It's better if you hear it from Birdie. It's her story to tell."

What was this all about? "All right, I'll speak to her tomorrow if she's available."

Tallulah closed her eyes and nodded, seeming relieved.

"I assume Middleton, Bull & Vanderhorst drew up the will," I said.

"Yes," said Tallulah. "Alex Ireland. She's relatively new in the wills and estates department, but she came highly recommended."

"I don't know her." I bit my lip. "I doubt she's going to want to discuss the will with me."

"What do you need to know?" asked Tallulah. "I'm the executor."

"Oh." Interesting. I would've thought Eugenia would've used her attorney, or maybe one of her children. "Who all benefits from Eugenia's death?"

"No one who would've hurt her," said Tallulah. "Well, Everette does get a small bequest."

I squinted at her. "Everette doesn't inherit everything?"

"He does not," said Tallulah. "Although, their original wills stated that if either of them died, everything went to the surviving spouse, to be divvied up between the kids after both Everette and Eugenia were gone."

"So she changed her will?" asked Quinn. "When did she do that?"

"About a year ago," said Tallulah. "She set up a series of trusts. By South Carolina law, it's impossible to completely disinherit a spouse. Especially when one's spouse is a retired judge one was married to for forty-two years. But Eugenia did her best." Tallulah grinned.

"Tell me about these trusts," I said.

"Well," said Tallulah, "her children, of course, each have a trust. Gwyneth, the daughter, is the oldest. She lives in California. Married to a movie producer. They have three children, a boy and two girls. The oldest is six. They all have trusts.

"Eugenia's son, Harrison, lives in Silver Springs, Maryland. He works for NOAA. He's married to his job, no kids. Eugenia rarely sees any of them. You know how it is. They're all busy with their own lives. Anyway, all their trusts are irrevocable. Which means neither of the children had a financial motive to kill Eugenia. They're already getting their money, and the amount won't change. I can't conceive of any motive they might have, for what it's worth."

"And everything else goes to Everette?" I asked.

"As a matter of fact, no," said Tallulah. "There's a large trust for Cornerstone Community Church. There's a trust to manage annual donations to several other charities. And then there's the one dealing with the house." Tallulah looked at Fish.

"Yeah, I know I'm going to need to move soon. The kids will want to sell the house." Fish dug a hand through his hair. "Do you know how long I have?"

Tallulah said, "Moving won't be necessary, Fish. Eugenia set up a trust for the house. You're the sole beneficiary. Provision has been made for maintenance, taxes, et cetera. I'll go over everything with you in detail later."

Fish looked stunned. He sat heavily in the closest chair. "I can't believe it. Why would she do that? The house is worth—"

"Because she loved you, Fish," said Tallulah. "You were her dear friend. You stood by her when she needed you most."

He shook his head. "I never would've expected—"

"She knew you didn't expect it," said Tallulah. "That's one of the reasons she did it. Now, the house is yours, and you can do anything you like with it except sell it or mortgage it."

"I'm flabbergasted." Fish drew a long breath and let it out slowly.

"How about other relatives? Eugenia was an only child, she told me that. So, no nieces or nephews on her side of the family. Any on Everette's who might've expected to inherit something?"

"Everette is the third of five sons," said Tallulah, "which more or less tells you why all the money was Eugenia's. His family was well-to-do, but what they had was divided five ways, with the biggest share going to the oldest in the form of the family business —some sort of technology company. I don't think any of Everette's brothers are still in Charleston. He was never close to any of them. They all did pretty well, from what I hear. But no,

Everette's family wouldn't've been expecting anything from Eugenia. They hardly knew her."

"So then, what does Everette get?" I asked.

"Everette gets one third of the estate," said Tallulah, "which is the minimum the law allows."

"Tallulah, you sure do know a lot about all of this," said Sarabeth.

"I had to learn, didn't I? Eugenia entrusted *me* with managing her estate. Which calls her good judgement into question, doesn't it? Anyway, as I was saying, it's substantially reduced by all the irrevocable trusts. They come out first precisely because they're irrevocable. Technically, those are gifts Eugenia gave before she died, and they aren't affected by her death. Alex Ireland set all this up. She's quite sharp. Everette will receive the tiniest sliver of a fraction of what he expected."

"And you're sure he didn't know about this? He thought he got it all?" I asked.

"Oh yes," said Tallulah. "I'm quite certain."

Would things have been different if Eugenia had told him? Maybe. But then again, maybe not. Everette might not've had the same motive then, but he'd've still had a motive to kill Eugenia —rage.

Chapter Twenty-One

Fish took down the crime scene tape across the front door, and we went inside.

"Her office is this way." He walked through the foyer and started down a hallway to the left.

The house had a closed-up feel, and at the same time a preternatural tension hung in the air. I stepped towards the kitchen.

"Hadley, they haven't let me have the cleaners in." Fish moved quickly, tried to slip in front of me. "You don't want to see this."

"No, I don't," I said. "But I need to." Eugenia's beautiful kitchen, where she'd doctored my hives, made us coffee, and put breakfast together only a week ago was a scene from a horror movie. I snapped a few photos, but I didn't cross the threshold.

I was shaking as I turned away.

"Here," said Fish. "This way." He put a hand at my lower back and escorted me down the hall to Eugenia's office.

A large modern desk floated in front of a wall of windows dressed in white billowing floor-length drapes. Overstuffed floor-to-ceiling bookcases lined the wall to the left. Two club chairs sat in front of the desk, and a deep white sofa with an orange throw tossed across one end anchored the righthand wall. Tables with lamps flanked each end of the sofa. On the coffee table rested a New Oxford Annotated Bible with a bookmark.

"I don't know what I was thinking," said Fish. "Of course the police took Eugenia's laptop. That's what she used to log in to the security system."

"Do you know the user id and password?"

"She'll have it written down in a little notebook in the top drawer."

I sat at Eugenia's desk and slid open the center top drawer. Nothing but office supplies, and those seemed disheveled. I checked the other drawers. Everything had the look of being rifled through. "I think they must've taken it."

"I think I have it written down." He hesitated. "Will you be all right here for a few minutes?"

"I'll be fine."

He nodded and backed out the door, giving me a worried look. "I won't be long."

I gave a closer look to the contents of Eugenia's desk. In the bottom right-hand drawer were four books: a copy of the novel *Atonement* by Ian McEwan, *Mere Christianity* and *The Screwtape Letters* by C.S. Lewis, and *The Five People You Meet in Heaven* by Mitch Albom. Another drawer held only a blank notepad and a pen. I suspected Cash had taken anything remotely helpful.

I walked over and picked up Eugenia's Bible. On closer inspection, I saw that there were two bookmarks. The first was in Deuteronomy. Eugenia had highlighted the first few verses of chapter 21, which had to do with how to handle a body found lying in open country. What in the world? I was mostly a New Testament girl myself and was rusty on Deuteronomy. I read the chapter notes at the bottom of the page. There was that word again: atonement. This passage dealt with atonement for an unsolved murder. Why had Eugenia highlighted this passage?

I turned to the second bookmark. 1 John . . . chapter two, verse two. Eugenia had highlighted: "and he is the atoning sacrifice for our sins, and not for ours only but also for the sins of the whole world."

I flipped through the Bible. Eugenia had highlighted numerous other passages, mostly in the Gospels. I walked back over to the desk, opened the bottom drawer, and pulled out the books I'd found. They all had the look of books that had been read more than once. I opened *Atonement* and flipped through the pages. Eugenia had highlighted the following passage: "How guilt refined the methods of self-torture, threading the beads of detail into an eternal loop, a rosary to be fingered for a lifetime."

Eugenia, what were you thinking about when you drew the yellow marker through those words? Why were you torturing yourself? For what did you seek atonement? And did that have anything to do with your death?

Fish came back into the room. "Here you go." He handed me a piece of paper torn from a notebook with the login information.

"I can look at this on a larger screen later," I said. "But I'll just make sure I can get into the account. I can do that from my phone."

Fish nodded. He didn't sit. He looked supremely uncomfortable.

I navigated to the CPI website and accessed Eugenia's account. There were only two outdoor cameras, in the front and back yard, and none indoors. I pulled up the footage from Saturday night. The camera by the front door captured a grey Honda Accord arriving at 2:25 a.m., but then there was a skip in the recording until 10:14 the next morning, when it recorded police cars out front.

"Someone clearly disabled the cameras," I said. "Who turned them back on?"

"Detective Reynolds," said Fish. "He asked to see the security system, and when he went to the panel, he discovered the cameras, glass breaks, motion detectors—all the alert devices, had been turned off. Normally, even when the system isn't armed, the cameras and all still monitor things and send alerts to Eugenia's phone. She only arms the system—like so you hear an alarm if a door or window opens—at night, or if she's out of town. When the police checked the system, everything had been turned all the way off."

Why didn't Fish mention this earlier? "Who all knew how to turn it on and off?"

"It's a CPI system. Anyone who has one of those, or ever has, would know *how* to operate it. But having access to do that, that's something else altogether, isn't it? If you're standing at the panel, it's easy enough, but you still have to have a code. From the driveway, you can do it with an app. If you have the code."

"I can think of several ways it could be done without the passcode," I said. "But someone would have to know their way around these systems."

"Hard to imagine Kateryna would have that skill set," said Fish.

"It is, isn't it?" What in the name of common sense was Cash thinking?

"Who besides you, Eugenia, and Everette knew the codes?" I asked.

"No one that I'm aware of."

"Where's the safe you mentioned?" I asked.

"In the closet." He pointed to a door in the corner near the end of the sofa. "No one's found a combination. I honestly have no idea what might be in there. I didn't even know she had a safe."

I walked over, opened the closet, and flipped on the light. Shelves held more office supplies: printer paper, ink cartridges, and the like. Baskets arranged artfully on a few of the shelves held smaller items. The modem and router sat at eye level. A small but sturdy safe sat on the floor in the corner. I tried the door just to be thorough, but of course it was locked. It had a keypad rather than an old-fashioned combination lock. I opened the electronic case file saved to my desktop from my phone and tried Eugenia's birthday, her and Everette's wedding anniversary, and the birthdates of their children, with no luck. What did you keep in here, Eugenia?

Beside the safe was a four-drawer file cabinet. I pulled on the handle of the top drawer. It was unlocked, but empty. The other drawers had likewise been cleaned out. Cash must've just grabbed everything from bank records to electric bills. I walked out of the closet.

Fish looked decidedly uncomfortable. "Get what you needed?"

"Not entirely," I said. "You mentioned Eugenia's jewelry was all accounted for. So that's all in her bedroom?"

"Her dressing room, yes," said Fish. "Of course, I can't swear nothing is missing, but there's no empty spot in her armoire. Tallulah said all the important pieces were there."

"Jewelry would be the logical thing to keep in a safe," I said.

"Could be bonds, maybe? Some cash? She had some in her desk drawer, about five thousand dollars. The police had me sign something that itemized what was taken. But she could've had more money in the safe, I guess."

"Maybe," I said. "I'll need to come back when I've collected a few more combinations to try."

"Anytime," said Fish. "Just let me know."

"Fish, I need to ask you something, and I don't want you to misunderstand . . ."

He nodded. "You want to know why I was living in Eugenia's pool house."

"Yes . . . and more about the nature of your relationship with Eugenia. The police must've asked you this, didn't they?"

"They did . . . Eugenia and I went way back. We grew up near each other. Our families were friends. We ran with the same crowd all through school, well, up until she left for college, anyway.

"I was my parents' only son. They died in a plane crash when I was thirty-three. I inherited quite a lot of money. I was nonfunctional from grief for about a year. Then I had an epiphany of sorts. My parents had done all the right things—they worked hard, were on several charity boards . . . they were on a business trip when they died. Their whole lives, they worked, and for what? They missed out on so much. So I decided I wasn't going to miss a thing.

"I quit work and embarked on the grandest of adventures. I bought a yacht and a plane, and I traveled the world with a series of entertaining women. I experienced everything that came to mind, and I traveled every continent. And I went through a fortune. I blew every nickel of it and came home penniless.

"Eugenia took pity on me and took me in. We were never anything but the very best of platonic friends."

"Were you and Everette close?" I asked.

He shrugged. "Not especially. Well, I suppose we were in school. By the time I came home broke, Everette and I had little in common."

"How did he respond to Eugenia taking you in?" I asked.

"He didn't care for the arrangement and thought it was unseemly. The more he carried on about it, the more determined Eugenia became. She and I were good company for each other. If he'd've been a better husband, she wouldn't've been so lonely."

"Indeed," I said. "Thank you for sharing that."

"My pleasure to assist. And Hadley?"

"Yes?"

"I had no earthly idea she planned to leave this house to me. But if I had known, it would've never been a motive to kill her. Eugenia was my best friend. I don't know how I'll ever manage without her."

Chapter Twenty-Two

When I first found out I had a brother, J. T. and I were sixteen. Up until that point, we'd both thought we were only children, and we were instantly fascinated with each other. We've been close ever since. It was the late nineties, and J. T. was listening to, among other things, a lot of Will Smith's music. To this day, his ring tone is the chorus of one of Big Willie's songs. I was in my office setting up the case board a little after nine when my phone sang out, "Gettin' Jiggy Wit It."

"Hey, little bro." He was only younger than me by two days, but younger was younger.

"That's right, this is your one and only little brother. Your only sibling, in fact."

I sat back in my chair and looked at the ceiling. "What do you want?"

"You know what I want, Sis."

"What? Oh—no. No, we've been over this, J. T." We'd been over it several times since I'd received the engraved invitation on heavy ecru card stock.

"Why are you so freakishly stubborn?"

"Freakishly? Really? You think I'm *freakishly* stubborn? As opposed to the normal degree of stubborn you are, I suppose?"

"Something like that. Look . . . I just want to toast turning forty with my sister. And frankly, it hurts my feelings that this is something that not only didn't even occur to you, but you're digging in your heels against it."

"Ah, crackers, come on, J. T." I loved my brother. I did. But . . . "I have told you a dozen times already, I would be thrilled to drink champagne with you anytime. Even though you're well aware that I don't celebrate my birthdays, I will happily toast yours, and we can mark the occasion any other way you like. Just as long as Swinton is not part of the equation."

"Hadley Scott Drayton Legare Cooper, I am positively shocked to hear you don't want a birthday dance with our pater familias."

"Pigs will first fly."

He laughed. "You don't want to dance with Dad? That's perfectly fine. But come dance with your brother. The only one you have, or ever will have."

"I bet Judith has invited half of Charleston. You won't even notice I'm not there."

"Wrong on both counts. It's an intimate gathering of two hundred and fifty or so close friends and family. And you're one of the few people I actually care about seeing. Please say you'll come."

I drank in a long breath, then let it out. "I would do almost anything for you. You know that. But I can't do this."

"You don't even have to speak to Dad if you don't want to. Although, that will kill him a little bit. But I guess he's not expecting anything any different. I'll talk to him."

"J. *Teeeee* . . ."

"Or—here's an idea. If you come, you can smash another one of his cars. Any one you like."

Now he'd pissed me off. To his credit, he figured that out fast.

"I'm an idiot. I apologize. Please forgive me. *Dammit.* It was only a matter of time before I said something stupid. Trying to discuss Dad with you . . . it never fails."

"Which is why you should know better than to try it."

His tone went serious. "Hadley, this is important to me."

I so did not want to go to Swinton's house . . . into his lair. But I did love my brother. I sighed deep and long. "I know beyond a shadow of a doubt I will regret this."

"You'll come?" The joy in his voice shamed me.

"I'll come."

"This will be the best birthday ever."

"You'll have some eye candy on your arm. You'll forget I'm even there."

"Nope. I'm not bringing a date, except you."

"What? No. Look, there's enough talk about us as it is. I will not be your date, J. T."

"Who talks about us? This is all in your head, by the way."

"You bring a proper date. So it's clear I'm *not* your date."

"I'll bring one if you do."

"If you'll recall, I was just epically dumped. I have no date to bring."

"Oh please, any man over twelve in Charleston would give his left nut to be your date to a tractor pull, and this, if I say so myself, is one of the highlights of the social season. The party favors . . . two words, Hadley: cake pops."

"Cake pops you say? How many?"

"Four in each bucket."

"I want a dozen. Made with healthy flour and natural sweet-eners—no refined sugar."

"Done. Your bucket will have a dozen—two dozen—of the healthiest, most naturally sweetened cake pops ever baked."

"Fine."

"But I'm not bringing a date unless you do."

Who on earth was I going to get to escort me to a fancy party five days from now? "Gavin. I'll bring Gavin."

"Nope. Has to be someone born in the same generation as us."

"Stop adding conditions. I can't afford to be picky."

"You're my sister . . . hey, a few of my friends from college are going to be in town—"

"No. Uh-uh. Not happening. You will not fix me up. Not with anyone."

"So you'll find your own date then? Is that what you're telling me?"

"Fine."

I hung up the phone and drained my wine glass.

Chapter Twenty-Three

I took another glass of wine and waited near the pool, just outside the breakfast area. North was early that night. At ten thirty, he walked up the path from the beach, opened the gate, and crossed the pool deck. He was far too skinny, but in board shorts and a t-shirt, he looked like any other beach lover coming back from a nighttime stroll.

"I'm torn about this place," he said.

"What do you mean?"

"On the one hand, it's so over the top. I mean, who needs something that cost as much as this must've cost to build, right?"

I drew a long breath, nodded. "It's excessive. I'll give you that."

"On the other hand, the way the house is designed . . . You have to admire the way it becomes one with the landscape, blending the indoors with the outdoors. And you just feel so peaceful here by the ocean, like you're so close to nature you're just sitting on God's lap. Parts of this island are pretty wild anymore."

"Yeah, you better watch out for coyotes and other critters. Snakes. All kinds of things living in the bushy parts. There're laws protecting all that accreted land."

"You don't have to worry about that on this end of the island, but . . . it's kinda nice. The new wilderness that's building by a few grains of sand every day. Anyway, if anyone deserves this house, it's you, Hadley."

I shook my head. "Now that's just crazy. And it's not my house. It belongs to a New York banker."

"Figures."

"He's a nice guy, actually. As far as I can tell, anyway. The good news is we're sitting in the outdoor kitchen. There are two refrigerators built into that island over there. One will always have food for you, and the other, drinks—water, tea, some healthy sports drinks."

"Hadley, you don't have to do all this."

"But I want to. I want you to feel at home here, North. Check out the open-air bathroom around the corner behind the palmetto there." I pointed to my left. "When you need it, the fire pit operates on remote control. I'll leave the remote right here on the shelf underneath this table."

"Hadley . . ."

"I hoped you'd like it here."

He winced. "I appreciate you. You know I do. But this is your temporary home. It's not a good idea for me to get too comfortable in one place."

I'd rushed things. I mentally smacked myself in the head. I knew better. You could overwhelm North very easily. And let's face it, anyone would be overwhelmed by this place. Time for a subject change.

"Hey, I wondered if you'd help me out tomorrow," I said.

"What do you need?"

"I need to be in two places at one time." I could easily have asked Joe or Gavin—or both of them—to help me with surveillance. But North needed to be needed. And I needed a reason to pay him.

"I can help with that. Where's the one you want me at?"

"In Charleston. Meet me in Washington Park. I need you to

follow someone. See where he goes and if he meets with anyone." Washington Park was a little more than a block from Everette's Tradd Street house.

"Who am I tailing?"

I told North about Eugenia, about Everette. And about how Cash was the lead detective on the investigation.

"Are you sure this is a good idea? You working on an active police case—Cash's case?"

"No, I'm not sure of that at all," I said. "But this is something I have to do."

He nodded. "What time do you need me there?"

"About eleven. I'll need to be able to reach you. And I need you to get pictures of anyone he meets." I'd tried several times to give him a cheap phone so he could reach me if he needed to. So far this effort had met with flat refusal. North was adamant about not taking anything from me. Even the food he kept a tally of and insisted on working off. I laid the older model iPhone I'd had for at least a year on the table.

He looked at it but didn't take it.

"North, I need you to take this. You can't do the job I need you to do without some way to take pictures. And you have to be able to call me if he's headed home." I had a tracker on Everette's car, but often he left home on foot.

North hesitated, made a face that told me he was only cooperating under duress. "I'll ride my bike over early."

"Thanks, North."

Chapter Twenty-Four

Tuesday morning, I walked on the beach as the sun came up, spent thirty minutes in the exercise room next to my office working out with the punching bag, then made myself a smoothie —my favorite, one I called my brain smoothie—for breakfast. I needed all the help I could get that morning. My brain smoothie is a bit like a science experiment I've perfected over the years. It has, among other things, wild blueberries, beet juice, kale, oats, and cacao. It helps me think.

I carried my smoothie with me and settled into my office to mull the case board. Already, I thought of it as *my* office. Better not get too used to this chair, all this room, or this view. The night before, I'd listed all the possible theories of the crime I could think of on my case board. I kicked back in my chair, propped my feet on the desk like I owned the place, and celebrated on the hypothetical narratives.

Cash had apparently found a theory of the crime he liked awfully fast. *He* rushed to judgement. I would not make that same mistake. I would carefully consider all the possibilities and eliminate them one by one until I was left with the only possible solution, which of course would be that Everette was guilty as sin. I sighed and reprimanded myself harshly.

People kill for all kinds of reasons, but most often, they do have a reason. Random murders are rare, which is why they get splashed all over the news. It's especially rare for someone to be the victim of a random killing in their own home. Particularly when the jewelry was left behind. Eugenia was almost certainly killed by someone she knew. Given that, my pool of suspects was relatively finite. Motives tend to repeat, with money and love, or what passes for it, at the top of the list.

I'd started my list with Eugenia's family—and those connected to them, like Jordyn Jackman—then Eugenia's closest friends, and worked outward to acquaintances, like Kateryna. For each, I listed any conceivable motives they might've had. To be thorough, and in the interest of documenting the case, I listed even those people I considered almost certainly innocent, like Eugenia's kids. At the very bottom of the list was the least likely scenario, that Eugenia had been killed by a stranger for the thrill of it, or in a fit of rage which somehow involved Eugenia. My case board that morning looked like this:

Suspect — Motive
Everette Ladson — Money, freedom, love, lust, rage, hate
Jordyn Jackman — Money, love, lust, rage, hate
Gwyneth Ladson-Cartwright — Unknown Motive
Harrison Ladson — Unknown Motive
Hamilton "Fish" Aiken — Money, love, lust, rage
Birdie Markley — Unknown Motive
Vernon Markley — Unknown Motive
Tallulah Wentworth — Unknown Motive
Camille Houston — Unknown Motive
Sarabeth Boone — Unknown Motive
Libba Graham — Unknown Motive
Quinn Poinsett — Unknown Motive
Kateryna Petrenko — Rage

Anson Gibbes Jones — Love, lust, rage (on behalf of
Kateryna)
Unknown Friend — To keep a secret, rage, love, lust
Unknown Friend or Acquaintance — Burglary of specific
item, revenge
Unknown Stranger — Thrill, rage

As I worked the case, I would probably uncover additional
motives, and possibly additional suspects. This was typical,
anyway. My list was a working document. I would update it every
day. I was an adherent of the Sherlock Holmes school of thought:
when you've eliminated the impossible, whatever remains, no
matter how improbable, is the solution. Generally, I started every
investigation by quickly ruling out those things that were impossible. This first step typically saves me time. I begin by gathering
alibis and eliminating everyone who has a solid one.

My problem was that, as alibis go, Everette's was strong.
Really strong. If he'd killed Eugenia, and I was absolutely
convinced of it, he had to've hired someone. I needed to access his
financial records to see if I could suss out who he'd recently paid a
large chunk of money to. Of the many things I could find in one
of my subscription databases, or even in public records, financial
transactions was not one of them. Now, I'm technically pretty
competent. I could maybe hack into a bank if I put my mind to it.
But that's a whole other level of criminal activity, and a risk I'm
not willing to take. There are limits, even when I'm working for
the greater good.

I needed to remove the cameras from Everette's house before
Cash found them anyway. While I was there, I'd have a look
around for anything that might point me to who Everette had
hired. How would your average person even find a contract killer?
Then again, Everette wasn't your average person at all. He was a

retired judge. All manner of criminals had crossed his path over the years. Had he found the solution to his problem in one of his old cases?

Chapter Twenty-Five

On my way into Charleston, I tried calling Gavin.

His ancient answering machine picked up. "State your business," said Gavin on the recording.

"I need some help, if you've got time," I said. "I'll give Joe the details."

Then I called Joe Vincent. My mentor may've been retired, but he seemed awfully happy whenever I asked for help—as long as it didn't interfere with his fishing schedule.

"Do you have time to run down some alibis for me?" I asked.

"Sure. Whatcha got?"

I briefed him on the case.

He whistled, long and low. "Twinkle . . ." There was admonishment in his tone.

"I know. I know. It's an active police investigation. It's a distinctly bad idea for me to get involved. I get it, and I don't disagree with a thing you're thinking. But Eugenia was a friend. I have to do this, and that's that." That's when I told him about Cash going to work for SLED, and how this was his case.

Joe was quiet for a minute. I could tell he was pondering all the angles. Finally, he said, "How is Cash? It's been a while." His tone was neutral, but I knew exactly what he was thinking.

"He's fine. Joe, look—don't get your hopes up here. Cash and I decided a long time ago we're just not meant to be. This case is not going to change anything between us."

"Of course not. What? You think I've got fairytales spinning around in my head? Heaven's sake, Hadley. Who do you think you're talking to?"

"Oh, I know exactly who I'm talking to. And you don't fool me one bit. Besides, if anything, this case has already shined a bright spotlight on all the reasons Cash and I are apart."

"How's that?"

"Cash rushed into an arrest," I said. "And I'm convinced he's arrested the wrong person. I'm working with her attorney. We're on opposite sides of this thing, Joe. Again. As always."

"No, not as always. What are you talking about? Both of you want the perp in jail, don't you?"

"Yes, of course. But—"

"That's what I thought," he said. "The two of you just need to give each other the benefit of the doubt a little more, that's all. And listen to the way you're talkin', would you? 'Cash rushed into an arrest. He's got the wrong person.' A body would think Cash is a mall cop or some fool thing instead of a decorated, experienced detective. Show some respect, for goodness' sake. Now, I'm not saying he's right. But what I am saying is you know darn well he didn't just go off half-cocked and arrest the first person he came to."

"I never said that."

"He deserves your respect if nothing else," said Joe.

"Oh please. Joe, look, I can't do this right now. Actually, there's not going to be a good time. Cash and I are over. You need to accept that. We both have."

He blew out his breath in a scoffing noise. "Whose alibis you want me looking into?"

Good. Back to business. "Let's start with Gwyneth Ladson-Cartwright and Harrison Ladson—Eugenia's children. I spoke with the executor of Eugenia's estate. They both have generous irrevocable trusts, as do Gwyneth's three children. The executor is unaware of any motives either of the children might've had. If they have strong alibis, I can cross them off my list."

"What's the window?"

"Sometime between midnight and four a.m."

"I'll widen that by a couple hours on either end. Best to err on the side of caution if you're going to rule them out. Anyone else you want me to look at?"

"If you have time, you could go through a list of her friends. Again, these are very long shots. But—"

"But this is a murder investigation, and we don't assume anything."

"Exactly. I'll text you a list."

"I'm on it. Maybe I'll get Gav to lend a hand, if he's not baking cookies this morning. We can knock your list out pretty quick."

"Yeah, I left him a message. Thanks, Joe."

"You bet, kiddo. Give Cash my best. And give him the benefit of the doubt, why don't you? Maybe talk things through over dinner. It wouldn't hurt you to have a nice steak every now and again. A man loves a good steak." He hung up before I could respond to that.

Sitting at the last stoplight on Highway 17 before I headed across the Cooper River Bridge, I knocked my head against the steering wheel.

I parked in the garage on the corner of Queen and King, grabbed my backpack, then hustled over to meet North in Washington Park. It was closing in on eleven a.m., and the Carolina sun pressed down hard. The temperature dropped perceptibly as I stepped into the shade of the towering oaks that bordered the walkways leading to the forty-two-foot model of the Washington monument. North waited for me on a bench just inside the Chalmers Street entrance.

"I'll wait here," I said. "You ride your bike over to Tradd Street, just down from Everette Ladson's house. Make like you're fixing the chain on your bike or something. And wait. He's been leaving for lunch around eleven thirty. Text me as soon as he's out the door.

"Some days he drives, and if he leaves in his car, I'll get an alert on my phone. If you can follow him on your bike to get photos, that's great. If you lose him, don't worry about it. We can only do what we can do. And I have to get some equipment out of the house stat."

"I won't lose him."

"More than likely, he'll be on foot, so you should be fine. But if he's driving, please don't take any risks."

"Had, I don't know if you've noticed, but traffic moves pretty slowly around town. I'll be fine."

"He's likely meeting friends for lunch. Take a few snapshots of who, and if you can, capture where, just in case it's something. But I'm really most interested in anyone he hands a package to. And if he's walking, I need you to let me know when he's headed back to the house so I can get out in time."

"Roger that."

I knew North could only follow Everette to where he was going. He couldn't follow him inside. I used to try periodically to get North to come indoors. I thought if I were patient enough, I could coax him back to a more normal lifestyle, one that involved sleeping inside. The last time I did that ended with a trip by ambulance to MUSC. North collapsed in a trembling heap, gasping for breath, his heart rate off the charts. If he ever crossed another threshold, it would be because it was his idea, not mine.

For a few minutes, I kicked myself for not thinking this through far enough. I should've gotten Joe to follow Everette that morning. He would only pay his hitman once. It was too late to think about that now.

North left on his bike, and I waited on the bench until he texted me twenty minutes later.

Just left on foot

I picked up my backpack and hurried down Meeting Street to Tradd. In less than five minutes, I let myself in with the key Eugenia had given me and checked the alarm, which Everette hadn't bothered to set.

First things first. I started upstairs with the master bedroom and deinstalled the cameras I'd put in place with such high hopes on Friday. It seemed like a month ago. When all the cameras were secure in my backpack, I texted North.

> Sit rep?

> Lunch at Millers All Day. By himself. No contacts.

Millers All Day was less than a five-minute walk away. The good news was that it had large windows, and North was clearly able to see Everette from the sidewalk. I texted him back.

> Need to know the second he walks out the door.

> Roger that

It seemed to me a retired judge like Everette would have a home office, or a study. Some sort of classy man cave, with leather furniture and dark woods. I hadn't run across such a room last time I was in the house. But I also hadn't climbed the stairs to the third floor. I scrambled up to check it out.

The first door at the top of the stairs was a narrow bedroom. Just beyond it, I found what I was looking for. Paneled in what might've been mahogany, but I'm no expert, Everette's office gleamed with old-money style. I crossed to the massive desk and perched in the buttery-soft leather chair. What I needed most was the one thing I couldn't get anywhere else: financial data.

The large desktop computer was on, but the screen saver had launched. I moved the mouse sideways and a box appeared asking for the password. I plugged the thumb drive with the hacking software I used into the back of the computer. Three minutes and thirty-two seconds later, I was in.

I clicked on the Bank of America icon on the desktop. Thankfully, Everette's password to that was saved on the computer and automatically populated. A few clicks later, I was looking at Everette's checking account.

Which had $256.47.

I scanned the transactions. Monthly deposits were made from a pension account in the amount of $3,300.00. The account was frequently overdrawn, but the charges were reversed each time. Everette paid his utilities, bought gas and groceries, and ate at a few local restaurants. But there definitely wasn't enough money here to finance a hit, and no suspicious transactions in the last ninety days.

I went back to the account list. The savings account had less than $500, and the last withdrawal was a transfer to checking of $200. The highest balance the account had had that year was $987. There was a credit card, but it appeared to have been maxed out for years, with Everette only paying the minimum. I went back to the desktop. There were no other banking applications. Was it possible Everette, who gave the appearance of having money and enjoying a life of leisure, lived hand-to-mouth? How long had he lived this way? Had Eugenia cut him off when they separated? Well, except he lived in a house that she inherited.

Had he paid someone to kill his wife some other way? Done someone a favor as payment? But since he'd retired, he wasn't really in a position to grant the kind of favors that would buy a murder. I copied a year's worth of statements to the thumb drive, then opened his email.

I scanned for a cell phone bill. Verizon.

I opened a browser window and went to the Verizon website. Bingo—Everette had saved his login and password. A few clicks later and I was looking at his call history. I copied the last twelve bills to my thumb drive.

My wrist vibrated with a text from North.

He's on the move

I had to get out of here.

I glanced at Everette's inbox, scrolling, looking for anything that caught my eye.

There was so much of it. Clubs, charities, advertising emails from a long list of stores. I knew he wouldn't be stupid enough to have a contract for murder in his email. But there might be something that gave me a clue as to how he'd pulled this off.

A subject line caught my eye: Dinner in Greenville. I opened the email. It was from a Leland Marchant.

Ev,

Sounds good. I'll make a reservation at Soby's for six p.m.
Mike wants to talk about the Jocassee project we
discussed last year. Timing might be right. I'm asking
Bryce Brashier to join us as well.

Leland

The email trail showed an ongoing conversation about getting together in Greenville for dinner. This was apparently something they did periodically. I scrolled through the older emails. Last time was in February. What was interesting was that they had originally planned to meet again in May, but Everette had postponed. They'd rescheduled for July, but then they must've had a conversation or two that wasn't reflected in the emails, because suddenly they were getting together on Saturday, June 12.

I took photos of the entire email exchange. Then I closed all the applications, closed down the computer, grabbed my thumb drive, and scanned the desk area to make sure I'd left no trace. I raced down the steps and out the front door.

I passed Everette on Tradd Street. He smiled happily, nodded at me, and said "Good afternoon." He was the picture of Southern graciousness. Funny, he didn't look much like a grieving widower.

People grieve differently, I admonished myself. Don't be so judgy.

But I couldn't offer Everette the benefit of the doubt. I didn't know how he'd done it, but I was certain he'd killed Eugenia. And with Kateryna charged, he was probably feeling pretty smug right now. That was fine with me. Smug people made mistakes.

Chapter Twenty-Six

On the northeast end of Sullivan's Island where I currently resided, the street closest to the ocean—that ran more or less parallel to it—was Marshall Boulevard. If you were driving southwest towards the lighthouse on Marshall, the street ran out at Station 28. A quick jog right, then left, put you on the next road over, Bayonne, which runs down to Station 26, where you do another little jog to get on Atlantic Avenue.

Atlantic Avenue is the closest street to the ocean for a large swath of the island, interrupted by the elementary school and the lighthouse near Station 20. Atlantic Avenue ends at Station 16, near the nature trail established by The Town of Sullivan's Island on the densest part of the maritime forest that flourished on 190 acres of protected land between Station 12 and Station 29.

At the northeastern most part of the beach, nearest Breach Inlet, the forest consisted of dune grasses and flowers. As you walked southwest on the beach, you started to see a few small shrubs. Then the shrubs became thicker and taller, and trees started to appear, and before you knew it, there were patches of forest between the beach and the row of beachfront homes. Whether this was a blessing or a curse depended entirely upon who you asked. The accreted land with all its various vegetation belonged not to the oceanfront property owners. Their lots didn't expand as Mother Nature enlarged Sullivan's Island. This newly birthed part of the island belonged to the Lowcountry Land Trust, whose mission was to protect it.

Birdie and Vernon lived on Atlantic Avenue near Station 24, in a home that was once oceanfront. They were expecting me, and they both came to the door.

"Well, Tallulah wasn't exaggerating for once." Vernon Markley raised both eyebrows and gave me a slightly lascivious look.

"*Vernon.* Sweetie, don't mind him. He's old and crazy. I'm Mary Evelyn. Folks call me Birdie. This is my cross to bear in life, Vernon. Come in, come in."

"Hey, I'm Hadley Cooper. We spoke on the phone."

"It's lovely to meet you. Let's get comfortable, shall we?" Birdie led me through the foyer and into a large family room with large windows and several sets of French doors that opened onto a pool deck.

The name Birdie suited her. She was delicate, fine boned, and had pale, luminous skin. Her wavy light brown hair had a few grey streaks. It was long, and she wore it pulled over her left shoulder and tied loosely with a ribbon. Birdie's decorating style appeared to have been influenced by the modern farmhouse trend, with neutrals in several shades. "Please have a seat. What can I get you to drink? Iced tea?"

I took a spot on the loveseat. "Well, only if you're getting some for yourself."

"I keep a glass at all times," said Birdie.

"Hides the bourbon." Vernon grinned.

"Vernon, you know very well I don't put bourbon in my glass until after five o'clock. I'll just be a moment."

"I understand you're our newest neighbor," said Vernon.

"Temporarily." I didn't want anyone to get the idea I was parading about as someone who owned property on Sullivan's Island. "I'm house-sitting for a client."

"Do you have a . . . jungle situation?" He looked around, as if checking for eavesdroppers.

"I beg your pardon?"

"Are the bushes and trees and scrub sprouting up everywhere? Taking over everything like kudzu?" He gestured wildly with both hands as he said the word "sprouting." His eyes shone with a wild gleam.

"No, I'm far enough north I may have the opposite problem." I wasn't exactly sure where the line was—where erosion stopped and accretion began. But I thought I lived close to the border.

"Keep a close eye," said Vernon. "It's best to catch it early. At first, it's all sea oats and wildflowers, and you think, 'well, that's nice.' But then you wake up one morning and you can't see the ocean and snakes are sunning on your walkway and varmints are procreating in bushes so thick you can't see if it's raccoons or possums or teenagers. Keep a close eye."

"I'll do that," I said.

"Vernon, for Heaven's sake." Birdie set a glass of iced tea on a coaster to my right. "Hadley didn't come to hear you whine about your jungle woes."

"I'm just trying to help the girl," said Vernon.

"Don't you have something you need to be doing?" Birdie looked at her husband. "I'd like to have a nice chat with Hadley. Girl talk."

"I'd like to have a nice chat with her too." He looked petulant.

"Vernon." Birdie spoke sternly to him.

"Oh, all right." He stood. "You ladies enjoy yourselves. I'll be downstairs if you need me."

"Vernon?" Birdie smiled when she looked up at him, but her tone still carried a warning.

"Yes, dear?"

"Keep the pets indoors, won't you?" Butter wouldn't have melted in her mouth.

"Of course. It's too hot out in the midday heat for—"

"We'll catch up with you later," said Birdie.

He muttered something under his breath as he walked out of the room.

"Men," said Birdie. "Sometimes I think I married a toddler. Is your iced tea all right? You need some lemon?"

"It's delicious, thank you," I said. "Tallulah said you wanted to speak with me?" I had questions for her as well. But I was curious as to what was on her mind.

"Yes, well. We're all quite close. Tallulah and Eugenia and I have been friends forever. But I suppose you'd say Eugenia and I were best friends. Our mothers were close. They raised us together. I can't imagine what I'll do without her." She looked down, blotted her eyes with an embroidered handkerchief.

"Sounds like she was practically a sister," I said. "I didn't know her for very long. And I regret that, very much. I think we would've been close friends."

"Eugenia thought a lot of you," said Birdie. "It was like her, to make fast friends. As her oldest friend, I think it falls to me to tell you what she can't."

I tilted my head at her, gave her a questioning look.

"You noticed, I guess, how Eugenia likes to fix things . . . people, actually. Take Kateryna, for example."

"She certainly was trying to fit her to a proper pastor's wife." I laughed.

"Yes, she was, at that. Eugenia cared quite a lot for Kateryna. That was the thing about Eugenia. The more she tried to meddle in your business, the more she loved you. She never bothered with people she didn't like. But she loved her newest project best."

"What was that?" Something crawled around the edges of my stomach.

"You."

"Me? How was I her project? I mean, she hired me to do a job, but—"

"And she was sincere in that. She thought you were the ideal person to get the goods on Everette, and it certainly sounds like you did. But Eugenia had something else up her sleeve when it comes to you."

"What's that?"

Birdie smiled, shook her head slowly, then sighed. "Eugenia told you that she and Judith were old friends, right?"

"She did, yes."

"Well, that's part of the story. The whole truth of that situation is that Eugenia and Everette and Judith and Swinton were quite close for many years. It started in middle school, I suppose. Around the time people start pairing off boy-girl. The four of them, and to a somewhat lesser extent Vernon and me, and Fish and a long list of girlfriends, ran together as they say, throughout high school and college—and into our thirties, I guess. Some of us gradually drifted away after that, but then someone would throw a party, and we'd all be right back together."

"Why wouldn't Eugenia have told me that?" I asked.

Birdie sighed. "You look so much like your father."

I inhaled slowly, tamped down my irritation. I needed Birdie to talk to me about Eugenia. I couldn't alienate her. But I seriously did not want to discuss Swinton. "I've heard that."

"He's a good man, Hadley. A very decent, honorable, nice man."

"I'm sorry, I can't—"

"Please just listen to me. It's all wrapped up in why Eugenia did what she did. Or what she was planning to do rather. She didn't actually do anything. Yet."

I closed my eyes for a long moment, then cleared my throat. "All right."

"Eugenia had it in her head that no one had ever told you the truth about your parents. And so she decided she should be the one, only she was biding her time when she ran out of it."

"And what is the truth, exactly?" My voice might've been a teeny bit frosty.

"Judith and your father were high school sweethearts. But

their relationship was complicated. Their families encouraged the match. But Swinton always saw Judith as more of a best friend."

"I really don't see—"

"Judith adored him. He's always been the love of her life. Your mother, Hadley, was the love of Swinton's life. And Judith has always known that."

"I don't understand—"

"The point to all of this is that your father is a good man. He didn't mistreat your mother. She broke his heart. He married Judith on the rebound. Oh, I suppose there was a short period of time right before the wedding when he held out hope, was thinking maybe he could work things out with Vivienne. She must've wavered, considered saying yes to a life with him. And then she changed her mind. And I'm supposing a few things here, because I guess one can't explain away you and your brother, born two days apart. But Swinton never cheated on Judith. They broke up. The wedding was off. And then it was back on. And he didn't know he had a daughter until you were sixteen."

I focused on taking deep breaths.

"Did your mother not tell you any of this?" Birdie asked.

I sipped my tea, set down the glass. "No. She didn't talk about my father at all. I didn't know who he was until she got sick. It took a lot out of her, talking about him. So she didn't. She needed to focus on her health."

"Eugenia just thought it was so tragic. And I have to say I agree with her. You lost your mother all those years ago, and your father adores you, but you seem to despise him. Now, I don't presume to know all of your business. But here's what I do know. Here's what Eugenia knew, that she was trying to figure out how to tell you without having you run away from her too: I've rarely in my life met a finer man than Swinton Legare. He never cheated on your mother. He didn't cheat on Judith, though back in the day you'd hear a lot of people in Charleston claim he did, mostly out of loyalty to Judith. They don't know what they're talking about. And Judith surely took him back quicker than most women would've. Swinton has always been a good and faithful husband, and he's been a good father to John Thomas."

I felt a tear slip down my cheek. "And all I know is that my mother died alone except for me and a family friend. If my father loved her so much, why did he not lift a finger to get her the best of treatments?"

"Now that I don't know the answer to," said Birdie. "But, if you recall, at the time, he'd been married to someone else for more than sixteen years. He, and Judith, had just learned that he had another child, one your mother had kept from him all those years. I said he was a good man. I never claimed he was a saint. I'm sure your mother had her reasons for what she did. If you'll pardon my frankness, it seems to me she had the life she chose."

"Is that it? Eugenia just wanted to speak up for poor Swinton?" My tone might've been a touch sarcastic.

"Eugenia wanted to mend the relationship between you and your father. For your sake as well as his. She just thought the two of you needed each other. And after she died, and Tallulah came up with the idea that we should all hire you to look into Eugenia's death, well, I knew that you were going to talk to people who would tell you exactly how close we all were. I figured you should hear it from me. And I thought I could try to honor what Eugenia wanted. But I'm no good at fixing people. That was her gift."

"I don't think I need to be fixed, actually," I said.

"Just promise me you'll give all of this some thought."

"I'll do that." I doubt I meant that exactly how she would've liked. I couldn't see how I could *not* think about all of this. But I had no plans at that point to reconsider my opinion of my father.

I cleared my throat. "Back to Eugenia and Everette . . . Can you shed any light on their financial arrangements?"

"Well, most of the money was Eugenia's. I guess she told you that. They were one of those couples who always kept their finances essentially separate. I mean, I understand they did have a few joint accounts for most of their married life. But Eugenia moved her money out of those during the last year or so. After she knew for sure he was cheating. And, well I mean, he was such a jerk to her when she was sick. Do you know he refused to be seen with her in a headscarf? She was fighting for her life, and he was basically absent, and when he was around, he was indifferent or worse, downright cruel."

"We certainly agree on the content of Everette's character." I gave her a wry smile. "So did he live off of his money then?"

"That was my understanding," said Birdie. "He has a pension. And it's not like Eugenia tossed him out on the street. He lived in the Tradd Street house. I don't think he had other sources of income, though. He made decent money as a judge, but he spent what he made. He wasn't one to squirrel money away. Everette has always liked to live well. And I think he always felt like he had something to prove, money wise."

"Can you think of anyone, aside from Everette, who might've had a motive to kill Eugenia?" I asked.

"Goodness gracious, no." Her hand went to her chest, a horrified look on her face. "And I'm certain it wasn't Kateryna. Why, the idea is absurd."

"Do you think it was Everette?" I asked.

Birdie tilted her head in thought. "I do. And yet, it's hard to see how he could have. Tallulah told me he was in Greenville. That you were certain of that."

"I am. I wish I weren't. I'm operating on the assumption that he hired someone. Perhaps someone he ran across in the courtroom?"

"I've never personally hired a hitman. Lord knows the thought has crossed my mind a time or two. Vernon does try my patience. But I'm guessing that's quite expensive. Especially if you're a retired judge and relying on the discretion of criminals. It's hard for me to imagine how Everette could've pulled that off. He was on a very short leash, financially speaking."

"But if it wasn't Everette, then who?"

"I can't think of another soul who had a motive," said Birdie.

"Was she worried about anything?"

"Not to my knowledge. Well, aside from the fact her husband of forty-two years was having an affair in her ancestral home. That worried her."

"Was there anything new in her life?" I asked.

"Not really. She did change churches, but that happened . . . I guess she's been going to that new church in Mount Pleasant for about a year, maybe longer. The pastor there could tell you for sure." Something about the way she said pastor gave me pause.

"Have you ever been to Cornerstone Community Church with Eugenia?"

"Oh, no. That's not my style. I'm not saying there's anything wrong with it. But I'm a lifelong Episcopalian."

"Eugenia was too, right up until recently, right?"

Birdie half chuckled, shook her head. "That Fish. He's the one who put that idea in her head. Hey, different strokes and all that. I say go to church wherever you feel led. I just personally don't feel led to services with tambourines and guitars."

"And what was that pastor's name?" Of course I knew this. But it was important to keep the conversation flowing. And by that I mean keep Birdie talking.

"Jones. Anson Gibbes Jones. That's a made-up name if you ask me. Eugenia raved about him, but I believe members of the clergy need proper training."

"Did he not study theology?"

She scoffed. "Well, here again, it's more about where he studied, and the church having a proper hierarchy. Listen, I know I'm old fashioned. And this was Eugenia's choice. I was happy for her. I just . . ." She shook her head. "It just wasn't for me, that's all. Give me the Book of Common Prayer."

"But you don't have any reason to suspect anyone at the church of any chicanery? Trying to get Eugenia's money maybe?"

"No, nothing like that. Oh, Eugenia gave them plenty. And that really stuck in Everette's craw. But no. I think Eugenia would've seen that a mile off."

Eugenia's reading material occupied a shelf in the back of my mind. "Birdie, can you think of anything Eugenia felt guilty about? Something she perceived she needed to atone for?"

Birdie's eyebrows drew together, and she frowned. "Why, no."

Just then I was thinking there may have been secrets Eugenia kept even from her almost sister. Either that, or there were things Birdie had decided I didn't need to know, perhaps to protect Eugenia's memory.

"Birdie, are you certain?" I asked. "This could be important."

"How fortunate a woman is if she can look back and not find anything that brings her pain. I don't believe I've ever had the pleasure of meeting anyone that virtuous. But if anything in particular weighed heavily on Eugenia, she never confided in me about it. And I was certainly never a witness to anything she did that would warrant such guilt on her part. Everette. There's your guilty party right there."

On my way out to the car, I turned off the "do not disturb" feature on my phone. I had four text messages from Tallulah, the last of which caught my attention:

> Meet us at Charlie Vanderhorst's office at four.
> *** 911 ***

Chapter Twenty-Seven

Prioleau (PRAY-low) Street ran parallel to East Bay from Vendue Range down to East Elliott, where it dead-ended into a parking lot. On the corner of Prioleau and Middle Atlantic Wharf sat a two-story brick building that looked like it might house horses and carriages, but no—it was lawyers. Middleton, Bull & Vanderhorst occupied the space. In addition to the named partners, the group employed a few associates and a gaggle of paralegals who always seemed stressed to me.

The firm specialized in criminal law—all flavors, from traffic tickets, to murder, to white collar crimes—as well as family law, personal injury, wrongful death, and estates and wills. Charlotte "Charlie" Olivia Rutledge Vanderhorst was one of the named partners. Charlie practiced family law, and I had worked a number of her cases. Charlie was also handling Eugenia's divorce. The morning Eugenia died, I'd told Fish to contact Charlie for two reasons: 1-Her client, who was in the middle of preparing to divorce her husband, had been murdered, and 2-I knew she had partners who were criminal defense attorneys, and she'd know who best to send over to protect Fish and Tallulah when they were vulnerable on account of suffering such a shock.

Why Tallulah had summoned me there that afternoon was

indeed a mystery. Charlie's assistant showed me right in. In her signature pantsuit and sneakers, Charlie sat in the middle of the sofa by the window, Tallulah, and Camille in chairs to her left. Tallulah and Camille clutched their pearls. Charlie wore a furious expression, a look not foreign to her. Charlie was a flamboyant, cantankerous, fifty-year-old, divorce lawyer who'd seen too much of marriage to ever take the plunge herself.

"Hadley." Charlie looked at Tallulah, a question in her eyes.

"I thought it best to keep her in the loop," said Tallulah.

"Why is that?" asked Charlie.

"These ladies and a few of their friends have retained me to help prepare Kateryna Petrenko's defense." I took the empty chair to Charlie's right.

"I wasn't aware of that." Charlie sounded disgruntled.

"We're keeping it strictly hush-hush," said Camille.

I said, "Ladies, it's best to not keep secrets from your attorney. Charlie, I assume you represent one or both of them?"

"Tallulah retained me on Saturday," said Charlie. "Camille, give me a dollar as a retainer."

"I don't carry cash," said Camille. "And you're a divorce lawyer. Neither Tallulah nor I are currently married."

Tallulah handed a twenty and a withering look to Camille. A slightly befuddled Camille handed the twenty to Charlie.

"Charlie dabbles in all kinds of law when it suits her," I said. "Right now, we apparently need to have a very private conversation."

"Yes," said Charlie. "I represent them both. You work for them both, and for me. This conversation is covered by attorney-client privilege. Shall we bring Hadley up to speed?"

"I think I mentioned Eugenia had planned her services in great detail a while back," said Tallulah.

"You did." I nodded.

"She arranged for the pastor of her church to conduct the funeral there. She wanted to be cremated, and have her ashes interred in the columbarium in the Cornerstone churchyard. She also arranged a big party—a celebration of life—for all her friends and family, a catered affair with an open bar at her house. She paid for everything in advance."

"Sounds lovely," I said.

"It would've been, I'm certain," said Tallulah. "But *Everette* has taken over everything."

Of course. He'd want to play the role of grieving husband. "How can he do that?" I asked.

"He's the surviving spouse," said Charlie. "They weren't divorced. They weren't even *legally* separated. The presumption is that he has the right to attend to her final arrangements. The coroner released her body to Stuhr's Funeral Home on Everette's behalf."

"I'm certain he's shown Stuhr's her original will," said Tallulah. "He's making arrangements with St. Michael's. Eugenia was a member there all her life until a year ago. Everette's just acting like nothing ever happened—no separation, no affair, no change in churches."

"Okay, but wait," I said. "Isn't this covered in her new will?"

"Of course," said Tallulah. "But Everette hasn't seen that, and he doesn't want to."

"So he doesn't know about the arrangements Eugenia made?" asked Charlie.

"Oh, he does," said Tallulah. "I told him. I also told him he should ask her attorney for a copy of her will. His story is that he has her last will and testament. Any other document anyone might supposedly have is fraudulent."

"Alex Ireland in our estates department is handling the will," said Charlie. "She's in court today, which is how this meeting landed in my office. But we typically don't discuss the estate with the family until after the funeral. In this case, I suppose Alex needs to get ahead of it. I'll talk to her. But I would bet Everette will contest it."

"Oh, I'm quite certain he will," said Tallulah. "It will be an absolute brawl. But Eugenia's mind was quite sound and her wishes quite clear. Ms. Ireland covered all the bases. The will is solid. But I'm afraid Everette will have Eugenia buried at Magnolia Cemetery in the family plot before this all gets sorted out."

"Alex can appeal to the court for relief," said Charlie. "In the meantime, she can have a chat with the folks at Stuhr's."

"Oh, that would be a big help," said Tallulah.

"This is all for show," I said.

"Why, of course it is," said Camille.

"Everette wants to make a big display of public grief to protect him legally and in the court of public opinion," I said. "He's using Eugenia in the most abhorrent way."

"We'll do our best to put a stop to this," said Charlie.

"In the meantime, no one knows which funeral to plan to attend," said Tallulah. "Everette has it on the calendar at St. Michael's for two p.m. on Thursday—that's day after tomorrow, with visitation tomorrow night at seven at Stuhr's downtown chapel. Pastor Jones has his service scheduled for the same time, with the party afterwards. But of course, it can't be at Eugenia's. It's been moved to my house. We could hardly have an open bar in the church fellowship hall."

"The Episcopalians are fine with that sort of thing," said Camille.

"Well, the Cornerstone Community Church is not," said Tallulah.

"It would be awful if all the confusion meant some of her friends missed saying goodbye to Eugenia," I said. "It's like he's holding her hostage."

"Indeed," said Charlie. "I'll talk to Alex as soon as she's out of court for the day. Just in case, I would plan on going to Stuhr's for visitation tomorrow. With any luck, we can get the word out there about the change in plans for Thursday."

Chapter Twenty-Eight

I walked through Gavin's door at five till six.

"Hey, Babe. Wanna take a ride on the red rocket?"

"*Rudi* . . ." Gavin drew his name out in a warning.

"Up yours, Colonel Dickhead," said Rudi.

"Mouth off to me all you want. But you be nice to Twinkle here, or I'll make a nice stew outta you," said Gavin.

"Ah, that wasn't so bad. I'm Babe today." I hugged Gavin's neck then reached for Joe. It was Taco Tuesday at Gavin's house. He didn't always make tacos, but he made something with a Mexican or Tex Mex vibe every week. I came as often as I could. Gavin's homemade queso is a magical, luscious concoction, second only to his gravy.

"State your business," said Rudi.

"Be a damn shame if that bird escaped," said Joe, in a tone that advertised he'd given some thought to opening the cage and the front door.

"You'd better hope that never happens. I'd know precisely who to thank." Gavin headed towards the kitchen. "Y'all fix us something to drink. Dinner's almost ready."

"Who do I have to screw to get a drink?" Rudi cawed.

"I'll make you a cyanide martini," said Joe. "Want me to cover 'im up?"

"Ah, leave 'im alone. He'll quieten down," called Gavin.

"Semper fi," said Rudi.

Gavin set plates piled high with veggie enchiladas, sweet potato and black bean taquitos, and cilantro lime rice in front of us. I picked up the bright blue gravy boat and poured queso all over everything.

Joe gave the gravy boat a skeptical look. He picked up a taquito and dribbled some of the sauce on the end and took a bite. He squinted harder at the queso. "What did you say this stuff is made out of?"

"Oatmeal and red peppers," said Gavin. "A few other ingredients."

"No cheese?" Joe's face was painted with a mix of disbelief and confusion.

"None whatsoever," said Gavin.

"It's the dangdest thing," said Joe. "I'd swear that's nothing but pure cheese—good cheese."

"And you'd be wrong," said Gavin. "Yet again."

Joe shrugged and doused his plate with the sauce. "We made quick work of running down those alibis. No joy there, depending on which way you look at it, I guess. Every one of them checked out."

"Thanks, guys. It's a huge help to be able to cross all the long shots off my list."

Gavin gave me a sideways look that let me know he disapproved of something, and I knew what. "Twinkle, this just isn't a path you need to be traipsing down. Open police case, high profile. Cash's case." He gave extra weight to the last two words.

"Gavin, I understand where you're coming from. I do. And you're not wrong. But that's just one side of the thing. Eugenia was my friend."

Gavin raised his eyebrows and shrugged. "I guess you know what you're doing. How is Cash?"

I forked a bite of enchilada, looked at him sideways. "I suppose he's fine. Listen, I need to ask you something."

"Shoot." He took a bite of a taquito.

"I know this is out of the blue, but . . . do you remember when Mom was dating my . . . Swinton?"

His eyebrows lowered. "Of course. Why do you want to know about that?"

I sighed, studied the ceiling. "I don't know. I probably don't. But it turns out Eugenia and her husband, who, by the way I'm reasonably certain is the one who killed her, were old friends of Swinton and Judith's. This case rubs up against my life in more than one way, it seems."

"Interesting." Gavin chewed thoughtfully, then sipped his iced tea. "What was the question again?"

I was having trouble getting it out. "He broke Mom's heart, right?"

Gavin set down his fork. "It was a complicated situation. I suppose, in a manner of speaking, their situation broke her heart. But I can't honestly say he did that. To tell you the truth, I expected you to ask me these questions twenty-three years ago."

"I thought I knew all the answers."

"You and she were awfully close," said Gavin. "When you never asked, I guess I figured she told you everything you needed to know."

"I thought she did. Someone said to me, recently, that she was the one who broke his heart. Can that be true?"

"I never knew Swinton well. He wouldn't have confided that sort of thing in me." After a long moment, Gavin nodded. "I expect that's the truth of it."

Something clutched at my heart. "I don't understand. She never had another serious relationship her whole life. I thought she pined away for him."

Gavin winced. "She did. Like I said, it was complicated. Your mother loved Swinton. But she hated the world he was born into. I think she was intimidated by it more than anything else. Felt like she would never be at ease there, wouldn't fit in with all the South-of-Broad types. She knew he couldn't change that. And she loved him enough that she didn't want to force him to choose. So she ended the relationship."

"And he married Judith on the rebound?"

"Now, I can't tell you why he did anything," said Gavin. "Your mother was like a daughter to me. We were tight. You know that. But you'd have to ask him about that. I'll say this much. I think after you came along, it got worse."

"What do you mean?" I asked.

"After you were born . . . You were her entire world. She raised you like you were her sister, or her best friend. You always spent too much time with adults and not enough with kids your own age, if you ask me. I don't mean to criticize her. You know I adored her. But . . . it's like she kept the two of you in this bubble. She never moved forward, past Swinton. She drove the car he bought her and listened to the music they listened to for the rest of her life. It's what you still listen to."

"What—"

"Not that there's anything wrong with it," said Gavin. "Listen to whatever you like. But my point is that Vivienne was stuck in time. And she held you awfully close. I think she was very much afraid that if you met your father, you'd be drawn to everything he could give you. She was afraid of losing you to him. Which is why she hid you from him for sixteen years. I didn't agree with that, mind you. But it was her decision."

"She didn't think he'd be a bad father?" I asked.

"Not that she ever mentioned to me," said Gavin. "Look, Vivienne was a good mother. But, she wasn't perfect, Twinkle. She'd be the first one to admit she made mistakes. Maybe let her down off that pedestal you keep her on."

"Thanks, Gavin." Sixteen years later, when he found out he had a daughter, Swinton didn't owe my mother anything, I supposed. But a decent, honorable man with unlimited resources would certainly have provided lifesaving healthcare for the mother of his child, wouldn't he?

We ate quietly for a few minutes.

When Joe had endured all the silence he could stand, he said, "So you like the husband? For the murder?"

"I'm certain he did it," I said. "I just don't know how."

"You just mind yourself," said Gavin. "Be cautious. A man who would kill the mother of his children has no conscience, no value for human life whatsoever. He's a sociopath. He'll kill anyone who gets in his way, and it won't cost him a millisecond of sleep."

"I hear you. I'll be careful."

"You'll figure out how he did it," said Joe. "Probably hired someone."

"He had to've," I said. "But he doesn't have the resources."

"Maybe he was banking on his inheritance," said Joe. "Talked someone into doing it now for a payoff down the road."

"Layaway murder?" Gavin screwed up his face. "Who'd be dumb enough to do that?"

"Damn hippies," squawked Rudi from the living room.

"Pipe down, Rudi," said Gavin. "What would you do if he didn't pay up? File a complaint?"

"I never suggested he hired a smart criminal," said Joe.

"I appreciate the idea," I said. "I've been wracking my brain for how he pulled this off. It's a possibility. Which is more than I had before dinner."

Joe beamed while Gavin rolled his eyes.

We ate in silence a few more minutes, then in a softer tone, Gavin said, "Listen, Twinkle . . ." He leaned towards me. "Your mother let fear get the best of her. It cost her an awful lot. The thing about fear is, it's temporary. You can get past your fear. Regret is forever." He gave me a meaningful look.

"What are you saying?" I asked.

"I'm saying be careful you don't repeat your mother's mistakes," said Gavin.

"Are we talking about me having a relationship with my father, or are we talking about Cash again?" I felt my cheeks flame.

Gavin gave an exaggerated shrug, looked sheepish. "Well . . . maybe it's that second thing. Maybe you ended that relationship out of fear. I'm saying, you were afraid of other things, maybe, than her. But fear is fear."

"Gavin—" I gave him an admonishing look.

"I'd just hate to see you spending your life alone like she did," said Gavin.

"She wasn't alone," I said. "She had me. And you."

"And family is everything," said Gavin. "Except maybe she coulda had a bigger family, am I right? *May*be she coulda spent her life with the man she loved. And maybe you should think about that."

"State your business," said Rudi. "Semper fi."

Later that evening, as I was sitting by the pool, mulling over everything Gavin had said, my watch buzzed an alert. Everette was leaving his house in the car. I opened the app on my phone and watched as I sipped a glass of an inexpensive red blend I'd picked up on sale at Publix. Beck had three floor-to-ceiling six-feet-wide wine coolers tucked away near the pantry, one filled with red wines from Italy, France, and California, and one with white wines, and one with sparkling wines. He hadn't mentioned the wine, and I wasn't going to touch it. More than likely, he'd send someone to move it to Manhattan or Telluride.

I kept my eye on the screen—and Everette—but my mind drifted back to my mother. I had a magical childhood, mostly because Momma saw to it. She read to me from an early age, then encouraged me to pick out my own books. We played board games and always had a puzzle going. She worked hard—she was a waitress at Alex's Restaurant, which was where Page's Okra Grill is now—but no matter how tired she was, she made time to play with me. Momma was so young when she had me, it was almost like we grew up together. When I went through my Barbie doll phase, she made furniture for my dolls from oatmeal boxes and cereal boxes—upholstering the furniture with fabric scraps. She made my dolls the finest wardrobe of clothes. Gavin wasn't wrong. My mother *was* my best friend.

I worried a lot about her being alone, I remembered that. She never dated, never went out with friends. Of course I never knew what my parents were like together, but I never knew her to love anyone else. Oh, there were always candidates lining up to ask her out, even though she was a single mother. But no one ever really got her attention. Her attention was always on me.

She taught me so much. It was almost like she was trying to download everything she'd ever learned. She was so kind, and she taught me to be. She'd say, "Hadley, always be mindful of the needs and feelings of others." I try my best to honor that.

Honestly, she probably got that from someone else. Mother was always so self-conscious about not having a proper education, as she put it. I think she was always trying to teach me things, but a lot of her material came from dubious sources—it was bumper sticker philosophy. And that didn't make it wrong, maybe just oversimplified.

"Never complain, never explain . . ." Mother said that a lot. She said it was a Katherine Hepburn quote, and Mother idolized Katherine Hepburn. On Saturday nights, we used to watch old movies, sometimes a double feature. Mother would make us sandwiches. Before she got sick, they'd be bacon or bologna with lettuce, tomato, cheese, and mayonnaise on toasted bread. We'd get in her bed with our sandwiches and big glasses of iced tea and watch movies. Those were precious memories.

Everette was crossing the Cooper River Bridge. Was he heading towards Sullivan's Island? No . . . I watched as he bore left onto Highway 17, then continued to the Mark Clark Expressway. Where was he going?

Five minutes later, he took the Daniel Island Exit, then parked near Daniel Island Grill. Who was he meeting? I curbed the urge to drive over and see what he was up to. I was on my second glass of wine. I kicked myself for that. But I'd long ago come to terms with not being able to watch someone twenty-four seven. Tracking was nearly as good. I knew where he'd been anyway. That was a start.

As Scarlett herself said, tomorrow was another day.

Chapter Twenty-Nine

~~~~~

I made it my business to be at Ensemble, a consignment store on King Street, when they opened at eleven Wednesday morning. I needed a couple of things before Saturday night, and a dress to wear was the second-most important. There was nothing in my closet appropriate for the gala that would be J. T.'s birthday, and if I was going, I did *not* want to embarrass my brother.

That said, I was necessarily thrifty. I bought most of my clothes at the Salvation Army Store. You'd be amazed what you can find there. I mean sure, you have to pick over things. But I've found brand-name jeans there with the tags still on them. It wasn't unheard of to find nice dresses there too. But I was short on time, and when I needed something nice, Ensemble was my go-to. Did they even have formal wear? I'd honestly never looked.

Ensemble wasn't your typical consignment store. It felt more like an upscale boutique, with an energetic vibe. Shopping there was a splurge for me. When I walked through the door, "Ladies in the 90s," by Lauren Alaina was playing. As always, the woodsy scent of an essential oil floated on the air. Focused on my mission, I made a beeline for the dress rack, praying there'd be something that would do.

"Hey, how are you?" The young woman with dark hair and a

big smile welcomed me. They were real friendly here. And helpful —or at least they tried to be. I tended to be shy when trying on clothes.

"Hey, I'm good, thanks." I returned her smile and continued towards the dresses.

"What brings you in today?" she asked.

Maybe today I didn't have time for shy. "I need a dress for a formal party on Saturday."

Her name tag read "Kristen." "You're in luck, I think. We don't typically have many formal gowns. Is it black tie?"

"Mm-hmm." I nodded. I had no idea what I was doing. The invitation had said black tie. But that confused me. Women wore floor-length gowns to black-tie affairs. That was the more traditional thing, right? But then I'd seen photos of women wearing short dresses with men in tuxedos on their way to fancy affairs. Okay, these were mostly Hollywood types I saw when the images flickered across the screen as I was changing channels. The truth was, I didn't go to many black-tie affairs myself.

So I'd texted J. T.

Long or short?

Wear whatever you want. Just bring your boogie shoes.

Typical man. What I wanted was to look like I belonged there, so I'd Googled it. In case you need to know, Emily Post was no help at all. According to her, black-tie attire for women can be either a floor-length gown, a cocktail dress, or your dressiest little black dress. I needed specific directions. The consensus of the other authorities I consulted on the Internet is that while cocktail dresses "can be" appropriate for black tie, a floor-length dress is the more "elevated choice." I definitely wanted to be elevated.

"What size do you typically wear?" asked Kristen.

"Usually a two. I'm pretty bony."

"You're kidding right?" Kristen raised an eyebrow and smiled.

I scrutinized myself in the mirror. A stick person looked back, hard and angular rather than soft and feminine. "Well, in some things I take a zero, other things a four—"

Kristen laughed. "No, I believe you're a size two. And many women probably hate you for that. You're not bony."

"You don't think?" I was pretty sure I was bony.

She shook her head. "No. And I can't wait to see you in these dresses." She scooted some of the clothes left and pulled out a pink ball gown. "So we have this Oscar de la Renta."

"Wow. That's gorgeous. I'm not sure . . ." The de la Renta was a bright pink shade that probably had a fancier name.

". . . and this sort of whimsical boho beaded gown. It's an Adrianna Papell."

Such a pretty shade of blue. "Oh! It's exquisite."

"It does have a softer look," said Kristen. "And then we have this Michael Kors number."

I gasped. "Oh that's—"

"You can't tell a thing until you try them on." She whisked all three dresses over to a dressing room. "Let me see them, okay?"

I drew a deep breath as I closed the door. I tried them in the order she'd shown them to me. I changed into the pink floor-length Oscar de la Renta. I'd never worn a dress that cost as much as this one probably did. I stared at the woman in the mirror, who seemed to be someone else.

"Do you have one of them on?" called Kristen.

Wordlessly, I stepped outside the dressing room.

"That looks amazing," said Kristen. "What do you think?"

"I feel pretty." I smiled at her.

It did make me feel pretty. But there was a lot of it. And it had a little train in the back. "I'm thinking this one is a little over the top."

She tilted her head back and forth in an "I don't know about that," kind of way. "Let's see the others."

I changed into the blue Adrianna Papell and waltzed out for inspection. It was also floor length. "I really love this one."

"It is gorgeous," she said. "What's the occasion?"

"My brother's fortieth birthday."

"Try the Michael Kors," she said.

Obediently, I went to change. I might've stared at the mirror too long, because the next thing I knew, Kristen was standing behind me, looking over my shoulder in the mirror.

"Wow," was all she said.

It was a slip dress made from silver metallic lace fabric covered in sequins. With spaghetti straps, a thin belt, and a slit in back, it left virtually nothing to the imagination. The skirt fell to my midcalf.

"This seems pretty . . . bare."

Her eyes met mine in the mirror. "You will kill it in this dress."

"It's not too . . ." I searched for the right word.

"Oh no." She shook her head. "It's just the right amount. Of everything. You should definitely buy this dress."

"You think?"

She seemed very sure. "Yes, I think."

"But the party is black tie. This dress isn't floor length."

"This is Charleston, and it's summertime. It will be hot. I'll bet you at least half the women there will be in shorter-length dresses. Maybe all of them."

"Really?"

"Really."

I looked at the mirror uncertainly. "How much is it?"

She winced. "New, that dress was nearly six thousand dollars. It's been worn once, by a friend of mine, actually. I've had it for ninety days. I was going to donate it this weekend. Dresses like this . . . sometimes they're harder to move. What's your budget?"

It was my turn to wince. "I know this isn't reasonable, but I was hoping to find something for a hundred. Or less."

She bit her lip. "You and this dress were clearly meant to be. I tell you what . . . let's find you some shoes and accessorize you. Are you willing to let me Instagram you?"

I might've looked like I was going to bolt.

"I'll let you have the whole thing . . . dress, shoes, and accessories . . . for a hundred IF you let me take some pictures and use them on social."

I stared at the mirror. I'd apparently recently been a YouTube sensation. What would it hurt to have my picture on Instagram? "All right. Just don't use my name, okay?"

"Deal."

I walked out of the store and down King Street an hour later carrying the dress in a garment bag in one hand and strappy silver high-heel sandals, sparkly earrings, a matching necklace, and a cuff bracelet in a bag in the other. I felt giddy. I did feel awfully pretty in that dress. "Pretty Woman" might've been playing in my head as I was walking down the street, and I hate to admit that because it sounds like I was full of myself, but believe me when I tell you, that's highly unusual, and it was a fleeting thing.

I'd parked way down King Street, past Birlant Antiques. After circling the block a few times looking for a spot, I'd just taken the first place I came to. So I was strolling back down towards my car. I crossed to the other side of King Street at John. It was a glorious day, with a bright blue sky, not too hot. Birds were probably singing. There was a spring in my step. Just after I crossed Fulton Street, as I passed in front of Sara Campbell, I saw them coming straight towards me.

Dylan, of "It Ain't Me Babe" fame, and Faith—a woman who I had thought was a friend, who had clearly been inappropriately named—on his arm and cuddling up to him in a most familiar way, whispering in his ear. They were wrapped up in each other and hadn't seen me yet.

I panicked.

At that point, I didn't care what—or who—Dylan did. Really. But it was just so raw, so recent, the humiliation. And he was with someone, and I wasn't. Right then, I needed Brad Pitt on my arm.

And that's when I saw him.

Not Brad Pitt, of course. But he did look a little like him, actually. He was sitting in a red Mercedes convertible, parked on King Street, right in front of 167 Raw.

I did the only sane thing I could possibly do.

I put my packages in the back seat, opened the car door, and climbed into the passenger side, smiling at a shocked-looking Dylan, who looked up from his new dish at just the right moment. He stumbled, caught himself, and looked over his shoulder as he walked on by.

Then I turned to look at Brad Pitt.

"Well, hello," he said, in this calm voice that sounded friendly and not at all put out.

I tried so hard to make the smile I gave him not look crazed. "Hey, I'm Hadley."

"I'm pleased to meet you, Hadley. I'm Owen Callaway. No connection."

"No connection?" I smiled brighter, could feel how much like a crazy person I looked.

"To the golf company. Have we met before?"

"Actually, I don't think so. Do you play golf?"

"I do. But I was actually just meeting someone for lunch."

"Oh. I am so, so sorry. If you'll just give me a minute, I'll get right out of your car."

"Hadley, are you in trouble? Is someone bothering you?"

"Yes." I nodded. "Yes, they are."

He craned his neck, looking around. "Should we call the police?"

"No, I just . . . please, can I have a minute?"

"Of course. Take all the time you need."

"You're not a serial killer, are you? A psychopath? An insurance salesman?"

"No, I'm a heart surgeon."

I gave him a look that said, oh, pu-*leeze*. "Is that supposed to be a pickup line of some sort? No, seriously."

"Would you like to see my business card? Maybe some ID?"

He seemed quite sure of himself.

Oh, good grief. "No. I'm so sorry. I mean . . ." I blew out a long breath. "I don't know what I mean at all. I'll just . . . I'll just get out of your way."

"Hadley."

"Yes?"

"I'm in no rush. I have lunch with this same group of men every Wednesday. If I miss the whole thing, it's really perfectly fine. Why don't we get you something to drink? Are you hungry? How about lunch?"

He really did look like Brad Pitt, from certain angles. He was somewhere in the vicinity of my age. And maybe he was a heart surgeon. "Are you married?"

"No, ma'am. Are you?"

I laughed, possibly a bit manically. "No."

"Why not?"

"If I'm going to tell you that story, we're going to need liquor."

"Well, all right then. I'll just let the guys know something's come up. Is 167 Raw okay? They have very nice cocktails. And they're quite convenient." He nodded to the restaurant we were parked in front of. "That's not where my friends will be, by the way."

"167 Raw is fabulous." I smiled at him again. I was smiling too big and too much. "I mean, I hear it is. I've never actually eaten there. I only eat plants."

"Oh, well, we can go anywhere you like."

"No, 167 Raw is perfect. I hear they have excellent potatoes."

"You are a very interesting woman."

And that's how I found the number one thing I needed for Saturday night.

A date.

Chapter Thirty

Roger Riddle, Kateryna's neighbor—the one with all the cameras —left me a message during lunch. By the way, the midday meal turned out to be fun and truly delicious. I confess I was intrigued by Owen Callaway. He was just a very kind man, or at least he seemed to be. Oh, you could bet your grandmother's silver I would be running background on him before five thirty p.m. Saturday, when he'd be picking me up, provided of course he turned out to be an upstanding citizen. But first, I had work to do.

I drove through Southern Shores and parked in Roger's drive- way, next door to Kateryna. He must've been watching for me, because he opened the door and walked out on the small front porch of his older but well-kept single-wide mobile home. He waited, his hands on his hips.

Something about Roger Riddle reminded me of a banty rooster. Maybe it was the way his chest was stuck out in an aggres- sive posture. Or maybe it was the ponytail, silver with red streaks, that stuck out from underneath the helmet he wore, which might've once been a football helmet, but the face mask had been removed. What appeared to be aluminum foil covered the outside. Roger wasn't a large man, maybe five nine or ten, and scrawny. He wore a tattered Lynyrd Skynyrd T-shirt, baggy shorts, and sneakers with tube socks that came up to his knees.

"Mr. Riddle?" I called as I got closer.

"Who's asking?"

"Mr. Riddle, I'm Hadley Cooper. We spoke on the phone?"

"I'll see some identification." He lifted his chin.

I produced a leather fold-over wallet with my PI license and my driver's license and held it open for his inspection.

He leaned forward with raised eyebrows and studied my credentials, then looked me up and down. "S'posing you are who you say you are, what can I do for you?"

I looked up the street, then down. A group of three women walking dogs passed by, chatting happily. The Riddle residence was far enough off the street we could speak privately on the porch. I wasn't a hundred percent sure about the wisdom of going indoors with Mr. Riddle just yet.

"Do you know your neighbor, Kateryna Petrenko?" I asked.

"I knew Oscar. He was a long-haul driver, like me."

"He was Kateryna's friend," I said.

Roger was quiet for a minute, then shrugged and nodded. "I s'pose that's right."

"I think someone broke into Oscar's house and took something from her. Would you help me figure out who did that?"

He rolled his lips in and out. "I take it you noticed my cameras."

"I did. Very nice setup you have there. Motion activated?"

"Naturally."

"How long are recordings saved?"

"I save them on a hard drive indefinitely," he said. "You can't be too careful."

"I'd sure love to get a look at your activity for the last month or so," I said.

He drew his face up in a pained-looking wince. "I'm afraid that's not possible."

"Oh?"

"Hasn't a woman crossed my threshold since Merlene moved on."

"I'm so sorry for your loss."

"Weren't no loss a'tall. She was a mean woman. Used to be a bingo caller in Vegas, but she didn't have the disposition for it. Anyway, I said she *moved* on, not passed on. But she did keep the place clean. I don't have time for housekeeping and such."

"Oh, I'm not picky about that sort of thing." This was likely the biggest lie I'd ever told in my entire life. And I was not at all sure I wanted to see what the inside of Roger's house looked like. But I was absolutely certain I needed to see his outdoor video footage.

Roger regarded me with suspicion. "You're one of those dadgum visiting angels, aren't you?"

"I'm sorry?"

"Oh, you're good." He nodded. "You go right back to where you came from. And tell Ruby Jean I am just fine, thank you very much. I do not need a visiting angel or any other dang thing. I am not senile. Do you hear me? If she is so worried about her daddy, maybe she should take the time to come and see me herself."

"Mr. Riddle—"

"And I have said it before, and I'll say it again . . . no more doctors. I will never see another doctor, do you hear me?"

"Yes, sir. I hear you. I do. It's just—"

"I'll have you know, in certain circles, I'm a doctor myself."

"Is that right?"

He nodded. "And in other circles, I'm the second-best snake preacher in the South."

I might've taken a step back. "That's . . . impressive."

"Tell Ruby Jean the doctors didn't do nothin' but ruin what was left of her momma's life, and they dang sure aren't going to ruin my golden years. I'm going to fish and play cards and play my banjo and have a drink whenever I feel like it. You see this helmet?" He knocked on the shell.

"Yes, sir, I do." You really couldn't help but.

"They're all so worried I might fall. It's your head you have to worry about. This right here protects my head, just in case. Oncet you get to be fifty, every . . . dang . . . time . . . you see a doctor, they will ask you if you have fallen recently. And if you ever answer back and say you did, it goes in your file. They watch that. It counts against you."

"But Mr. Riddle—"

"No doctors. No drugs. No angels."

"Sir? I'm afraid we've had a misunderstanding."

"Eh?" He drew back. "Oh—and no more lab work. Ruby Jean is forever asking, 'Daddy, when's the last time you had labs?' I tell her the same thing every time. I did it myself. I peed in a mason jar. Swirled it around. Looked at it. Looks fine to me. That's all the labs I need."

"But back to your security system . . ."

"Eh?"

"Sir, it would just help me so much—help Kateryna so much —if I could just look and see if your cameras captured anyone breaking into Kat—Oscar's house recently."

"Hmm." He was quiet, considering. "S'posing I help you? Will you speak to Ruby Jean?"

"Yes, sir, absolutely." Provided she was a real person, and not a figment of his fevered imagination.

He squinted at the sky, stroked his scruffy beard. "There was something a while back . . . I got an alert. Checked the footage, but it weren't no one messin' with *my* property. I didn't pay it no attention. Didn't hear anything about a break-in, so I thought . . . Well, I didn't think on it, I guess, is the point. You wait here," he said. "I'll burn you a copy of the last sixty days."

"Oh, that's perfect. Thank you so much." I was relieved, for the moment. I wouldn't have to see what Roger considered a messy house.

He backed away, fumbled behind his back with the door, and disappeared inside without turning his back on me. When he came back ten minutes later, he handed me a thumb drive and an index card. He held onto the index card, pointed to it as he spoke. "This here is Ruby Jean's cell phone number. You tell her what I said, hear?"

"Thank you, Mr. Riddle. I will. I'll speak to her this afternoon."

"There's not a dang thing wrong with me." His eyes went large and round and wild looking. Then he winked and grinned. "That's a nice car you got there. 1966?"

"Thank you, yes, it is."

He sighed, shook his head. "She reminds me of the one I had, back in the day. You name her?"

"Yes, sir. Her name's Jolene."

"That's a good one. Mine was Elvira." He got a wistful look in his eye. "Don't never let no one talk you into sellin', not for a million dollars."

"No, sir, I won't."

"Car built like that'll last a lifetime. Not much else will, these days. If you want some more advice, I'll give it to you. Save your money, pay with cash. And don't never carry a broke heart to Vegas."

Chapter Thirty-One

Peach tea is my weakness, specifically, Bai Narino Peach tea. But it's expensive, and there's no room for it in my grocery budget. Also, it comes in plastic bottles, so there's that. But I love the stuff, so I keep trying to match the recipe, with mixed results. I took a glass of my most recent attempt to my office with a dish of pretzel-and-nut mix. I needed brain food.

I settled in at my desk and stared at the ocean for a spell. A body could get used to this. Watching the waves relaxed my mind and helped me think. Reluctantly, I pulled myself out of my reverie and called Ruby Jean, who assured me she would be by that very afternoon to check on her daddy.

"He's not half as crazy as he acts," she said. "He likes the attention. I was just over there this weekend. But I'm a trauma nurse. I work long shifts. I can't run over there every day, and he won't have anyone else in his house."

I murmured something sympathetic and extricated myself from the conversation. Roger was Ruby Jean's situation. I had my own. A vision of Gavin and Joe wearing aluminum foil-covered helmets passed through my head and made me snort peach tea.

I popped the thumb drive Roger had given me into the back of my Mac and opened the folder. Roger's motion detectors were sensitive. There were clips of the mail carrier, a few neighbors, dogs, cats, and squirrels. It took me an hour to find what I was looking for: someone dressed all in black creeping across Roger's yard and into Kateryna's, then around Kateryna's house carrying a backpack.

I zoomed in on the image. The figure was male, for sure. But he wore a ski mask, so it was impossible to tell who it was. I scrolled through a dozen clips from Monday before last, at eleven thirty p.m. That was the day I'd met Eugenia—the day she'd had a public quarrel with Kateryna. But Kateryna had worked during the day. She must've gone out that night.

The figure entered Kateryna's house through the screened porch. Once he was inside the porch, I couldn't see how he'd gotten inside the house. A set of sliding doors opened from the living room to the screened porch, I remembered that from when I'd gone to see Kateryna. Did she leave them unlocked?

The man was inside less than five minutes, then came out the way he'd gone in, slinked around the house, crossed Roger Riddle's yard, and disappeared. He was the right size and build to be Everette. He wasn't doing anything Everette wasn't capable of doing. It easily could have been Everette, and he certainly could have swapped Eugenia's chef's knife for Kateryna's and then later taken Kateryna's knife—with Kateryna's fingerprints— and put it in Eugenia's knife block. Or he could've just held onto it and given it to his hired help to use the following Saturday night.

I needed to get this footage to Cash. He'd have to collect it himself from Roger to avoid a chain of custody issue. But by itself, it didn't prove anything other than Kateryna had had a break-in. I needed more.

Who might've helped Everette pull off the nearly perfect murder? I knew who he'd been spending time with in Greenville . . . Leland Marchant and someone named Bryce Brashier. But they were more likely additional alibis than anything else, by virtue of the fact that they, like Everette, had been four hours away when Eugenia was killed. Who was Leland Marchant, anyway? I opened a database query window.

Moments later, I knew that Leland Marchant was a prominent Greenville Attorney. When I queried his name along with Everette's, I quickly found that they'd been college roommates. Bryce Brashier, a Greenville doctor, appeared to have no connection to Everette aside from their common friend, Leland, and a business deal they'd apparently been discussing with someone named Mike involving land on Lake Jocassee. A few queries later, I had a short profile of Michael Gambrell, an Upstate realtor. Better to know who all the players were.

I spent the next hour importing data from Everette's cell phone logs into a spreadsheet. I sorted it by phone number and pulled a search on each phone number from my subscription database. In the six months prior to Eugenia's death, Everette had called only a dozen numbers. They were all identified friends and family, including the three friends he'd had dinner with in Greenville, or local clubs or businesses—no unidentified numbers. No burner phone numbers. But then again, how many cases had Everette watched where a criminal was caught because of his phone history? If anyone knew better than to create a phone trail, it was a retired judge. He was probably a walking reference library on stupid things not to do to get caught.

He was an evil rat bastard.

If he'd killed Eugenia—and I remained convinced he had—it almost surely had to've been a barter or pay-me-later situation. And he'd clearly been smart about it.

I dug my fingers through my hair and massaged my scalp, trying to get some oxygen to my brain. Then I noticed the time. Visitation at Stuhr's started at seven. It was five after six.

I bolted for the shower.

Chapter Thirty-Two

J. Henry Stuhr's downtown chapel was a red-brick affair with white columns, on the corner of Calhoun and Smith. I arrived at precisely seven o'clock, and the parking lot was overflowing. I circled the area a few times and finally scored a metered street spot on Rutledge near Cannon Park. I hurried the block or so to Stuhr's. Had Tallulah and Camille settled the matter of Eugenia's service for tomorrow?

Eugenia had certainly drawn a crowd. I was torn between wanting to mourn my friend with others who loved her and needing to work—to find out the who, the why, and the how of Eugenia's death. A line of folks waiting to pay their respects snaked out the door. I moved to the back of the line.

Forty minutes later, I'd made my way inside and down the hall to the first of three connecting parlor rooms forming an L shape. Traditional furnishings, wingbacks, sofas, and armchairs dotted the rooms, which were stuffed to capacity with folks paying their respects. After an hour, I arrived in the third room, where Eugenia lay in her casket between the United States and South Carolina flags. In front of a pair of burgundy wingbacks with floral throw pillows, Everette, along with Gwyneth and Harrison,

Eugenia's children, and Gwyneth's husband, accepted condolences.

Something clawed at my stomach. I hated seeing people I'd cared for in a casket. I knew it wasn't Eugenia—that she wasn't there but had gone to a far better place. Somehow it just felt wrong for the body that remained to be on display. It hit me then that Eugenia was the first person I'd seen in a casket since my mother passed away.

When I arrived in front of the family, Gwyneth's husband shook my hand and said, "Thank you for coming." I knew that his, Gwyneth's, and Harrison's alibis had checked out. They'd been in other states when Eugenia was killed, and none of them had any sort of a motive. I was in line only to pay my respects.

I gave him a sad smile, nodded, repeated the procedure with Harrison, moving all the while, and then stopped in front of Gwyneth. We'd never met, of course, but I felt a connection to her and specifically wanted to speak to her.

"Your mother was my friend," I said. "I will miss her so much. My deepest condolences."

She reminded me of Eugenia. Her long blonde hair hung past her shoulders. In a black sheath with a long-sleeved cardigan, and minimal makeup, she was elegant and composed. "Thank you so much for coming. I know Mother would appreciate your being here."

There was more I wanted to say to her, about how special Eugenia had been, and how I would personally see to it her killer was brought to justice. But this wasn't the time or the place for all that.

And then I was in front of Everette.

I would rather have petted a snake than shake his hand, but there was nothing else to do. "Thank you for coming," he said. He was subdued, but struck me as stiff, like he was acting out a part. If he happened to be innocent of Eugenia's murder, this was grossly unfair of me, to judge him. But I remained convinced he was the lowest of the low. He'd killed my friend, robbed his children of a mother, his grandchildren of their grandmother—and he expected to profit from it.

I didn't trust myself to speak, and you can get by with that, in a funeral home because so many people are overcome with emotion. I lowered my eyes so he couldn't read what was in them, nodded, and moved away.

I navigated through the knots and strings of people who'd stopped to chat along the way and into the adjoining room. It was way too full of people. In a far corner, Tallulah, Camille, and Sarabeth huddled. I made my way towards them.

"Hadley." Camille caught sight of me, and they all turned.

We all said our hellos and so forth.

"Everyone holding up?" I asked.

"As well as can be expected," said Tallulah, "in the circumstances." She glared in Everette's direction. "Did you speak with Birdie?"

"I did." I was still chewing on our conversation.

"Everything all right?" asked Tallulah, in a tone that indicated she knew full well it wasn't.

"It will be," I said. "Tallulah, are you up for a question?"

"Of course," she said. "I'm up for anything that will help you get to the bottom of this."

"Eugenia seemed to feel guilty about something," I said. "She had atonement on her mind. Can you think of any reason why?"

Tallulah's face wrinkled up. "Eugenia? Heavens no."

"She did give a lot of money to the church," said Sarabeth.

"That was just Eugenia." Tallulah waved the thought away. "She's a lifelong tither."

"You mentioned she left a trust to manage annual donations to several charities. Would you mind getting me a list?" I asked.

"Well, I can tell you who they are," said Tallulah. "It was the Charleston Animal Society, the Cancer Society, and well, there's ongoing contributions for the care of Meryl Simons, for the rest of her life."

"Who is that?" I asked.

"It's a sad story," said Tallulah. "Her twin sister was a classmate of ours. Amelia Simons. Amelia was killed when we were teenagers. Boating accident on the Stono River. Anyway, as she got older, the rest of Meryl's family passed away. She has MS. She never married or had children, so there's no one to care for her. Eugenia has always made sure she was taken care of, I think out of fondness for Amelia."

"You said they were twins," I said.

"That's right," said Tallulah.

"But only one of them was your classmate?" I asked.

"Meryl was always homeschooled," said Tallulah. "She wasn't well enough to attend class regularly."

"Hmm . . ." I turned that over in my mind.

"If there's more to the story, Eugenia never told me," said Tallulah. "You might ask Birdie about it."

"I will," I said.

"There's Birdie and Vernon now, in line," said Sarabeth.

I followed her gaze. Great. Birdie and Vernon were chatting with Swinton and Judith. "I'll speak with her later."

Tallulah raised an eyebrow at me but kept her peace.

Slowly, I scanned the room, searching faces. Who among them knew something that would help me solve Eugenia's murder? Who held a piece to the puzzle? I needed to settle into a chair in a corner and do a little people watching, perhaps some eavesdropping.

Swinton's eyes caught mine and registered surprise. He must've wondered what on earth I was doing there. I did not trot over to explain myself.

"Tallulah, did you tell Hadley about tomorrow?" Camille's expression was layered with import.

"I meant to ask you about that," I said. "Which funeral should I attend?"

Tallulah flashed Camille a quelling look, then turned back to me. "Come to Cornerstone Community Church at two. I understand they may be late starting, but be there before two to get a seat. I'm certain it will be standing room only."

Chapter Thirty-Three

Thursday, June 17, 1:30 p.m.
St. Michael's Church, Charleston, South Carolina
Mrs. Josephine Huger (you-JEE)

I always make it a point to arrive early at weddings and funerals. Otherwise, you run the risk of having to sit in the back where all you can see is the backs of a roomful of heads. In any case, if I hadn't arrived early to Eugenia Ladson's funeral, I would've missed it—not the funeral, mind you, but what happened before.

Arthur had a doctor's appointment. It was for a procedure, one of those that's difficult to reschedule, so I was by myself. We have friends who live just down Meeting Street, and I parked at their house. The weather had been quite nice for the last week or so, but I decided against walking from home in a suit with stockings and heels.

I was walking towards the church on Meeting Street. The hearse was parked at the curb in front of the church, right there on the corner—on Meeting—where it usually parks, and everything appeared normal. I've been to quite a few funerals at St. Michael's these last years. They all go pretty much the same way.

So I was passing in front of the entrance to the churchyard, when I noticed two women speaking to the driver and another man—I don't know what you'd call him, but I suppose he worked for the funeral home. They were standing out near the front end of the hearse. Now, the women had their backs to me, and I couldn't say for certain, but I'm reasonably sure one of them was Tallulah Wentworth. The other woman I didn't know, but she had red hair, and they were both dressed appropriately for a funeral. I couldn't tell you why, but I stopped right there at the gate, and I guess it's a good thing I did.

Tallulah and whoever it was with her, they were clearly distraught, and the gentlemen were apparently trying to assist them in some way. I thought at the time something must be terribly wrong, because Tallulah is not given to public emotional displays. Well, about this time, Tallulah's friend fainted dead away —just hit the asphalt, rather hard. At our age, a fall like that could easily break a hip. And I'm sure that's what the gentlemen with the funeral home must've been thinking, because they hopped right in, trying to revive her.

At that same moment, a big crowd of people—I assumed it was one of those walking tours, with a guide going on about the history of the church—filled up the sidewalk and gathered around the sides of the hearse. Some of these people were in the street. It was the strangest thing, really bad form if you ask me. Surely, they could tell there was a funeral about to start. Had it not been for Tallulah's friend fainting, I'm certain the men from the funeral home would've asked these people to move along, but as it was, they had their hands full. But this crowd of people completely blocked the view of what was going on with the hearse, is what I'm telling you.

And then out of nowhere, this hippie van—one of those Volkswagen Microbuses, bright orange—pulled up behind the hearse. I have the strangest feeling I've seen that bus before, but I cannot put my finger on where. It's about to drive me crazy.

Anyway, out hopped four . . . men. I suppose they must've been men . . . dressed in grey coveralls, wearing *clown masks*. Clown masks. Well by this point, I was just about to faint myself. I have just never in my life.

These clowns dashed up to the back of the hearse. I should mention, I suppose, by that point I had stepped inside the churchyard gate, out of the way. I had to peer out from behind one of the brick columns to see what was going on.

One of the clowns from the hippie van opened the back of the hearse, and the four of them pulled the casket out and carried it back to the microbus. They opened this large window in the back and slid it in. And then they climbed back inside, and off they went. I honestly don't know how all four of them fit in there with the casket. Anyway, the crowd parted for the microbus, and then all those tour group people just dispersed in all different directions. The whole thing couldn't have taken a minute.

Well, I was in shock. Speechless. I have just *never* in my *life* . . .

The next thing you know, Tallulah's friend recovered. She hopped right up and brushed herself off, and the two of them scurried off down Broad Street like nothing had happened. I don't know where they were headed, but I was thinking they weren't going to get a good seat for the funeral, and Tallulah was one of Eugenia's very best friends from what I understand.

I waited for a moment to see what might happen next, and then I went on inside the church. Frankly, I needed to sit down. I know I should've spoken to the men from the funeral home and told them what I'd seen. But Arthur always says it's better to give any situation that might turn litigious a wide berth. And let me tell you, there's not a doubt in my mind that both criminal and civil proceedings will be forthcoming. Eugenia was a judge's wife, after all.

Now, normally, they bring the casket inside the church for the funeral. That wasn't possible, of course. But her funeral was quite moving nevertheless, though I will say, I was surprised the turnout wasn't bigger. And there were a few people in particular I was surprised weren't there—Swinton and Judith Legare, for starters. I know for a fact they were in town. And they must be the oldest friends Eugenia and Everette had.

No one ever offered an explanation as to why Eugenia wasn't there. They just carried on, as if nothing unusual at all had happened. But then again, what would one do in such a situation? I suppose it was fortunate the burial at Magnolia Cemetery following the service was arranged to be private to begin with—just the family. It'll be easier to reschedule it for after they find Eugenia. If they find her. I guess it depends on why the clowns took her to begin with. I wondered if they were holding her for ransom. I declare, I don't know what this world is coming to.

Chapter Thirty-Four

Cornerstone Community Church had a newish campus near the corner of Church and Hibben in Old Mount Pleasant. The inside of the sanctuary was filled with light, with pale stained woods and pews with comfortable, sand-colored cushions. The most striking thing was all the floor-to-ceiling windows, with lush planting beds on the other side of the glass that served as privacy screens. There was an overwhelming aura of peace, like you could discern the presence of God. I reflected on how I hadn't been to church in a while, and I missed this feeling.

I'd arrived early as Tallulah instructed and was seated in the fourth row near the middle. A pianist played softly, and the ushers slowly escorted people to their seats, then hustled back to the next folks in line.

By quarter till two, the church was filled to capacity. Eugenia's friends crowded into the pews and stood in the back and around the sides. She was clearly well loved. I was shocked, though maybe I shouldn't have been, that one of the six pall bearers was Swinton. The only others I recognized were Fish and Vernon Markley.

The service was a joyous celebration of life, and my first impression of the Reverend Anson Gibbes Jones was that he was sincerely a man of God. I've met ministers who seemed more like businessmen, to be honest. But Reverend Jones had this peaceful, happy glow about him that seemed to signify and inspire confidence in the Divine. He gave Eugenia a fine send-off. We sang "Amazing Grace," "Morning Has Broken," and "How Great Thou Art," along with a few other hymns I wasn't as familiar with.

On my way out, I waited in line at the door to introduce myself.

"Hadley." His voice came from behind me.

I turned to see Cash sliding through the crowd.

"Hey." I scrambled for something intelligent to say.

"I thought I might see you here," he said.

I should've known he'd be here—of course he was. I mustered a smile. "Well, Eugenia was my friend."

"Right. I don't know if you heard. We've made an arrest."

"I did. I heard, actually," I said. "I need to speak with you. Whenever it's convenient."

"I'm headed to the reception at the Wentworth house. Do you want to ride over there together?"

"That's not far from me," I said. "Why don't I meet you back at my place? We can walk from there."

"All right, I'll see you there." He touched my arm and disappeared down the aisle.

When would the sight of him stop affecting me so?

Someone muttered what might've been a Ukrainian curse. "Imbecile."

I turned to see Kateryna on my right.

I patted her on the arm and resisted the urge to defend him. Cash would go where the evidence led him. Sometimes maybe he needed to validate the evidence a little better.

By unspoken agreement, Kateryna and I hung back, letting others go in front of us. If anyone was upset by Kateryna's presence at Eugenia's funeral, they hid it well. Several of the congregation offered her sympathetic nods and pats on the arm. Twenty minutes later, we stood in front of the reverend with no one behind us in line.

Kateryna said, "Hadley Cooper, please meet Reverend Anson Gibbes Jones. My fiancé. Anson, this is the detective I told you about. Eugenia's friend."

"I'm so pleased to meet you." He wore a sincere expression. "We're grateful—"

Everette appeared in front of Reverend Jones. "I will see you in jail for this."

Reverend Jones wore a confused expression. "For conducting a funeral service for your estranged wife?"

"For . . . *theft*. For tampering with a corpse." Everette seethed.

"I assure you, I've done no such thing." Anson was calm, an aura of peace around him.

"Where is my *wife*?" Everette snarled.

Anson looked bewildered. "The folks from the funeral home have taken her to be cremated, according to her wishes."

"*What*? Who? Who has taken her?"

"I just told you," said Anson. "The gentlemen with the funeral home have escorted her to the crematory."

"On whose authority?" Everette was in the reverend's face.

"On my authority." Charlie Vanderhorst stood a few feet away. Tallulah and Camille hovered just behind her, like wingmen. "Everette, I'd back off if I were you. You're on the verge of an assault charge."

Everette spun in Charlie's direction. "You authorized this desecration?"

Charlie held a folded set of papers. "I am honoring my client's last wishes. I have a notarized copy of her new will, dated March 11, 2020, along with a document appointing the executor of her estate, Tallulah Wentworth, as custodian of her body. She specifically prohibits you, Everette, from making any decisions about her final arrangements. Eugenia left very specific instructions. You, Everette, have been unlawfully interfering."

Everette advanced towards Charlie, sneered at her. "This is far from over."

Charlie didn't budge. Tallulah and Camille both snugged in closer to her, as if to back her up. "Now here we agree," said Charlie, cool as a cucumber. "In lieu of a formal reading, I'm having copies of Eugenia's will delivered to her heirs. Your copy will arrive this afternoon by courier. If you have questions, call my office and make an appointment."

His eyes glittered, and he appeared on the verge of foaming at the mouth. "I have a copy of Eugenia's will. She and I drew up our wills years ago. Whatever trumped-up document you have is invalid."

"If I were you, I wouldn't count on that," said Charlie.

"I will see you in court," said Everette.

"Perhaps, eventually," said Charlie. "But in the immediate future, you have one week to vacate the Tradd Street house. Pepper Townsend, as you know, was hired by Eugenia to sell the house."

"That house is now mine," said Everette.

"I'm afraid you're wrong there," said Charlie. "And it's certainly your legal right to contest Eugenia's will. But you, of all people, know just how expensive that will be. I don't think you have the cash, Everette."

He drew back like the big bad wolf preparing to huff and puff. Then he seemed to think better of it. He sneered at her one last time and stormed off.

I looked at Tallulah. "What was he talking about? What's happened?"

Tallulah looked innocent. "On advice of counsel, I assert my fifth amendment rights."

Charlie kept her eyes on Everette. "Let's just say some friends gave Eugenia a ride to the church while we got the paperwork sorted out."

Chapter Thirty-Five

Cash was parked in my driveway when I got home. I pulled past him into the garage, then walked back out to the foot of the steps leading to the porch.

"I need to show you something," I said. "Come inside for a minute?"

"Sure." He nodded, then followed me up the steps and to my office.

I sat behind the desk and pulled up the footage from Roger's security cameras. Before I clicked "play," I said, "I know you're not going to like this. Actually, I don't much care for the situation myself. But some of Eugenia's friends have hired me to assist in Kateryna's defense. And for the record, I can't believe you didn't even mention you suspected her when we sat right downstairs and I told you everything I knew about this case."

He squished up his face in a confused expression. "Why would her friends want to help her killer?"

"Well, that would be because none of them believe Kateryna killed Eugenia."

"I get that her friends are upset, maybe not thinking straight right now. And it follows that they wouldn't want to believe someone they know is capable of murder. No one ever wants to think that. But you're a professional, Hadley. I'm surprised you would go along with this."

"It turns out, I don't believe Kateryna killed Eugenia either."

"Her fingerprints are on the murder weapon."

"About that." I clicked 'play.'

"What am I looking at?"

"Security camera footage from Kateryna's neighbor, Roger Riddle. From Monday evening, June 7. The Monday before Eugenia was killed."

"What, you're suggesting the knife was stolen from Kateryna's kitchen?"

"No, I'm not suggesting that. I'm telling you that's what happened."

He watched it with me, leaning in when the figure appeared on the screen. "Rewind that, would you?"

I played it for him three more times.

He rubbed the back of his neck. "You can't tell whether he went inside or not. You can't see anything once he goes inside the porch."

"I bet you have technicians who can improve the quality of the video," I said.

"Probably. Look, Hadley . . . I'll go talk to this Roger Riddle, okay? I'll get a copy of the video and have our best video people see what they can do. But I still believe Kateryna is guilty. Even if someone broke into her house, we don't know what he did while he was in there. He probably stole something. That's usually what burglars do. Did she report anything missing?"

"Not that I'm aware. This has to be Everette. Kateryna has a set of knives identical to Eugenia's. Eugenia bought them for her." I explained the gift.

"And you think Everette knew about that? They were separated. I seriously doubt they chatted about chicken bog."

"She must've," I said. "I don't know the scenario, but she had to've told him."

"I think you're grasping at straws. Look, the knife is not the only physical evidence we have."

I raised my face to his with a question.

He sighed, shook his head. "I shouldn't be telling you any of this."

I thought of what Joe had said. "Why not? We both want the same thing, right? The killer in jail . . ."

"Of course we do . . ." He rubbed a spot below his right ear with his left hand, something he always did when he was stressed, or thinking hard. "We found a few of Kateryna's hairs in the kitchen near the body."

"Those could've been planted too, you know."

"Obviously, if anything was planted, it all could've been. There was also a book with a stamp from Eugenia's personal library found at Kateryna's residence."

"That doesn't prove a thing," I said. "She could easily have leant her a book."

"Maybe, but some of Eugenia's hair was also found at Kateryna's residence. She claims Eugenia was never there."

"And that's more evidence that could've been planted," I said.

"And then there's the matter of her car at Eugenia's house during the window when Eugenia was killed," said Cash.

"Do you have any idea how many grey Honda Accords there are in South Carolina?"

"No, do you?"

"Many. There are *man*-ee. Her car is hardly unique. Fish never said it was her car. He said it was a grey Honda Accord. With stickers Kateryna doesn't have on her car."

He winced, pointed to the screen. He was wavering, I could tell. "Run that for me one more time."

He leaned in, watched it closely, then straightened. "I'll have it analyzed, see if we can get anything else."

"You ready to head over to Tallulah's house?" I asked.

"You know Mrs. Wentworth?"

"Eugenia introduced us. Tallulah is the ringleader of the group that hired me."

"That's just great." Cash wore a grim look, one I recognized. He doubted himself.

"Listen, I forgot I need to make a stop somewhere else before I head over there," I said.

"Related to this case?" He raised an eyebrow.

I smiled. "What would you have said if I'd told you before I went that I was going to Roger Riddle's house looking for proof someone had broken into Kateryna's house and planted evidence?"

He shrugged. "That it was a waste of time."

"Exactly. It's better if you just go about your business in blissful ignorance. If I find anything helpful, I'll let you know."

"What if you find something that's helpful to my case, but not to your theory of the crime?"

"Like I said. We both want the same thing."

Chapter Thirty-Six

Magnolia Cemetery, where Everette Ladson's people were laid to rest, occupied a former rice plantation on the upper neck of the Charleston peninsula. The sprawling garden backed up to the Cooper River, roughly where the Wando River flowed into the Cooper. Dating back to 1850, the cemetery's residents included many a dignitary from historic and modern-day Charleston.

I drove through the white painted brick columns and wrought iron gate. It was a picturesque, park-like place, with grounds divided into several sections. A series of roads and paths wended through and around marshes, lagoons, and forests. I proceeded towards the Greenhill section, and the Ladson plot.

Given Everette's display at Cornerstone Community Church, the fact that I knew Eugenia's body was en route to the crematorium, and that a private family burial had originally been scheduled for four o'clock, I was curious to see what, if anything, was going on by the grave that would apparently remain empty.

At first, I thought I had the entire place to myself. The Greenhill section was in the back, more or less isolated. As I drove, I took in the landscape. Massive live oaks draped in Spanish moss dotted the grounds, some performing improbable acts of contortion. Before long, the road turned to dirt and gravel. Elaborate monuments—crosses, angels, and spires—many much taller than me, stood inside iron fences and stone borders marking family plots. Presently, I came to a sign pointing right to Greenhill.

As I approached the Ladson plot, I slowed to a roll. Everette had certainly expected to get away with hijacking Eugenia's funeral. A fresh grave had been dug inside the low wrought iron fence that marked the Ladson perimeter. A canopy stood nearby with half a dozen folded chairs set up underneath. But no one was there. I'm not sure what I'd thought I would find, actually. I'd had an urge to have a look, to check the box on the day's itinerary. It appeared I'd wasted my time. I circled around and made my way towards the exit.

On the far side of the Greenhill section, a lone figure stood at a grave, a trim woman in a black suit. Something about her was familiar. I kept moving, trying not to attract attention, but slowed. A late model Cadillac was pulled to the side just beyond where she stood. I rolled past her, then peered in my rearview mirror just as she headed back to her car.

It was Judith. If she'd noticed my car, she gave no indication of it. My impression was that she seemed preoccupied, though I didn't get much of a look, honestly.

Surely, she'd just come from Eugenia's funeral. Where was Swinton? Whose grave was Judith visiting?

Rather than following the road out, I turned, making another loop. By the time I'd made it back around to where I'd seen Judith, she and her car were gone.

I parked and made my way to the headstone she'd been standing in front of. It read:

Amelia Caroline Simons
Beloved Daughter
May 15, 1956–June 17, 1973

Amelia Simons. Tallulah had mentioned her. Eugenia had set up provisions for the care of her twin sister. Meryl, that was her name. Amelia was a classmate of Eugenia's, and of course, Judith's as well.

Today was the anniversary of Amelia's death. Judith—or perhaps someone else who'd been here earlier—had laid a bouquet of pink lilies and roses with white daisies on Amelia's grave. Maybe Meryl had been here. Was she able to drive herself? Tallulah had said Meryl didn't have any family left.

Amelia and Judith must've been very close. Forty-eight years had passed since Amelia's death. Judith had a full calendar today with Eugenia's various funerals and receptions. And yet she'd made time to visit Amelia's grave all these years later. That was unexpected.

Chapter Thirty-Seven

Tallulah Wentworth's beach house was on Atlantic Avenue between Station 21 and Station 22, maybe ten doors down from the Markley's. A traditional raised beach house with deep porches and a shiny metal roof, Tallulah's home was welcoming. By the time I arrived, the reception had evolved into a full-blown party.

Tallulah greeted me just inside the door. "I'm honoring Eugenia's wishes. She wanted a celebration of life, not a sad affair. Her instructions were quite specific."

"I don't doubt it," I said. "You're a good friend."

"Let's get you a drink. There's a signature cocktail. I bet you can guess what it is."

"A prickly pear margarita?"

"Naturally. The bar's on the pool deck." She pointed in the general direction of the Atlantic. "Hadley? Fair warning, Darlin'. Your father's here, though I'm certain you expected he would be."

"I'll just grab that drink." I made my way through the foyer, a wide hall, and across a large family room. Several sets of French doors had been thrown open wide to allow the party to flow freely from indoors out.

I'd imagined a makeshift bar at a folding table. What I found was a permanent outdoor kitchen combination tiki bar that would've looked at home on the pool deck of a hotel. The bar was manned by two bartenders in tie-dyed T-shirts, a man and a woman, who appeared to be working hard. I waited my turn.

Adjacent to the bar was an extravagant buffet of all manner of Southern and Lowcountry favorites: fried chicken, country ham biscuits, chicken bog, shrimp and grits, macaroni salad, potato salad, corn salad, pimento cheese, and on and on. A separate station featured an ice sculpture of a mermaid and offered a sumptuous display of chilled seafood. A tiered table with tiered cake plates served up mini trifles, banana puddings, chocolate mousse, macaroons, and strawberry shortcakes, and those were just the things I recognized.

And of course, there was a table with a sign that read "WFPBNO." I was possibly the only person who knew what that even meant. The food looked delicious—skewers of grilled vegetables, hummus and crudités, sliders, crispy roasted potatoes with dip, and a massive fruit display. They might not know what the sign said, but folks had been enjoying the picked-over platters.

Butlers passed trays of hors d'oeuvres to hold folks over while they sipped their signature cocktails. Bob Marley sang "One Love" in the background. It was a sight, I'll tell you what. I'd never seen a funeral reception like it, but it had Eugenia's fingerprints all over it.

When I had my prickly pear margarita in hand, I surveyed the outdoor crowd, most of them still in funeral clothes. Some of the faces I recognized from the funeral home. A few of the people I knew. Sarabeth, Libba, and Quinn chatted with gentlemen I assumed were their husbands by the hot tub.

Kateryna and the Reverend Jones spoke with a group of people I hadn't met by the French doors that led to the family room. Reverend Jones wasn't making eye contact with the person he was chatting with. He nodded and scanned the crowd. Was he on the lookout for trouble? Unlike the church, not everyone here was a member of his flock. Perhaps he anticipated trouble. There were likely those among us who considered it odd for Kateryna to be here.

Camille, Tallulah, and Birdie sat by the fire pit with their heads together. The three of them were probably a skosh past tipsy.

Fish had changed into board shorts and a faded Tommy Bahama shirt. He stopped by on his appointed rounds. "Hello, Miss Hadley." He seemed glassy eyed, but then, if pressed, I couldn't recall seeing him otherwise.

"Hey, Fish. Quite the turnout."

"Eugenia was well loved," he said. "You missed the toasts, I'm afraid. Oh, on a more painful topic, I should let you know, the police gave me the go-ahead to get the house cleaned. Apparently, there's a company who specializes in such nightmares. They were there all day today. Should you need access to the house for your inquiries, it's safe to go in now."

"Thanks. I would like to spend some more time in her office, maybe her bedroom as well. Is tomorrow morning okay?"

"Sure, whenever you like. Stop by the pool house, and I'll give you a key."

He meandered on around to the far side of the pool, where he chatted with Swinton and Judith. She must've just beaten me to the reception. Vernon Markley joined the group, gestured extravagantly, and appeared to commence telling them a story.

I made my way towards the fire pit and took a seat by Birdie. "What are you ladies up to?"

"We'll never tell," said Camille.

"I'm probably better off not being an accessory," I said.

"Where's Charlie?" asked Tallulah. "We'll need attorney-client privilege to discuss it."

They all hooted with laughter.

"Birdie, I wondered if I might come by tomorrow," I said. "I have a few more questions for you."

"Why sure, that's fine," said Birdie. "Or you can ask me whatever you like right now. I don't have any secrets from these two.

No time like the present. You never know when I might decide to shoot Vernon, and there's always a chance he'll get the first shot off."

"Well, all right then," I said. "I'm just dotting all my i's . . . I was taking a look at the provisions of Eugenia's will, specifically the charitable and special provisions. What can you tell me about Eugenia's relationship with Meryl Simons and her sister Amelia?"

Birdie's expression darkened. "Oh, that's such a sad story."

Tallulah said, "I'm going to leave y'all to this. I'm afraid I can't handle another sad story just now. I'm trying my best to stay upbeat, as Eugenia wanted. I need to speak with the caterers anyway. We need replenishment on a few items."

Camille said, "I'm just going to powder my nose."

The two of them took their leave, and Birdie recounted what Tallulah had already told me about Amelia and Meryl. "It was such a tragedy. Amelia had dated Charles Butler for ages. Her parents had a home on the Stono River. She grew up on that river. Knew it like the back of her hand. Both of them were very experienced boaters. But somehow, they lost control of their boat. They were both thrown out near Limehouse Bridge.

"It happened between our junior and senior years in high school. I think there was a pall over our entire class after that. Nothing was ever the same, really, for any of us."

"Did Eugenia know Amelia or Charles well?" I asked.

"As well as any of us, I suppose. I mean, we all grew up together. They weren't close, you understand. But Eugenia always did feel badly for Meryl. Her parents sold the house on the river after the accident. Meryl loved it there, but of course, none of them could bear it afterwards. And of course, Meryl was sick . . . she has MS, you know."

"I heard that. Were Judith and Amelia close friends?"

"Not that I recall," said Birdie. "It's like I told you. Eugenia and Everette and Swinton and Judith were close. Eugenia and I were like sisters, and Vernon and I spent a good deal of time with them. As did Fish and whoever he was dating at the time. Everyone else was sort of on the periphery, I guess you'd say."

And yet forty-eight years later, Judith was putting flowers on Amelia's grave. I needed to speak to Judith. I scanned the area on the other side of the pool. Fish and Vernon burst out laughing, slapped each other on the back, and appeared to be holding each other up. Swinton and Judith were no longer there.

Birdie continued, reminiscing, "There for a while, especially I guess during our junior year, the six of us were really into boating too. Judith's family had a house on the Stono River, and we used to take her daddy's boat down to Kiawah and spend the day at the beach. It was glorious, being young and feeling so free on the water. After the accident, we kind of all were put off spending time on the river.

"Actually . . . now that I'm thinking about it, that very same day—the same day as the accident, we were all supposed to take the boat down to Kiawah. But it was Father's Day. Somehow or another, it worked out that everybody's daddy was out of town except Vernon's. Vernon adored his daddy, and his momma always threw a big picnic, so we went to that instead, and then I guess the plans just fell apart. But if it hadn't've been for that, we might all have been on the river when it happened. For a long time, I wondered how things might've been different if we'd been there. Could we have helped Amelia and Charles? Or would we all have ended up dead?"

Chapter Thirty-Eight

Fish was in the garage when I arrived at Eugenia's the next morning, polishing a vintage orange VW van. "What year is that?" I asked.

Fish grinned. "This is a twenty-one-window 1967 Samba Deluxe microbus."

"She's a beauty."

"She's my pride and joy. I've never been passionate about classic cars. Not like your father. But something about this old bus captured my heart. She and I have been together now for . . . oh, I guess it's going on ten years. Well, what do you know about that? My longest relationship with a woman." He reached into his pocket. "Here's the house key. Keep it. You never know."

"Thanks. Hey, Fish . . . do you know of anything that was troubling Eugenia?"

"I do." He continued rubbing the car but flashed me a sardonic look over his shoulder. "Her husband was having an affair with another woman."

"Anything besides that? Maybe something she felt guilty about?"

He straightened, shook his head slowly. "I can't imagine what that would be. Now, Eugenia always had a philosophical streak.

Always. One might argue that became more pronounced after her cancer diagnosis. However, as far back as I can recall, she waxed poetic about doing unto others, loving your neighbor, and making amends. Some people considered Eugenia overbearing. That wasn't it a'tall. She had the biggest heart of anyone I've ever met. Would do absolutely anything to help a friend . . . or a stranger, for that matter. Perhaps Eugenia struggled to contain her zeal for helping others. One didn't want to stand between her and a good deed."

"That sounds right," I said. "I'll be inside if you need me."

I spent the next three hours going through Eugenia's bedroom and bathroom. I ran my hands along the underside of drawers, pulled out dressers and checked behind them, and checked for hiding places in the floor. I felt closer to Eugenia when I finished, but there was nothing there to help me better understand her state of mind in the days and weeks leading up to her death.

I made my way back to her office and perused her bookcases. She'd had eclectic reading tastes, with novels by a diverse range of authors from Ann Patchett to Dean Koontz to Nora Roberts. Her collection included many Southern authors, including, of course, all of William Faulkner's novels. I pulled out a copy of Jane Austen's "Sense and Sensibility" and flipped through the pages. It bore Eugenia's personal library stamp.

Her nonfiction shelves held titles by C. S. Lewis, Billy Graham, and Lee Strobel, among others. She owned several bibles and a Book of Common Prayer. Why was I here?

I knew in my core that Everette had killed Eugenia, and I knew why. It was the how that escaped me. The answer to that question was almost certainly not in Eugenia's office. But something pulled me here. Was that Eugenia, guiding me from beyond the grave? Okay, I'm not saying I thought that, but I didn't completely discard it either. My mind was open to the possibility.

What was in that safe? I wandered back to the closet. If she'd wanted what was inside found, she'd've left the combination somewhere. Just in case I'd entered something wrong before, I tried Eugenia's birthday. A red light flashed on the lock.

And then a fanciful notion floated across my mind, likely put there by some hodgepodge of seeing Judith at the cemetery the day before and my conversations with Tallulah and Birdie. I typed in zero, six, one, seven, one, nine, seven, three—June 17, 1973. The date of Amelia Simons and Charles Butler's accident on the Stono River.

The light flashed green, and the lock disengaged.

I gasped. *Sweet baby Moses in a basket.*

I ran back into the office and grabbed gloves from my purse. I slid them on, carried my phone with me into the closet and took a picture of the unopened safe.

I swung open the door and took another photo.

Dangit, the safe looked empty.

I ran my hand along the lower shelf, then the top.

There . . . on the top shelf, I found a single faded photo.

Six teenagers in swimsuits smiled for the camera. Eugenia, with long blonde hair and long arms, held the camera and they all crowded in—a selfie, before selfies were a thing. I recognized Everette, Swinton, and Judith. The other two had to be Amelia Simons and Charles Butler. I flipped the picture over. On the back, Eugenia had written all their names, Kiawah Island, and the date, June 17, 1973.

The boating trip down the Stono to Kiawah hadn't been canceled after all. Birdie and Vernon went to his family's Father's Day picnic, but the others went to Kiawah, and took Amelia and Charles instead. Or had the four of them gone, then ran into Amelia and Charles at Kiawah? Either way, for some reason, Eugenia and the others had told Birdie and Vernon they didn't go at all.

Perhaps that was just a white lie to keep Birdie from feeling left out. But there was a reason this photo was in Eugenia's safe— a safe with a very specific date as the combination. Eugenia must've known or suspected something to do with Amelia and Charles's accident.

Did this photo have anything at all to do with Eugenia's death?

Meryl Simons shot to the top of my list of priorities.

Chapter Thirty-Nine

Amelia Caroline Simons and Charles Hamilton Butler, who I learned was Eugenia's first cousin, died in 1973. There was very little from that long ago in my online databases. I spent the early part of that afternoon in the main branch of the Charleston County Library on Calhoun Street, digging through newspaper archives and city directories. I was working old school. Specifically, I needed the names of the sheriff's deputies and officers from the South Carolina Department of Natural Resources involved in investigating Amelia and Charles's deaths.

I found the accident coverage in the newspaper easily enough. It was front page news for a few days. Another boater found Charles's father's Boston Whaler floating adrift. The bodies weren't found until two days later. It was a tragedy that devastated two local families and the rising senior class at Ashley Hall and Porter-Gaud. There was no indication anyone ever thought it to be anything other than a horrible accident. No other names were mentioned.

From several days' worth of articles, I pulled a list of four sheriff's deputies and two SCDNR officers. But when I ran the names through my database, I discovered five of the six men were no longer with us. The accident had happened forty-eight years ago, so I'd expected as much.

Just when I was about to give up, I got a hit on the last name I ran. Zane Norton, one of the SCDNR officers who'd worked the case, was alive and living in Edisto, as recently as a year ago anyway. If he was still there, he was now eighty-eight years old. I crossed my fingers he would be willing to speak with me and would remember the case. I found a phone number in another database, then went out to my car to make the call.

"Hello?" His voice was clear and strong.

"Good morning, Mr. Norton, my name is Hadley Cooper. I'm a private investigator from Mount Pleasant. I wondered if I might speak with you."

"Seems you are," he said in a matter-of-fact tone. "Speaking with me, that is."

"Would it be possible for us to speak in person? Perhaps tomorrow morning?"

"Hold please. Let me confer with my secretary."

Surely, he was pulling my leg. He was closing in on ninety. I smiled. "All right, then."

After a moment he said, "I can do ten o'clock. After that, my day gets impossible."

"I'll see you at ten."

"Err . . . private investigator you say? What's this in regard to? Not that it makes a difference, mind you, as long as it's entertaining. But I am curious."

"The deaths of Amelia Simons and Charles Butler in 1973."

"Well, now," he said. "This is an interesting turn of events. Very well. I'll see you in the morning, young lady."

Chapter Forty

When people have something to hide, they grow adept at showing you only what they want you to see. I needed to speak with Meryl Simons. But before I did that, I needed a baseline for her. I needed to see the person she was when she thought no one was looking. So when I finished at the library, I went to Daniel Island to do some reconnaissance.

Much the same way downtown Charleston is nestled between the Ashley and Cooper Rivers, the community of Daniel Island—which is actually part of the city of Charleston—resides between the Cooper and the Wando. All of the land used to be owned by the Harry Frank Guggenheim Foundation, back when it was used for farming and a private hunting reserve. These days, the land is occupied by a master-planned community, complete with single family homes, condos, apartments, restaurants, boutiques, businesses, medical offices, parks, sports complexes, schools, a private club with two golf courses, and a ferry to Waterfront Park in downtown Charleston. There's literally everything you need. I've heard there are people who only leave when there's a mandatory evacuation.

Meryl Simons's two-bedroom condo was situated in the heart of the nouveau hamlet, off Seven Farms Drive. A corner unit on the top floor, it offered views of the Wando, and convenient access to shopping and restaurants. It was a nice area, not anyone's idea of bargain real estate. Had Eugenia paid for Meryl's condo?

My online digging hadn't turned up an employment history for Meryl. Birdie had said she was homeschooled, so my expectation was that her health was fragile. Her parents had left her enough money for the average person to live modestly without having to work. But this wasn't an especially modest condo, and an MS patient might well have expenses an average person didn't have.

Tallulah had provided me with Meryl's cell phone number, but I hadn't been able to find a landline. She had no social media accounts I could find, but I did score a driver's license photo, so she was still driving it seemed. I'd pulled the make and model of her car—a gold, 2018 Subaru Forrester—from a subscription database. That afternoon, the Subaru was parked next to the elevator in the garage on the first level of the building. Unless she'd left on foot, she was at home. I drove around and parked on the street nearby.

So much of my job involved waiting I was practiced at it. But if Meryl was a shut-in, I could potentially wait here for weeks, and she wouldn't come out. I needed to force the issue, but I had to be careful here because I didn't want to be recognized later when I interviewed her. This is what I was thinking.

I had my hand on the door, just about to open it to go around back and grab a wig, when a woman came out of the garage on a bike pulling a lime-green kayak on a cart. I was focused on the contraption she was pulling, which is how I almost missed her.

Then I caught a glimpse of her waist-length, wavy brown hair. In her driver's license photo, I'd noticed it was streaked with silver, but you'd hardly notice it from a distance. It was Meryl, and she certainly looked healthy, though I knew with MS, you could have long periods of remission.

She turned down Seven Farms Drive, and I had a decision to make. Clearly, she was going paddling. She'd be gone a while, and

I wouldn't be able to follow her far. Also, it was doubtful she would be doing anything relevant to my case in a kayak. Following her wouldn't be productive.

But knowing she'd be out for a while gave me an opportunity to explore her condo. I knew she'd never married, and her name was the only one on the deed. But it was entirely possible she had a roommate. Buildings like this had security—cameras in the hallways at a minimum. At that point, I'd gotten what I came for. I'd seen Meryl when she didn't know I was looking. After I spoke with her, if I needed to, I could come back another day and search her condo while she kayaked.

Chapter Forty-One

Happy hour was in full swing in the beach cabana when I arrived at five fifteen. Everyone was there that Friday, even Birdie. I'd considered showing the photo I'd found in Eugenia's safe to Birdie and Tallulah and asking them what they made of it. But something held me back. After my last conversation with Birdie, and of course, seeing Judith at Amelia's grave, I was convinced the person I really needed to speak with was Judith. I was still deciding how to handle that.

Fish had left an empty space in the middle of the tent where Eugenia's chair used to sit. He sat to the right of her spot, beside Tallulah. When he saw me walking down the beach, he rose and poured me a prickly pear margarita.

He handed me my glass. "Hadley, please tell us you come with good news."

I settled into my canvas chair between Tallulah and Camille. "I wish I could say I did, Fish. But I'm nothing if not tenacious."

"Don't hound the girl, Fish. These things take time," said Tallulah. "What we need is a distraction. Something happy to think about."

"I assume supper club is on hiatus this month," said Quinn. "Out of respect for Eugenia?"

A thoughtful look slid over Tallulah's face. "It seems to me that's the last thing Eugenia would want. Anyone who hires a karaoke DJ for her funeral reception definitely has an appreciation for carrying on."

"Wait," I said. "There was karaoke? How did I miss that?"

"You left too early," said Camille. "It didn't start until ten."

"You missed it," said Sarabeth. "Fish does a remarkable Frank Sinatra."

"My dear, you flatter me," said Fish. "Our Sarabeth stole the show with her Miranda Lambert numbers."

"Ten o'clock?" I asked. "What time did this shindig end?"

"Last call was at two," said Tallulah.

"I know you're exhausted," said Birdie. "But you really gave Eugenia quite the send-off. I'm sure she's well pleased, curled up on a cloud somewhere like a fat old cat who just lapped up a bowl of cream."

"Well, she planned everything," said Tallulah. "That was the easiest party I've ever hosted. And I do think the caterers did a fabulous job. I'll use them again, perhaps for my own farewell party."

"So we are having supper club?" asked Sarabeth.

"We are," said Tallulah. "Hadley, I'd love for you to join us. Perhaps you'll take Eugenia's seat."

"That's so sweet of you—thank you. When is it? And what should I bring?"

"The Sullivan's Island Supper Club meets on the last Saturday of every month, unless I change it," said Tallulah. "It's always at my house."

"So it's a week from tomorrow," said Libba. "And the theme this month is the Casbah."

"I'm sorry, what?" I felt my face squinting.

"There's always a theme," said Tallulah. "This month's theme is the Casbah. Think Moroccan-inspired tapas."

I'd need to do some research on that. "Okay then. Is there anything else I should know?"

"I don't think so," said Tallulah. "But I'll need your date's name for the place cards."

"Date?"

"Will you be bringing a date?" asked Camille.

"Can I get back to you on that?" I asked. Owen Callaway might prove to be someone I went out with more than once. But the jury was still out on that.

"Of course," said Tallulah. "And we're happy to assist with that if you like. Between us, we know a lot of people."

"Oh . . . I—" There weren't many things I disliked as utterly as being fixed up.

"My, yes," mused Tallulah. "I think we've hit upon a worthy distraction—something fun."

"Wait—"

"This is so much safer than the Tinder," said Camille. "Everyone we know has been thoroughly vetted."

I had to stop this train. "But I may actually have a date. I've met someone new."

"Really?" asked Sarabeth. "Tell us everything."

"Everything?" Where to start?

"Yes," said Birdie. "Everything."

So I started with my recent public humiliation, backtracked to Cash, and then told them about how I'd been in desperate need of a date for tomorrow night and had miraculously found one on King Street.

"And you're certain he's a doctor?" asked Camille. "Because he very well could've been lying in wait for you. This could be an elaborate scheme to kidnap you."

"Oh, Camille, for heaven's sake," said Tallulah. "Do you hear yourself?"

"Young women can't be too careful these days," said Camille.

"I've done a thorough background check," I said. "He actually is a very highly respected heart surgeon."

"And he's not married?" asked Camille.

"Nope," I said. "Never been married. Like me."

"He may be your Prince Charming," said Birdie.

"But if he isn't," said Tallulah, "we can arrange for a well-vetted dinner escort."

"Tallulah, who are you bringing this month?" asked Quinn.

Tallulah glanced at Fish, and he nodded.

"Fish was always Eugenia's date for supper club," said Tallulah "well, in recent times anyway. He's agreed to accompany me a week from Saturday."

"Tallulah brings a different date every month," said Libba.

"No sense in getting their hopes up," said Tallulah. "I've already had the love of my life. My husband passed away five years ago. There'll never be anyone else for me. But that doesn't mean I can't enjoy a gentleman's company."

"And I'm honored to escort you," said Fish.

"Do let us know on Sunday what you decide about the heart surgeon," said Tallulah. "I have several single doctors in my address book."

Chapter Forty-Two

I threw together a salad with mixed greens, roasted sweet potato, mixed berries, pear, avocado, and glazed pecans, and topped it with an oil-free fig balsamic dressing. This was one of my favorite salads. I took it outside and ate by the pool. It was such a sweet indulgence, eating where I could hear the ocean and inhale deep lungfuls of salt air. I would miss this, when Beck no longer needed a house sitter. Best to keep in mind he'd be selling this house, and not get too spoiled.

After dinner, I retreated to my office and spent time updating the case board, crossing off names. When I finished, I was aggravated with myself. The only real progress I'd made was in eliminating the names of the folks whose alibis Gavin and Joe had verified, and adding a possible motive to an unknown suspect.

My case board that evening looked like this:

Suspect — Motive
Everette Ladson — Money, freedom, love, lust, rage, hate
Jordyn Jackman — Money, love, lust, rage, hate
Hamilton "Fish" AikenMoney — love, lust, rage

Kateryna Petrenko — Rage

Meryl Simons — unknown connection to sister's death

Unknown Friend — To keep a secret, rage, love, lust

Unknown Friend or Acquaintance — Burglary of specific item, revenge

Unknown Friend or Acquaintance — Related to Simons/Butler deaths

Unknown Stranger — Thrill, rage

I didn't consider Fish a suspect, but as he'd been alone in the pool house—very nearby—at the time of the murder, he had no alibi. By my own rules, I couldn't cross him off my list. Kateryna was likewise not a serious suspect in my mind. It was either Everette or Jordyn—or the two of them working together—or someone unknown to me.

Given that Eugenia considered the accident that killed Amelia Simons and Charles Butler so important she used the date as the combination to her safe, it seemed plausible to me that there was a connection between their deaths and hers. I needed to speak with Judith as soon as possible. That wouldn't be until after J. T.'s party.

I also needed to speak with Meryl Simons. Perhaps she could shed some light on why Eugenia was apparently haunted by this tragedy that happened so long ago. Surely, she was aware of Eugenia's motives in providing for her care. There had to be a connection here.

And I needed to focus on Jordyn Jackman. She could be the key to how Everette pulled this off. If he didn't have money to hire someone, perhaps he somehow convinced Jordyn to help him. Or, maybe she was the one who convinced him that Eugenia stood in the way of their happily ever after.

I had my game plan figured out, starting with my conversation the next morning with Zane Norton. He'd seemed a bit of a character on the phone. With any luck, he wouldn't be wearing a foil-covered helmet.

Chapter Forty-Three

I took a glass of wine out to the pool at ten thirty. The sky was cloudless, a quarter moon glistening off the water. It was one of those warm June nights when the air felt like silk against your skin, and you gave serious thought to sleeping outside.

North walked through a group of palmetto trees and across the grass at ten forty-five. It was rare for me to see him that early. He wore a broad smile, also a rarity. Perhaps living beside the beach soothed something inside North the same way it did me.

"You have some interesting neighbors." He walked over to the outdoor kitchen and pulled out a turkey sub and a bottle of water.

"Oh, I'm aware of that," I said.

"There's this guy down the beach . . . He keeps goats inside his house. He lets them out after dark to graze in the accreted area between his house and the beach."

That had to be Vernon. I laughed and shook my head. Poor Birdie. "He's a character."

"I don't understand why he waits until night and lets the goats out surreptitiously. I checked the website. There's a *long* list of animals you can't keep or maintain here, including horses, pigs, cows, and baboons. But goats aren't on the list." He wolfed down the sub.

"I imagine his wife prefers he lets the goats out at night. You have a computer?"

"Yeah, a laptop. Why? I charged the battery here. I hope that's okay."

"Of course it's okay. Do you need the Wi-Fi password?"

"Hadley, please . . . you wound me."

I looked at him for a long moment. "You already hacked it?"

"Consider it a security audit. *I* was able to hack it. But I'm reasonably confident no one else can, unless there's a reason why you're thinking hackers with military-grade skills would be snooping on you."

"Not that I know of. But I'd like it better if it was unhackable."

"Me too," he said. "I'll do some tweaking."

"I could use your skills on a regular basis, you know."

He lifted a shoulder. "Anytime. Let me know what you need."

"I'll take you up on that." I needed to tread carefully. "Are you liking it here?"

"Of course," he said. "I'd be crazy not to. Have you seen the hidden garden?"

"What hidden garden?"

"Come on, I'll show you."

I set down my wine glass and followed him across the swath of grass to the left of the patio and beyond the trio of palmettos. A line of staggered magnolias marked the border between the yard and the path, or so I thought. North led me between two of the magnolias.

"Are you taking me to the jungle?" I asked.

"Not a chance," said North. "I know you better than that."

And then we were in a pocket garden completely hidden from both the yard and the path on the left side of the house. It was completely enclosed by magnolias, tea olives, and a variety of trees and shrubs I couldn't name, with the only openings the offset gap between the magnolias and the window to the sky. "Well, my, my . . . Would you look at this?"

Border beds to the left, raised in places and ground level in others, burst with vegetables—tomatoes, peppers, squash, and on and on . . . and the herbs! I could smell the cilantro. "This is unbelievable."

"I've weeded the vegetables," said North. "There's a gardener who comes on Thursdays, but I didn't want them to take hold."

"Good idea," I said. "Is the gardener picking the vegetables?"

"No, I wanted to ask you about that . . . I can pick them."

"Thanks," I said. "I'll double-check with Beck, but we can't let them go to waste."

I was still taking it all in. Nearest the house, a small shed built to look like the rest of the house offered a tin-roofed overhang with a swing on one side and a hammock on the other. In between the two, against the wall sat two chairs with cushions and ottomans, and a weather-proof storage chest. "What's in the shed?" I asked.

"A few gardening tools, though the guy who comes brings his own. There's storage. A sink. But you can access the outdoor bathroom from just behind the far side of the lean-to. And just beyond that is a door that leads into the utility room of the house, or that's what it looks like, anyway. I didn't go inside, obviously."

"Obviously." I was still slack jawed.

It was as if someone had thoughtfully designed a space for North, one where he could have everything he needed without ever having to go inside. But then they'd left a way for him to quickly come inside if he needed to. He had shelter from the elements, a choice of outdoor beds, a comfortable place to sit, and access to a bathroom.

Nearby was an outdoor living room and kitchen.

How could this be? Suspicion crept inside my gut and curled up. Something nagged at me. But North looked happier than I'd seen him in years.

"Look up," said North.

Above us, billions of stars were scattered across the velvet night. Waves crashed beyond the lush green walls. It was like we were in our own secluded world, safe from whatever might be on the other side of verdant sentries that guarded this haven.

"There're quilts in the chest," said North.

"What are we waiting for?" I asked.

We spread quilts in the lush grass and stared at the stars, pointing at constellations, and arguing about which planets were which until finally we were quiet long enough I dozed off to sleep.

North nudged me. "You snore, you know that?"

"I do no such thing."

"You're going to scare the wildlife."

"Fine. I'll go sleep in my own bed."

Chapter Forty-Four

Zane Norton lived in a small condo on the golf course at Edisto Beach. I knocked on his door at ten o'clock the next morning.

"You're punctual," he said when he opened the door. He had the posture and twinkle in his eye of a much younger man.

"I do my best," I said. "Thank you for seeing me so soon."

"Come in, come in. Would you like something to drink? Tea, water, beer, bourbon?"

"No, thank you. I'm good."

"Have a seat." He gestured to a denim sofa. The room was neat, with a minimalist vibe.

I sat where instructed, and he settled into a chair to my right.

"I canceled on my golf buddies this morning," he said. "I usually win, so they're not too tore up about it. What can I do for you?"

"Okay, well, I'm looking into a recent death in Sullivan's Island."

He nodded. "Ladson woman."

"Yes, I suppose you've heard about it in the news."

"Could hardly miss it. It's made all the networks. Probably be on *Dateline* before it's over with."

"I wouldn't bet against it," I said. "I'm wondering if there's a connection to the deaths of two friends of hers, Amelia Simons and Charles Butler. You recall the accident?"

"Of course I recall it," he said. "It was the most heart-wrenching case I ever worked. Two young people, with their whole lives ahead of them . . . just . . . I saw things I couldn't unsee."

"What caused the accident?" I asked.

He shrugged. "No way to know that. Coulda been anything. Kids, you know . . . coulda been going too fast. Honestly, we didn't look too hard at that. It really didn't matter. We did our best to make it as easy on the families as we could. Wrapped things up as quickly as possible."

"I understand," I said. "Was there anything about it that bothered you?"

"Everything about it bothered me."

"What I mean is, was there anything you thought needed further investigation? Anything that maybe wasn't in the newspapers?"

He screwed up his face, like maybe he'd bit into a lemon. "You're not trying to dig this all up, are you?"

"Only if it has a bearing on the murder I'm currently investigating."

"Frankly, I don't see how that's possible," he said.

"Did you speak to any of Amelia or Charles's friends?"

"No, couldn't see the need." He sighed deeply. "Look, there's only one piece of information that was withheld. It was in consideration of the families. Some things just don't need to be in the newspaper."

I waited while he conducted an internal debate.

"And I can't see any possible connection to your case. But I'm an old man, and on the outside chance I'm wrong, I don't want to take this tidbit with me to my grave. I'm the only person still breathing who knows this—well, the only law enforcement officer, anyway—and I suppose there would be some relief in passing this on to someone else. Just in case."

I raised my eyebrows, ducked my chin in an inquiring expression.

He rubbed the back of his neck and winced again, shook his head. Finally, he said, "The Simons girl . . . she was pregnant, about six weeks."

Chapter Forty-Five

Before I pointed Jolene towards home, I stopped by Tortuga's Mexican Grill on Jungle Road and had a veggie burrito, no cheese, no sour cream, extra cilantro, extra jalapeños. I needed thinking food. The day was one of those gifts from God, when the humidity in the Lowcountry had been dialed back from sauna, and the thermometer was only forecast to reach the mideighties. I put the top down, shuffled my driving playlist, and headed out Highway 174 to the tune of "Black Water," by the Doobie Brothers.

All the way back to Sullivan's Island, I pondered Amelia Simons and Charles Butler, and how their deaths—and that of their child—might conceivably be connected to Eugenia's. I knew for certain Eugenia was still dealing with what happened all these years later. Perhaps she took the accident harder because she knew Amelia's secret. Clearly, Eugenia was scarred by the tragedy. But what was murkier was if that had a connection to her death. I had no stomach for dredging up people's private matters when there was no call for it.

The only possible connection I could see between the accident forty-eight years ago and Eugenia's very recent death was if Eugenia held a secret that someone didn't want exposed. But why now, after so long, would anyone be concerned that a secret kept for forty-eight years was suddenly at risk? And who was still alive to protect this secret?

I called Meryl Simons and made an appointment to speak with her the following day. Then I refocused my attention on the Jordyn and Everette angle. I'd removed the cameras from Everette's house, but there was a window of time between when I installed them on Friday around lunchtime, and when I took them out the Tuesday following Eugenia's death, I hadn't reviewed. Probably nothing relevant there. Everette and Jordyn had just seen each other on Thursday. But you never knew, and I was scrambling for a clue, a breadcrumb, a sliver of information that would unravel Everette's scheme.

I'd initially slid the video to the back burner because I'd installed the cameras looking for something to use in a divorce suit which was now irrelevant. But what if I'd captured a conversation between coconspirators? It couldn't be used in court, of course. Eugenia had authorized the installation of the cameras in her own home, but because she died during my contract with her, things got very murky. Nevertheless, if there was something on the cameras that helped me figure out what happened, I could worry about how to prove it in court afterwards.

I was crossing the peninsula on the Septima Clark Parkway when Dana Smalls, Kateryna's public defender, called.

"You found anything yet?" she asked without preamble.

"Good afternoon to you, too."

She huffed at me. "I don't have time for a tea party. Do you have anything relevant to my case?"

"I have someone on camera sneaking into Kateryna's house. I'm reasonably certain it's Everette, but he's wearing a ski mask. I think he stole one of Kateryna's kitchen knives, maybe planted some evidence that would make people think Eugenia had been there." I explained about the knives and the chicken bog.

Dana was quiet for a minute. "That's useful. Anything else?"

"Nothing else as firm," I said. "But I think I'll have something tomorrow."

"How the duck does that work?" She didn't actually say duck.

"Do you kiss your mother with that mouth?"

"Look, Mary Poppins, call me the minute you have something concrete. She might be out of jail for the moment, but my client still has this hanging over her head. She's terrified about her immigration status. I'm not sure which she fears more at this point, going to jail or going back to Ukraine."

"I am every bit as concerned about Kateryna's situation as you are," I said.

"I highly doubt that."

"I will call you when I have more. If you can manage to keep a civil tongue in your head."

She hung up on me. Dana Smalls needed lessons in manners, or possibly ten milligrams of something I couldn't offer her. I turned up the music. Tom Petty and the Heartbreakers sang "Refugee." The Cooper River glistened in the sun as Jolene climbed the Arthur Ravenel Bridge.

At home, I grabbed a glass of peach tea and took it upstairs and settled in at my desk. It would be easier to scan the footage from the cameras I'd installed at Everette's house on my laptop. The three cameras, from the kitchen, living room, and bedroom, each had different tracks, but the software on my computer allowed me to stream them concurrently, in separate boxes on my screen. Motion detectors switched on the devices, which recorded both audio and video.

The first thing captured was at one forty-five, less than two hours after the devices went live. Everette stormed through the living room, barking at someone on the phone. I caught the words, "open house" embedded in a long, colorful string of profanity, before he disappeared, then appeared in the next box on the screen seconds later as he passed through the kitchen and into the sunroom. The cameras stopped recording after thirty seconds with no movement. Everette must've finished his conversation in the sunroom.

The next activity was thirty minutes later. Everette passed through the kitchen into the dining room, then into the living room a minute later with a highball glass with a generous pour of something dark. He sat in one of the chairs by the window, put his feet up on the ottoman, and sipped his liquor while he studied something on the wall across the room. After a bit, he took his drink and walked towards the foyer. He must've gone upstairs, but the camera in the bedroom didn't activate until nearly midnight. Everette must've taken his drink to his office. If only I'd had a camera there, I could've heard any phone conversations he might've had the day before Eugenia was killed.

As it was, between Friday around noon and Tuesday, the cameras captured a lot of Everette traipsing around the house while he was home, the cameras switching on frequently, to catch him in the act of him filling a glass with filtered water, walking from one room to the next, and other such riveting activities. Of course, there was a big gap during the time he was in Greenville.

But the most promising thing I captured was taped Saturday morning during the open house. Pepper Townsend arrived at eight thirty, an hour after Everette left. Just after nine, Jordyn Jackman arrived. The living room camera activated as the two of them passed through and into the kitchen.

"Congratulations on scoring this listing." Jordyn looked around as if she were touring the house for the first time. "I had no idea it was coming on the market."

"It was rather sudden." Pepper's down-home accent, her somewhat over-styled platinum hair, and her dress, which wasn't too small, but hugged her curves closely, gave a first impression that maybe she was less than sophisticated. Eugenia had mentioned that this led people to underestimate Pepper, and she used this to her advantage.

"I'm shocked the family would let this one go," said Jordyn. "It's been in the Ladson family for centuries, hasn't it?"

"No indeed," said Pepper. "It's been in the *Butler* family for quite some time. Eugenia Ladson was a Butler."

The women passed into the sunroom, and no matter how I tried to enhance the sound, I couldn't make out what they were saying. Were they friends? It made sense that they knew each other—they were both local realtors. But how friendly were they?

"Hel-*loooo,*" a woman called out, and then she appeared on the living room camera. She was tall, close to five ten, with short blonde hair and glasses. "I don't see anybody."

A man of about the same age—I'm guessing these folks were in the fifty-five to sixty-five range—followed behind her, then a younger couple and another guy. Of the five people in the group, four of them had some sort of LSU Tiger logo somewhere on them.

Pepper hurried back through the kitchen and met them in the living room. "Good morning. I'm Pepper Townsend. The fact sheets for the home are on the table in the foyer. Please sign in on the signup sheet. And please do let me know if you have any questions at all."

"Thank you so much," said the blonde woman. "We'd just like to take a look around."

"I'll be in the garden," said Pepper. "Y'all should really see that. It's just gorgeous."

"I'll sign the sheet," the woman said to the man I assumed was her husband.

The younger members of the group followed him as he moved back into the foyer and presumably upstairs. After a minute, the blonde woman crossed the living room and went into the kitchen, where she took her time admiring the fireplace mantel and the woodwork. A few minutes later, she had a seat at the small table and bent over to remove a tennis shoe.

Pepper appeared at the door to the kitchen, looked around, and apparently missed the woman, who was at the far end of the room attending to her foot, and disappeared back into the sunroom.

The blonde woman looked inside her shoe, like maybe there was a rock or something in there. And then an odd look passed across her face. She squinted and turned towards the sunroom. Her eyes grew in surprise. Then the expression turned to alarm. She shook out her shoe, then shoved it back on her foot and tied it. Hopping up, she called out loudly, "Allen, you ready?"

He met her in the living room, a questioning look on his face.

"Kids?" she hollered.

"Coming," yelled the young woman.

"What—" the man tried to ask.

"We'll talk outside," she said.

And then they were gone.

Why had they left so abruptly?

Pepper had been in the sunroom. Jordyn was most likely with her.

What did the blonde woman hear that caused her to leave in such a hurry?

Chapter Forty-Six

Owen Callaway was punctual. He rang my bell at exactly five thirty. Now, Owen was a handsome man in a button down and pressed khaki shorts the day I climbed into his car on King Street. But if ever there was a man God created to wear a white dinner jacket, it might've been Owen Callaway. I might've gasped a little when I opened the door.

"Hadley, you are stunning." His look was one of appreciation. I wished I could trust that I looked appropriate for the occasion. Ever since I'd put the silver sequined number on, I'd worried it was too much. I desperately wanted to fit in at this party. Well, Owen would definitely fit in. Maybe arriving on his arm would buy me a little grace.

He escorted me to the car and opened the door, the perfect gentleman. So far, so good. All the way into Charleston, I agonized over what I was wearing. Why, oh why, did I agree to this? I would be so out of place. Anxiety crawled from my stomach into my throat.

"Are you and your brother close?" Owen asked as he turned the car down East Bay.

I was so caught up in fretting, I was being rude. And I should probably give Owen a bit of background. "We are. He's my half brother, actually. We have the same father. It's complicated. But I don't have a relationship with my father at all. It probably won't come up, but I guess you should know, in case. I'll try my best to avoid him."

"The party is at his home, isn't it?"

"Yes."

Both of his eyebrows hitched up a bit. "I'll just whisk you onto the dance floor whenever I see him coming."

"Oh . . . I'm not the best dancer, actually. I mean . . . I love to dance. I'm just not very good at it."

"Nonsense. Anyone who loves to dance is a natural. You can't do it wrong. It's an expression of joy."

I felt my eyes widen as I inhaled slowly. "I'm pretty sure you can do it wrong."

"Hadley, how can we get you to relax? Do I need to write you a prescription for something?"

I laughed. "No, I just need to take a few more deep breaths." I needed to keep my wits about me this evening, so as not to embarrass J. T.

Owen and I drove past Rainbow Row in silence. The late evening light dappled through the crepe myrtles along the sidewalk. East Bay became East Battery, and along the Battery, families, couples, and folks grabbing a late afternoon jog or walk, moved at varying paces, some stopping to watch the sailboats on the harbor, or point to Fort Sumter. We turned on Murray Boulevard at Oyster Point. A couple spread a quilt beneath a live oak in White Point Garden to our right. The Ashley River spilled into Charleston Harbor on our left. The Carolina sun retreated in front of us, bathing the evening in a soft, magical glow. I was nearly faint with anticipation.

"Listen, we need a signal," said Owen. "Anytime you're uncomfortable and you want to leave, you can say the word, and I'll spirit you away."

"Turnips."

"Turnips?"

"That's the only vegetable I don't like."

"Turnips it is. Should the word cross your lips, we'll disappear into the night."

And then before I was ready, we were parking in front of the massive brick Charleston Colonial Revival mansion. I had an overwhelming urge to flee the scene, but it was too late. In front of us, a couple arrived in formal attire on a golf cart. I felt like I was having an out-of-body experience. Like Owen was opening the door for another woman, offering her a hand, then his arm. I smiled and thanked him as I was swept by the current into the evening.

"Summertime's Calling Me," by the Catalinas played from the lawn to the right of the house. A salty breeze spiked with jasmine wafted by. Elegant couples climbed the steps to the portico. I focused on breathing.

We walked through the gate and moved through a dream to the doorway. Heavy wooden double doors stood open, and we followed the crowd into a foyer with white marble tile with black diamond accents. I'd been inside the house before, but it had been many years. Built in 1913, it was one of the first waterfront homes along Murray Boulevard. Though it wasn't an historic home, it radiated with character.

The woodwork alone was a work of art. Columns with intricate carvings at the top marked the pass-through to a hallway with a wide staircase. A large stained glass window above the stairway caught my eye. Everywhere I looked, there was something beautiful, but somehow it wasn't stuffy. It felt like someone's home, though never mine. I'd always felt like a poor relation here.

"Lovely," murmured Owen.

"Hadley!" J. T. appeared, wearing the widest grin I'd ever seen. "I was worried you'd back out." He hugged me, then held me at arm's length. "I'd better get a gun."

"What on earth for?" I asked.

"The way you look, there's no way we'll get through this evening without me having to shoot somebody."

"Hopefully, that won't be me," said Owen.

"Oh! Where are my manners? J. T., this is Owen Callaway. Doctor. Doctor Owen Callaway. Owen, this is my brother, John Thomas. Everyone calls him J. T."

They shook hands and exchanged nice to meet yous.

"I was kidding about the gun," said J. T.

"Oh, no, I think it's wise of you to arm yourself. Say, do you have a spare? I seem to have left mine at home. We should be prepared. In that dress, your sister is positively a duel waiting to happen."

J. T. laughed good-naturedly. "I'm happy to know you stand ready to defend her honor. First things first, there are two bars, one on the piazza, through the living room over there. And one outdoors near the guest house." He looked at Owen. "If you drink bourbon, I recommend the signature cocktail. It's a black Manhattan. Come on, I'll show you around."

We followed him past the staircase and to the right, along the gallery, through the sunroom, out a set of glass doors, and down the steps into a magical fairyland that might've been a yard on ordinary days.

A million white lights were strung overhead. On a stage at the edge of the yard, with the Ashley River as a backdrop, a band awaited someone's signal to play. In front of the stage was a dance floor that had been carefully fitted inside the contours of the landscaping, so that it was bordered by shrubs. On the edge of the dance floor and scattered all around the lawn were cocktail tables and stools with bamboo backs. Potted trees with white lights were artfully arranged in groups of three. Savory smells floated by on the breeze as butlers passed trays of hors d'oeuvres.

"So the bar is this way," J. T. headed down a brick-lined path, and we followed.

"J. T.?" I said.

"Yes, Sis?"

"I'd love to meet your date. You do have one? You'll notice mine . . ."

"Perfect timing." J. T. stopped behind a woman with long blonde hair and waited for her to finish what she was saying to the couple in front of her. He touched her on the arm, and she turned around.

I sucked in a lungful of air.

It was the woman I'd seen having lunch with Swinton at Rodney Scott's Whole Hog BBQ.

"Hadley, this is Alex Ireland. Alex, my sister, Hadley Cooper. And this is Owen Callaway."

We all said our hellos and how are yous.

"You work with Charlie Vanderhorst?" I hadn't adequately quashed the amazement in my voice. Could she merely have been discussing Swinton's estate with him over lunch?

"I do," she said. "Do you know Charlie?"

"We go way back," I said. "I work with her too, actually. Oh, I'm not a lawyer. I'm a private investigator."

"*You're* the investigator," said Alex. "I've heard a lot about you, but I had no idea you were J. T.'s sister. It's great to meet you. Charlie's a piece of work, isn't she?"

"She is indeed," I said. "You and I have a client in common. Eugenia Ladson."

Alex's face fell. "I'm still in shock."

"No talking shop tonight, you two," said J. T. "Tonight we feast, we have entirely too much to drink, and we dance like nobody's here to watch."

"Of course." I smiled and mentally slapped my head very hard. Stupid, stupid. Civilized people didn't discuss murder at nice parties. "So how long have you two been dating?"

"Alex and I are good friends," said J. T., in a way that announced that's all they were. I wondered how Alex felt about that. She didn't seem to mind.

We all followed J. T. to the bar at the back corner of the yard.

"What can I get you?" The bartender smiled.

"I'd like one of the signature cocktails," I said.

"Which one?" he asked.

I tossed J. T. a questioning look.

He grimaced, looked away, then back. "There are actually two signature cocktails." He looked at the bartender. "The ladies would like Holy City Smokes. I'll have a black Manhattan." He looked at Owen who ordered a black Manhattan.

I stared at my brother. "You did this?" Not many people knew how much I loved the mezcal drink created by the bartender at Hank's.

"I wish I could take credit for it," said J. T. "I did provide the requested information."

"What's going on?" asked Owen.

"My birthday was two days before J. T.'s," I said. "The Holy City Smoke is my favorite cocktail."

"Ah, well, that's lovely, isn't it?" Owen's voice was calm and soothing, and he made an excellent point. It was a sweet gesture, and there was no need for me to behave childishly. I may feel a bit like I was in hostile territory—Swinton's territory—and I may *feel* like a fish out of water, but Judith and J. T. were doing everything they possibly could to make me feel welcome.

When we had our cocktails, we found a standing table along the edge of the yard to set our glasses on. The crowd was building. The Tams sang "Be Young, Be Foolish, Be Happy." I took it all in.

"This is . . . utterly . . . amazing," I said, trying not to notice no one else seemed to be wearing sequins, or silver dresses for that matter. Most of the ladies wore fitted dresses in summery colors. I'd never seen so many toned women. These ladies took fitness seriously.

J. T. laughed. "Yeah, I think Mom got tired of waiting on me to get married so she could throw an engagement party and a rehearsal dinner. Our joke is that this is my debut. One way or another, Judith was going to throw a big party. Though, between you and me, Dad was uncharacteristically enthusiastic about the whole thing."

I sipped my drink, which was perfect.

"There seem to be a preponderance of young women here," said Owen.

"Yeah." J. T. shook his head. "I think Mom has a glass slipper somewhere she wants them all to try."

Alex picked up her drink and smiled. "To successfully avoiding institutions."

Apparently, she was happily unmarried, which was a good thing, because J. T. had no interest whatsoever in domesticity. Poor Judith.

"The band's ready to start playing," said J. T. "Dance with me, Hadley." He held out a hand.

"Oh, J. T., really . . ." I shook my head.

"It's all I want for my birthday." His eyes twinkled mischievously. "You to dance with me. Come on, Had."

He stood there with his hand outstretched.

I downed my drink. "Fine."

I took his hand and let him lead me to the parquet dance floor.

The opening notes of "Gettin' Jiggy Wit It," played over the sound system.

"Really?" I laughed in disbelief.

"What, what, what, what?" He sang along with Will Smith. "Just dance. The band will play the next song."

So I just forgot where I was and danced with my brother to Will Smith for his birthday. I lost myself in the tune and laughed with him. And I didn't worry who was watching or what they thought. It felt delicious. Perhaps I should do this more often—refuse to worry what people might think of me.

When the song finished, the band started playing "Carolina Girls," as if their cue had been to play it when "Gettin' Jiggy Wit It" was over. J. T. took my hand and spun me around, and the next thing you know, he was shagging, and I was fake shagging, which is something I usually only do after two drinks, or maybe three. I've never had lessons. I don't really know any of the steps. But J. T. did, and he was an excellent leader. I didn't notice until the song stopped that no one had joined us on the dance floor. But when we stopped dancing, they all clapped and cheered.

I froze like a thief in the spotlight. Jesus, take the wheel. *What* was I thinking?

J. T. bowed and gestured to me. Somehow, I slapped myself out of my panic attack. I did a little curtsy, and we both laughed, and he escorted me back to our table.

"Clearly, you have misled me," said Owen.

"What do you mean?" I offered him a happy smile.

"You're an excellent dancer. Come with me."

He took my hand, and then I was back on the dance floor dancing to "You're More Than a Number (in my Little Red Book)," and then "Hold Back the Night."

"Would you like something to eat?" asked Owen when the last strains of "Hold Back the Night" played.

"Yes," I said. "Let me powder my nose first."

"J. T. and Alex have gone mingling, I suspect." Owen was looking in the direction of the table we'd occupied earlier. "I'll find us a spot with chairs."

I climbed the steps and made my way back through the sunroom and found a powder room just off the living room. A painting—a seascape—in the next room caught my eye as I was on my way out. I stepped over to get a closer look. I was close to the other bar—the one through the living room—wasn't I? I should get us fresh drinks. That was through here . . .

"Just keep your ducking wits about you, and everything will be just fine." The voice was low and laced with menace. He did not say ducking.

I ducked into a short hall.

Everette Ladson shot his cuffs and strutted towards the foyer in front of me.

Who had he been talking to?

I waited.

Moments later, Swinton walked by. I waited a three count, then peered out from my spot. They'd come from the study, with its massive dark wood desk, leather chairs, and whiskey decanters. Swinton's study. No one else was in there.

I would love to've been a fly on the wall for that conversation. What on earth was that all about? I knew they'd been friends years ago, but there was nothing friendly about Everette's tone. *Does he have something on you, old man?* What the actual heck was Everette doing here to begin with? He was supposedly grieving. He had no business whatsoever at a black-tie affair.

I found my way through the living room to the piazza. A woman around Judith's age who looked vaguely familiar stood at the far end of the bar, by a window. Who was she? Should I know her? I smiled and waved as I waited for our drinks, and she gave me a little wave back, but I just couldn't place her. I collected our drinks and went to find Owen. He'd scored a table with chairs on a patio near the front of the guest house.

"I brought refreshments," I said.

"How very resourceful you are." He took the glasses and set them on the table.

"I have strategically scouted food," he said. "I think we should start with the main buffet. There are duplicate lines by the house. Then we can check out the specialty stations. I calculate there's enough food here to feed the guests for a month."

"Well, we should do our part then. Lead the way."

Once in a blue moon, I deviate from my food protocol. That night, I'd given myself permission to eat whatever I wanted. But as it turned out, there were ample vegan options on the buffet. Judith, being thoughtful again. I felt a touch guilty eating the non-vegan food, but nevertheless, threw caution to the wind and had some of nearly everything.

The buffet was laden with several kinds of biscuits—sweet potato with ham, cheddar scallion with fried chicken, and butter-milk with cheddar bacon—pimento cheese, shrimp salad, cucumber, and chicken salad tea sandwiches, chilled asparagus with dill dip, mini tomato pies, spinach and artichoke dip with toast rounds, hummus with fresh vegetables, black-eyed pea salad, meatballs, and a massive cheese and charcuterie spread. We piled our plates high.

"I'm afraid we'll have to hit the seafood station next trip," said Owen. "The crab cakes the butlers were passing were delectable. We can't miss the ceviche or the shrimp. After that, I'd like to try the tenderloin—it has its own station. And then, of course, we have to plan for our desserts."

"We may have to dance some more after this plate before we eat anything else." Was that really me suggesting that we dance?

"That's it—strategic eating. You are quite clever."

I rolled my eyes at him as we made our way back to our table.

And there was Judith, standing nearby, as if waiting to speak to us. She was lovely in a pale pink gown, her chin-length blonde hair swept back from her face. Her smile was warm and genuine. "Hadley." She waited until I'd set my plate down, then reached for both my hands. "I'm delighted that you're here, Darlin'."

"Thank you so much for having me—for going out of your way for me. I really appreciate it. You're very kind. Oh—Judith, this is Owen Callaway. Owen, this is Judith Legare, J. T.'s mother."

They both said their nice to meet yous.

"I can't tell you how happy it made me for you to open the dancing with J. T.," she said. "It just did my heart so much good."

"Is that what we did?" I smiled. "We were just having fun. This is an amazing party."

She hesitated. "Hadley, if you could just speak to your father . . . It would mean the world. I don't mean to push."

I inhaled and exhaled. "Of course. I haven't seen him yet. But I will make a point to speak to him." I actually had *seen* him. It just wasn't a good time. Not that I'd been looking for an opportunity.

"Thank you, Sweetheart."

"And Judith, I have a favor to ask you," I said.

"Yes?"

"Could we meet—soon? I need to speak with you about

something. It's rather urgent, actually, but I don't want to get into it tonight, of course."

"By all means. When would you like to do it?"

"Would tomorrow work? Maybe late afternoon?"

"Certainly. Five o'clock?"

"That's perfect. Thank you so much."

"I'll see you then. Enjoy your dinner. And happy birthday, Darlin'."

I smiled my thanks. Judith had no way of knowing my birthday situation. No, that wasn't right. J. T. would surely have told her. It didn't matter. I did what I did to honor my mother. I shouldn't expect every other person I knew to do the same. Especially not Judith.

Owen and I tucked into our food, sampling and taking turns saying, "Try this." Everything was delicious. I'd skipped the charcuterie but had picked up some pickled okra from the display. I'd just bit into a piece when I saw Cash and nearly choked on the okra.

What in the name of sanity and prudence was *he* doing here?

He was walking across the lawn, a drink in his hand, looking better than was good for me in formal attire. A shadow passed over my happy.

"Everything all right?" asked Owen.

"I just nearly inhaled a piece of okra."

"Well, it is tasty."

I smiled, pushed some food around on my plate. I guess it made sense. Of course J. T. and Cash knew each other. They were friends when we were dating. I just didn't think they still kept in touch. J. T. hadn't mentioned it. But he wouldn't, would he?

I watched Cash stop to talk to Alex. Did he know her? It would appear so.

"Shall I get us another drink?" Owen asked.

I smiled at him, perhaps too brightly. "That sounds great, actually."

He gave me an odd look, then touched me lightly on the shoulder as he passed behind my chair.

I tried not to watch Cash and Alex move to the dance floor, looked away when he took her hand. I'd been having such a lovely time. A sadness settled into my chest, and unwelcome tears welled up in my eyes. Get a grip, Hadley.

I made my way to the bathroom, and I know I stayed in there with the door locked, focusing on my breathing and making sure there were no telltale tears pooling up, for longer than was polite in the circumstances. I smiled my apologies to the woman waiting when I came out. I just needed a few more minutes alone.

I wandered out through the living room, past the bar on the piazza, and down the steps to the pool deck. My plan was to just take the long way back to the party, take a few minutes and gather myself. I meandered by the pool, around to the pergola, and just as I was ready to round the corner to the gravel driveway that leads back to the lawn on the other side of the house, I heard a woman talking.

"I'm at a party. This isn't a good time."

Now, most people would have continued on their way, I know. But my professional inclinations take over sometimes—I can't help myself. I'm predisposed to eavesdrop. I peeked around a palmetto. It was Alex, standing on the driveway between the pool deck and the lawn by herself. She must've come straight here after they finished their dance. Where was Cash?

"That's not possible," she said. "Beck—"

Beck? I caught my breath.

"Look, just calm down," she said. "Everything is fine. You are imagining things . . . Well, if that happens, it's not your fault . . . No, I certainly won't blame you . . . I appreciate your telling me, but it's really not a problem. Trust me. I would know if she'd figured it out. Look, I've got to go. Stop worrying."

I waited a five count and walked around the corner. She'd gone.

I retraced my steps, sat on the end of a lounge chair by the pool, and stared at the water.

Alex was Swinton's estate attorney—*and Eugenia's*. Alex was very talented with trusts and whatnot, had set up some very creative vehicles for Eugenia. Alex and Beck, my client, who I was housesitting for, were just on the phone discussing something he was concerned someone had figured out. My mind swiveled back to the secret garden, so perfect for North. Such an unusual feature . . . not to mention all the things about the house that seemed designed just for me. I'd known something was off, too precise. I'd left a message with Beck's assistant earlier saying it was urgent that we speak. Which had clearly spooked him.

Somehow, I had missed something when I did Beckett Driscoll's background check. Could Eugenia possibly be behind the house on Sullivan's Island? Did it really belong to her? She'd given Fish her house, and had arranged for Meryl's care . . . Had she, for some reason known only to her, decided to give me such a beyond extravagant gift? Maybe to keep Everette from getting more of her estate?

No. I couldn't believe that. Surely, she'd want most of what she had to go to her children. It made no sense, anyway. I hadn't known Eugenia long enough for her to know so much about what I liked. She couldn't know about North Pickens, much less anything about his condition. She couldn't know what my fantasy house looked like, that I dreamed of living on Sullivan's Island, or that I loved punching a bag for stress relief. Something else was going on here.

I needed to get myself together and focus on not ruining J. T.'s birthday party. There would be time enough to sort this out tomorrow. I took a deep breath, stood, and made my way back to the table.

"There you are," said Owen. "I was beginning to think someone had absconded with you."

I smiled at him. "Let's dance."

He took my hand and led me to the dance floor. The band

played "I Only Have Eyes for You." I swayed to the music with the sweetest doctor I'd ever met, one who might even like me—a man who was the fantasy of every unattached, heterosexual woman in the country.

And I searched for Cash in the crowd over Owen's shoulder.

Chapter Forty-Seven

Saturday, June 19, 8:15 p.m.
Charleston, South Carolina
Mrs. Josephine Huger (you-JEE)

Well, first, I have to say, Judith Legare is the absolute consummate hostess. Arthur and I had a wonderful time at John Thomas's birthday party. Practically everyone we know was there. Hamby's did an excellent job with the food, as they always do, and Judith selected a nice variety. Arthur particularly enjoyed the tenderloin, but of course he would. I rarely let him have red meat anymore.

You should have seen the floral arrangements. Simply exquisite—I meant to get a closer look at those. There were white hydrangeas, but then an unusual mix of greenery and some woodsy looking accents—mushrooms, dried okra, lotus pods and millet. I imagine the idea was to keep them from being too feminine, and it was brilliant, if you ask me. Judith had a large arrangement on the table in the foyer, plus several smaller pieces scattered around the house, and then, of course, the buffet arrangements.

Between the food, Judith's silver trays, and the flowers, those buffet tables were magnificent.

And the band—you've heard the East Coast Party band, I know you have. Between you and me, I think they're the best band in the area for . . . Well, all right, most people do book them for weddings. Some might say it was a mite over the top, having a black-tie affair, with a nine-piece band, and what could've easily passed for a wedding cake for a fortieth birthday, but I say why not? Why not celebrate your only son, who's doing a fine job gradually taking over his daddy's business, not getting into drugs, not going through wives like they're harem girls, *not* causing his momma to lie awake at night worrying herself sick, driving her to prescription pills. That's something to celebrate if you ask me. We have friends who have spent many times more than Judith and Swinton spent on that party on bail and rehab.

Anyway, I personally didn't find the party itself out of line at all, though I will freely admit it was much more like a wedding reception than a birthday party. What was shocking was that Everette Ladson was there. We just buried that man's poor wife not two days ago. Well, I suppose they buried her eventually. I understand she was cremated. Apparently, there was a misunderstanding with the arrangements? But there Everette was, in a white dinner jacket, strutting around like a peacock, without a care in the world. It was unseemly. And that was before the incident.

Now, whatever you do, don't breathe a word about this. Whatever was going on, I want no part of it. I had gone to powder my nose, and I told Arthur I would meet him by the bar outside. Well, I meant the one on the piazza. I was waiting for him down at the end, by a window, and I suppose it was the window to Swinton's office. Eavesdropping is not something I approve of, and I would never do that on purpose. But I was standing there when Swinton walked into the room and Everette came in behind him and closed the door.

I couldn't make out everything that was said—not that I was trying to do that, mind you. But I couldn't help but overhear Everette threatening Swinton. I couldn't believe it. They were friends, I thought, for as far back as I can remember. Like I said, I didn't hear everything, but one thing I distinctly heard Everette say was, "For Judith's sake, you will do what you've done for nearly fifty years and keep your mouth shut, or I will destroy all of you." He threw some bad language in there as well, but that's certainly not worth repeating.

I just can't imagine what all that was about. I was completely flustered a few minutes later when Swinton's daughter came out on the piazza to order drinks. She waved at me, but I don't believe we've been introduced.

Now, I am here to tell you, there was not a lovelier woman at that party, and it was positively packed with beautiful women. Hadley—that's her name. I was having trouble remembering, but Judith reminded me of it. Hadley was wearing a silver sequin dress, and you know how sometimes sequins can approach unladylike? Well, this dress toed that line beautifully. She was simply stunning, and every inch a lady. She surely stood out from the crowd, but in a good way. Arthur agreed she was definitely the belle of that ball. There were quite a few young women there who were happy to learn she was John Thomas's sister, let me tell you. Especially after they danced together to kick things off.

Oh—and I have to tell you just the sweetest thing. When Hadley and John Thomas were dancing? You should have seen Swinton and Judith. They were standing right beside Arthur and me, and I have never seen either of them as happy as they were to see those two children dancing together. I could've sworn I saw Swinton Legare dabbing at his eyes, and that's something that stays with you. He's never been one for emotional displays.

Judith's smile was . . . Well, it brought tears to my eyes. She was positively joyous. And I couldn't help but think, that's just Judith—she is simply good to her core. A lot of women would've resented Hadley. Most women would not have wanted her at their son's birthday party. But there she was, hugging Swinton and smiling, and at one point, they did this little high-five. She went out of her way to include Hadley. It was almost as if she threw the party for the both of them.

But back to Hadley . . . She had a date, a doctor, as I understand it. A very handsome man, and he seemed quite attentive. But remember the police officer who I told you came and sat with her at Hank's a couple of weeks ago? After the singing and harmonica playing? Well, he was there too, the police officer, not that fool with the harmonica. I suppose the police officer and John Thomas are friends. But what was interesting was the way he barely took his eyes off of Hadley all evening. I know what a man in love looks like, and that young man is positively smitten. And let me tell you, he did not care for that doctor one bit.

I enjoy people watching, especially at parties. Hadley and the doctor were a striking couple. But there were times I noticed her watching that police officer exactly the same way he was watching her. There's a story there, you mark my words. I hope they work it all out before he ends up in Alcoholics Anonymous. Towards the end of the evening, he pulled up a stool at the bar on the piazza, I guess so he didn't have to keep walking back over there. Young people have too many choices if you ask me. When things get hard, they walk away instead of fighting for each other. In my day, you worked things out. Why, where would Arthur and I be if we'd given up the first time we disagreed? No place good, I can promise you that.

The other thing that will be interesting to watch is whether John Thomas finds a wife among the bevy of young beauties Judith made sure were at the party. He had a date. Alex Ireland, the attorney? You remember, I mentioned her before? She's a beautiful girl. But Judith says they're just friends, and Judith is well past ready for grandchildren. I wouldn't be surprised to learn John Thomas had Alex on his arm for the sole purpose of keeping the rest of the women at a safe distance. But she strikes me as quite the smart cookie.

If she's set her cap for John Thomas, she hides it well, as one does.

Chapter Forty-Eight

The morning after J. T.'s birthday party, my mind churned like a multivortex tornado. I had to school myself to focus on what was most urgent—finding out who had killed Eugenia and clearing Kateryna. My messy personal life would have to wait.

I took the elevator to the fourth floor of Meryl's building, found her condo, and rang the bell.

The door opened immediately, as if she'd been standing there waiting.

"Hi, I'm Meryl. You must be Hadley." She looked me straight in the eye and displayed a very forthright manner. As had been my impression the day before, she looked the picture of health, and a much younger woman than the sixty-five-year-old I knew her to be. Her wavy, dark brown hair hung loose. Barefoot, in a long bohemian-looking print skirt and a white tank top, she wore a relaxed air.

"I am. Thank you so much for seeing me."

"Come in, come in." She opened the door wide. "The living room is right through here. Please, make yourself at home."

A bar with a row of stools separated the kitchen to my left from the living room. Wide-planked hardwoods gave the space a warm feel. The room was tastefully decorated with an uncluttered, coastal style. I took a seat in one of the cream-colored club chairs, and she sat to my right on a tweed sofa.

"You're here about Eugenia." It was a statement.

"Yes. She was a friend of yours, I understand."

"She was a good friend *to* me," she said. "We really didn't become friends until after my twin sister passed away. You know about the accident?"

"I know what was in the papers. Is there anything you can tell me that wasn't covered?"

"Well now, you get right to the point. I like that. I don't know much that wasn't printed. I'll tell you what I do know. But I have to say, I can't see what this could possibly have to do with Eugenia's death. I hope you aren't thinking—with the provision in her will—that I had anything to do with this?"

"Oh, no. Of course not." I can lie straight faced when the job calls for it. "I do know she was still bothered by what happened that day, all these years later."

"Let's just get this all out on the table right now. Eugenia saw to it I had what I needed while she was alive, and her will provides for my care after her death. There's nothing I get with her dead that I didn't get while she was alive."

I nodded and smiled. She seemed to have some steam, so I waited for her to keep talking.

She tilted her head from side to side in an acknowledgment. "That's true, about Eugenia being bothered by the accident. She was. Eugenia was bighearted. My father died of a broken heart not three years after my sister's death. Mom had a stroke a year later, and I lost her too. Eugenia got in touch with me after my mother's stroke. I had the impression she'd been keeping tabs on me. She cared that I was by myself. She made it her business to see to it I was taken care of." She laughed. "The first thing she did was get me on a better diet, get me to exercising. I'm a whole lot healthier than I was back then, I'll tell you that."

"You have MS, is that right?" I asked.

"I do, but I've been in remission for years."

"You said you didn't become friends with Eugenia until after your sister passed away. Was Eugenia close friends with your sister?" I knew what Birdie thought. But I also knew there were things Birdie didn't know.

"No, I don't think she was." Meryl wore an odd expression.

I waited to see if she would elaborate, but she didn't.

"I understand Amelia and Charles spent a lot of time boating and were very familiar with the river."

"That's true, but it's like the South Carolina Department of Natural Resources officers said at the time. Sometimes the strongest swimmers drown. Sometimes the best boaters have bad luck. They get thrown into dangerous situations. Things happen fast on the water."

"Do they know what caused the accident?"

"No, there's really no way to know. I think that drove my father crazy. He wanted answers, but there just weren't any," she said. "They were both thrown from the boat. It was found near Limehouse Bridge, so that's where the accident happened. Of course, it's not the same bridge that's there today. They replaced it in 2003. Amelia and Charles weren't found until two days later, and the current had moved them a good ways downriver. But it wouldn't have mattered. The coroner told Daddy Amelia drowned at the time of the accident, or close to it anyway. Charles must've been thrown against the bridge support. He died of head trauma, also at the time of the accident." She stared at a spot over my shoulder.

"I'm so sorry to ask you to revisit such painful memories," I said. "You mentioned there were things not in the newspaper."

She hesitated. "I really don't see why this matters now."

"Was your sister expecting a baby?" I asked.

A troubled look crept into her eyes. "How could you know that?"

"I spoke to one of the DNR officers," I said. "He thought that someone else should know."

"Yes, well, that's the only thing they didn't report. No point in it. Daddy asked the officers to keep that quiet, and they respected his wishes."

"Did Charles know she was expecting?" I asked.

Meryl shook her head. "No." She studied her hands in her lap. "I suppose, like the officer said, maybe someone else should know this . . . It wasn't Charles's child."

A spot in the back of my brain tingled, and I held my breath.

"Charles was raised very conservatively. His family went to church twice a week. He wanted to marry Amelia, he said. But he wanted to wait until they were married . . . for sex. Amelia was not one for waiting, for anything."

"Do you know who the father of Amelia's child was?" I asked, though I already knew the answer.

Meryl sighed. "Everette Ladson."

"Are you certain?" Did Eugenia somehow know this? Is that why she was haunted by the accident? Because Everette's child had perished? How did this fit into the picture?

"Yes, of course. It could only have been him. He was the only man my sister ever knew, in the biblical sense. Eugenia and I never discussed this, you understand. There was no point, really. Why tell her things that would only hurt her? Everette and Amelia had been seeing each other for a while behind Eugenia's back. He told Amelia he was going to end things with Eugenia. He had a kind of spell over my sister, I think. I'm not proud to say she kept Charles dangling, but she fully intended to break up with him. She said Everette was going to marry her; he'd promised. But there's no point in airing all that dirty laundry now, is there?"

"Was there ever any suggestion that your sister and Charles Butler . . . that someone else was in the boat with them the day of the accident?" I asked.

"Not so far as I'm aware," said Meryl. "Mom and Dad and I were in Baltimore. I had a doctor's appointment the next morning, at Johns Hopkins. We left that morning after breakfast. The last time I spoke to Amelia, she and Charles planned to spend the day together, just the two of them, on the boat. I urged her to tell him . . . to break up with him, at least. I think she was finally ready to do that."

"Meryl, does anyone else know your sister was carrying Everette Ladson's child?"

"Not that I'm aware."

There was so much I hadn't figured out at that point. But I had a strong conviction Meryl was in grave danger. "Listen to me carefully. Go pack a bag. We need to get you on a plane to anywhere else."

She gave me a look that called my sanity into serious question.

"Something about this accident was troubling Eugenia. I haven't worked out what just yet. But, if I'm right, Everette killed her—a woman he was married to for forty-two years—to keep her fortune. Her will is a huge problem for him, and he's going to be contesting it in court. If he believes you or anyone else holds knowledge that can hurt him in the eyes of the court, or in the court of public opinion, I seriously doubt he'd hesitate to kill again."

It took me a while to get her to agree. Eventually, she conceded that while I almost certainly suffered from an overactive imagination, perhaps erring on the side of caution was the best idea.

While she packed, I bought a one-way ticket in her name to Seattle, Washington—a place I chose randomly because there was a direct flight leaving soon—then I dropped her at the airport. Maybe I *was* overreacting. But I'd rather laugh at myself later than forever regret not keeping Meryl safe when I had the chance. Taking care of her had been important to Eugenia, so it was important to me.

Chapter Forty-Nine

I was headed to Charleston. Whether I liked it or not, Swinton and Judith were the only ones who could tell me what the picture in Eugenia's safe meant. If there was a connection to Eugenia's death, they would know. I had an appointment with Judith, but not until five. This couldn't wait. When I stopped at the light at International Boulevard and 526, my phone rang. Snakes on a popsicle stick. It was Swinton. This was danged strange. Did he get some sort of alert I was headed his way?

"Hello?" I said like I had no idea who was calling.

"Miss Cooper?" The voice was female.

"Yes?"

"This is Marigold Williams calling. I'm Mr. and Mrs. Legare's household manager."

"What can I do for you?"

"Mrs. Legare asked me to let you know she'll need to reschedule your appointment this afternoon."

"Is she available?" I asked. "It's urgent I speak with her."

"I'm afraid not. Will Wednesday afternoon work for you instead?"

"No . . . listen . . . I'm so sorry. I don't mean to be rude. But this may literally be a matter of life and death. I need to speak to

Judith as soon as is humanly possible. I'm actually on my way there right now, so—"

"I'm afraid she isn't here," said Marigold.

The light changed. I was moving through the intersection.

"When will she be back?"

"I'm afraid I couldn't say."

I gripped the steering wheel with both hands, my frustration building. "What about Swinton?"

"Mr. Legare isn't home either."

"Where are they?" They hadn't been planning to leave town last night. Judith had agreed to talk to me. Had she spoken to Swinton, and he decided that was a bad idea? Did this have anything to do with the tail end of the conversation I'd caught last night between Everette and Swinton?

Marigold Williams hesitated, then said, "Mrs. Legare is being seen at MUSC."

That stopped me cold. "Is she all right?"

"I believe so," said Marigold. "She had a seizure this morning. They're treating her, getting her blood sugar stabilized. At this point, they haven't said whether they plan to keep her overnight. But she was worried about having to reschedule your meeting. She wouldn't have done that under any other circumstances."

I felt like a heel. "Of course she has to take care of herself. Please let her know I'm thinking of her, and I hope she feels better soon."

"I certainly will. Will Wednesday work for you, then?"

Apparently, I had no other choice. "Yes, of course. But would you ask her to let me know if she happens to feel up to talking before then?"

"I'll let her know."

I changed lanes and headed towards Mount Pleasant on 526.

Chapter Fifty

Pepper Townsend was next on my list. I called her, and she agreed to meet me at her office at four. I hadn't eaten since breakfast and was starving. I grabbed a veggie burrito, fresco, from Taco Bell and ate it in the parking lot of Pepper's Coleman Boulevard office.

She parked her Mercedes beside Jolene at three forty-five.

"Are you Hadley?" she approached the driver's side window.

"Yes. Thank you for meeting me on such short notice."

"Well, you may as well come on in." She'd evidently been showing houses. She was dressed in a suit and heels similar to the outfit she'd worn for the open house.

By the time I made it to the door, she had it unlocked. "My office is this way."

I followed her past the reception area to a large office. She dropped onto a yellow leather sofa and gestured towards a matching chair. "Make yourself comfortable. I have got to get out of these shoes." She slid off her impressively high heels.

"Now, what can I do for you?" she asked.

"As I mentioned on the phone, I'm investigating Eugenia Ladson's death."

"Poor Eugenia." She shook her head. "I still can't believe what happened."

"Yes, it is shocking. And I am bound and determined to see to it that whoever is responsible spends the rest of his life in jail."

"What can I do to help?" she asked.

"Do you know Jordyn Jackman?"

A confused look flashed across her face. "Well, yes. I make it a point to know my competition."

I nodded. "Would you say the two of you are friends?"

"I suppose so."

I had to make a decision here. I could ask her straight up what she and Jordyn were talking about the morning of the open house. But then she might get spooked, clam up, and not let me see the sign in sheets. Pepper had a professional reputation to protect.

I changed gears. "It's possible one of your guests witnessed something the morning of the open house."

"What on earth would that be?"

"I have reason to believe one of the parties involved in the murder actually came to the open house." This was true. She just didn't sign in.

"You don't mean it? You think they were casing the joint?"

"It's possible. Could I see the sign-in sheets? Just to eliminate this as a possibility?"

"Well, I don't see why not. You're not going to spam these people with emails, are you? That's what most of them are worried about."

"I promise not to do that."

"Hang on a minute," she said. "I'll make you a copy. We had a good turnout, overall. Slow at first. But the afternoon got busy." She walked over to a light-toned wood credenza, opened a file drawer, and walked her fingers back to the folder she needed. She pulled out a piece of paper and made a copy, then handed it to me. "Here you go. I hope this helps."

"I think it will. Thank you so much."

Chapter Fifty-One

Poe's Tavern is on Middle Street on Sullivan's Island, near Station 22, in a white house with a big front porch and a metal roof. The front yard is encircled by a white picket fence with a wide border that explodes with brightly colored blooms year-round. Tables with big navy canvas umbrellas with Shock Top logos are scattered around the yard, and big fans keep the air circulating.

By eleven Monday morning, my patience was done for. I arrived at Poe's ten minutes before they opened. As soon as the hostess appeared, I asked for a table outside. She carried two menus to a table by the fence under the shade of a large crepe myrtle. My guest would arrive at eleven thirty.

I'd known the woman I was looking for would be the first name on the list. Lisa Hudson had helpfully filled in the requested phone number on the sheet. It was a Mississippi area code, and I held my breath until she answered and confirmed they were still in the area and graciously agreed to meet me at Poe's for lunch.

The waitress brought me a glass of iced tea, and I sipped it and watched for Lisa. When she appeared at the gate of the white picket fence that encircled the front yard of the restaurant, I stood and waved. Her face split into a big friendly grin, and she headed in my direction.

We introduced ourselves, ordered Lisa some iced tea—half and half—and studied the menu. I knew what I wanted, but I also knew she needed a moment, so I looked at mine too. When the waitress came back, I ordered my usual, a veggie Amontillado, no cheese, no sour cream, extra pico de gallo, extra guacamole. Since I was stress eating, I splurged and got the fries. Lisa ordered the shrimp salad sandwich with fries. Finally, that was done, and the waitress took our menus and hustled away.

"How long are y'all in town for?" I asked.

"Until Saturday," she said. "My husband, Allen, and I are here with our kids, April and Cal and April's husband, Sam, for two weeks. We're celebrating our anniversary. One of the milestones."

"Congratulations," I said.

"Thank you." She nodded, sipped her tea.

"I know you're curious what this is all about," I said.

"Well . . . yeah." Lisa laughed.

"You went to an open house Saturday before last on Tradd Street."

An uneasy look crossed her face. "We did. I'm the daughter of a retired realtor slash builder slash broker slash property manager and the wife of a general contractor. Allen is also a gifted finish carpenter. We love looking at houses. We're interested in the craftsmanship and the trends. It's just something we do on vacation. We flew in early on the 12th. We couldn't get into the condo until three o'clock. So, we drove through Charleston looking for open houses. That's the first one we came to."

I nodded, smiled. "I love looking at houses too. Did anything unusual happen while you were there?"

She took a sip of her tea. "Unusual, like how?"

"Did you see or hear anything that disturbed you?" I asked.

She drew a long breath and exhaled slowly. "It was nothing, really. I'm sure this happens."

"What do you mean?"

"I mean realtors are people too. I don't want to cause trouble for anyone. She seemed really nice."

"Pepper?" I asked. "She is very nice. She's a friend of a friend of mine. Our friend—her client—was recently murdered."

Lisa's brown eyes were so dark you couldn't see the pupils. They widened with surprise. "I'm so sorry to hear that."

"I'm investigating the murder," I said. "And this is very important to my investigation. Whatever you heard, or saw . . ."

Creases appeared in her forehead. "How do you know I heard anything at all?"

I rolled my lips in and out. I was going to have to trust her if I wanted her to trust me. "My client, who owned that house on Tradd Street, asked me to put cameras in the house. She thought her husband was unfaithful. It looks like he was."

I could see the implications registering on her face.

I continued. "I had a camera in the kitchen, but not the sunroom."

She nodded. "Okay, well . . . believe me when I tell you, the last thing I intended to do was to eavesdrop."

"Oh, of course."

"I had gotten a pebble in my shoe. I sat down in the kitchen, took my shoe off. And then the realtor and another lady came in from the garden. They were in the sunroom chatting. One of them said something about it warming up outside. Neither of them were really dressed for being outdoors in the heat.

"Anyway, before I knew what was happening, the realtor—Pepper, was saying something like, 'Yeah, poor thing, she found out her husband was having an affair. But that's okay, she's going to nail his hide to the barn. She got herself a private investigator to follow him everywhere he goes.'"

I absorbed that. Pepper had told Jordyn Jackman that Eugenia had hired a PI. She told her that Saturday morning. Jordyn would certainly have called Everette immediately, or rushed to wherever he was to tell him. At the time, I was under the delusion that the cameras in the house would do the job for me within a week or so. I was settling into the house and getting ready to have lunch with J. T. at Gnome Cafe. Those were my plans anyway.

Everette knew that Eugenia had hired me.

He knew I was following him.

This changed everything.

"That's all I heard," said Lisa. "I put my shoe on as fast as I could and got out of there. It was none of my business. And it made me uncomfortable, that they'd see me in the kitchen and know I'd overheard. We left and did our own walking tour of Charleston until time for lunch."

A server dropped off our lunch. Lisa and I chatted about what they'd done and planned to do on vacation while we enjoyed our burgers. But I was multitasking. One part of my brain was planning my next steps.

After lunch, I thanked Lisa, climbed in Jolene, and shuffled my thinking music playlist. I headed towards Greenville with "Already Gone," by the Eagles playing on the stereo.

Chapter Fifty-Two

Soby's was likely busy every night, but maybe Mondays was the least busy. I was there thirty minutes before opening and managed to speak with Brookelynne, a helpful hostess. While Brookelynne was sympathetic to the plight of a young woman from Ukraine wrongly accused of murder, she couldn't, of course, share anything that might compromise a guest. She did, however, insist on seating me at Table 301—the upstairs table with an amazing view for which the restaurant group was named. Table 301 was quite near where Everette and his friends had sat the evening they dined at Soby's. Brookelynne neither winked nor nodded, but I had a good feeling.

After she seated me, she said something to a waiter on her way down the stairs. He looked my way, then hustled over to my table and poured me a glass of water.

"Good evening, I'm Jeremy. I'll be taking care of you this evening. Can I start you off with a cocktail?" A gentleman of somewhere in the vicinity of fifty, Jeremy had the polish of an experienced waiter.

I knew Jeremy would be in a much better frame of mind if I started with a cocktail. A single diner . . . mine wouldn't be his biggest check of the evening. That's what he was thinking at that moment, anyway. The least I could do is order a cocktail. As it happened, they had a mezcal drink on the menu. "I'd like a Smoke on the Horizon, please."

"Excellent choice. I'll be right back with that."

Moments later, when he set the drink in front of me, he said, "What brings you in this evening?"

"Jeremy, let's say I'm writing a book."

"Oh, that's amazing. What's the book about?"

"It's about a man who needs an alibi for something horrible he's about to do. He plans a dinner with several friends, and while the others are drinking heavily, he has the waiter bring him drinks that look like bourbon, but they're something else entirely."

He seemed to be mulling that.

"By the way, I'm ravenously hungry. I'm also a vegan. What would you recommend?"

"We've got you . . . chef could put together an appetizer of the veggie components from a few of our appetizers . . . some crispy potatoes, Brussels sprouts, maybe a little pickled okra. For a salad course, we could do the strawberry fields salad without the goat cheese. And for an entree, we have the Ponzu marinated tofu bowl."

"That all sounds amazing. I'll have that, please."

"All of it?"

"Yes, please. And I'll want some dessert as well."

"Perhaps some mixed berries?"

"That sounds perfect. And one more thing, Jeremy?"

"Yes, ma'am."

Thankfully, I had called Tallulah on the drive from the Lowcountry, and she'd approved what I was about to do up front. "I'm doing a pay it forward challenge this evening. I'd like to pick up the check for every table seated right now. But discretion, Jeremy, is so important to me. So that everything is fair, as well as discreet, I will of course tip the waiters and waitresses thirty percent, and I'd like to add your tip of thirty percent on the total as well."

Perhaps for the first time in a distinguished career, Jeremy was speechless. I gave him a moment. Eventually, he nodded. "How very generous of you, ma'am. I'll take care of that."

"Thank you, Jeremy."

"And about your book . . ."

"Yes?"

"That very thing actually happened to me on a Saturday night two weeks ago."

"On the twelfth?"

"That's right."

"Go on . . ."

"I had a party of four. One of the gentlemen excused himself to go to the men's room. He pulled me aside, said he was embarrassed for his friends to know he was in AA. He said they'd all order bourbon, likely quite a lot of it. And I should charge him for bourbon, but bring him tea instead, in a bourbon glass. He also tipped me quite well. But not well enough that he should get away with something horrible."

I opened my phone and showed him Everette's photo. "Is this him?"

"Yes, ma'am. It surely is."

Chapter Fifty-Three

To say that Leland Marchant, Everette's college roommate, was initially reluctant to speak with me would be an understatement. But Leland was an attorney, and seemed absolutely convinced he was the smartest person in any conversation. In the end, I think he decided he could "handle me" for Everette. I made sure to tell him twice that if he spoke to Everette before he met with me—or after —he could expect SLED agents at his door within the hour. That was a bluff, but an effective one. It was a risk he couldn't take. Because I knew the kind of people Leland called friends, we met at the entrance to Falls Park.

I stopped by Spill the Beans and got some sorbet, then took a seat at one of the cafe tables by the rock wall overlooking the park. It was public enough for me to feel safe, and private enough for a conversation. I opened the Voice Memos app on my phone, tapped record, and spoke clearly into the mic. "Meeting with Leland Marchant, entrance to Falls Park, Greenville, South Carolina, Monday, June 22." Then, I slid my phone in the side pocket of my purse, microphone end up.

At ten past eight, he stopped at the edge of the patio and scanned the area, a tense look on his face. He wore pressed khakis, a golf shirt, polished loafers, and a smug veneer. I lifted a hand to signal him, and he walked over and took the chair across from me.

"Want to get some ice cream?" I licked my cone of sorbet. "It's delicious."

He made a face designed to communicate his utter distaste for me and all my ancestors. "I don't know what you hope to accomplish here, Ms. Cooper."

"Seriously? I would've thought you'd've figured that out riiight off." I spoke slowly.

He rolled his eyes, gave his head a dismissive shake. "Don't waste my time."

"Your friend, Everette, is going to jail. You will not stop that from happening. You have a very small, minuscule, in fact, window of opportunity to save yourself. You, Mr. Marchant, don't waste *my* time."

His eyes took on a wary look.

I continued. "SLED will arrest Everette before dawn tomorrow. You can be a witness, or an accessory. The choice is yours. Decide now."

"Who are you again? How do you fit into this? Because SLED doesn't typically give subjects a warning. And you don't look like a SLED agent to me."

"Oh, I'm not a SLED agent," I said. "I told you, I'm a PI. I'm the PI Everette used to fabricate an alibi, and I'm highly ticked off about that. I'm the person, Leland, who knows what happened here on Saturday the 12th."

"I had dinner with my college roommate—a retired judge— and two other friends, an award-winning local realtor, and a doctor. I don't know what you think you know, but there was nothing clandestine about it. We had dinner at Soby's. We all had too much to drink. I Ubered home, as did Mike and Bryce. Everette stumbled over to the Westin Poinsett."

"And then what happened?" I asked.

"Not a ducking thing." His language was much more colorful than that.

"Who does the Honda belong to?" I asked. "I couldn't find one registered to you. And frankly, that's not really your style, is it?"

His face screwed up in a mocking expression. "What?" He laughed an ugly laugh. "What the duck does the Honda have to do with anything?"

"Who does it belong to?"

"A car lot over on Wade Hampton Boulevard. A neighbor of mine owns it."

"Where did you leave it?" I asked.

"In the parking lot of Second Presbyterian Church on River Street. What does a secondhand Honda have to do with anything at all?"

"You really don't know?" I had a pretty good crap detector. I almost believed him.

"Know what?"

"Oh, come on, surely, you're not this dense. Everette's wife was murdered in her home several hours later. Surely, you read the news coverage."

"Of course I know his wife was killed—by an immigrant woman. That's what the newspaper said."

I shook my head. "No, Kateryna Petrenko was framed. Everette asked you to leave the Honda in the church parking lot?"

"Well, yes, he did. But it had nothing to do with any murder."

"Why?" I asked. "Why did he tell you he needed you to leave a grey Honda Accord in a church parking lot, several blocks from the hotel he was staying in?"

"He wanted to test drive it, have it checked out by a mechanic. He was doing a favor for a friend who wanted to help her maid out. She needed a reliable car, and they thought a Honda was a good, reliable choice. Everette found it online. He knew the guy who owned the lot was my neighbor. Why are we talking about a ducking Honda?" He might've been foaming at the mouth a little bit. "The church parking lot was a convenient place where

Everette wouldn't run up a big parking bill or have to feed a meter." As he talked, doubt crept into his voice.

I nodded. "Did you know that Kateryna Petrenko, the young woman who was arrested, drives a grey Honda Accord?"

His face flushed. "No."

"A witness saw a grey Honda Accord in Eugenia Ladson's driveway the night she was killed."

"Look . . ." He stammered. "This has to be a coincidence. There is no way Everette could've driven to Sullivan's Island that night. He could barely walk. He was drunk, for crying out loud."

I nodded. "I fell for that act. But no, he wasn't."

"What—"

"He asked the waiter to bring him tea instead of bourbon. The waiter has made a statement." I might've left out who exactly the waiter had made his statement to, which could've led Leland to jump to the conclusion that the waiter had given an official statement to law enforcement . . . But, I never said that.

All the blood rushed from Leland Marchant's face. You couldn't manufacture that kind of reaction.

I said, "Everette Ladson drove a car you surreptitiously left for him to Sullivan's Island. He killed his wife, drove back, and slipped back into his hotel room."

"No." He shook his head. "That's not possible."

I took one of Cash's cards out of my pocket, laid it on the table, and slid it towards him. "I'm afraid it is. And if he used you without your knowledge, I suggest you call Agent Reynolds immediately and get that on the record."

He lowered his voice, looked away. "How much do you want?"

"Oh, no. This isn't about money."

"Everything always is."

"I feel sad for you." I pulled a pad and pen out of my purse. "What's the name of the car lot?"

"Reliable Rides."

"Is the car still there?" I asked.

"How would I know?"

"Listen to me good. If you tip Everette off . . . Well, you know better than I do how many crimes you could be charged with. Be smart."

I drove by the car lot before I headed back to the Lowcountry. A grey Honda Accord sat on the back row, with a stick-figure family sticker on the back and a "Low Mileage" sign on the front. I took plenty of pictures.

Chapter Fifty-Four

I called Cash right after I left Greenville.

He answered on the first ring. "Hadley?" I would analyze what sounded like hope in his voice later.

"Cash, hey. Listen. If you get a call from a number you don't recognize—one from the Upstate—take the call."

"What's going on?"

"Everette Ladson knew I was following him. He deliberately used me to create the illusion of an ironclad alibi. He didn't drink alcohol the evening before Eugenia's murder. His friend left him a grey Honda Accord a few blocks from his hotel. Everette drove the Honda to Sullivan's Island. Cash . . . Everette Ladson killed his wife." I resisted the urge to add, *Like I told you.*

"Where are you now?" he asked.

"On 385 headed home."

"Walk me through it," he said.

So I did. I told him about Lisa Hudson at the open house, Jeremy the waiter, and Leland Marchant and the Honda.

"But the video—the footage where you think he was breaking into Kateryna Petrenko's house. Whoever that was . . . that incident happened the Monday before that. Lisa Hudson didn't overhear the conversation between the realtors until Saturday morning. The timeline is wrong."

"I think he must've already had a plan. Then two things forced him to execute it. One, he witnessed the fight between Eugenia and Kateryna at Dunleavy's that Monday, giving him the perfect setup. That's when he swapped the knives. Then, finding out an investigator was following him . . . He couldn't pass up an opportunity to have the perfect alibi and use Eugenia's own investigator against her."

"Does he know that you're the investigator?" he asked.

"I can't imagine how he would," I said. "I don't think Eugenia told Pepper Townsend my name. She didn't recognize it when I asked her for the sign-in sheets. She couldn't have told Jordyn something she didn't know."

"Even so. Best to lay low until I get all this sorted out," he said. "I'm getting a call. This may be your guy. Good work, Hadley."

"Thanks." I won't lie, that gave me a warm, fuzzy feeling.

Traffic was light on the way home, and I made good time. Cash didn't call me back, which disappointed me a bit. I wanted to hear him say he was on his way to arrest Everette.

Where was Everette, anyway? Would Cash be able to find him, or was he somewhere with Jordyn Jackman? How could I tip Cash off to Everette's location without letting on I'd been tracking his car?

I had crossed the Cooper River and was at a stoplight on Coleman Boulevard when I opened the tracking app to see if Everette was at home. He had known I was following him, but he must not have known I had a tracker on his car. Surely, he would've removed it if he had. The screen loaded, and it took me a moment to register Everette's current location.

His car was on Murray Boulevard.

He was at Swinton and Judith's house.

I made a U-turn and headed into Charleston.

Chapter Fifty-Five

I circled the block and found Everette's BMW parked on Limehouse Street. I pulled in behind him, then called the land line. What was Everette up to? What was he doing here at one in the morning? Was anyone else in the house?

This could be completely innocent. They've been friends their whole lives.

Everette was a murderer. He'd said something that might've been a threat to Swinton Saturday night.

I called Cash.

It went straight to voicemail. *Helen of Troy. Are you on the phone?*

I tried again. It rang and rang. *Pick up the phone.*

The third time, it went to voicemail again, and I left a message telling him Everette was at Swinton and Judith's, and I was going to see what was going on.

But what if they were having nightcaps and toasting old times? Swinton and Judith didn't know Everette was a psychopath. Or did they? They'd known him a lot longer than I had. These were the things swirling in my head.

Lights were on inside the house. I tried Judith's cell—no answer. J. T. lived in a beach house at Folly, but he would surely know what was going on with Judith. Had she been released from the hospital? I tried J. T.'s cell, but no luck there either. Finally, in desperation, I called Swinton's cell, but it went straight to voicemail. Where the actual heck was everyone?

I had to assume bad things were going down inside the house. If I was wrong, well, I'd look like an idiot. If I was right, I could interfere and play for time, at the very least. I could live with looking like an idiot. I could not live with myself if I walked away and later found out Everette had hurt Judith . . . or Swinton.

I'd worn a sundress to dinner at Soby's, and that wasn't going to cut it. I popped the trunk and grabbed the tote with extra clothes. A pair of cargo shorts, a tank, and one of those fancy fishing shirts with all the pockets would give me places to put things. There was no one else in sight. I slid into the shorts and tank under my dress, then pulled it over my head and slipped into the shirt. From the weapons tote, I filled my pockets with every gadget Joe and Gavin had bought me that would fit—mace, bear spray, a tactical pen, a stun gun. Then I started a voice memo and buttoned my phone into my front shorts pocket. With the long-range pepper spray gun Joe had gotten me for my birthday tucked in my back waistband and hidden under my shirt, I headed down the pebble driveway that ran along the back of the property.

The small white rocks crunched under my feet. Time slowed, and I focused on breathing in and out. Palm trees lined the drive, the scent of gardenias floated in the air. I passed behind the pool deck, then beneath the kitchen windows. Ahead, the driveway dead-ended at a row of bushes. I went right, onto the patio adjacent to the dining area and family room off the kitchen. Two sets of glass doors opened onto the patio. The doors were tall, maybe ten feet. But the wooden panels on the lower third gave me cover. Keeping to the right, I crept up the wide brick steps.

Judith was in the family room, on a grey sectional sofa.

Swinton stood across the room, by a chair. He was talking to someone to his left.

There . . . Everette was seated at the end of the dining table.

I couldn't hear what they were saying, but they all looked tense.

I waited, breathed in, breathed out.

And then I plastered on a bright smile, stood, and walked up to the glass door. I knocked and smiled and waved, like it wasn't at all unusual for me to show up at one a.m.

They all stared at me.

A frown crossed Swinton's face. He seemed to be solving a complicated math problem in his head. Then he walked over and opened the door.

"Hadley," he said in an even tone. "What a nice surprise."

Judith didn't stand. She was trying to tell me something with her eyes. It might've been, "Run!"

"Darlin', I'm so sorry I couldn't make it this afternoon. Is everything all right?" she asked.

"Oh, sure," I said. "No worries."

Swinton had not stepped back to welcome me inside. I stepped around him.

My eyes settled on Everette. "I'm so sorry to interrupt. I didn't realize you had a guest."

"Everette was just leaving," said Swinton, in a tone that said, get the hell out of my house, Everette.

Everette looked from Judith, to Swinton, to me. "So this is the daughter I've heard so much about. Nice to finally meet you."

"Nice to meet you," I lied. "I'm sorry, what was that last name?"

"Ladson," said Everette.

"Everette, as I said, I'm afraid I can't help you," said Swinton. "Now, if you'll excuse us, I'd like to speak to Hadley."

Everette's grin was malevolent. "Now, Swinton, I know you better than that. You'd never turn your back on a friend in need. Especially one who you have such a long, long history with. There's nothing like old friends, am I right?"

"Regardless of whether I'd like to help you," said Swinton,

". . .or *not*, J. T. took the company jet to New York this morning. I simply can't help you, Everette."

Everette wanted Swinton to fly him somewhere in the corporate jet. He was making a run for it. Had Leland Marchant tipped him off? Surely, he was smarter than that.

"I'm afraid I don't believe you." Everette's voice held menace.

"Be that as it may—"

"And it's irrelevant," said Everette. "You have access to several other planes. Friends, business associates—people who owe you— own planes, Swinton. And *you* owe *me*."

Swinton's face filled with disgust. "Everette, we're done."

Everette barked a bitter laugh. "Oh no. We'll never be done."

Judith looked weak. "Everette, Swinton's told you he can't help you. I'm not well. Please leave."

"Oh, you're not well?" asked Everette. "Like you weren't well that night on the Stono River?"

Swinton growled, "That's enough, Everette."

"You want me to keep quiet?" asked Everette. "Like I've done all these years? I've been a good friend to both of you. Now you be a good friend to me."

I deliberately baited him. "I think Delta has some early flights," I said. "Not all of them are direct, of course. Where're you headed?"

Everette flashed an annoyed look my way. "You'd be well advised to stay out of my business."

Swinton was looking at me, I could see that from the corner of my eye. He was likely trying to signal me to hush up. But I had Everette in my sights. And I wanted to get as much out of him as possible.

"Why's that?" I gave him a ditsy look. "Are you going to kill me too?"

"*Hadley.*"

Involuntarily, I turned to Swinton.

He telegraphed me an urgent warning.

I turned back to Everette, who scowled at me. "What are you talking about?"

"Not what," I said. "Who. Her name is Eugenia. She was a friend of mine."

Everette screwed up his face like he was about to spit. "That hot-headed Ukrainian bartender killed my wife."

"No," I said matter-of-factly. "Oh, I know that's what you wanted people to think. You went to a great deal of trouble to incriminate her . . . planting a knife, a book, some hair . . . getting your friend to borrow a car just like hers . . . and setting me up as your alibi." I stared at him hard.

"Hadley, please." Swinton sounded tired now, like he realized the protest was futile.

"You?" Everette drew back in disbelief. "*You're* the PI? You can't be serious."

"Oh, trust me. I'm quite serious."

Everette laughed. "You're just a girl playing Nancy Drew. A piece of fluff."

"Well, this piece of fluff has you figured out, you slimeball," I said.

"Is that a fact?" Everette still looked amused.

"Who called you? Was it Leland?" I asked.

"What the hell is going on?" demanded Swinton.

Everette's expression changed to one of confusion. "You're the one who met with Leland in Greenville earlier this evening?"

"That would be me. I'm the one who figured out your girlfriend tipped you off that a PI was following you. You led me on a merry chase to Greenville. Bribed a waiter to bring you tea while your friends drank bourbon after bourbon. You pretended to stumble to your room. Then you snuck out the back and hurried over to a nearby church parking lot and picked up the car your buddy left there for you—one exactly like Kateryna Petrenko's—and you drove it to Sullivan's Island, where you, Everette, killed your wife."

Judith gasped. "Everette? Surely that's not true."

"Trust me, Judith," I said. "It's the stone-cold truth."

"I want to hear you say that you are not capable of such a thing, Everette," said Judith.

Everette leveled a dangerous look at her but said nothing.

Something tickled my brain, and I decided to throw some gas on the fire to see what might explode. "Judith," I said casually, "what I wanted to ask you, was this: can you think of anything related to the deaths of Amelia Simons and Charles Butler that Eugenia would feel guilty about? A reason she'd leave money in her estate to provide for Amelia's sister's care?"

Judith turned to me, confused. "I don't understand."

"Judith, please," I said.

She looked down at her hands, then up. "She blamed herself."

"Why?" I asked.

"I'd like to hear that myself." Everette sounded both amused and confused.

Judith sighed. "Eugenia knew Everette had been messing around with Amelia. When the four of us left on the boat that Sunday afternoon, we drove past Amelia's family's house just as she and Charles were getting in their boat. Remember, Swinton, Eugenia's the one who told you to stop?"

"I remember," said Swinton.

Judith continued. "Eugenia was playing a game. She thought if she put Amelia and Charles on the boat with the rest of us . . . well, she was taunting Everette, I suppose. She didn't mean any harm by it, not really. She just wanted to see how Everette would react, and how Amelia would. It was a game with her."

"Who knew?" asked Everette. "All these years, I had no idea she's the one who set everything in motion, or why. I'd forgotten it was her suggestion, stopping to see if they wanted to come with us."

"She knew." Judith's voice cracked. "But what happened wasn't her fault, none of it."

"What happened, Judith?" I asked gently.

"Yes, by all means," said Everette. "Let's tell the girl what happened."

"We went down to Kiawah and spent the day on the beach," said Judith. "Eugenia was in a fine mood, poking at Everette and Amelia. Amelia kept giving Everette these desperate looks. Charles was oblivious to the whole thing.

"Anyway, on the way back, I was driving the boat. It was my father's boat, and I'd had less to drink than any of us. We were almost back to Limehouse Bridge, when another boat came barreling straight towards us. They were going too fast. I can't imagine . . . maybe the driver had been drinking. We'll never know. I swerved to miss it. I nearly hit a bridge support, and I overcorrected. It all happened so fast. Amelia was thrown from the boat. Charles jumped in to help her.

"I guess I'd gone too long without eating. That, and the adrenaline, I think, triggered my blood sugar to drop all of a sudden. I passed out."

"Eugenia and I were taking care of Judith." Swinton stared at Everette hard. "Everette jumped in the water. He said Charles was taking too long, needed help."

I had a really bad feeling about where this was headed.

No one spoke for a long moment.

"But you never found either of them, did you, Everette?" Swinton looked at Everette with disgust.

"No, I never did," Everette said in a "how about that" tone.

"You convinced me we needed to get help for Judith. There was no helping Amelia or Charles."

"Did Eugenia know Amelia was pregnant with Everette's child?" I asked.

"What?" Swinton's voice was sharp.

Judith gasped. "No. Is that true?" She looked at Everette.

His face darkened. "You may be too smart for your own good, Nancy Drew." He pulled a gun out of his jacket pocket and laid it on the table.

"You killed them both, didn't you?" Swinton growled. "All

these years, you let Judith grieve thinking they'd died in an accident she felt responsible for. And Eugenia thought it was her fault. You let both of them carry the weight of two—three—deaths, while you pretended to help protect them both. What happened, Everette? Amelia expected you to marry her?"

Everette nodded, shrugged. "She did. And there was no way that was going to happen. Eugenia had qualities Amelia lacked."

"Her father's fortune," said Judith.

"Precisely," said Everette. "Not that Amelia was penniless, mind you. And she had other interesting qualities. That girl was imaginative. Mmm, mmm, mmm."

"You are one disgusting SOB," said Swinton. "Get the hell out of my house. Don't ever make the mistake of letting me see your face again."

Everette laughed. "Come now. We've gone way past the point of no return here. Get on the phone and find me a damn plane. Do it now. As we've hashed through here, I've already killed three people. Some might say four, if you count Amelia's unborn child. Two of those people I liked a whole hell of a lot more than I like you." He pointed the gun at Swinton.

"Wait now, tell me how it ended," I said, like we were talking about a movie. "How is it that the authorities found Charles's father's boat?"

Swinton said. "I drove us back to Judith's family's house and called for an ambulance. I went with her to the hospital. Everette stayed behind. He later told us he'd fixed things like none of us were ever there. He said he did this to protect Judith. For forty-eight years, he pretended he did that to protect my wife."

Everette shrugged. "I took a kayak with me on Charles's father's Boston Whaler. Set the boat adrift and paddled back. Nothing to it."

"I just can't believe it," said Judith. "Everette, how is it possible you're really capable of killing our friends? Of killing *Eugenia*?" Judith looked at him, a question in her eyes.

Everette laughed, a low, evil laugh. "Needs must, Judith.

Needs must. Eugenia changed these last few years. She was having an attack of conscience. She was already paying for Amelia's sister's care. It was only a matter of time before she confessed we were all together that day. Inconvenient questions would've been asked. Things were unraveling. Apparently, Eugenia has a photo from that day somewhere. She made the mistake of taunting me with it. I couldn't let that photo see the light of day, now could I? Swinton, I need that plane ride. Now. I wonder, how much do you care about your bastard daughter?" Everette raised his gun and pointed it at me. "Make the damn call, Swinton."

Everything that happened next happened all at once, in a jumble.

My phone rang.

Swinton darted across the room.

He jumped between me and Everette, right as Everette fired that gun.

Swinton fell to the floor.

Judith started screaming and rushed to him.

And I must've instinctively pulled out that birthday pepper sprayer, the one with the laser pointer to help people like me, who've never fired a weapon and don't really want to anyway . . . because before my father hit the floor at my feet, I unloaded four shots of pepper at Everette's face.

He dropped the gun, screaming, coughing, and gouging at his own eyes.

I scrambled in my pocket for my phone.

Doors on both sides of the family room burst open, and Cash and I don't know how many SLED agents burst into the room.

And I collapsed next to Judith at my father's side.

Chapter Fifty-Six

I told Cash everything while Judith, J. T.—who had actually not gone to New York—and I, held on to each other in the surgical family waiting room. Cash told me he'd been taking a video statement from Leland Marchant when I was trying to call. Leland had not tipped Everette off, but he had talked to Mike Gambrell. Mike, who was under the mistaken impression that Everette had money and was eager for him to invest it in some property on Lake Jocassee. In possession of only a few of the facts, Mike had tried to curry favor with Everette by telling him a PI had been asking questions.

Somewhere, in another part of MUSC, medical personnel tended to Everette Ladson's eyes. He would be fine, and would stand trial for the murders of Amelia Simons and her unborn child, Charles Butler, and Eugenia Ladson. Alex and Charlie were taking steps to prevent Everette from using Eugenia's estate to pay for his defense. Cash called Dana Smalls to let her know all charges against Kateryna would be dropped.

At seven fifteen that Tuesday morning, the surgeon came to tell us they'd removed a bullet from my father that had narrowly missed his aorta. He was being moved to the intensive care unit. We comforted each other, saying we thought that was normal.

Didn't they always do that after surgery? We moved to the ICU waiting room.

I had done everything in my power to deny him a place in my life, and he'd taken a bullet for me, reflexively. At the first sign of a threat, he'd jumped between me and a psychopath with a gun. He had been unable, for twenty-four years, to convince me that he loved me. But he'd shown me, irrefutably, in an instant.

Sitting in an ICU waiting room gives you plenty of space to reflect on all the things you need to say to a person you're praying will wake up to hear.

"Hadley." J. T. spoke to me in a gentle tone, put his arms around me and held me still. "Shhh. You're rocking back and forth."

I must've been doing it in such a way that drew attention, perhaps concerns about my grip on reality. I stilled. And I prayed and prayed. God, please give me the chance to set this right. I'd misjudged my father . . . Had judged him harshly and refused to listen to anything he'd tried to say. Because Gavin was right. I'd put my mother on a pedestal. And I had steadfastly refused to consider the possibility that there was any legitimate perspective that sprinkled the least bit of tarnish on her memory.

After twelve hours in ICU, they moved him to a room.

They let us go in one at a time. Judith went, then J. T.

Finally, it was my turn.

I stood in the doorway. He was hooked up to so many machines. So many things could still go wrong. I sent up another prayer.

"I won't bite." His voice sounded normal, if a little on the cranky side.

I grinned, walked over to the bed. "Sorry I caused so much trouble."

"What are you carrying on about, girl?"

"Showing up after midnight, poking a psycho with a stick, getting you shot . . ."

"Whoa, now. You're not responsible for any of this mess. The way I see it, you jumped into a pond with an alligator and tried to draw his attention away from Judith and me."

"Says the man who literally jumped in front of a bullet."

He reached for my hand. "I'd do it again in a heartbeat."

I leaned in and hugged him as best I could.

"I love you, Hadley. You're my only daughter."

"I love you too, Dad."

Chapter Fifty-Seven

By Thursday evening, Dad had twisted his doctors' arms, and he was home. Judith insisted I come for supper. For the first time, the four of us sat around a table together. It was the same table Everette had been sitting at when I made my entrance.

It was oddly not odd, well except for the fact we were still all talking about Everette, Eugenia, and what Everette had done all those years ago. J. T. was more than a little miffed at me for not telling him everything well before it ended in a shootout. As I told him, things came together so fast I never had the chance.

To make me feel at home, Judith had asked their chef to prepare a plant-based meal. The Asian brown rice noodle bowls with stir-fry veggies were delicious.

"What is this we are eating?" asked J. T.

"They're called vegetables," said Judith. "Eat them. They're good for you."

"Tastes pretty good to me," said Dad.

"I'm glad you like it," said Judith. "After the scare you've given us, you'll be adopting every healthy thing I can come up with. Starting with eating your vegetables."

After supper, I asked Dad if we could speak privately. I'd

thought J. T. would give me trouble about leaving him out again, but he actually seemed pretty pleased with the situation.

We went into the study and sat on opposite ends of the leather sofa.

"I need to ask you something." I suppose I wore a nervous grin that may have tipped him off.

He scrutinized me for a minute, then said, "Dammit. What gave it away? It was the outdoor room, wasn't it? I knew that was too much. I shoulda curbed my urges there."

"I don't understand," I said. "Why would you go to so much trouble to give me such an over-the-top extravagant gift?"

He sighed. "Hadley, I hope I have many years to spend getting to know you. But I'm not a young man anymore. It's an uncertain world we live in. I needed to be sure you were taken care of. It was your fortieth birthday. J. T. got control of his trust when he turned twenty-five. I didn't know another way to give you at least part of what I wanted you to have."

"But how did you know so much about me?"

"You made that a challenge, for sure," he said. "But it didn't happen all at once. I've been studying up on you since you were sixteen, and I first found out you existed. And don't be mad at him, but J. T. gave me some pointers about what you like. Well, he gave them to a designer."

"J. T. knows about this?" I felt my voice and my blood pressure rising.

"Now, now . . . his heart's in the right place. He told me when we first started this project, he would never lie to you. And I'm willing to bet he didn't."

"It never occurred to me to ask him about it," I said.

"Well, there you go. I think he enjoyed helping with it . . . putting in things he knew you'd like."

"Did he tell you about North?" My mind went back in time, cataloging what I'd told J. T., and when.

Dad winced. "No, now that I learned initially from an investigator. Back when it all first happened. I'm really sorry we couldn't get a better outcome."

I stared at him. "You sent the attorney from Middleton, Bull & Vanderhorst to Atlanta?"

He nodded. "I knew North didn't drink, knew he couldn't have been responsible. And I knew how important he was to you. I only wish I'd been able to do more."

"I just can't believe it." I shook my head. "What else?"

"Hmm?"

"How many other times have you been behind the scenes taking care of me?"

He shrugged elaborately.

"College of Charleston . . . that was you, wasn't it? My 'financial aid package?' That was all you."

He nodded his head sideways, right, then left. "Well, all right, yes."

"Thank you," I said. "Thank you for everything. But especially for what you tried to do for North."

"You're welcome, Hadley. You're my daughter."

After a minute, I asked him, "Did you love my mother?"

"She was the love of my life. Now, don't get me wrong, here. I love my wife. Judith is my best friend, my partner. She's J. T.'s mother. Judith has stood by me through an awful lot. But your mother . . . you only get one love like that, and only then if you're very, very fortunate."

"Did you break her heart?" I asked.

"Well, I guess that's complicated. I suppose she would say it broke her heart that we came from different worlds. But I did not end our relationship, as I may have mentioned to you a time or two. She did that. I wanted to marry Vivienne. She told me she couldn't live in my world. She felt too out of place. She said that *she* was not what I needed.

"So, I proposed to Judith. And then, right before the wedding, I tried one last time to convince Vivienne that we should be together, no matter what. That's where you came in. But ultimately, your mother told me I should marry Judith. So, I did. And then we had J. T., and I never looked back. I swear, I didn't know about you until after your mother got sick. Only then did she tell me I had a daughter.

"I think she was afraid she'd lose you. She wanted to hang onto you as long as she could. And then she ran out of time. But one thing I need you to know, Hadley. I tried every way I could to get her to go to MD Anderson for treatment. But one thing I was never able to do is to change Vivienne's mind once she'd made it up. And she had it in her head that because her mother had the same cancer, there was no hope for her. She wanted to spend what was left of her time with you, not across the country in a hospital. And I had to respect her choice."

"I guess I just needed someone to blame," I said.

"Could you not have picked someone else?" He smiled at me.

"I'm just so incredibly sorry . . ." I teared up.

He grimaced as he leaned forward to pat my arm. "Now, now. None of that. This is the happiest day I've known since . . . well, I guess since the day I found out I had a daughter. And I'll tell you something else . . . something that for me shed some light on what your mother was thinking, the day you were born, anyway, even if she dropped a ball or two when she was sick."

"What's that?"

"If she'd ever intended to keep us apart forever . . . If she wanted to make sure we never had a relationship . . . If she just thought I'd be a lousy father . . . your mother would never have named you the way she did. Her intentions are right there on your birth certificate. She named you for all four of your grandparents, Hadley Scott Drayton Legare Cooper."

"Yeah, she did." I reached out and took the hand that was on the cushion nearest me.

He squeezed it tight.

Chapter Fifty-Eight

Everyone was at the cabana for happy hour on Friday.

"Hadley, I have a doctor on call for tomorrow evening," said Tallulah.

"I'm sorry?" I sipped my prickly pear margarita.

"For your date? For supper club?" Camille piped in.

"Oh . . ."

"How was your date Saturday evening?" asked Sarabeth. "In all the excitement, I haven't had a chance to ask."

"Yes," said Tallulah. "Tell us about the heart surgeon."

I sighed. "Well, he's just really a nice man."

"Oh dear," said Tallulah.

"Kiss of death, right there," said Fish. "Nice guys can't get a break."

"It's not that he's a nice guy," I said. "It's . . . complicated."

"It always is." Camille nodded.

"I'll just let Charles know to pick you up at six tomorrow then," said Tallulah.

"That's not—"

"Oh, don't think a thing about it," said Tallulah. "I know a lot of people. You can have dinner with someone new every month, like I do. Keep your options open."

"Hold that thought just for a minute," I said.

I dialed Cash, who answered on the first ring. "Hadley?" There was that hopeful note again.

"Hey Cash, are you free for dinner tomorrow?"

"As a matter of fact, I am."

"Would you like to come with me to the Sullivan's Island Supper Club?"

"I don't know what that is, but I would very much like to have supper with you, whenever and wherever you like."

"Maybe afterwards we could take a walk on the beach. I have a lot to tell you."

"That's the best news I've had in years."

I couldn't seem to stop smiling when I hung up the phone.

The weekend would be the fullest one I'd had, possibly ever. I was having dinner (at lunchtime) tomorrow with Gavin and Joe. I had a lot to tell them too. Of course, a lot of what happened had been in the newspaper, and I'd spoken with Gavin by phone to let him know I was all right. But there was much I needed to fill in. They'd be happy to hear that dad and I had a breakthrough, though they wouldn't be one bit pleased about how that had all come about. They would no doubt try yet again to get me to carry a gun.

Honestly, the situation with Everette crystalized for me exactly why I would never carry one. I'm not certain I could've fired a gun at Everette. I'm afraid I might've hesitated to use lethal force. If I thought about it long enough, yeah, of course I would decide it was worth it to save us, even if I might kill Everette. But you don't have that kind of time when someone is pointing a gun at you. If I know what I have in my waistband isn't going to kill anyone, I won't hesitate to use it when I need to. But we'd hash all this out at dinner tomorrow, and often, no doubt. Gavin and Joe would always be my family, no matter how many new family members I was blessed with.

Sitting under Eugenia's cabana with all my new friends, I teared up thinking about how blessed I truly was. Eugenia had brought all these wonderful women into my life, and she'd even managed to fix things with Dad and me. She was a force to be reckoned with, and I would forever be profoundly grateful to have known her and called her friend.

Acknowledgments

Above all, I thank God for the doors He's opened for me, and also for the ones He's kept firmly closed because He had something else in mind for me. I am indeed grateful for unanswered prayers and for the many gifts in my life.

I've never lived on Sullivan's Island, but I once lived close enough that I could ride my bike across Ben Sawyer Bridge and down the beach after I dropped the kids off at school. It's a magical place, and it's always fascinated me. The seed of an idea that became this book, and the books to come in the Carolina Tales series, came to me years ago. I've since had numerous conversations with friends, family, friends of friends, and people who were kind enough to speak with me when I intruded, unannounced, on their day.

Thank you so much to everyone who contributed to the fabric of this novel. Special thanks for your time and insights Gervais Hagerty, Everette Presson, Kristen James, owner of Ensemble Consignment Boutique, Mary Poole, Jacquelyn Gypin, Becky Williams, and Linda Ketner. The things I got right are because of y'all. Any mistakes are purely my own.

Huge thanks to Dariia Demkiv, who inspired the character Kateryna Petrenko. Dariia is an excellent nail tech—not a bartender. Her life is very different from Kateryna's, but they share the experience of winning the immigration lottery.

As always, my heartfelt thanks to each and every reader who has connected with my novels. You make it possible for me to spend my days doing what I love—making things up and writing them down. I am truly grateful.

And, as ever, I'm so grateful to every book seller who has recommended my books to a customer or hosted me for an event. I love bookstores, and I'm so happy to have discovered a long list of unique book boutiques to browse as I'm traveling about in an effort to meet readers face-to-face.

Thank you, Jill and Lee Hendrix and Melissa Oates at Fiction Addiction bookstore, for everything.

And, as always, thank you, to my husband, the man who first encouraged my dream when the company I had long worked for went out of business, and he said, "Why don't you give the writing thing a try?" I did that, and I've never looked back. Thank you, Jim, for being a "patron of the arts," for being my fiercest advocate, for endless encouragement and enthusiasm, and for always serving as my sounding board.

Thank you, Christina Hogrebe at Jane Rotrosen Agency for your guidance and expertise in the publishing industry and for believing in my work.

Thank you, Kristen Weber, my developmental editor, for your insights and encouragement. Trish Long, thank you for your sharp eye, careful copy editing and proofreading, and your patience with my many questions.

Thank you, Elizabeth Mackey, for the lovely cover design.

Thank you, MaryAnn Schaefer, my able assistant, who seems to work all the time, and must have the lowest hourly wage in the country. Thanks to Veronica Adams at 1852 Media for all the lovely graphics and general marketing savvy. Thank you, Rachael Palasti, for joining the team.

Thank you, Kathie Bennett, at Magic Time Literary Publicity, for working me until I nearly drop, but stopping just short of killing me.

Thanks to Marc Duroe at New Wave Media Design, for excellent website design and maintenance.

Thank you, Ginger Jacks, caterer extraordinaire, for your creativity in bringing the flavors of the book to the launch party.

Thank you to Lisa Hudson. She and her family appear as characters in this book because Lisa won a contest, and her family are good-natured sorts. With the exception of a few minor details supplied by Lisa, their story here is wholly a product of my imagination.

Writing is a solitary occupation, and this past year has brought many changes for me. Thank you to my writer friends who've served as a sounding board for issues small and large, who've helped me make the transition to independent publishing: Gretchen Archer, Debra Clopton, Grace Greene, Pamela Kelley, Karen McQuestion, Liz Talley, and Tess Thompson.

Thank you to all the members of The Lowcountry Society, for your ongoing enthusiasm and support.

As always, I'm terrified I've forgotten someone. If I have, please know it was unintentional. I am deeply grateful to everyone who has helped me along this journey.

About the Author

Susan M. Boyer is the USA Today best-selling author of twelve novels. Her debut novel, *Lowcountry Boil*, won the 2012 Agatha Award for Best First Novel, the Daphne du Maurier Award for Excellence in Mystery/Suspense, and garnered several other award nominations. Subsequent books have been nominated for various honors, including Southern Independent Booksellers Alliance Okra Picks, the 2016 Pat Conroy Beach Music Mystery Prize, and the 2017 Southern Book Prize in Mystery & Detective Fiction. Susan and her husband call Greenville, SC, home and spend as much time as possible on the Carolina coast.

Never miss a new release—sign up for Susan's newsletter on any page of her website at susanmboyer.com.

Also by Susan M. Boyer

CPSIA information can be obtained
at www.ICGtesting.com
Printed in the USA
BVHW030837070423
661949BV00004B/86